Praise for
BUTTERFLY GAMES

"Lyrical and passionate, this historical novel illumines a little-known countess with a big story. Drawn into a treacherous game of politics, betrayal, and forbidden love, young Jacquette must choose between her heart and her loyalty. A tale that reels you in and doesn't let you go."

—Jude Berman,
author of *The Vow*, a 2024 *Kirkus* Best Indie Book

"In this novel of love and betrayal, Jacquette grapples with Swedish court politics, while her mistakes, resolve, and sacrifice make her the true heroine of this sweeping tale."

—Michelle Cameron,
author of *Beyond the Ghetto Gates* and *Napoleon's Mirage*

"Complex, captivating characters. Immersive prose. Glittery royal court intrigue. Based on the true, ill-fated love story between a countess and a prince, *Butterfly Games* unfolds with all the dramatic intensity of a Shakespearean tragedy."

—Joan Fernandez,
author of *Saving Vincent: A Novel of Jo van Gogh*

"Set against the turbulent backdrop of Napoleonic-era Sweden, this richly woven tale follows Countess Jacquette Gyldenstolpe through passion, political intrigue, and heartbreak. Blending deep historical insight with irresistible drama, this is a romance that lingers long after the final page."

—Anna-Lena Berg, noted biographer
of Jacquette Gyldenstolpe (*Jacquette Gyldenstolpe*)
and Gustav af Wetterstedt (*Grand Tour*)

BUTTERFLY GAMES

BUTTERFLY GAMES

a novel

KELLY SCARBOROUGH

SHE WRITES PRESS

Published in 2026 by
She Writes Press, an imprint of The Stable Book Group

32 Court Street, Suite 2109
Brooklyn, NY 11201
https://shewritespress.com

Library of Congress Control Number: 2025918557
ISBN: 979-8-89636-050-6
eISBN: 979-8-89636-051-3

Interior designer: Katherine Lloyd, The DESK
Maps courtesy of Erin Greb

Printed in the United States

To Mom, for supporting my work
and inspiring my dreams.

Fjärilsleken

[fjar ils lek·en]

"The Butterfly Game"

A term that describes fleeting sexual affairs between lovers who frivolously change the objects of their affections.

CONTENTS

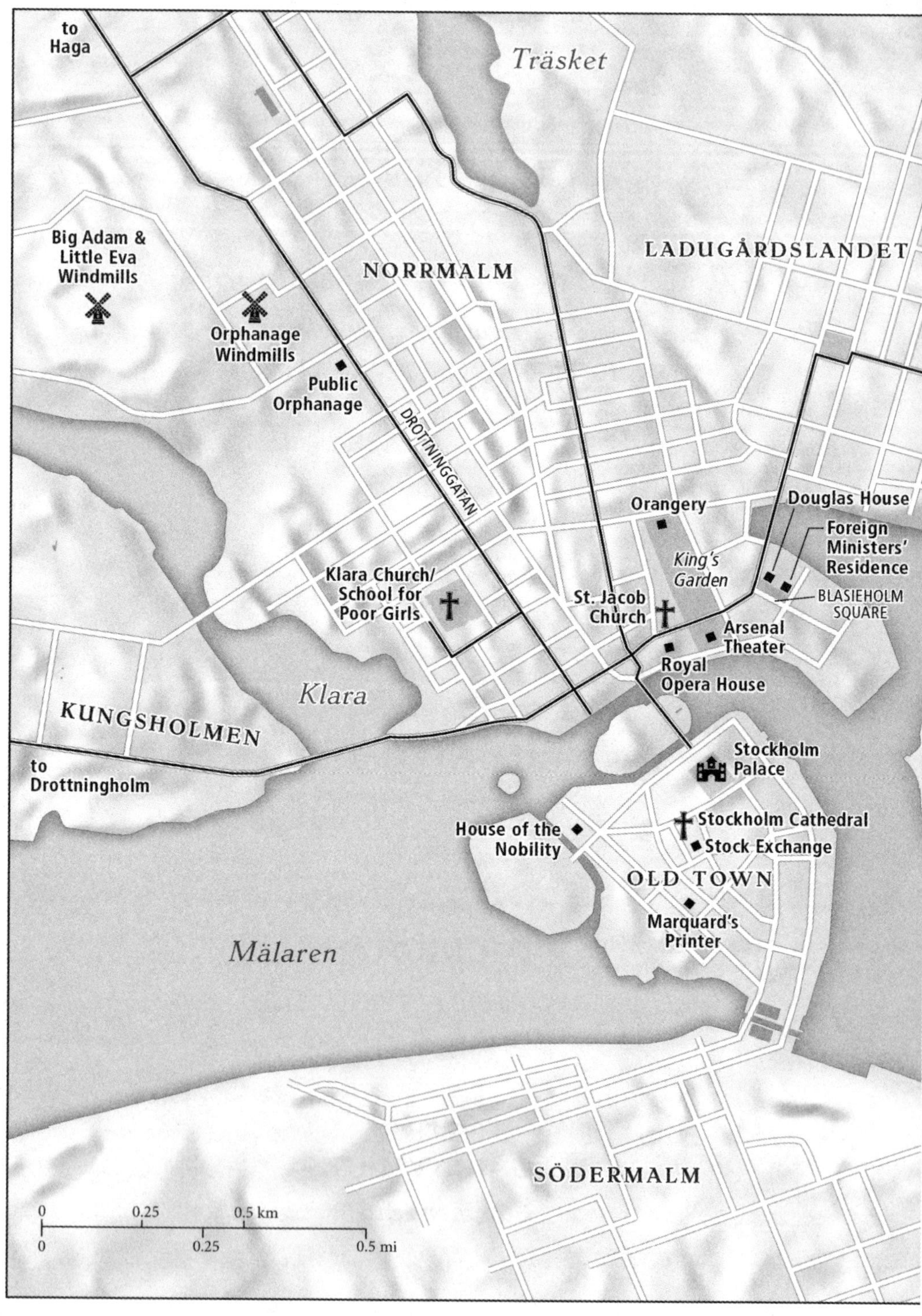
to Haga
Träsket
Big Adam & Little Eva Windmills
NORRMALM
LADUGÅRDSLANDET
Orphanage Windmills
Public Orphanage
DROTTNINGGATAN
Orangery
Douglas House
Foreign Ministers' Residence
King's Garden
Klara Church/ School for Poor Girls
St. Jacob Church
BLASIEHOLM SQUARE
Arsenal Theater
Royal Opera House
Klara
KUNGSHOLMEN
to Drottningholm
Stockholm Palace
House of the Nobility
Stockholm Cathedral
Stock Exchange
OLD TOWN
Marquard's Printer
Mälaren
SÖDERMALM
0
0.25
0.5 km
0
0.25
0.5 mi

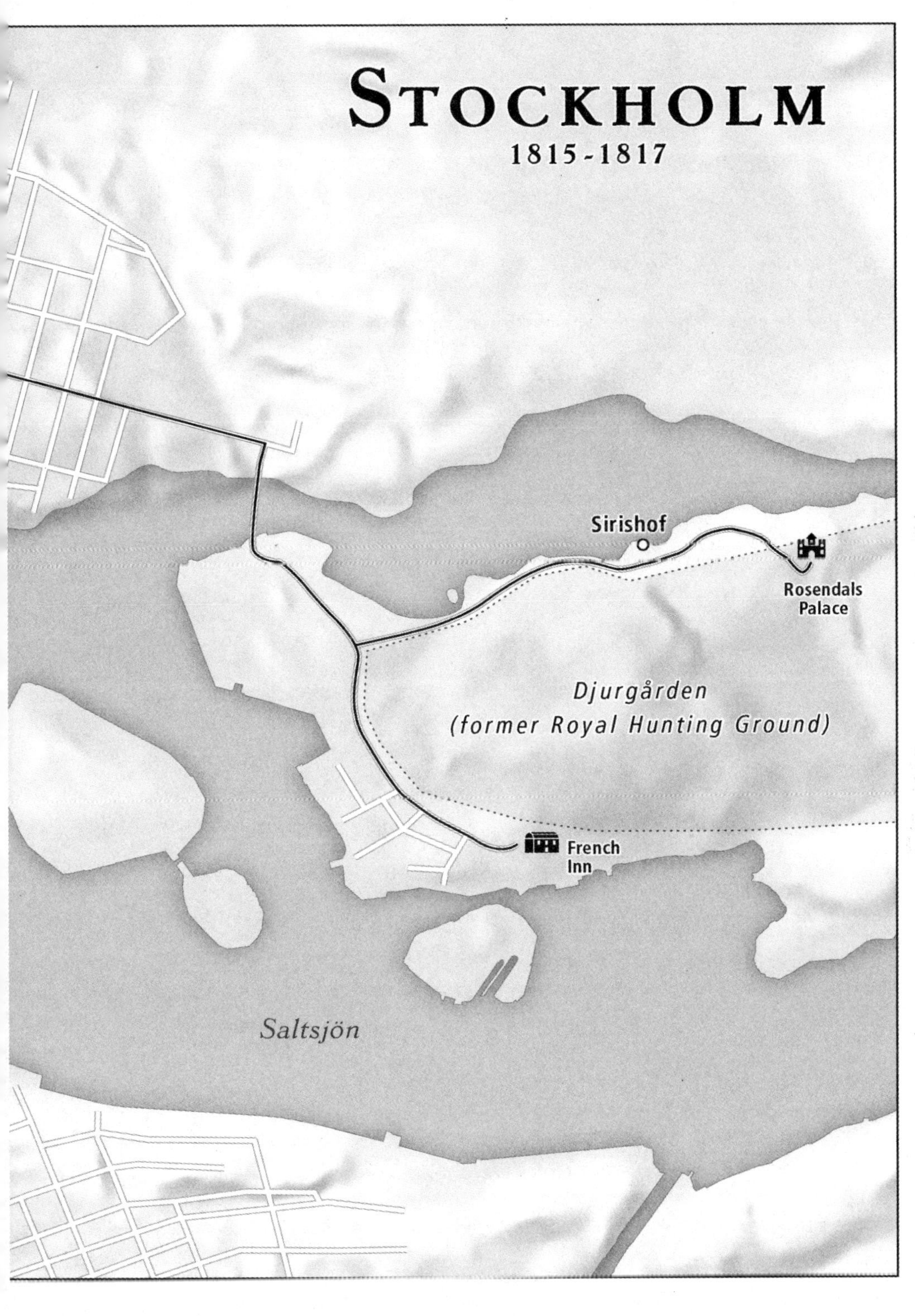
STOCKHOLM
1815-1817
Sirishof
Rosendals Palace
Djurgården
(former Royal Hunting Ground)
French Inn
Saltsjön

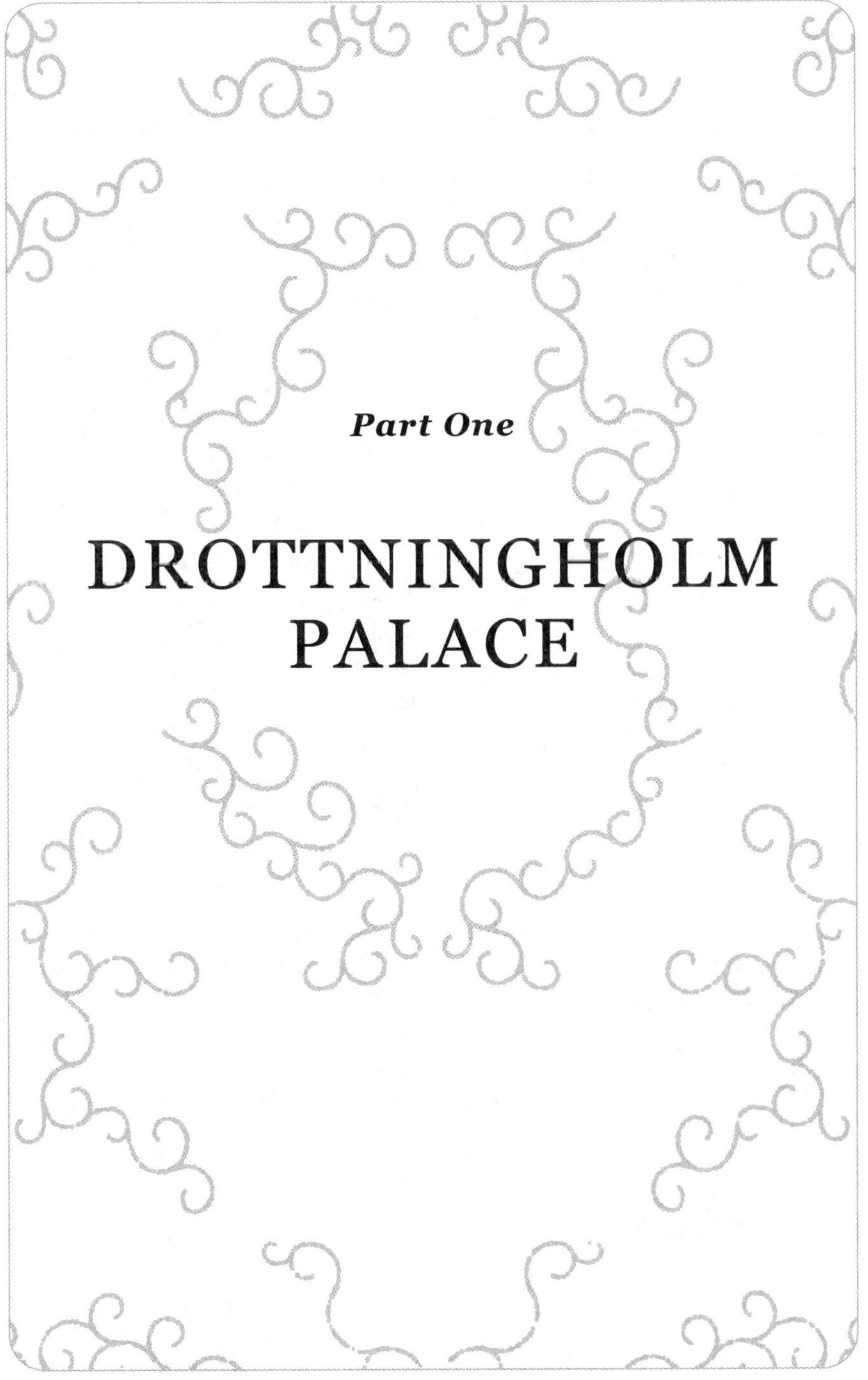

Part One

DROTTNINGHOLM PALACE

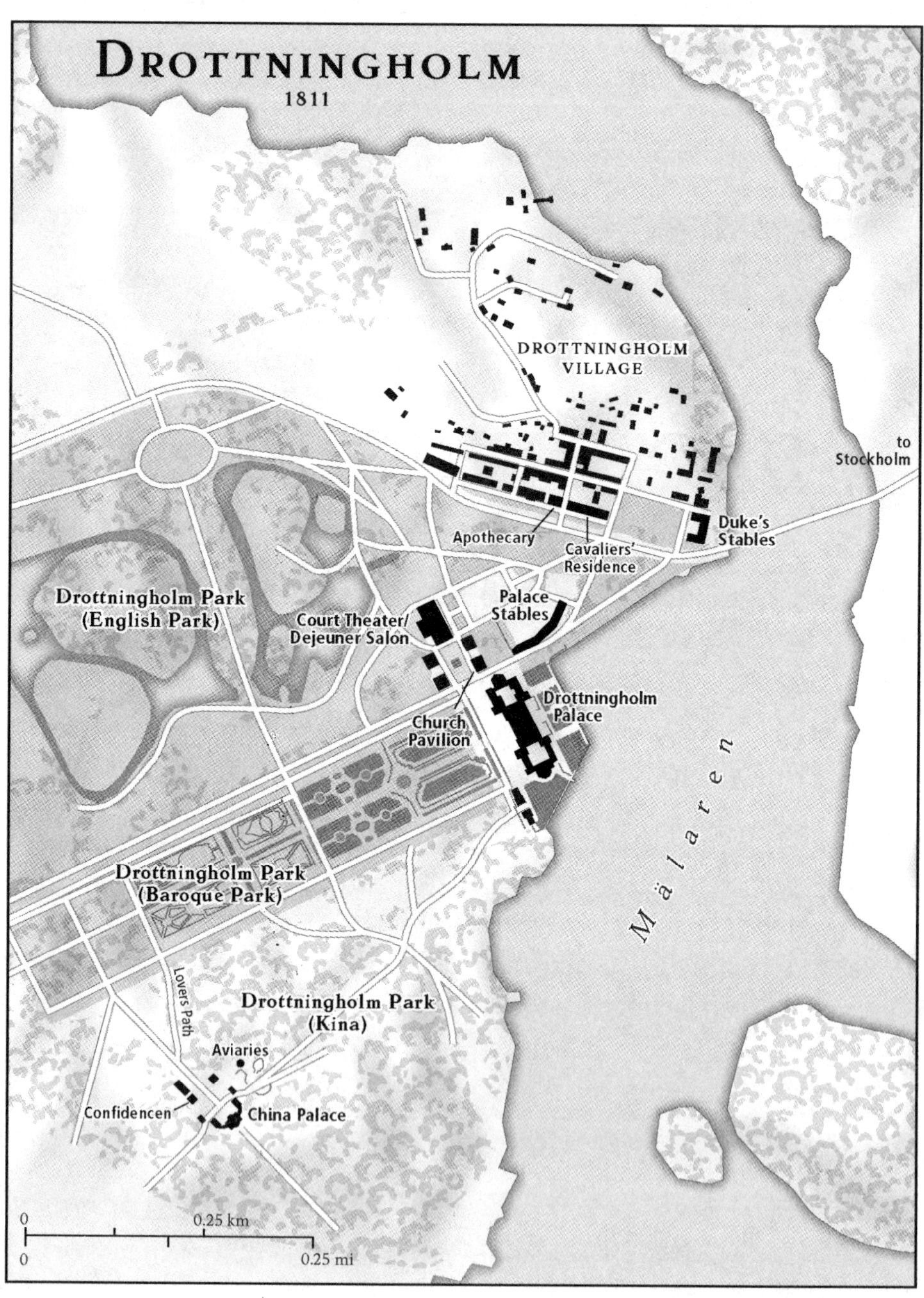

Drottningholm
1811
DROTTNINGHOLM VILLAGE
to Stockholm
Duke's Stables
Apothecary
Cavaliers' Residence
Palace Stables
Court Theater/ Dejeuner Salon
Drottningholm Park (English Park)
Drottningholm Palace
Church Pavilion
Mälaren
Drottningholm Park (Baroque Park)
Lovers Path
Drottningholm Park (Kina)
Aviaries
Confidencen
China Palace
0
0.25 km
0
0.25 mi

CHAPTER ONE

Church Pavilion at Drottningholm Palace
One Swedish Mile from Stockholm
June 24, 1811

Jacquette lingered at her dressing table on her first day at Drottningholm, unprepared to face the Chatterati. Not a single member of the vicious clique had ever shown any interest in her existence, yet they seemed to hate her with an inexplicable vehemence. She'd arrived last night to learn that four of them, the most merciless of the queen's young maids of honor, would be lodged with her for the summer in the Church Pavilion, a tiny biscuit-colored house with a red mansard roof just a few steps away from Drottningholm Palace, where the royal family was summering. The Birdcage, as everyone called the house, looked so innocuous, so delicately last century, like a place where genteel courtiers might sip tea and exchange pleasantries in sweet voices. But like everything else at the royal court, it was a lie. Jacquette was to live here among the Chatterati all summer, and they would make these eight weeks a miserable, lonely purgatory.

The injustice of this persecution was that it had nothing to do with her. This was Aurora's fault, Aurora's scandal. Jacquette's mother was at the center of such an intrigue that people could speak of little else, which was why she'd chosen to travel with her lover this summer and leave Jacquette here. She offered up her daughter to answer for her sins.

It was past ten o'clock when Jacquette descended to the breakfast room, long after the aroma of fresh bread had wafted through the still air to her tiny room in the attic. All four Chatterati were there, their voices giddy and full of hubris, as they were whenever they escaped the strict rules of Stockholm Palace. Jacquette had been naive to imagine she could avoid them.

Huddled at one end of the table with their heads pressed together, they were of a breed—gray daytime court gowns, hair pulled taut to the nape of the neck, square-toed black slippers. Each wore a diamond brooch with Queen Charlotte's cipher—two *C*'s entwined like serpents, the mark of a Chatterati. Averting her eyes and toying with her bracelet, Jacquette skirted past them to the end of the table and dropped into a wobbly chair, relieved to be ignored.

She would breakfast at dawn tomorrow morning, she told herself. And she would spend her days alone, and hope the dinners were brief and uneventful. It would be over in August; Aurora had promised her that.

The Chatterati buzzed on as she made quick work of eating her strawberries, pushed away a tray of herring, and laid her fork across her porcelain plate. Today was Midsummer Eve, and two Chatterati were about to come to blows over the flowers for their garlands while the other two were whispering behind their newspapers and taking sides. Seven different flowers from seven different fields, one said, but the others disagreed.

Jacquette peeked at them over her teacup and set it down, intending to make her exit. But the heel of her hand tipped her saucer so that her spoon clattered onto the table, an ornate lacquered piece that looked like it belonged at Versailles. A chorus of stares met her from around the now-silent table. Four Chatterati holding tiny French porcelain cups pursed their lips, regarding her as they would a bruised apple in a market stall.

Their leader, a tall, sturdy young woman named Erica, folded her napkin and donned her spectacles. "I see your mother deposited you here alone. In the night. But pray, tell us her news. We so miss Aurora's leadership."

They all nodded, and two giggled.

The Chatterati liked nothing more than gossiping about Baroness Aurora De Geer, Jacquette's mother, although as a court mistress, Aurora well outranked them.

"I didn't travel alone. I have a companion, Madame Love, and a new maid, Brita." Jacquette tried to keep her voice light and pleasant, not wishing to provoke them.

Another Chatterati snickered. "Aurora was too busy to come herself and do her service."

"Perhaps Chancellor Wetterstedt needed Aurora's services more than the queen did," Erica mused.

Chatterati rarely wasted time getting to the heart of a matter, and Aurora's decision to travel with Wetterstedt this summer was almost as scandalous as her divorce from Jacquette's father last year. But Jacquette did not deserve their scorn, and neither, in fairness, did Wetterstedt. He had waited years for Aurora to be free and was always sweet and kind to Jacquette, writing letters to her, sending for her favorite black boots from England. Though he was not wholly blameless, this mess was not Wetterstedt's creation.

The plump blonde one, Hedda, gave an indignant nod of her head. "They divided your mother's hours among us. We all are working harder so she can travel around the countryside with Chancellor Wetterstedt."

Nothing could make Chatterati more furious than extra work.

"You would think she would want to be with the queen, especially after the king's stroke. The man could die," said Erica.

"Aurora gets what she wants. She wanted Wetterstedt, so she divorced Count Philip. Who knows how she managed that?" This from a wisp of a girl with freckles who was reputed to have the quickest intellect of the group. And the sharpest wit. Jacquette thought her name might be Diane.

This question appeared to confound the others, who looked to Jacquette for an answer. She counted crumbs on the tablecloth, not wanting to meet their eyes. She never spoke of her father.

Erica took over. "Wetterstedt is not all Aurora wanted. She wanted Finspång Castle, and she traded your brothers to Count Philip so she could keep it. But your father didn't want you, did he, Jacquette?"

It was true, and her father hadn't even bothered to deny it. Last year, after Jacquette's father, Count Philip Gyldenstolpe, and her mother, Aurora, signed the paper that allocated their children like chattels, he'd come to Finspång to take away her brothers. She had been standing alone in the entry hall, crying, when he stopped and placed his hands on her shoulders. She'd hoped he would comfort her, even invite her to come to his home in the north. Instead, he'd warned her that she was cursed with the blood of the De Geer women and would turn out no better than her mother if she were not careful.

She mumbled, "Finspång has always belonged to my mother's family, not to his. I can't imagine why our laws would have given it to him."

It was the wrong thing to say to Erica, who responded instantly. "Because she married him, dear. That's what it is all about. Well, now that Wetterstedt is going to buy your aunt and uncle's shares, Aurora will have it all—the castle, the cannon foundry, everything. If I were you, Jacquette, I would worry she will sacrifice you for something she wants."

There are so many ways one can be sacrificed, Jacquette thought. *This is just one.*

Diane shrugged. "About the marriage, I fault them both. Count Philip was more unfaithful than Aurora. He played his butterfly games since they were newlyweds. After years of tolerating other women, who could blame Aurora for taking Wetterstedt to her bed? He's a new man, not the son of some washed-up ancient family."

"I am more peeved about having to stand in to cover Aurora's service weeks than I am by her indiscretions," said Hedda.

Erica frowned at Hedda, who seemed chagrined at the rebuke. Erica usually delivered the vulgar insults herself.

Jacquette didn't want their pity. "I grew up at Finspång and rarely saw my father or mother. They were at court, and I guess I just stopped thinking of them as parents."

Erica changed the subject, lest Jacquette improve her position with the others, who were looking at her with interest. "Did your mother send you here for a reason? Give you something to do?"

It was the very question Aurora had advised her not to answer. The best way to placate Chatterati, Aurora had said, was to offer what they valued most—information. Jacquette folded her hands on the table.

"Of course not. She and Wetterstedt don't need me sitting in the carriage between them. They have much to discuss. You see, he proposed at Easter. Theirs will be a fall wedding, I think."

"Once they marry, do you think Aurora will send you back to the country? She left you at Finspång for how many years?" Diane asked.

Jacquette would have liked nothing better than to return to Finspång, but she suspected Aurora had other plans for her. "Six. It has been about a year that I have been at Stockholm Palace with my mother." These girls knew it well; they all lived on the floor beneath Aurora's palace apartment and snickered whenever they passed Jacquette in the corridors.

Erica ran her finger around the rim of her teacup. "Just remember, there were other girls—maids of honor—who were sent home for the summer because you got the attic room. You'll get no special treatment from us."

Everyone nodded, and the fourth girl, Johanna, a sharp-faced brunette with a long neck and rounded shoulders, added, "Being pretty won't help you."

So far in Jacquette's fourteen years, it had only seemed to hurt.

Diane folded her hands on the table and dipped her chin. Looking directly at Jacquette, she said, "This might not be her last summer at The Birdcage if what I hear is true. They say Aurora wants her named a maid of honor now that she is turning fourteen. Aurora was fourteen herself when she first came to court."

"One of us?" asked Hedda.

If there was one thing her short, fractured life had taught Jacquette, it was that she must stay away from the royal court. A summer would be bad; a lifetime would be intolerable. She would never accept a position in the royal household, not as a maid of honor, not as a court mistress. Not if the queen offered it, not if her mother pushed and cajoled. She wanted no part of that world. For it was there that royals and nobles broke their marriage vows, ruined innocents, and trampled hearts without a thought for the consequences. Their way of life even had a name. Everyone called it the Butterfly Game, and it had ripped her family in two.

She stood to leave the room. "I cannot imagine such a thing. Never." For at least the fiftieth time that day, she condemned her mother for arranging this. And it was not yet noon.

A pockmarked Life Guard captain appeared in the doorway, blocking her path. Jacquette recognized him from Stockholm Palace.

"Ladies," he said, "may I trouble you to pay attention? I have orders signed by the regent." He pointed at Jacquette with his staff. "Countess Jacquette, would you join the others?"

Jacquette walked to the end of the table and stood behind the Chatterati, who were in a flurry of disorder. Erica, who seemed to have had a change of heart, patted the chair next to her and said, "Sit with us. And do be quiet and listen."

With two junior officers flanking him, the Life Guard unfurled the order and read aloud:

> *All items that bear the name or likeness of any member of the exiled former royal family shall be surrendered to the palace guards forthwith for destruction. Anyone failing to comply shall be brought to justice and punished in accordance with the law.*
>
> *Signed, Crown Prince Charles Jean, Regent*

"He cannot mean paintings of Crown Prince Gustav, can he? He was only a boy when he was exiled," said Hedda, pushing an enameled bracelet inside her sleeve.

Jacquette had seen bracelets like Hedda's before and knew what she was trying to hide. The gold cuff had a miniature of Gustav on a medallion.

The captain flipped his staff over and rammed its head into the floor planks. "Come forward," he ordered.

Hedda presented herself.

"For your information, Gustav is no longer our crown prince."

She stammered a bit, eventually getting out the words. "I misspoke, Captain. *Former* Crown Prince Gustav. I forget sometimes."

It had been two years since Gustav and his parents were exiled and his childless aunt and uncle were placed on the throne. Some people had accepted the change more readily than others.

The Life Guard did not relent. "Call him what he is—a pretender to the throne."

"Yes, Captain. Pretender."

"You may sit."

Hedda returned to her seat, and Diane wrapped her arm around Hedda's shoulder.

The front door slammed, and Jacquette heard raised voices in the entry hall. One of the Life Guards went to investigate and reported back.

"Captain, the chief court mistress is in the library."

Sighing, the captain put on his gloves.

As soon as the officers left, Erica said, "Crown Prince Charles Jean didn't write that order. I can assure you he doesn't know a word of Swedish and just fired his language tutor."

Jacquette did not doubt her. The new crown prince was as French as they came. He was one of Bonaparte's generals and wasn't even born noble, she had heard. And since the king's stroke, he had been regent, in charge of everything.

"And Wetterstedt isn't even here to be his scribe," said Diane.

"The crown prince does rely on Wetterstedt," said Jacquette.

"Maybe Wetterstedt and your mother advised Charles Jean to seize our bracelets," Hedda said. "It isn't fair. They were gifts for our service."

The stony glares told Jacquette the Chatterati would blame even this, the seizure of their jewelry, on Aurora.

"Couldn't the Estates of the Realm have elected someone other than Charles Jean?" Hedda asked. "Even a Dane would have been better."

Erica shook her head. "The king is old and has no heir, and the French are threatening to invade. Who better to protect us from Bonaparte than a general who knows his war plans?"

Someone coughed, and Erica jumped to her feet.

Jacquette's Aunt Lotten, a stern, terrifying woman, marched up to the table. She put her hands on her hips and stared down a footman until he pulled out her chair, then sat. Tall, big-chested, and blonde, she was a typical Gyldenstolpe, and Jacquette's brothers looked much like her. She did not appear pleased this morning.

"Ma'am," said Erica, looking demure. The others murmured greetings. The Chatterati had never seemed so relieved to see their chief court mistress.

Erica took Jacquette's hand, and Jacquette had to restrain herself from snatching it away.

"Tell your aunt we want to keep our bracelets," she whispered.

"I'll try," Jacquette whispered, "but I don't think she likes me. She took my father's side after the divorce—he's her younger brother, after all—and she hasn't forgiven my mother yet."

Lotten began issuing directions. "All of it. Go to your rooms, gather the contraband, and put it in the library. Every note, every letter, every gift and portrait, even if it is scrawled on a theater program."

Hedda, who seemed incapable of silence when nervous, asked, "Even miniatures of Gustav? He's only eleven years old."

Lotten rolled her eyes. "*Especially* Gustav," she said. "The rebels would do anything to make him crown prince again. One cannot speak his name in Crown Prince Charles Jean's presence without risking a treason charge. Take this seriously."

It made no sense to Jacquette. As children, she and Gustav had been friends.

"Aunt Lotten, Gustav did nothing wrong. No one should be called to account for the bad conduct of their parents."

Everyone was watching. Everyone had heard. Everyone knew she was really talking about herself.

When Lotten spoke again, her voice was husky. "I must have your word, ladies. Go and collect everything."

She rang a bell on the sideboard, and the Life Guard captain returned. "Tell the crown prince it will be done," she said.

He bowed low and backed out of the room, nearly tripping over his sword as it grazed the floor. The Chatterati mounted the stairs with dour expressions.

"Jacquette, a moment," said Lotten, extending her hand. "I have something for you to do. Come to the library."

"Ma'am?"

The Birdcage's ordinarily tidy library was in disarray. Torn canvases with half-finished portraits of the exiles leaned against the walls, and stacks of letters covered the floor. Trinkets were piled everywhere, and there was even a teapot painted with Gustav's hounds. From this disorder, Lotten extracted a coffin-shaped wooden box with gold trim. She brushed it off and handed it to Jacquette.

"Take this to the China Palace, would you? You'll find a wall cabinet upstairs in the yellow drawing room. Press the little door and it will open. Just leave this on the shelf, and mind you close the wall panel tight. But don't let anyone see you. They are preparing for the king's luncheon there today."

Jacquette knew this letter box—she had seen it before at Stockholm Palace. On its mother-of-pearl lid was a miniature portrait of Crown Prince Gustav in a gilded frame. It was precisely the type of thing the Life Guard had ordered them to surrender.

"But this belongs to the queen."

Lotten patted her shoulder. "Gustav is her nephew. She deserves a memento of him, doesn't she? It's only an empty box. Now go on, child, if you wish to be useful." As the words left Lotten's lips, a hint of a smile replaced her exasperated look. "I don't know why I didn't think of you before. You are just the person to do this."

Drottningholm no longer seemed as uninteresting as it had before breakfast. If Jacquette could earn Lotten's trust, the Chatterati would have to accept her.

With the queen's writing box tucked under her arm, Jacquette climbed the hill at the edge of the castle park, where a narrow dirt track called Lovers Path led through a forest of spindly pines. The Mandarin, Crown

Prince Charles Jean's secret police, would never search the China Palace. Tucked into a corner of the palace grounds, it was the king's private summer retreat, a tiny pleasure pavilion in chinoiserie, a spot for parties and luncheons and card games. It was the perfect hiding place.

Finding the park and the woods largely empty, she blessed her luck, for a great mob of people would soon arrive to celebrate Midsummer Eve. She reached the top, a bit winded, and paused in a patch of brilliant sunlight where the trail joined a wider gravel-paved avenue that ran along a ridge. As she started turning toward the China Palace, a flash of light from the opposite direction caught her eye. She walked toward it.

She knew what was here—two abandoned aviaries, octagonal structures with tall, narrow cupolas. Elaborate follies from an earlier time, they were painted a dull eucalyptus color with mustardy trim. Their two-tiered roofs were made of thin rolled iron stained green with linseed oil paint. The iron had wavy fluted edges. In her grandmother's day, exotic birds—canaries and parrots and turtledoves—had sung behind the now-disintegrated nets.

At a gap in the tall hedge near the entrance to the aviaries, she found herself looking down at a lanky boy with dark shoulder-length curls. He had fine features—a straight, narrow nose and rounded brown eyes. *So typically French*, she thought. It was the new prince; there were portraits of him in half the rooms at the palace. His name was Oscar, and he was Crown Prince Charles Jean's only son. Had she made a list of people to avoid at this moment, his would have been one of the first names she added, right after his father's.

She looked down at the box. It was contraband, and she needed to hide it.

CHAPTER TWO

Prince Oscar appeared not to notice Jacquette, or not to care. She was tempted to ask why he was alone here, sitting in the dirt with his back against a rock; why he was staring at something he clutched between his hands; why his horse, untied, was grazing in an overgrown patch of herbs. Why he didn't look or act anything like Gustav. Like royalty.

She knew all the answers. It was because he was French, a commoner, and had never set foot in Sweden before last winter. One could tell he was no prince simply by looking at him. His crisp officer's jacket, blue with shiny gold buttons, was stiff with starch and too long in the sleeves. Small-boned across the shoulders, he was not ruddy and stout, as Gustav had been. But something about his white silk shirt drew her eyes and held them. Untucked from his trousers, it hung in graceful folds over his narrow hips. He was as delicate as a dancer, beautiful in a way.

He was her junior, but only by two years, and should have known better than to ride off by himself. She would be wise to hold her tongue, though, as he would someday be king. And more than anything, she needed to send him on his way before he figured out what she had under her arm.

A gust of wind parted the spruce branches, and the flash of light reappeared. It came from the item in the prince's hands, something familiar. The unmistakable silver medal, an eight-pointed star with a round blue center, was the insignia of the Royal Order of the Seraphim. The young prince was flipping it into the air and catching it with one hand, then the other.

Receiving this medal was a rare honor, Sweden's highest, and he was tossing it like a toy. One of her uncles had earned his Seraphim Star by losing an arm in the Finnish War. This so-called prince had done nothing to earn his medal. What if he allowed the Gustavian nobles to see him treating it with so little respect? If he did, he would be the next one sent into exile.

Suddenly, the box felt heavier, a burden rather than an opportunity.

"Your Royal Highness. Are you well? Where are your guards?" she asked.

His eyes met hers, and the Seraphim Star clattered onto the stone path. The prince clamped his lips in a grim line and looked away, brushing locks of hair from his face with long, tapered fingers.

She retrieved the medal and rubbed off the dust between the folds of her skirt.

"My guards are fighting among themselves," he said in soft Parisian-accented French as he climbed from the ground, sweeping pebbles from his uniform. He was at least a head taller than she was. "My father assigned me a new Swedish cavalier who dislikes my tutor, and the two of them argue all the time. They did not even notice I left."

Most royal persons would not have offered any explanation. Jacquette knew the prince's tutor, a Frenchman named Lemoine, but had not heard about any new Swedish cavaliers.

She placed the medal in the prince's hand and watched him fasten it to his jacket. "Are they nearby?"

In a few hours, the royal family would assemble at the China Palace to celebrate Midsummer Eve with the villagers, and the prince must soon return to the main palace to dress.

He shrugged in the direction of the forest. "In the guard tent. They don't want me around."

Jacquette listened for horses coming from that direction but heard nothing. If his guards were not coming to get him, she would persuade him to go back to the palace.

"Oh, that cannot be right."

"They are arguing about whether my father will change sides and don't want me to hear. They think I'll tell him."

"Change sides?"

"You know, break Sweden's alliance with France."

She rolled her eyes and sighed. "Would your father go to war against his homeland?"

He threw a pebble over the wall. "For a man like him, a vow doesn't mean anything. Bonaparte is my godfather, you know."

She remembered the box under her arm. "Well." She curtsied. "It has been an honor to meet you, sir. I've not been presented at court yet. I'm Countess Jacquette Gyldenstolpe."

"I know who you are. Your mother is soon to marry Wetterstedt. Are you walking out here alone?"

He held her gaze with a boyish intensity, but she could not tell him that she was on a secret errand to hide contraband from his father. "My maid was walking with me, but she stopped down there—"

His eyes shone with amusement, and he laughed. It was an honest sound from deep inside, the laugh of a soldier's son. "You are such a poor liar. What do you have there? You're hiding that box from me, aren't you?" He tried to grab it, still smiling.

She hugged it against her chest. "It's just something my aunt asked me to bring to the China Palace. They want it for the luncheon, probably to hold the silver or something."

While stepping back toward the hedge, she caught her heel, perchance on a root. The branch she grasped for support gave way, and the box slipped from under her arm. She felt herself teetering, the spiky shoots and thorns coming nearer.

The prince caught her by the side of the waist, and she turned toward him. As they righted themselves, she was conscious of his other hand, which was wrapped around her bare arm below the short puffed sleeve of her dress.

His face reddened, and she looked away. Through the dense leaves, she saw the box perched at the intersection of two branches.

"Oh, no—the box."

He released her, and they looked into the hedge. The box was turned sideways, and Gustav's portrait was hidden, but the lid had opened a sliver, and some papers were jutting out.

Aunt Lotten had told her the box was empty. Probably just a mistake, but Jacquette needed to find out what was inside before the prince did.

He said, "I think I can reach it."

There was nothing she could do to stop him. He was royal, or so the Estates of the Realm had decreed. She couldn't touch him. She couldn't tell him no. With her heart pounding, she stepped aside.

He tore off his jacket and draped it over the gatepost. "You'll have to give me a hand. Just for balance."

She laced her fingers between his, then clasped her other hand around his wrist for reinforcement. As he reached deep into the hedge, the tail of his white silk shirt caught the wind and billowed above his trousers.

"I think I have it," he said. "Voilà."

As he lifted the box, she saw the picture of Crown Prince Gustav emerging from the leaves. He was certain to notice it any second, and she did not know what to do. His own father had decreed that possessing any object relating to the former royal family was a crime. A crime serious enough to disgrace her family. Imagine what the Chatterati would say about that.

She opened her fist, releasing his hand, and he fell headfirst into the hedge.

"Ouch. Why did you let go?" Some of the smaller branches snapped, and the prince's head moved closer and closer to the hard earth.

"I'm so sorry. I—my hand slipped."

He managed to climb out by bracing himself on the thicker limbs, but when he stood, tiny green boxwood leaves were stuck in his hair. As he brushed off his coat, he looked cross.

She laughed. "Your hair, sir."

He shook his long curls, and a shower of leaves fell to the ground. The irritation drained from his expression, and he propped his hands on his thighs, looked up at her, and smiled. It was a broad grin that filled out the sharp edges of his face and made her forget the solemn boy he had been only moments before.

"It's fine. Really, it is. I haven't been tossed into the bushes since I came to Sweden. My cousins used to do it." With a shy smile, he shook more leaves from his hair and shoulders. "That's not the only thing I've missed about Paris, but don't tell anyone."

Jacquette picked up the box while the prince was still brushing boxwood leaves from his jacket.

"Let me see," he said.

Clutching the box, she showed it to him.

He traced his lower lip with his index finger, staring at the miniature portrait of his father's rival, then surprised her by flashing a sarcastic grin. "I don't think they will want to display the dessert spoons in this. All the new ones have my father's picture on them."

Ack, there was nothing she could say. She had lied to him, and he had found her out.

The head of a horse emerged from the trees. Its rider was a wisp of a man, Oscar's tutor, Lemoine. As Oscar walked toward him, Jacquette looked inside the box. It wasn't empty. There were papers inside, and it took only a glance for her to understand what they were. Horrified, she closed the lid and latched it again.

Oscar was shouting to Lemoine. "I'll come up to the China Palace in a minute."

"That won't do. Carl will have my head if I leave you here—oh, Jacquette. What are you doing so far from the palace?"

"An errand for the chief court mistress, monsieur."

Jacquette felt Prince Oscar move behind her. He whispered, "Go ahead. Take your box wherever it needs to go. I'll handle Lemoine."

She didn't move.

Oscar walked toward Lemoine, who had dismounted. "Don't worry about me. I will come over with the countess. Fifteen minutes."

The tall white plume of a Swedish cavalry officer's helmet emerged from the trees. Jacquette did not know the rider, who was about twenty with a waxed mustache and closely curled dark brown hair cut short at the temples.

Lemoine groaned. "It's Carl Löwenhielm."

"Lemoine, there you are. Do I hear you speaking French? You know the prince's father forbids it. And what is he doing here? You were supposed to take him back to the palace."

"Come now, Carl. There is plenty of time," Lemoine replied.

Prince Oscar whispered to Jacquette, "That's my new Swedish cavalier, the one I was telling you about. Carl Löwenhielm. He's causing a lot of trouble, especially with the men who came with me from France."

Löwenhielm shrugged and said to Lemoine, "As you wish." He shifted forward in the saddle, and his horse cantered off toward the China Palace.

"He's up to something," said Oscar.

Lemoine frowned. "I am afraid so, but at least he is gone for now. You can walk with Jacquette for a short time. There is something at the stables I need to attend to."

Prince Oscar smiled at him. "Is her name Hedda?"

Lemoine reddened. "Just assure me, sir, that you will be back in fifteen minutes. Carl seems intent on having me dismissed, and I am sure your father will hear about this."

"Don't worry. And thank you, Lemoine."

After the tutor rode away, Jacquette turned to the prince, unsure what he intended to do about the box. He could report her to his father, or seize it, or something worse.

The prince spoke first. "We'll tie up my horse here, and I will walk with you."

"But you must return to the palace, sir—I mean to say, the carriages will be leaving for the luncheon at noon, and everyone is probably looking for you."

"They don't need me." He tied his horse and began to walk. She hurried to match his long strides.

"But your whole family will be there."

The prince blinked his eyes.

Too late, she realized that was untrue. Only a fortnight ago, Oscar's mother, Crown Princess Désirée, had returned to Paris. There was talk of a quarrel between Désirée and Charles Jean, and no one knew if or when she would come back. Jacquette could imagine how lonely Prince

Oscar must be. Her parents had done the same thing—left without a thought of her, wrapped up in their own selfish concerns.

"It's fine. Let's not talk about my mother now." His fingers drummed on the side of his left thigh. He pointed at the box. "Let's talk about that. I know it belongs to the queen. Tell me, what was Gustav like? You were acquainted with him, I trust?"

Since Charles Jean's arrival last year, no one spoke of the exiles. This new prince probably knew little or nothing about him.

"Crown Prince Gustav? Forgive me—I keep calling him that."

"That is what he was when you knew him."

"We were very young; he is the same age as you, and we played together in the royal nursery."

"Was he a scholar? I'm not very good."

"I don't really know," Jacquette said. "But it's hard to be a crown prince."

"Sometimes I don't even want to be a prince."

"That's why I can't see why everyone is so afraid of Gustav. I doubt he really wants to come back and take your father's place."

"My father certainly fears him."

"I cannot imagine your father fearing anyone, Your Royal Highness."

"Do you know what I dislike most about being a prince? Ever since I left Paris, no one calls me by my name."

"How awful that must be."

"Call me Oscar. Please."

She nodded. "Oscar."

Jacquette took a step toward the China Palace, but Oscar moved in front of her.

"I really must finish my errand now," she said.

"Not so fast."

He was trying her patience, this mock prince.

"Oscar, I must."

He grinned. "You're probably worried I'll tell my father I saw you carrying around a portrait of Gustav."

"Somewhat. Not that much."

"Why not?"

"Just a feeling I have about you and him," she said.

Perhaps, she thought, *I should be more concerned, given what is in this box. The picture is nothing, but the documents, mon Dieu.*

During the dozen or so seconds when Oscar had spoken with Lemoine, Jacquette had looked through them. Pages and pages of notes and plans, apparently written by supporters of Gustav—the same people who sought to overthrow Charles Jean and Oscar. And right on top was the written statement of a chamber servant swearing that Gustav's father was legitimate, despite the many rumors to the contrary.

She knew how important that was.

How had these papers found their way into the box? Did they belong to the queen? Aunt Lotten had left the box unattended in the library at The Birdcage amid the disorder that followed the arrival of the Life Guards. Someone else could have slipped them inside while bringing items into the library. Almost everyone staying at The Birdcage had a portrait of Gustav, or a ring, or a teapot with his name and picture on it. Any of them could have done it. Jacquette only wished the documents had not ended up in her hands.

Making sure to hold the lid closed, she walked down the path toward the China Palace, hearing Oscar's long strides behind her. As they neared Kina, the section of the castle park where several pagoda-style pleasure buildings were arranged in a clearing around the China Palace, she had an idea.

"I don't tell my father everything," he called. "You said you had a feeling about us. What?"

"That you don't always agree with him."

"What do you think about him?"

She thought for a moment, unsure whether to trust him. "I don't understand why the secret police are seizing pictures of Gustav. Why does your father keep such people around him?"

"The Mandarin? Because he's afraid he will fail."

It had the ring of truth.

At home, Wetterstedt was forever fretting about the shakiness of

Charles Jean's position. Everyone knew the powerful nobles in the Estates of the Realm had the power to replace Charles Jean with Gustav and send him and Oscar back to France.

"People who are afraid often act imprudently," she said.

Oscar's face grew grave, and he hurried to walk by her side. "He won't even tell me why my mother left."

Jacquette thought of her own family. "Every bit of gossip I hear about my parents' divorce adds to my worry. I don't listen."

"I don't want my father to be the only one who knows the reason."

"Ask your mother, then."

"She doesn't tell me the truth." He kicked the cobblestones with the pointed toe of his riding boot. "If I agree to keep your secret, do something for me."

Royals, even pretend ones, always wanted something. "What?"

"Always tell me the truth."

It was not what she had expected to hear. "All right, but—"

"The real truth, not what you would say to a prince."

To Jacquette, this did not sound difficult, particularly because Oscar was unlikely to remain a prince very long. "Of course."

"Then I won't tell anyone about your box. It's settled."

This was encouraging news, but it did not solve the problem of the documents, which he would be unlikely to ignore. "Follow me," she said. "Have you been inside Confidencen?"

"That one?" he asked, pointing at a building on the other side of the gravel clearing.

"Yes."

One of four small square structures that surrounded the China Palace, Confidencen had always reminded Jacquette of a miniature Chinese pagoda with a billowing green silk scarf draped on top. Resembling its larger and more elaborate neighbor in style and color, it had a flared moss-green iron roof and a marbled plaster exterior painted dull red. Its tall, arched windows—three on each side—had wheat-colored trim and carved cartouches above them, each with twenty rectangular panes of precious glass. On its roof was an open-sided lantern tower with a small round clock.

Oscar gazed at the little structure as if he had never seen it before. "I've not been inside, but I tried the door once. It's locked."

"I know a way," she said.

"How?"

"Gustav took me inside. Come on, I'll show you."

Jacquette led Oscar around the back. Confidencen was built on a hill, and from the rear side, its two-story basement foundation was entirely above ground. Still holding the box, she said, "Can you try that door?"

Without hesitating, he pulled the latch, and the old basement door creaked open.

"What is down here?" he said, squinting into the darkness.

A foggy light shone through the ventilation grates, revealing an enormous wooden wheel in the center of the tiny basement. Without hesitating, Oscar placed one of his hands on a crossbeam and the other on a peg to turn it.

"Don't," she cried, and pulled him away by the sleeve.

Brushing dust off his jacket, he gave her an indignant look. "I'll do what I wish."

"I don't think it works anymore. It's dangerous."

He looked up at the ceiling, where a wooden beam connected the wheel to the underside of the floor above. "What is it?"

"It's why this place is called Confidencen. In the old days, if the king wanted to have a private dinner, the servants would turn this wheel, and a big section of the floor would lower into this basement. The dining table would come with it. And down here, they would set the table with everything the king wanted to eat and drink, then turn the wheel to raise it up. And the king and his lover could dine upstairs, *in confidence*."

Oscar ran his fingers around the wheel. "Let's lower it."

"It's too heavy. Gustav told me not to touch it."

"I'll call my men." He started to leave the basement.

Ack, boys could be so predictable. She'd known Oscar would not be able to resist seeing it operate, and that was why she'd brought him here. With the wheels and pulleys distracting him, she would have time to hide the papers.

"I have an idea," she said.

"What?"

"The cupboards upstairs hoist up and down, too, but with pulleys. They're small, and not so heavy as the table."

"We shall try one of them."

She found the correct rope, and he helped her unwind it from its anchor, controlling the slack as it loosened. With a moan, the long-unused pulley turned.

"Run upstairs to the dining room. You will see it starting down," she said.

His eyes shone with interest. "Can you handle it yourself?"

"Of course. Go ahead."

"The door is locked. You saw that."

"There is a key on that hook."

He took it and ran out the door. In a few moments, Jacquette heard his steps upstairs in the dining room.

Rather than releasing the rope, she took the papers out of the queen's box. Seeing a wooden chest next to the crank wheel, a place for tools and such, she tried the top. It was unlocked. She put the papers inside and shut it, then arranged a group of pebbles in a circle on top of the lid. She would know if anyone disturbed it.

"Can't you lower it?" he called.

"Of course. I was waiting for you to be ready."

Steadying the pulley with one hand, she released the rope to control the cupboard's descent into the basement.

"Remarkable." As he came down the stairs, he wiped the back of his neck. He was covered with dust, but his eyes were shining.

She pointed to the now-empty box. "Now," she said, "I really must bring this to the China Palace."

He smiled. "I, too, must go. To meet Lemoine and change for the dinner."

As they walked through the gate, the warden of the China Palace came out of his quarters. For the day's events, he was dressed in his ceremonial uniform, a gold full-length silk shift topped with a blue velvet robe that had gold trim and wide three-quarter-length sleeves.

"Your Royal Highness," he said to Oscar, and bowed.

Without hesitating, Oscar clasped his hands at his back, greeted the warden, and said in perfect Swedish, "The chief court mistress has asked Countess Gyldenstolpe to deliver this box to the China Palace. I trust you will ensure she is not detained."

"Of course, sir, without fail."

Jacquette turned over the queen's box and looked at the bottom. On it, someone had painted a quotation in neat French script. It said, *If a tree dies, plant another in its place.*

On the fourth of July, Jacquette followed her reluctant chaperones, the Chatterati, to the court theater for Oscar's birthday presentation. It was her birthday, too, a detail she had not told him when they met on Midsummer Eve in the park. It had not seemed important, and she had not lied about it—or not exactly. She'd just left things unsaid. Like the fact that they had the same birthday. And that she'd discovered those Gustavian papers. In any event, she had not told a single person about their secret friendship, except for her new maid, Brita. She didn't want anyone to ruin it.

Making it clear they wanted nothing to do with her, the Chatterati abandoned Jacquette near a potted orange tree in the small ballroom called the Déjeuner Salon. Through the tree's dense, waxy leaves, she saw Dorothea, the foreign minister's daughter, dancing and twirling in a tiny white ball gown. When Jacquette had last seen Dorothea in Stockholm, the girl's Polish mother had clothed her in bright, shimmering hues that did nothing for her complexion. In white, she looked like an angel.

The pale child was the reason Aurora had sent Jacquette to Drottningholm. Jacquette was to gather as much information as possible about the foreign minister and pass it on to Aurora, who intended to use it to undermine the poor senile man. More than anything, Aurora wanted Wetterstedt to become foreign minister, and she also wanted to persuade Charles Jean to elevate him from baron to count. Wetterstedt, Jacquette was certain, knew nothing of these plans.

When Dorothea saw Jacquette walking toward her, she stopped spinning. "Are the flowers in your hair forget-me-nots?"

Jacquette bent her head, allowing Dorothea to touch her wreath, and attempted a bright smile. "They're bluets. Like forget-me-nots, but the color is deeper. I cut them in a field just behind the China Palace and made the wreath myself."

"They match the trim on your dress."

Jacquette felt her smile fade. At the foot of her bed this morning, she had found her beautiful dress in a large birthday box wrapped in ribbons and silk. It was made of white muslin, high-waisted with blue trim and a wide blue sash. Blue, her favorite color. She'd spread it across her bed to examine it, hoping it was a gift from Aurora and Wetterstedt or perhaps even from her father. But no, Aunt Lotten had told her. It was from the queen, who gave a similar dress to all her future maids of honor when they turned fourteen. Her father had forgotten her birthday, and Aurora and Wetterstedt had sent her shoes.

A sharp voice startled Jacquette out of her daydream.

"Girls, *vite*. You are needed." It was the master of ceremonies. He carried four sprawling bouquets of purple and white orchids. Each had a ribbon around it with an engraved card attached. One of them, she saw, bore her name.

Jacquette took her bouquet, confused, and the man disappeared, leaving only Dorothea, who was rearranging her flowers.

"There," she said. "Let's do yours."

"What is all this about?" Jacquette asked.

"They are for the prince. The king will say a birthday blessing. Then we will give the prince the flowers." She frowned. "I was supposed to do it with Elise and Augusta, just the three of us. I don't mind that you were added, though."

"Well, I did not mean to offend. I knew nothing of this."

"Oh, it is only because you met Prince Oscar in the park on Midsummer Eve. He asked for you. My governess told me."

"Do not believe such talk," said Jacquette.

"No, it's true. The prince wanted you to do it instead of me, but my father spoke to the crown prince. I would not have cared so much whether I did it or not."

Had Oscar learned nothing about the royal court? Dorothea's father was Wetterstedt's superior, and so his young daughter had precedence over Jacquette.

"I have great respect for your father," Jacquette said, trying to be tactful.

"I am not allowed to walk in the park without a chaperone. Are you? My governess told me your mother and her sister, Emilie, used to do such things, too." She pulled a purple orchid from Jacquette's bouquet and added it to her own. "I like the purple ones."

Dorothea's mother appeared. Glaring at Jacquette, she took the bouquet from her daughter. As she placed it in Jacquette's hands, she leaned close and whispered, "Darling, Dorothea is much too young to be hearing your sort of gossip."

"But, Countess, I knew nothing about this flower presentation. And I only met the prince by chance," Jacquette said.

Dorothea's mother took her daughter by the arm and held her close. Absent a miracle, Jacquette thought, she would never again be allowed anywhere near the foreign minister's young daughter now that his wife had such a low opinion of her. And how did everyone know she had met Oscar in the park?

Lemoine would never have told; he was part of Aurora's circle. It had to be the Swedish cavalier, Carl Löwenhielm. Or Oscar himself.

She saw him at the end of the ballroom, encircled by a group of nobles, all laughing and offering birthday wishes. She wished she could ask him what had happened. But he was the center of attention, the cause for celebration, *le petit prince*. The boy who'd climbed into the hedge to help her had vanished, replaced by a smiling, carefree prince in a white waistcoat with gold epaulets and polished buttons. The sight of him made her sad.

He does not know how quickly they will expect him to grow up, she thought.

A sharp, strong elbow jostled her arm from behind, and her flowers tumbled to the floor.

"A million pardons. How unexpected that the prince chose you to present a bouquet! You really have used your time well while all of us have been working."

It was Erica, with the rest of the Chatterati a few steps behind her. She turned to Johanna and said, "Aurora's daughter, I understand, has been talking with the prince in the woods. Alone. Two statues from the same block of marble, didn't I tell you?"

"Cold and hard, like Aurora," Johanna replied.

"Not so hard, really. Easily broken," said Diane. "Marble, I mean."

The lovely orchids were still scattered about, and Jacquette stooped to retrieve them. She had a fervent desire for someone to find these girls husbands. Preferably short, old ones from Dalarna.

"Look! There's something written on the back of your name card." Dorothea retrieved the card from the floor, where it was lying among the flowers, and handed it to Jacquette. The neat French script on the reverse side said, *You should have told me we have the same birthday. O.*

"Who wrote it? What does it say?" Dorothea asked. Jacquette folded the card quickly, but not before Erica read its message.

"How sweet. Little notes from the prince," she hissed.

Before Jacquette could answer, Aunt Lotten motioned to them. "Come now. They are waiting." She straightened Jacquette's wreath and beckoned Dorothea forward.

Jacquette gathered her bouquet, tucked the card back inside, and shrugged at Erica.

They passed banks of skirted tables sagging under the weight of Oscar's birthday gifts. He would need someone to help him figure out what to do with the vast array, which included a set of antlers.

Aunt Lotten showed them a discreet spot where they would not interfere with the guests' views of the royal family. Charles Jean was speaking in French.

"He really does not know any Swedish, does he?" Dorothea asked.

Just then, Aunt Lotten jabbed Jacquette in the back, and she stumbled toward Oscar. No one had told her what to do, so she curtsied, still holding the bouquet, and waited to be presented.

The master of ceremonies took her arm. "Your Royal Highness, may I present Countess Jacquette Gyldenstolpe."

Oscar's smile was broad, even a bit mischievous. He seemed to be having fun. As she rose, he spoke to her.

"Do you plan to give me the flowers, or are you cross with me?"

"Yes, sir," she said.

He looked bewildered and opened his mouth, probably to ask which question she was answering. Aunt Lotten's fingers wrapped around Jacquette's shoulder, pushing her ahead. Her aunt was not about to permit this conversation to go on, and Jacquette was grateful.

"Let her stay a moment, Countess. If you would," Oscar said, and Aunt Lotten removed her hand from Jacquette's shoulder. "I'm sorry to have involved you in this flower thing," he said to Jacquette.

"Did you have to tell everyone you saw me in the woods? They're all talking about it." She waved a gloved hand in the direction of the Chatterati.

"I didn't tell."

She noticed Charles Jean glance in their direction. "Well, who was it, then?"

"It was Carl. He told my father that Lemoine left me unsupervised and is trying to have him dismissed."

Everyone was watching Oscar and Jacquette now, particularly Dorothea, who was still holding out her bouquet. She looked like she was about to cry.

"Thank you for your kindness in inviting me, sir. Happy birthday," Jacquette said.

"Good then," he said, low and fast. "We are still friends. Friends who share a birthday."

No one has told him, she thought. *Royals never apologize, and they do not have friends*. She whispered those words in his ear.

CHAPTER THREE

Church Pavilion at Drottningholm Palace
August 1811

The day Aurora returned from traveling, she strode into The Birdcage without acknowledging the kitchen maid who opened the door. After examining the foyer's appointments with a critical eye, she removed her French bonnet and pulled off her gloves. When none of the footmen appeared to collect them, her eyes finally rested on the unfortunate maid, a skinny farmer's daughter from Drottningholm Village, who had retreated into a corner. With apologies for her inexperience, the girl took the items, mumbling that she'd only happened to be passing by, heard Aurora's knock, and did not know where to store such finery as this. Jacquette, who had been watching from the adjacent sitting room, recognized Aurora's long, exasperated moan. It was time to intervene, if only to save herself from further embarrassment.

The confused maid willingly turned over the bonnet and gloves and darted toward the kitchen. Jacquette placed the items on the table. Despite all her mother's faults, Jacquette had missed Aurora and embraced her.

With a grin, she said, "Really, Mother? She's just a girl from the village."

"Is that the greeting I get after eight weeks?"

Wetterstedt's attentions apparently had not softened her mother's disposition.

"Tell me everything about this misunderstanding on the prince's birthday." Aurora lowered her voice. "It must have been the foreign minister's doing. Why else would Dorothea have been invited to the evening events and not you? You were paired with her at the ceremony in the afternoon, weren't you?"

Jacquette shrugged. "We presented the flowers and had lunch. Then, when I came back here to dress for the fireworks, Aunt Lotten told me the crown prince had decided I should stay in my room. But Dorothea went. I saw her from my window when she was walking there."

"How very odd."

Jacquette did not tell Aurora the reason for Charles Jean's change of heart. The rumor about her meeting with Oscar in the woods, started by that pompous cavalier Carl Löwenhielm, had not faded. The Chatterati were not about to forget it and, since July, had chided her constantly about being Oscar's favorite.

She raised another subject. "How was your trip?"

"Quette, praise God that I survived it. I was quite sick, but Wetterstedt took such good care of me."

"How is he?"

"If it were not for that dear man, the rebels would have taken the southern half of our country by now. I don't know what Charles Jean would do without him."

In the sitting room, Aurora selected the largest, most luxurious chair, the one where Erica usually sat. A servant appeared and removed her bookmark and spectacles from the side table. Mortified, Jacquette waved her hands in a gesture of apology.

Erica moved within earshot of Jacquette and grumbled under her breath, "Your mother outranks me. But you do not." She turned to Aurora. "Baroness, welcome," she said in a clipped, unfriendly tone. Aurora hated to be reminded that the divorce had lowered her title from countess to baroness. "The queen has been asking after you."

Eight weeks of summer court duties had only intensified the Chatterati's resentment about Aurora's trip with Wetterstedt. They saw it as the latest in a long list of royal favors, beginning with the king granting her divorce from Jacquette's father. But Aurora was adept at making others forget who she had been and what she had done, and she had regained her power, to the astonishment of everyone except Jacquette.

Unperturbed, Aurora replied, "Don't be silly. The queen knew all the details. There is a rebellion in the south, you know. We women must keep abreast of politics, or men will only think of us lying on our backs."

Jacquette sensed a trace of respect in the surprised expressions of Erica's companions. Only Diane, always ready with the most precise details, came to Erica's defense. "Actually, Baroness Aurora, you visited Ramlösa spa to take the waters. The second session. Was that to learn of politics?"

Ignoring her, Aurora continued. "I wrote to the queen from Skåne each third day. My absence was, of course, with Her Majesty's blessing." Thus ending the discussion, she drained a glass of sherry offered from a passed tray and turned her full attention to Jacquette.

With a thin smile, she said, "For strength. Well then, let us go to your room and find Madame Love."

Aunt Lotten, who had been standing in the corner having a loud discussion with the cook about a list of provisions for the house, spoke up. "My dear sister."

"Lotten," Aurora gushed.

Since her parents were divorced, it was less than evident to Jacquette how the two remained sisters, for they had only been sisters-in-law and were sisters-in-law no longer. It was obvious they were not friends.

"You should know that the only room I had for Jacquette and her party was upstairs."

"One room?" Aurora tapped her finger on the arm of the chair. "In the attic? For these two months, my daughter has been in an attic?"

Hearing Aurora's question, the other ladies fell silent. No one ever challenged Lotten's decisions.

"Jacquette can stay with me in the palace tonight. We will be leaving for Stockholm in the morning," said Aurora. "I have plenty of space. The queen assigned me rooms."

"Near mine?" As chief court mistress, Aunt Lotten always slept in a small room just outside the queen's bedchamber.

"Just down the hall, with a view of the park. Come, Jacquette."

As Jacquette opened the door to her room, Aurora said, "Let's see this attic." She pursed her lips, apparently disapproving of her daughter's small quarters.

"Aunt Lotten has tried to make us comfortable here."

"I hope you haven't been allowing her to bully you. She is still angry about the divorce. Though I can understand a sister who takes her brother's side."

Jacquette found it hard to see how anyone could choose a side in her parents' disastrous union. They both had lied, including to her, and they both had cheated.

"Where is your summer maid? I didn't hire her to flirt with the pages. What's her name?"

Brita came up the stairs, breathless. "It's Brita, Baroness Aurora. Welcome back."

About eighteen years old, Brita had straight blonde hair twisted into a crown of braids, and her eyes were a striking gray-green. Her skin was pale and even, without a hint of the reddish cast common among light-haired Swedes. Today, she was wearing lip tint and a necklace of seashells in soft hues. Standing as she did at least six feet tall, her plain dress hugging her slim figure without a pucker, she towered over Aurora and did not flinch under her criticism.

"Brita it is, then," Aurora said. She ran her hands down the sides of Jacquette's waist. "Jacquette's gown looks lovely. I know the clothes presses here are not what we have in the city."

"Thank you, ma'am."

"And Jacquette has so enjoyed your company. Haven't you, Jacquette?"

Jacquette nodded.

"Baron Wetterstedt and I have been talking, and we think it time that Jacquette had her own lady's maid. We wish to offer you the position."

Brita bowed her head, and when she looked up, she had tears in her eyes. "Thank you, Countess. And thank Baron Wetterstedt, too."

"Jacquette is only fourteen now, but we have every reason to expect that she will join the queen's household when the time is right."

"I won't," said Jacquette.

"I am talking to Brita, dear." Aurora turned to Brita. "What do you say? You will need to learn how to conduct yourself at court. There are many rules, but also many privileges."

"I'm sorry, but I cannot accept," Brita said.

"I pay well," said Aurora.

Brita nodded. "I have other plans for the fall. I want to learn baking."

"Baking bread? You can learn that in my kitchens," said Aurora with an incredulous look.

"No, pastries."

Aurora narrowed her eyes. "Oh, my dear, pastry chefs are men, and they are French. Suit yourself. You can return to your family, and without my letter of reference. You won't get a job anywhere, not even in a coffeehouse."

Brita put her hand over her mouth, stood there a moment, and then ran from the room.

"Odd girl," Aurora said to Jacquette.

"I like her." Jacquette wondered why she had not taken the time to get to know Brita better.

"I'll find someone else for you. Don't give it a thought. Tell me about Dorothea."

Jacquette had been hoping Aurora had forgotten about the foreign minister's daughter. "She's spoiled and unreasonable, and she hates me."

"I want to know everything. Every detail."

"There's nothing to tell. I walked ahead of her at the flower ceremony, and she wouldn't have anything to do with me afterward. They say she's a studious girl, and her head is always in a book. I don't know why you think my knowing her would help anything."

"So, you went first? And she walked behind, is that right?"

"What, at the flower ceremony?"

Aurora crossed her arms and glared at Jacquette.

"Yes, she was behind me."

"You should have allowed her to go first."

Before Jacquette could say anything more, they heard shouts coming from the stables through the open window.

"We can talk about this later," Aurora said.

Leaving Aurora wobbling down the stairs in her tight satin shoes, Jacquette ran to the building directly behind The Birdcage. The long three-story structure had iron gates set in rounded arches and housed the stables as well as barracks for the king's Life Guards, who slept upstairs. In front of one of the portals, Carl Löwenhielm, astride a tall gray stallion, was tapping the handle of his whip on his thigh and shouting at Lemoine.

"What did you think you were doing, letting the prince ride out alone?" Carl demanded.

Oscar was sitting on a bench between the stables and the shore of Lake Mälaren. He was doubled over, and two young Life Guards holding a collection of rags and glass bottles peered at him from close range. He motioned to Jacquette, then sat up to speak to the guards, who bowed and retreated toward the stable.

"What happened?" she asked. He rubbed his chest with the sleeve of his mud-covered riding jacket, and his face was streaked with dirt.

"It was stupid. I'm fine."

Hands on her hips, she bent to look him over. "Liar."

"All right, then. Do you know that stone wall in the English Park?"

"By the big lake?"

He nodded. "Odin must be getting lazy. I thought he could jump it."

"You fell?"

Oscar's breathing was ragged, and he coughed before he spoke. "I hit a tree branch, a low one. I was looking ahead to the wall, and I didn't see it."

"Where's Odin?"

"He's fine. They took him inside to rub him down. It's Lemoine I am worried about. Carl told him I was not to ride alone, and now he will have to answer to my father."

"Can't Count Löwenhielm leave him be?"

"He thinks he's always right and that everyone is out to get him." Oscar winced in pain. "But he works tirelessly. No one can handle the correspondence like Carl."

Aurora, after struggling across the bumpy drive outside the stables, joined them and fussed over Oscar as if he were her son.

Trying to smile, he said he was reluctant to see the palace doctor, lest the man jeopardize Lemoine's position by informing Charles Jean. With a motherly shake of the head, Aurora picked up one of the chilled cloths left behind by the guards and began mopping his forehead.

He shook her off and continued his conversation with Jacquette. "Carl's never let up since Lemoine allowed me to walk alone with you that day. But it was worth it. Don't worry. I'll take care of Lemoine."

Jacquette could not help but smile. He valued their bond.

Aurora's eyes darted from Jacquette back to Oscar, and Jacquette realized what her mother was thinking. She had to get her as far away from Oscar as possible.

It didn't work.

"Sir, perhaps we can help," Aurora said. "I can ask my doctor to see you. He is discreet."

"I would appreciate that," Oscar replied.

"Jacquette, let's go," Aurora said.

"Stay with me a minute, Q."

Oscar never should have called her that. Not in front of Aurora, who was gawking at them as if their clothes were on fire. But Oscar was young, and born a commoner, and could not have known her mother would devour their friendship like a cat with catnip.

Aurora stroked Jacquette's cheek and looked at her with a newfound keen interest. "My lovely girl, you stay right here with the prince."

After she was gone, Oscar moved over, and Jacquette sat with him on the bench. "Knowing me is not going to be easy for you. I am beginning to understand that," he said. "I think I gave your mother all sorts of ideas. I'm learning that mothers can be like that."

Easy or not, what was done was done. If there was ever a choice, a way to turn back, it had evaporated the instant Aurora heard Oscar call her Q. The innocent days of summer were past, and Jacquette knew it.

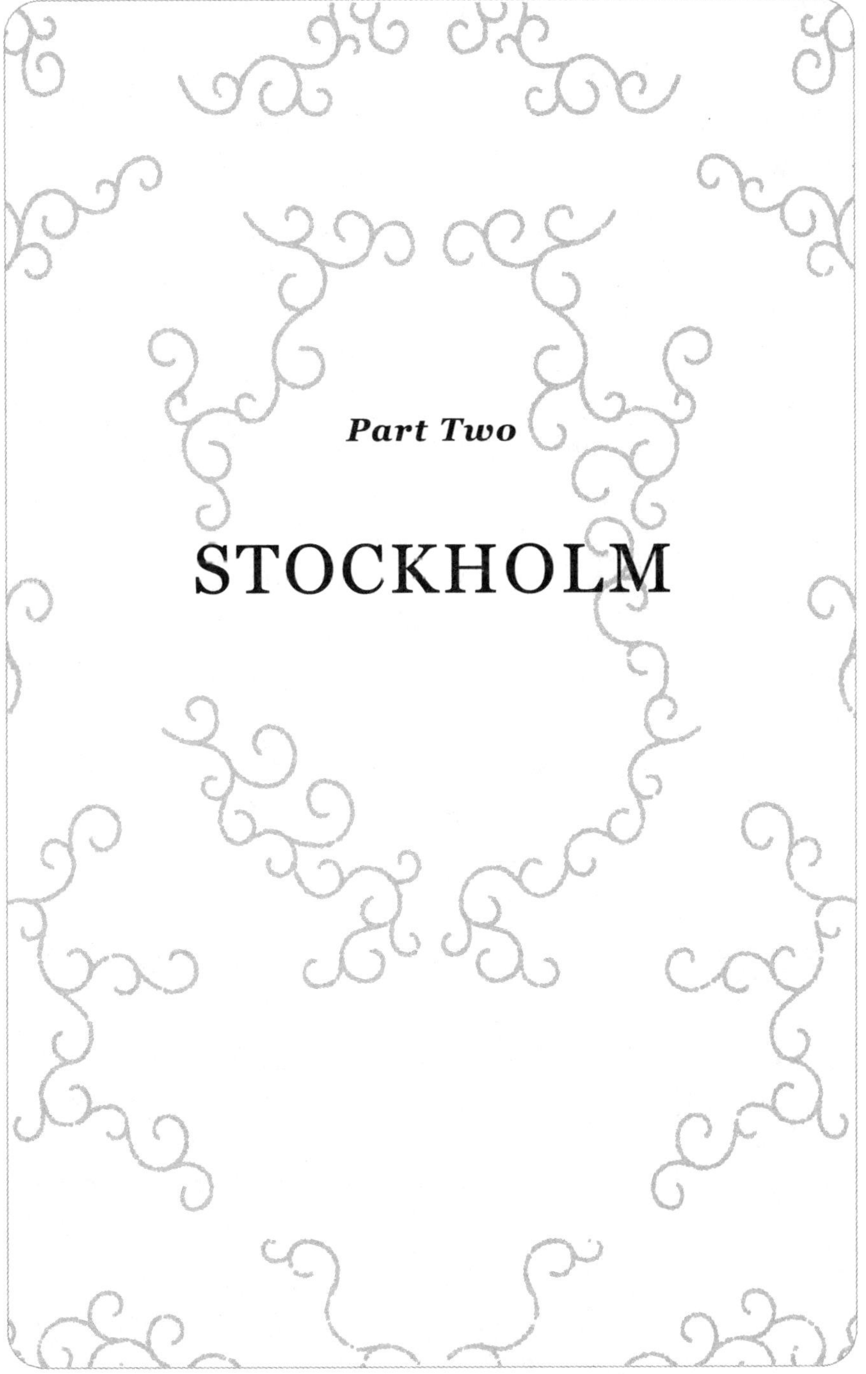

Part Two

STOCKHOLM

CHAPTER FOUR

Stockholm
Three Years Later
January 1815

The new year began in peace. On a snowy evening, Jacquette walked to the Stock Exchange from the line of carriages parked around Old Town's main square, nodding at the young door guard as he adjusted his chin strap and winked. The attention gave her a warm, pleasant buzz, and she wondered whether he remembered her from last year's Amaranth Ball, which had been held in the middle of the long war against Bonaparte. Then, with most men fighting Charles Jean's battles in Germany, society had come to a virtual halt, and Jacquette and Oscar had lived almost like ordinary people. On summer days, they would lie on the hill near the copper tents in the park at Haga Palace, united against the world, promising to remain the best of friends forever.

It was now a distant memory. After Charles Jean had defeated the French, Jacquette and Aurora sailed to Paris to celebrate with Wetterstedt. When they returned to Sweden, Oscar was in Norway, and Jacquette had not seen him in months.

"Come on. I'm freezing," Aurora said, putting an end to her daughter's thoughts of Oscar. Jacquette reveled in this weather, snug in a gray-blue gown the color of crusted Lake Mälaren ice, a pearly white pelisse with a high collar, and a fur-lined Bulgarian cape.

Aurora had regrettably high expectations for tonight's ball, which was being held to celebrate the new union with Norway, a wilderness Charles Jean now owned in the same way Jacquette owned her horse. Norway was Charles Jean's reward for defeating the French, and Wetterstedt's negotiating skills had secured the union between the countries. Charles Jean had proclaimed Wetterstedt's treaty a grand achievement, and Aurora said it was only a matter of time before he made his faithful chancellor a count.

Aurora brushed a curl away from Jacquette's forehead. "You're the loveliest girl here."

Was her mother just reassuring herself? Aurora believed physical beauty could compensate for almost any fault. Which of Jacquette's many inadequacies was troubling her mother tonight? Compliments from Aurora always made Jacquette uneasy.

In the ballroom, a tall officer escorted Jacquette to the receiving line. She waved to the dance master, who was arranging his cards, and reached for a fan, feeling the heat of the crowded room collide with the blast of cold air from the stairwell.

So, she thought, *I will begin this year by spending another night in an uncomfortably hot room dancing with lustful young counts who are bored with their interminable wait to collect inheritances from their very alive fathers. One of them will muster the courage to ask me to step outside in the frigid air, confident that his clumsy groping will lighten my surly mood.*

Ack.

She shivered, and the officer gave her a curious look. She did not want him to get the wrong idea, so she coughed and mentioned that she had just spent a month in bed with the chest grippe. He allowed the distance between them to grow.

She took a place at the end of the receiving line. The dispirited Norwegian delegates, who had been summoned to Stockholm to "celebrate" the Association, were standing behind a table examining their country's new flag, which, in truth, was the Swedish flag with a tiny red-and-white Norwegian cross in the corner. They looked displeased, and it was easy to understand why.

Aurora darted in and out of the line, chattering to one countess after another. Then Jacquette saw Oscar and drew in her breath. She touched the folds of her skirt, her hips, her throat.

He was at the end of the row of royals, only about ten feet away, separated from his father by a long empty space. Something was different about the tilt of his head, the knowing look in his lively brown eyes, the confident touch of his hand on the edge of the table. The childish softness in his face was gone, replaced by prominent cheekbones and a narrow, elegant nose. She could find no trace of the old tension in his slim square shoulders. His new posture was relaxed, a graceful, irreverent near-slouch.

No Swedish count could compare to him.

Eye to eye with a commander of the Life Guards, deep in conversation, he raised his eyebrows here and there with a half smile. His hands were never still, and she could imagine his soft, quick speech, perfect Swedish, but with *r*'s spoken from the base of his throat like the Parisian he was. When he tossed his tangle of dark brown curls, just as he had as a boy, two nearby ladies smiled at each other. Jacquette saw someone give him a sip of brandy and heard his muted laugh.

She had been so excited to see him, but something in his manner made her hesitate. So much had changed.

Vowing not to stare at him, she pretended to admire the gifts.

"I filled your card. Look." Aurora waved a white paper in front of Jacquette's eyes. She had been talking to the dance master. "Ledet gave you everyone I wanted." She pointed to a name, and Jacquette squinted.

"Count Hamilton?"

"Whom would you prefer?" Aurora's mouth narrowed.

"Is Adam Lewenhaupt here? I like him, and he doesn't ask every one of his dance partners to marry him." She stood on her toes and looked for Oscar.

"He's just a baron."

"So? You are just a baroness, Mother."

"You're seventeen. Almost eighteen. It's time you filled your dance card wisely."

"What does it matter? Let me see that." Jacquette ran her finger down the names. She would be Oscar's partner for the third dance, the first one after the ceremonial waltzes. It was a good position, one everyone would notice. She was pleased, despite the gossip it would cause.

"A countess should marry a count. Or better."

Lowering her voice, Jacquette said, "Father was a count, and you divorced him to marry a baron." She toyed with her white sash.

Aurora cocked her head and frowned. "Stop looking at the prince."

Jacquette shifted her gaze away from Oscar. "I wasn't."

Aurora held her fan up and lapsed into Swedish, which she spoke only to servants or when in distress. She was blunt. "Whatever is between you and the prince can never be more than butterfly games. And if you don't want his father to end it before it begins, you should do as I say and choose a husband."

"So you say."

"Oscar is a man now, and Charles Jean must look for a suitable wife for him."

"Am I unsuitable?" Jacquette asked.

"My dear, if you thought you had a chance—"

"Is it because you divorced Father? Or because Aunt Emilie was dismissed from court? Or because of Grandmother and her lovers? Is that why I am unsuitable? Because you are a De Geer?"

"You are a De Geer, too. I will not listen to an unkind word about your grandmother. Nor my sister."

Jacquette bit her lower lip, and the pain brought tears to her eyes. "I loved Grandmother, and you know how dear Aunt Emilie is to me."

Aurora continued, "Charles Jean has no choice if he wants to hold his throne. He is a commoner and needs to find a princess to marry Oscar. How can he begin a dynasty without royal blood? He will keep unmarried Swedish countesses like you as far away as possible."

Jacquette played with the fingertip of her glove. "But what has any of that to do with me getting married?"

"Oh, my young girl, it has everything to do with it. If I am reading you correctly, it is the only way for you to get what I think you want."

"And what is that?"

Aurora lowered her fan, and an adoring smile spread over her face. She was beaming at Oscar, who was looking in their direction. "Him. That is why your grandmother made me marry your father when I was fifteen."

"Why?"

"I had the king's eye. Just like you have Prince Oscar's."

"Stop imagining things, Aurora."

Aurora hated Jacquette calling her by her given name. She said it made her feel like less of a mother, which was precisely the point.

Jacquette tapped Aurora on the shoulder and whispered, "Look. The crown prince wishes to speak with you."

Aurora stepped out of the line, leaving Jacquette face-to-face with Oscar.

With a shy smile, he dipped his head and clasped her hands, squeezing hard. *Good*, she thought. *He is happy to see me.*

"Blue like your eyes," he said, pointing at her gown. "It makes them look almost violet."

"Thanks."

"From Paris?"

"Yes, I had some dresses made there. We came back in November. You were in Norway."

"Why haven't I seen you at the palace?" he asked. "Someone told me you had the chest grippe."

"It's just something I had to say. People ask questions."

He shook his head, but his eyes smiled. He was always scolding her for telling little lies.

"I couldn't leave the house. Emilie is in Stockholm. She's sick again."

"It's the cold," he said.

Oscar hated the cold. They argued endlessly about it.

"She's getting stronger, I think," said Jacquette.

"Good." He glanced in Charles Jean's direction, but the crown prince probably could not hear his son's soft voice. "Q, I wanted to talk to you about something."

Jacquette hated the way her heart quickened when he said her name. "*Absolut*."

Though she hoped he would ask her to walk around the palace

gardens with him on the next sunny day or accompany him to the queen's apartments after this infernal ball, he did not look like a young man ready to make an invitation. His easy smile was gone.

"Have you read the foreign newspapers?"

So, this was not a social conversation.

She waved toward her cousins on the other side of the ballroom. "Not for a month. I've been with Emilie. Will there be a written examination?"

"No, listen to me, I'm serious. The reason I asked you about the foreign newspapers is because my father cannot censor them. You know what he and Magnus are doing to the local press, don't you?"

"Oscar, just say what you mean. I don't know what you're talking about."

He spoke quickly, still watching Charles Jean. "My father and Magnus are using the Mandarin to seize every book, every newspaper, every pamphlet that criticizes the government. I was lucky and saw a French newspaper that reported some of the opposition's views."

"What did it say?" she asked, wondering how this concerned her.

He leaned close. "That some people want Crown Prince Gustav to return and replace us. My father is so over-fearful of Gustav, he even calls him the pretender. It's as if we are the Tudors or something."

She laughed. "Your father has never had more power. He defeated Bonaparte."

"Exactly," Oscar said. "The article I saw said Sweden has no need of us now that Bonaparte is gone. It's what my father fears most. And it said we spend all our money on the army and let the people starve. That we broke up farms and took the land. That we are foreigners, and I'm so weak I'm near death."

"You don't look like you're near death."

"What bothers me is that my father won't permit these opinions to be published. And he is cutting me out. He and Magnus look guilty as thieves every time I walk in on one of their meetings."

Jacquette knew how much Oscar envied Magnus Brahe, Charles Jean's young protégé, who was about a decade older than him. "Your father is right to keep him close. He's old nobility."

She meant that Magnus was dangerous. Gustav was not the first royal person the Swedish nobility had deposed. They could do it again.

Oscar's eyes moved across the room to Magnus, a vaguely effeminate man with close-set eyes and a pointed chin. Standing next to Charles Jean, he was ignoring a pair of baronesses who were trying, without success, to engage him in conversation. Since he'd entered Paris at Charles Jean's side after Bonaparte's abdication, Magnus had spent much of his energy driving away anyone who was close to the crown prince. Including Oscar.

"I thought things would change after we got back from Norway," said Oscar. "But my father won't give me any responsibility in the government or the army, and now he won't even tell me anything about this unrest. Some of it is directed against me. Seems like I have a right to know."

Diane, the cleverest of the Chatterati, was pointing in their direction. Instead of retreating to a respectful distance, Jacquette leaned closer to Oscar and smirked back.

"Forget them," Oscar said.

"How can I? They hate me, so I'm keeping them close. And I don't see what you can do about the opposition, anyway."

"You can help me. Wetterstedt oversees the censorship raids. Did you know that?"

Jacquette found this ridiculous. "Wetterstedt would never order a raid on the newspapers. The publishers come to my mother's salon every Sunday."

Oscar set his jaw. "Believe me, he is in charge of enforcing the Withdrawal Power. I'm not saying he wants to do it, but he signs the orders."

"Do you want me to talk to him?" She did not understand; Oscar could speak to Wetterstedt himself.

"No, don't. I'm not sure what I want you to do. Just keep your eyes open at home. If I could see what is being censored before the Mandarin destroys it, I would know what is going on, but I can't figure out how."

So that was it. Oscar wanted something from her. Had he even asked about her life, or what she had been doing? Had he missed her? He used to call her his best friend.

A tall young man in a plain black suit came and stood next to Oscar, evidently anxious to speak to him. His clear blue eyes were half hidden by wisps of straight blond hair that could not conceal the mischief inside him. Jacquette knew a rake when she saw one.

Oscar made the introductions. "Countess Jacquette Gyldenstolpe, this is Frederik Due from Norway."

Frederik kissed her hand and used his charm, as she had expected, speaking in fluent French. "Countess, I hope to see much of you. I'll be living in Stockholm now. The crown prince has invited me to be one of Prince Oscar's new cavaliers."

How curious of Charles Jean to choose this one, thought Jacquette. *He is plainly a commoner and has a bit of a sly look about him.*

"It is a pleasure," she said, not yet certain whether it was.

Oscar was keeping a close eye on his father, and Jacquette smelled brandy on his breath. Charles Jean, who was practically a teetotaler, would disapprove, but he was occupied with a guard who was delivering a message. As Charles Jean unfolded it, he touched his hand to his belt and looked at his right hip, frowning.

"You know what my father was doing, don't you? Reaching for his sword," Oscar said to Frederik. "I don't think he will ever get used to peace."

"We Norwegians could start another war if that would please him," said Frederik.

Oscar laughed. He liked people who amused him.

Frederik cupped his hand over his mouth and nudged Oscar, looking pleased with himself. "I spoke to the dance master."

"And?"

"He changed it around. She will be your third dance. First a brewer's wife, then the dowager queen, then she is yours."

Oscar's face lit up, and he slapped Frederik on the shoulder. "I knew you could do it," he said.

Who could Frederik be talking about? Jacquette's dance card was set. She was paired with Oscar for the third dance.

"Go tell her," Frederik said, nodding at a girl who was moving toward them in the receiving line.

Jacquette searched her memory for a name and finally remembered. She was Adelaide Frölich, a short, blonde countess from the north. Her father once had attended court, but Jacquette had never seen the daughter in Stockholm before. She looked about seventeen, her own age, and was wearing a blue velvet gown the same color as Jacquette's.

Had she really been bumped down the list by this country countess? She looked down at the blue velvet of Adelaide's skirts. It clearly came from Paris, and there was nothing like it in Stockholm. Who had dressed this new girl?

Oscar was staring at Adelaide, his eyes unfocused from the brandy. His face looked gaunt and hungry, reminding Jacquette of the counts who invited her into the garden. She pushed the thought away.

"Does my father know about the change?" Oscar asked Frederik.

"Not necessary," said Frederik. He was brash, this new Norwegian courtier.

"Have you met Adelaide?" Oscar asked Jacquette.

"Maybe a long time ago," mumbled Jacquette, trying to sound unimpressed.

"You don't mind giving up the early dance, do you? We will be partners in one of the country dances. It's a new one." She always knew when Oscar was nervous; he clasped his hands behind him, as he was doing now.

"From the English court," Frederik offered.

Jacquette rose to her full height and turned her back on Frederik, but not before giving him the most withering, hostile look she could muster. Apparently recognizing that he had waded into something that was not his affair, Frederik struck up a conversation with the commander of the Life Guards.

Oscar was persistent. "Don't be cross. You'll like Adelaide. You could tell her how everything here works. Be her friend, you know. She'll be here at court all winter and doesn't have any experience with the people here. The men, especially. Not like you do."

What did he mean by that? Was he talking about the rumors that had always followed the women in her family? Tears came to her eyes, and she faintly heard Oscar introduce Adelaide.

By the time she'd collected herself, Oscar was boasting to the girl, something about bullets flying over his head on a bridge during the Norwegian campaign. Jacquette doubted that anything of note had happened during his four-week march through Norway last summer, the only time he had been anywhere near a battle. Charles Jean would never have placed his only son and heir in danger. Oscar was just trying to impress Adelaide. The room seemed suddenly loud, and Jacquette's head began to ache.

"I must go dance with a brewer's wife now," said Oscar to Adelaide. He kissed her hand with an annoying little smirk, and she tossed her head, her blonde curls swinging past her round, pink shoulders.

Oscar took another timid step toward Adelaide, but someone blocked his path.

"Your Royal Highness." It was Carl Löwenhielm, the cavalier Jacquette had first met at Drottningholm nearly four years ago.

Carl Löwenhielm's breed of Swedish noble was familiar to Jacquette: counts from old families who died in the houses where they had been born. Still, despite his somewhat stiff and unrefined air, Carl, dressed in his deep blue Life Guards hussar's uniform, was not unattractive. He was older than most of Jacquette's officer friends, probably about twenty-five, and filled his jacket to perfection. The signature dozen or so white cords of the hussar uniform stretched taut across his chest, and the three vertical rows of tiny buttons lay flat and straight. Jacquette had known a few hussar officers, skinny young counts sent off to war in ill-fitting uniforms, their white cords drooping like sagging branches in an ice storm. Carl, she could see, was not one of those.

"Captain Due, may I see you for a moment?" Carl asked, his tone dripping with false civility.

"Call me Frederik, please," the Norwegian replied as he tucked a stray blond strand behind his ear and gazed at Carl without flinching.

With his sharp, pointed features and high cheekbones, Jacquette imagined there were a few Norwegian girls mourning Frederik's departure for Stockholm.

"We observe formalities in the prince's household, Captain," Carl replied.

Frederik shrugged and looked toward Oscar, who was still occupied with Adelaide. The couple had moved to the edge of the dance floor. Frederik said, "You've been on the Continent, Carl. For how long? Three years?"

Carl's face reddened. "There is no family that has served the Swedish crown like—"

"Yes," said Frederik in a calm voice. "We all know your uncle is in Vienna watching the Allies divide up the French Empire. But he's not at court to fight your battles, is he?"

"My point, Captain Duc, is that His Royal Highness is very particular about the people who surround his son. You might even find yourself back in Norway."

"The crown prince invited me to join his son's household, just as he asked you to do the same." With his boot, Frederik trapped a glass that was rolling toward him across the floor. "So, I'd say we are on equal footing now, wouldn't you? Things are changing, even in Stockholm." He smiled through perfect porcelain-white teeth.

"Don't encourage the prince to pursue that girl, I'm warning you," said Carl. He looked at Adelaide. "She is a fine young woman, and that kind of attention could ruin her reputation."

Frederik grinned. "Like a rutting stag, he is. There's no controlling him."

"Then take him to the inns."

"I think he's in love, Carl."

Frederik's words seemed to reach Jacquette from a distance. In love? Dancing with Adelaide was one thing. But Oscar simply could not be in love with that girl. He'd just admitted she knew no one and was uncomfortable at court. Jacquette refused to believe it.

She saw Aurora walking nearby. "Mother," she said, holding her head, "I must go home now. I am so, so sick."

"Now you call me Mother. But I hope it's not the same illness your aunt has."

"Oh, it is," Jacquette said. "Just as Emilie described. My head is pounding, and my throat is so dry."

Aurora looked around at the officers. "Count Löwenhielm, would you be so kind as to escort my daughter to Blasieholm Square? We live at Douglas House on the top two floors. Wetterstedt is probably working at the palace, but the servants will be there to receive her."

"Certainly," said Carl.

He offered Jacquette his arm.

CHAPTER FIVE

With a crinkle of her stiff black skirts, Aurora moved on after asking Count Löwenhielm to escort Jacquette home. Working on Wetterstedt's behalf, she would remain at the ball until the last dignitary left, seeking out influential people and entertaining, amusing, cajoling. As a pair, Aurora and Wetterstedt were like successive chapters in the same book, and one hardly knew where one ended and the other began.

Jacquette doubted she would ever enjoy a bond that strong with another human being.

Oscar had edged even closer to Adelaide, but Jacquette could not hear his words. The country countess probably could not understand his hushed, rushed, French-tinged Swedish anyway. It would serve him right to have to scramble for a dance partner after Jacquette went home. He deserved it if he really was in love with someone who would wear prim lace-up boots to the Amaranth Ball.

"Ahem."

Jacquette had forgotten about Carl.

He was a few feet away, not even pretending they were conversing. Lest people think she was alone, Jacquette moved next to him. She hoped this would not give Carl the wrong idea, but he didn't seem interested in that sort of thing. Instead of inspecting her waist or admiring her hair, as most men did, he looked past her, somewhere above her left ear.

"Shall I tell Baroness Wetterstedt you are recovered from your—what was it—headache?" he asked.

He thought she was lying. He was right. "Fine. Let us leave."

Outside in the square, Wetterstedt's black carriage was waiting, polished and outfitted for winter with blankets warmed over hot coals. Carl arranged one around her shoulders, then gave her his own for her legs. She braced herself as the driver took off with a loud whistle. As they bumped over the creaky wooden bridge from Old Town to Norrmalm, Carl did not speak a word.

She nestled her chin in the soft white fur of her cape. "It's from France. Do you like it?"

He replied as if reprimanding a child. "I'm a military man. I have no taste for expensive things."

Near the King's Garden, the driver hit a deep rut, and the jolt threw Jacquette off her seat toward the roof. She covered her head, anticipating a blow, but Carl rose and planted his large, calloused palms on her shoulders, pinning her down. His touch was coarse and indelicate, and she could almost feel the imprint of his fingers. It did not last long. He withdrew his hands with a look of surprise, and she mumbled some insincere thanks.

He rapped the ceiling with his sword handle. "Incompetent Stockholm coachmen," he barked.

How would this man ever work with Oscar, who never shouted at anyone? She said, "You must be pleased that the prince called you back to his household."

"Court service is not my preference."

"I see," she said. "You enjoy the army more?"

"Only when I ignore the favoritism. People are being promoted who have no business taking a command."

She suspected he was talking about Magnus.

"You will have your father's estate in Värmland, will you not?" Jacquette knew things such as this. There were not so very many counts in Sweden.

"Long Manor, yes, but my father is dragging his feet and refuses to turn it over to me. He behaves as if he will live forever. He probably will, just to thwart me."

"What do you mean?"

"What I mean, my lady, is that my father has opposed me in everything. I ran away to join the army after he refused me the proper military education. I had to enlist and earn my rank as an officer when that should have been my right as a noble. He is no less opposed to my court service with Prince Oscar, although he may not be so wrong about that. To make matters worse, he denies me my inheritance. He allows the manor to fall into disrepair just to punish me, I believe."

"Do you want to live there?" Värmland was a long way from Stockholm.

"Only if he gives me control. Until then, I'll spend as much time as I can with my regiment and serve at court when I must. But someday, I hope to become a diplomat."

Carl did not resemble the diplomats who filled Aurora's salon on Sundays, but his plans did seem quite definite, unlike Jacquette's own. "But now you are with the prince's household again."

His derisive laugh made her feel naive, something that was far from true. "One does not say no to Crown Prince Charles Jean. Prince Oscar has turned against me, I think; he is much changed since I served him last."

She blinked and opened her eyes wider. People tended to tell her things, and she knew how to encourage them. Particularly if they were men. And she very much wanted to hear this.

"How so?"

"He is boastful, for one thing. Did you hear him telling that girl how bullets flew over his head at the battle in Norway? He was nowhere near any flying bullets."

She was surprised to hear Carl's open criticism. Everyone knew she and Oscar were longtime friends. Maybe Carl did not know the happenings around court. "I haven't seen the prince for almost a year. What caused the change in him?"

"The company he is keeping, I would wager."

"I agree," she sniffed. "I don't think that girl he was with—Adelaide—has ever been to an Amaranth Ball."

Through his teeth, Carl said, "You misunderstand me, Countess. It is the young lady who is being wronged. If the prince does not ruin

Adelaide, she will be in high demand. But no man wants damaged goods or a wife with secrets."

"Who, then?"

"I was talking about his friend, Frederik Due. The new cavalier from Norway."

"Frederik Due? He made me laugh so much when he—"

Carl narrowed his eyes. "When he did what? When he passed that flask of *brännvin* to the prince behind your skirts?"

Carl's laugh had a cruel edge.

"Why are you laughing at me?"

His gruffness seemed to ease, and he offered up a half smile. "I'm not. It's not your fault that you find him amusing, given your education."

"What is wrong with my education? I have a French tutor, and I play the piano well."

"I know it has not been easy for you. Your mother is very busy at court."

"There are women at my house who pass the time with me. I'm not alone." Did this count disapprove of everyone and everything?

"You mean your mother's companions? Are they friends? Servants?"

Jacquette shrugged. It was a question she could not answer herself. "There's Christine Palmstierna. She's my age, and a friend. Her father's a baron, you know. She's my mother's . . . retainer, I guess you would say. A lady's companion. Unofficially."

"Yes, I have heard that her family has fallen on hard times."

Money was an ever-present concern, but in Jacquette's family, it was not to be discussed with strangers. "A lot of people lack means these days. My mother is trying to help her."

Carl sighed, obviously not sharing her view of Aurora's motives. Jacquette had an unsettling desire to prove him wrong.

"I do admire your brothers," he said.

She swiveled away from the window and faced him. "How do you know Nils and August?"

"I served with your father—not Wetterstedt, I mean your real father, Gyldenstolpe—in the Norwegian war, and I see him often on military business. Sometimes I speak with your brothers. When did you see them last?"

Tears burned her eyes. "Four years ago. Father took them north after the divorce. He has never even allowed them to visit."

"I'm sorry. They are exceptional young men."

Neither she nor Carl said another word until they arrived at Douglas House, where she had lived with Aurora and Wetterstedt since they married three years ago.

"You need not worry about me socializing with any servants tonight. Papa Wetterstedt is home." One of the palace coaches was in the carriage yard.

Carl snatched open the side curtain and pressed his forehead against the window. "You sound like you are close to your stepfather," he said, turning to face her. He was looking at her differently now, examining her face, eyeing the backs of her hands. She realized she had left her gloves somewhere and pulled down her sleeves.

"Why, yes, very. Papa is the most competent man I have ever met, and the most diligent."

Carl straightened his tall hussar's hat. "Well, here we are. I am honored to have been the one to accompany you tonight. May I help you out?"

She nodded, somewhat relieved to escape the confines of the compartment. She had always found this carriage large enough before.

In the carriage yard, servants were running everywhere, having seen the royal coach. Jacquette walked past the commotion and approached a man sitting astride a brown stallion. A slight figure in a black cloth suit and cloak, he dismounted, taking care to test his foothold in the stirrup, which was set a hole too long for him. With a wry smile, he scratched the beast on the withers, and it lowered its head and smacked its lips in his direction. Ever kind to horses, her stepfather did not like to ride.

A young groom hurried over, stumbling across the rough stones. "Apologies, Chancellor," the groom said in an uncertain voice. "I was—"

"Attending to your other duties, as you should do. Good fellow," Chancellor of the Court Gustaf Wetterstedt replied, handing the boy the reins. He pulled his white silk scarf up to his chin and wrapped his arms around Jacquette.

"Papa."

"My dear. What are you doing home so early?"

Jacquette buried her face in his cloak.

Bowing to Wetterstedt, Carl linked arms with Jacquette and patted her elbow. She stared at his hand.

"Chancellor, Baroness Wetterstedt asked me to escort the countess home. She is not well."

"Count Löwenhielm, thank you. A thousand times. My carriage is at your disposal for the night. I have more work to do now, but please accept my invitation to my wife's salon on Sunday. And, dear girl, you are ill?"

"I'm fine, Papa," Jacquette said. She peeled Carl's fingers off her elbow and backed away from him.

"Are you exhausted? Let's get you upstairs. And where is your mother?" Wetterstedt looked toward his carriage.

"She's at the ball." Jacquette could still hear the rustle of Aurora's skirts as she walked away. It was a sound she remembered from childhood. To her, it meant abandonment.

"Ah, my good Aurora." Wetterstedt beamed. He extended a hand to Jacquette. "Come with me, my dear."

Carl drifted along behind them toward the royal coach.

"Quette, I have brought home someone you know." Wetterstedt chattered as he walked, something he did whenever he was wavering over a decision.

"At this hour? Who is it?" Jacquette asked.

"It's Brita Nielsen." He pointed to the palace coach.

"Brita? Brita who was my maid?" Jacquette knew only one girl by that name and had not seen or heard of her since the summer of 1811 at Drottningholm.

Wetterstedt nodded.

"Why is she in the royal coach?"

Wetterstedt lowered his voice. "It seems she was arrested behind the French Inn and imprisoned in the palace jail on suspicion of prostitution. She had someone send word to me in the council room, asking for my help."

Jacquette heard Brita's unmistakable, fearless voice before she saw her. She was speaking to the palace guard.

"I must go back to the French Inn. There is a sledding party tomorrow. Please, Captain, please. I need to finish a cake. A very tall and elaborate almond cake. I do thank you for getting me out of there, but . . ."

The carriage door slammed shut, and Jacquette heard the lock slide into place.

Left standing on the step, the guard addressed Wetterstedt. "Chancellor, she's locked herself in."

"Leave it with me, son," Wetterstedt said. Though he had never been in the military, he treated soldiers with unfailing respect, having traveled in Charles Jean's entourage during the war against Bonaparte. He turned to Jacquette. "My dear, would you be so kind as to hold this?"

It was a folder labeled *Withdrawal Power*—the name for the censorship policy Oscar had spoken to her about at the ball. So, Oscar was right; Wetterstedt must have some part in Charles Jean's campaign to stifle opposing views.

She turned the label away from Carl and hugged it against her chest.

Wetterstedt tapped twice on the carriage window and spoke in his most calming voice, the one he used when Aurora was suffering one of her panicky spells. His tactic proved successful, for the door soon creaked open, and Brita appeared, her mouth set in a line.

"Do you know that woman?" Carl asked. He stared at Jacquette, then at Wetterstedt, as if in disbelief.

Jacquette nodded. "Brita Nielsen. She worked for us one summer at Drottningholm, but you wouldn't remember. You don't even recall me being there, do you?"

Carl looked puzzled.

"Never mind. After the summer, my mother asked Brita to stay on as my lady's maid, but she declined. Perhaps, like you, she'd heard about my inappropriate upbringing."

For whatever reason, it gave Jacquette pleasure to shock the stiff and unyielding count from Värmland, who failed to hide the flash of anger in his eyes.

"Just look at her. What kind of woman do you think she is?" he asked.

"I haven't seen her for almost four years."

"I can only hope you have not been around many such people."

"What kind of people?" Jacquette asked.

Carl didn't hesitate. "Prostitutes."

"Preposterous. You don't even know her," Jacquette said. "She told me she was going to find work as a pastry chef."

Admittedly, Brita's attire was unusual. Her garish yellow skirts were trussed up by red ribbons that tied on the sides, and a long expanse of slim lower leg was exposed to the January cold. She wore no gloves, bonnet, or shawl. But Jacquette could see the raised outline of a corset underneath her gown. She had been in Stockholm long enough to know that prostitutes didn't wear corsets.

Whatever Brita was, it was really no business of Carl's, and Jacquette left him standing with the household staff.

Wetterstedt was firm with Brita. "You cannot return tonight. The crown prince is adamant about medical examinations for all the women from the inns. If you don't stay here, you'll be sent to the palace jail. It's the law. But if you accept a position in my household, I can help you."

"I don't have any disease. I decorate pastries," Brita said.

"The crown prince makes no exceptions," replied Wetterstedt.

Brita looked relieved to see Jacquette join them. "Oh, ask the chancellor to let me go."

"What happened?" Jacquette asked. Emilie had told her all about Charles Jean's "morality police," who spent their time raiding the inns and arresting suspected prostitutes, releasing them only after they were "examined" for syphilis. No woman should have had to endure it.

Jacquette could see Wetterstedt was losing the argument.

"The only position open is parlor maid. I know it is not what you want," he said.

Brita turned and began to walk toward the square. "I'll not spend my days polishing the silver."

"Perhaps she prefers parting her legs," Carl said quietly to Jacquette.

She felt like the air had been squeezed from her lungs. She had not noticed him follow her to the carriage. And who was Carl Löwenhielm to make such a judgment?

"Papa," Jacquette said, "Mother once asked Brita to be my lady's maid. I still don't have one."

By the time she realized what she had said, Brita was nodding.

"It is my honor to take the position. Thank you, Baron Wetterstedt," Brita said.

⸙

Wetterstedt fished his spectacles from his pocket, as was his habit in matters resolved to his satisfaction. He patted Jacquette's cheek. "Good. Then it is settled. I'll see Count Löwenhielm off and meet you inside. Would you leave that folder on my desk?"

With an evil look at Carl, Brita sauntered over and straightened Jacquette's white fur hood. She extended her hand for the folder.

"I can take that. You'll have to show me where the office is, though."

"All right."

Brita pointed and frowned. "What's this Withdrawal Power?"

Jacquette did not have time to educate this new maid. "It's the censorship law," she said, hoping that the subject would bore Brita and put an end to her questions.

"And why are these addresses here?" Brita asked, pointing to the writing on the folder.

"They're print shops, I think," said Jacquette.

"I know that."

"How?"

"I walk past when I do errands for the pastry chef," said Brita. "Why are they on this list?"

"How would I know?" asked Jacquette, snatching the folder from

Brita. The string around it caught on Jacquette's bracelet, and one of the papers fluttered to the ground.

It landed face up, and they both examined it. A crude sketch, but unmistakably Oscar, lying dead on a table with his hands folded across his chest.

Brita grimaced at the pamphlet. "You're still tied up with the prince, I see."

"Come on, now. Hurry." Jacquette returned the pamphlet to the folder.

"Why?"

"I'm freezing."

"You don't act cold to me," Brita said.

Even in the dim light of the oil lamps, Brita's arms looked taut and lean, and there was a white powder caked under her fingernails. Maybe she had been telling the truth when she said she worked on cakes.

In the apartment, Sophie, Aurora's lady's maid, greeted Jacquette, but when Brita walked through the door, her voice turned shrill.

"Brita, isn't it? I remember you from Drottningholm. I thought you didn't want to work here."

"I don't," said Brita. "I'm a pastry apprentice at the French Inn."

A footman laughed, and a gratified smile spread across Sophie's face. "In that ensemble? You do look French—I'll give you that."

Jacquette pulled Brita into Wetterstedt's office and placed the folder on his desk. "Let's go upstairs now." She was hoping to get to the bedroom before an argument erupted.

Brita said, "Jacquette, help me leave this place. I'll get back to the French Inn on my own."

"You know I can't do that."

"Please."

"You should be grateful Wetterstedt got you out of the palace jail." Jacquette had heard wails and moans from the prisoners when she and Oscar walked the palace grounds. Oscar said there were all sorts of criminals down there.

"Men always expect gratitude for deciding what is best for us, don't they?"

Jacquette said, "But you can hardly stay on as my maid. My mother will never allow it. Particularly not if she sees you wearing that."

"The dress? It isn't mine. It belongs to a friend."

"A friend who is a prostitute?" Jacquette asked, not really expecting an answer.

"I don't see that the women in your family have a much better reputation. Just more money."

Jacquette had never encountered such an impertinent maid. "I don't see how you can question our reputations, not wearing *that*." She wrinkled her nose and looked at the threadbare dress.

"I'm not a prostitute, Jacquette. You'll not find a single person to say it. You might take a look in your own cupboard."

Jacquette was used to dismissing all sorts of gossip; it had been whispered and shouted at her from all corners ever since she came to Stockholm. Gossip about her Aunt Emilie resigning her position as a maid of honor in a scandal at the age of twenty-three. Gossip about Aurora's liaison with Wetterstedt, which had begun years before she divorced Jacquette's father. She knew better than to assume what was said about Brita was true.

One of the hall doors flew open, and Emilie emerged. She looked at Brita's dress and coughed. "Those are old stories. Haven't you heard any new ones about me? My sister is respectable now, or so they say."

Brita bent her head. "My lady, I meant no harm." She stared into the deep neckline of her frock.

Emilie slid down the wall and squatted on the floor. Jacquette sat on a silk-covered puff ottoman next to Emilie, pressing her hand to her aunt's cheek.

"What is the matter, Aunt? Are you not getting better?" Emilie had been Jacquette's only real parent from the age of six, when Aurora had left her three children at Finspång under her sister's care.

Emilie pulled a folded letter out of the satin belt she wore just under her bust. "A messenger brought this while you were at the ball." She crushed the cheap paper, and it crackled like the skin of an onion.

Jacquette plucked it from the floor and unfolded it. Someone had seen Emilie's husband, Clairfelt, at a brothel near the French Inn. With a woman.

"Who wrote this?" Jacquette asked Emilie.

"I . . . I don't know. Read it again to me."

In the quarter of the city where the French Inn is located, you will find Baron Clairfelt in the company of a woman of scant honor and repute. At the said disorderly house, he and the woman were seen entering a shuttered room together in high spirits. I regret to have caused you this pain and remain your devoted Servant and Friend.

Jacquette leaned against the wall to ponder the meaning of this news.

"A highborn person wrote that," Brita said.

"How can you be sure?" Jacquette asked, furious that Brita thought she knew everything.

"Look." Brita took the note from Jacquette and crouched next to Emilie. She pointed to a phrase. "Whoever sent this to you knew the right title for Baron Clairfelt, and the end here, this humble servant closing—to me, it seems a little old-fashioned. I know the people who work over by the French Inn, and none of them have the schooling to write something like this."

"Maybe it's a lie, then," Jacquette said. "Someone who just wants to injure us. Someone jealous of Clairfelt."

Clairfelt had just been named adjutant to Crown Prince Charles Jean. It would not be the first time, Jacquette knew, that such a promotion had led to cruel intrigues. But the flicker of hope in Emilie's eyes frightened her.

Brita stroked Emilie's thick red hair. "He's only a man; don't let him bring you to grief."

Emilie lifted her head and sat upright. "He brought me to grief months ago with his unfaithfulness. If he ever loved me, he doesn't anymore."

"This is not the first time?" Jacquette asked.

Emilie shook her head, and Jacquette could tell she was counting silently. "Seventh."

Jacquette and Brita looked at each other.

"You must divorce him, then," Brita said.

"Aurora has been pressing for that," said Emilie.

"Would it not be best?" asked Jacquette.

"No. I'll lose the children. Clairfelt will take them."

"May I give my opinion?" asked Brita.

"Who are you?" asked Emilie with a confused look.

"Brita. My new maid," said Jacquette.

Emilie shrugged. "Go on."

"There is nothing more certain to bring a woman to her knees than true love, and nothing better to save her soul than a child. Fight him. You are a De Geer."

Emilie nodded, and a smile crossed her tear-streaked face. "I hope you stay, Brita. Jacquette needs someone like you."

Having Brita at her side was beginning to look like a very good idea to Jacquette.

CHAPTER SIX

Douglas House, Stockholm
February 1815

For more than a fortnight after the Amaranth Ball, Jacquette avoided any gathering Oscar might attend, spending every morning at home with her harp, French, and dance tutors. In the evenings, she sat with Brita, Sophie, and Christine, stitching endless useless tablecloths and linens. Nestled with a novel in her favorite blue window seat one afternoon, she saw Aurora's long winter shadow glide across the salon's polished parquet floor.

"Go now. Change into the lavender gown," her mother said in a tone that left no room for discussion. "The crown prince and Oscar will be here in an hour."

So, Jacquette thought, *I will not be able to keep my distance from him any longer.*

When Oscar arrived, Jacquette was playing the grand piano in the library, making notes on an old copy of Herr Beethoven's easiest sonata. The piece her instructor had given her, *Appassionata*, was beautiful but difficult, and she did not want Oscar to hear her stumble over it. Whatever his other faults, Oscar's elegant, long fingers were made to roam the keys, and he was well aware of his talent. Piano was not a fair ground on which to compete with him, nor to impress him.

After tapping out a measure or two, she heard Oscar's quiet voice in the hall outside the library.

"I'll be fine on my own."

He dismissed offers from his guard, who always wanted to take up a post inside the room, and then the door latch clicked as he eased it back into place. Quick footfalls crossed the floor, barely audible.

They were alone.

She continued playing the sonata until the tart scent of lemon blossoms tickled her nose. He was standing close, perhaps an inch behind her, and when he leaned over to the music and turned the page, she felt his brass buttons graze her bare shoulder blades. She held her breath, enjoying his presence, and imagined having the courage to reach back and touch him.

"Did I frighten you?" His voice was teasing and lighthearted, as if he had not passed her over for Adelaide at the ball.

She was not about to let him charm her. "Is that how you persuade all the young countesses to fawn upon you? You take them by surprise?"

"I'll bring you the other sonata next time," he said. "*Appassionata*."

"No, thank you. I have it."

"Too difficult?"

"Of course it isn't."

"You left the Amaranth early the other night." He cocked his head to one side.

"I was sick."

"You weren't in the courtyard with your mother and Christine when I got here today, either."

"I'm still sick."

"Riding in a carriage with Carl Löwenhielm in January would tend to give one a chill," he said in a dry tone. He began playing *Appassionata* from memory. With one hand.

"Stop it." She closed the piano lid just as he snatched his hand from under it. She turned to face him.

"That would have hurt."

"How did you know I left with Count Löwenhielm?" Oscar had no business knowing everything she did, not while she had no window into his life.

He shrugged. "The guards were quite interested. Did Wetterstedt's driver really take two turns around the King's Garden? I imagine it would take that long for Carl to finish talking about himself." He poured a glass of wine from a decanter on the sideboard and drank. Like a peace offering, he passed her the goblet.

"You could have escorted me home."

Oscar's smile faded. "I can't come and go as I please. You know that."

"You were so captivated by that girl from the country—whatever her name is—when I left the Stock Exchange. I couldn't even have a word with you," she said and folded her hands in her lap.

"You weren't alone, either."

"Someone had to make sure I got home."

"Come on, Q. Don't be angry with me."

"Why would I be? You're free to do whatever you were doing with anyone you want, and it is none of my affair. But you should know that people are talking about you and that countess. Adelaide—I remember her name now."

He sighed. "All people do is talk about me." He pushed back a curl and sat, straddling the bench. "What's really wrong?"

"You could have taken some time to talk with me at the ball. I haven't seen or heard from you for almost a year."

He spoke in a sarcastic tone. "My apologies, Countess. I went to war, you know, and when I got back, you were in France. Everybody was in France, except me, which is ironic being that I'm French. You saw my mother in Paris?"

She nodded. "She sends her love. I think she misses you terribly."

"Then why does she stay away?" He rolled his eyes. "I know. She thinks my father will divorce her if she sets foot in Sweden."

No matter how he tried to hide it, Jacquette knew how much his mother's absence hurt. "It's not about you," she said.

"It doesn't matter. Not really. Are we friends again?" he asked.

She nodded, but she wasn't sure she meant it.

"My father asked me to read his opening speech to the Estates."

Jacquette did not try to hide her surprise. "He did? I told you he would eventually give in." Oscar would take the oath of allegiance in

April. He was second in line to the throne, and people were beginning to question why he was not more involved in the government. Some thought Charles Jean was jealous of his son's popularity.

"I don't think he has changed his mind at all. He needs me to read the speech. He's never going to learn to speak Swedish."

"Why don't you want to do it? It's the first chance he has given you."

"You wouldn't say that if you read what he made Wetterstedt write. It's a tirade against the press. I must preach the dangers of unbridled opposition. How censorship protects everyone."

"Is he still worried about Gustav?"

Oscar nodded. "He sees an enemy around every corner these days. He censors every newspaper that mentions Gustav or offers a hint of criticism of the palace. I want to see for myself whether the Gustavians are a real danger. If they are not, what my father and Magnus have been doing is just oppression."

"But you still haven't seen what the opposition is printing?"

He shook his head. "Only the French newspaper I mentioned to you at the ball. Once Wetterstedt signs the censorship order, my father has the Mandarin raid the printer, and they destroy every copy. Everything is burned. That was what I was trying to ask you the other night, Q. I think you can help me with this."

He rested an elbow on the smooth wooden cover of the piano. His eyes shone, as they did whenever he wanted something, but it reminded her of the way he'd looked into Adelaide's eyes at the Amaranth Ball.

She stacked up some sheet music and replied in her most sarcastic tone, "I don't know, Oscar. Why don't you ask Adelaide?"

"Don't be that way. You're the one who knows these things; Adelaide doesn't have a clue about court politics. She's an aristocrat, yes, but not like the people in your circle. And there is nothing going on between her and me. I told you. It's just talk."

"That's what my Uncle Clairfelt told Emilie, and it turned out he had seven other women."

Oscar raised a brow but did not give up. "I just want to show Adelaide the city. I told you, she is new here and doesn't know everyone like you do. That's all."

"She started at the top, then. She knows you," replied Jacquette.

Maybe it was the way Oscar was looking at her. Or the way he reached for her hand and kissed the back of her wrist, something he had done a hundred times before. Or that pamphlet in Wetterstedt's folder showing him dead. Suddenly, she wanted to prove to Oscar that there was no sliver of information, no gossip, no suggestion of a scandal that was beyond her ability to uncover.

She looked up. "I can find out what's in the pamphlets."

It was the only thing she could think of to say, but it was a lie.

"How? From Wetterstedt?"

She would never betray Wetterstedt. "No. Brita knows a printer."

"Brita?" he asked.

"You know, my maid."

"The one from Drottningholm? I thought she left."

"She's back," Jacquette said.

"And she knows someone who does printing for the Gustavians?"

"I think so. Yes." Jacquette could only hope she was right. Brita seemed to know every merchant and tradesman in the capital. She'd even recognized the addresses on Wetterstedt's folder.

The guard opened the door and told them dinner was served.

"I want to meet this printer. Tell me when you find him, and we will arrange a time. And you'll come to the party I'm having in a couple of weeks, won't you?" Oscar asked.

There was to be a soiree in Oscar's apartments, one of the first he had hosted. Jacquette accepted his invitation, pleased that the indifference he'd shown her at the ball had disappeared. But now, she had promised to introduce him to a Gustavian printer and had no idea if she could find one.

⁂

In the dim light of two bronze sconces, Jacquette followed Aurora up Stockholm Palace's East Stairs to Oscar's party. His five-room suite was some distance from the other royal apartments, and young princes who valued privacy had lived in these rooms for decades. Tonight, they were filled with noise and a sprinkling of the black gowns that were required at court, called *hovdräkter*. Everyone was drinking champagne from fluted crystal goblets, and there was no food in sight.

"If you spent more time in the queen's company, you would already be a maid of honor and would be wearing one of those yourself," Aurora said as she eyed the Chatterati's court gowns.

Jacquette grimaced at her mother.

"Did you hear the footmen talking in the guard room?" Aurora asked.

Jacquette ignored the question. "Where do you think the prince is? He must be here—he is the host."

Aurora pointed to a red-haired footman who had just entered the party with a tray of decanters. He turned his back to them and began arranging the brandy table.

"As we passed that footman in the guard room, I heard him making insinuations about Prince Oscar and that countess. What is her name? Adelaide?"

"What sort of insinuations?" Jacquette asked.

"That they went to the palace garden forty-five minutes ago. Alone. Charles Jean will be furious." Aurora craned her neck, probably hoping to find Charles Jean and tell him. Anything to gain favor.

"Would the crown prince care about such a trivial thing?"

Aurora lowered her voice. "Don't be naive. He is having difficulty finding a royal fiancée for Oscar. It turns out most of their fathers see Charles Jean as an upstart and predict Gustav is about to replace him. The last thing he needs is for Oscar to cause a scandal."

"I don't think Oscar will be his father's pawn," Jacquette said. "His mother promised him he would never be forced to marry."

Aurora laughed, and Jacquette knew what she was thinking. Oscar already was a pawn in so many ways.

"We'll see. I predict Oscar's little love affair will be over soon."

Jacquette could not put her mother's words out of her mind. Was it really a love affair? Frederik Due had said so, hadn't he? Through a window, she looked down on the snowy palace garden but could not see anyone. Her throat was dry, and she had not eaten anything since morning.

"My dear, are you all right?" Aurora asked Jacquette.

She didn't have to answer because Dorothea von Engeström appeared at Aurora's side, her celebrated peachy cheeks mottled with tears.

With a questioning glance at Jacquette, Aurora embraced Dorothea. "Your gown suits you so well. The simplicity."

Dorothea's drab gray poplin resembled the day dresses worn by the servants at Douglas House. And the poor girl, who was sobbing and clutching Aurora's sleeve, did not even realize she was being ridiculed.

Jacquette cupped Dorothea's face in her hands and wiped her cheeks. "What is the matter, dear?"

"It's my father," Dorothea sobbed.

"Is he—ill?" Aurora almost looked hopeful. Lars von Engeström was frail and unhealthy, and no one knew how much longer he could cling to his position as foreign minister.

"No, but the rogues in this city will go to any length to impugn the honor of decent people," Dorothea wailed. "Look." She handed Jacquette a piece of paper.

At the first mention of an intrigue, Aurora ordinarily would have snapped to attention. Instead, she shrank away.

Jacquette knew when to be suspicious of her mother. She read the unsigned letter, which attacked Dorothea's father for his "obvious stupidity." The nation, it said, had already made its judgment, and "at the Estates, a thousand voices will be raised against you, and your fall will be horrible." It offered the foreign minister a way out:

You are urged in the strongest possible terms to satisfy your duty to resign your post so that a more competent man can assume it.

Jacquette froze, mute with the sudden recollection of where she had seen this handwriting before. Aurora's lady's maid, Sophie, wrote this.

About a year after Aurora had divorced Count Philip, Jacquette and Emilie had been walking along the south wall of the King's Garden. There was no snow on the ground, and the dry, dusty road had been teeming with people carrying food and gifts for Christmas. A woman dressed in the charcoal skirts of a below-stairs servant had jostled Jacquette.

"You don't remember me, do you? Your kind only sees people of your own station."

Jacquette did know the woman. Once a maid in Jacquette's uncle's house, she had gone to the courts and revealed to all of Stockholm that Jacquette's father had made her pregnant and refused to support their baby. It was true, and the scandal that followed was the coup de grâce that finally persuaded the feeble old king to grant Aurora a divorce so she could marry Wetterstedt.

"I know all about you," Jacquette had replied.

The woman had reached into her coat and pulled out a paper, never looking at Jacquette. "You don't know how your mother brought your father low with her lies," she'd hissed.

"My mother? She has not wronged anyone. It was you who reported my father to the courts and caused his disgrace."

"Your mother paid me to accuse him. Go ahead. Read."

The letter had offered the maid money in return for reporting that Count Philip had impregnated her and refused to acknowledge the child.

You are urged, in the strongest possible terms, to satisfy your duty to file a criminal complaint to settle the matter of paternity.

Emilie had taken the letter from Jacquette's hands, given it back to the woman, and said to Jacquette, "Your mother's maid wrote this. Sophie."

The handwriting on the letter to Dorothea's father was identical. Even some of the words were the same. And it was well-known that Aurora had never given up her ambition to unseat the foreign minister so Wetterstedt could take his position.

Someone handed Jacquette a glass of champagne, and she drained it. When she turned to look for her mother again, Aurora was gone.

No one could be permitted to discover that Aurora had threatened the foreign minister; it could ruin them all.

Taking a deep breath, Jacquette wrapped her arm around Dorothea's shoulder and said, "Why don't we speak to the prince's cavaliers? They may have an idea who is threatening your father. Most of them gossip like kitchen maids."

A few of Oscar's men were talking at a nearby table, Carl Löwenhielm among them. Jacquette tried to engage her friend Adam, who'd recently joined Oscar's household, but Carl jumped to his feet.

He said, "Let's get away from here. My fellow cavaliers are apt to talk." He led them to a spot near the door in front of a bookcase.

"Tell Count Löwenhielm what happened," Jacquette said to Dorothea.

Dorothea recounted every aspect of the unfortunate event in painstaking detail.

Carl offered her his cotton handkerchief and told her to dry her tears, reassuring her that he would look into the problem.

"Now go check on your mother," he said, gesturing toward the door.

"I will," Dorothea said. "She will be so grateful for your help. And thank you, Jacquette. I hope you'll come call on us soon."

With Dorothea gone, Carl offered Jacquette his arm.

She said, "You certainly dried her tears."

"Don't think badly of me. Her father is still a powerful man."

She gave a little shrug. All courtiers played both sides. Carl would be loyal to the man who offered him more, whether it was the foreign minister or Wetterstedt.

At once, everyone stopped talking. The guests stood straighter, smoothing their sleeves, and stared at the doorway, where a flushed and breathless Adelaide had just appeared. Oscar was behind her, shamelessly whispering in her ear.

"There he is," Carl said. "The crown prince asked me to find out where the devil his son has been. His words, not mine."

"Have you not heard?" The words just slipped out of Jacquette's mouth.

"I have not." He looked skeptical, his arms crossed, his eyes narrowed.

"There is a man here, a footman, who is gossiping and needs to be told to hold his tongue."

Carl, obviously interested, asked, "Which footman?"

"There he is," Jacquette said. "By the telescope."

Carl moved toward Jacquette, crowding her against the wall, and she had a sense that he had forgotten all about Dorothea and her problem. "That one?" He pointed to the red-haired footman.

"Yes, him. He is spreading malicious gossip about the prince and Adelaide."

"What, exactly?" Carl demanded.

"That Oscar took her to the palace gardens an hour ago. He told all the officers in the outer guard room."

Carl rubbed his eyes and swore under his breath.

She reached out her hand to touch his sleeve and said, "I am sure he did not mean the prince any harm."

She didn't hear Carl's answer. When she looked up, Oscar and Adelaide were passing through the salon, and Oscar was not ten feet from her. Leaving Adelaide in the center of the room, he appeared at Jacquette's side and took her hand, holding it a little tighter than necessary. His cold, narrowed eyes never left Carl as he pressed his lips to her wrist.

"My good friends, together again," Oscar said. "May I see you for a moment, Countess?"

Erica, who was flirting nearby with Frederik Due, rolled her eyes and declared that Jacquette and Oscar were even beginning to look alike. Frederik led her away.

Jacquette's cheeks burned as Oscar closed his fingers around her upper arm. She lengthened her stride, lest the others see that he was practically dragging her across the floor.

"What's this all about?" Oscar asked, looking at Carl.

"I don't know what you mean."

"Carl. You."

What right had Oscar to disapprove?

"Nothing. Two people talking at a party, just like you and Adelaide," she replied, keeping her voice light and casual.

Carl was kneading his fists as if crumpling a wad of paper, apparently displeased about her private conversation with Oscar.

"Can we speak about anything other than Adelaide?" Oscar asked. "Did you ask Brita about her printer friend?"

"Not yet." *And perhaps never*, she thought, furious.

"My father and I are coming to your mother's salon next week. Maybe you will find time to ask her before then."

Adelaide cocked her head and curled her finger, beckoning Oscar to return to her. He frowned and shook his head, then turned back to Jacquette. Oscar's body had tensed when Adelaide summoned him, and Jacquette noticed. *He doesn't love that girl. Frederik was wrong.*

She moved closer to him. "I can do better than that. The printer will be there next Sunday, and you can meet him." This wasn't true, not in the least. Jacquette bit her lip, asking herself what she would tell Oscar when the man failed to appear.

"What's his name? Do you know where he works?" As he always did when something intrigued him, Oscar was firing off questions and speaking faster and faster.

Jacquette gave him her shiniest, most knowing I-told-you-so-Oscar smile, with her lips barely touching and her eyelids heavy. "I'll tell you everything soon," she said.

"I knew you would figure it out, Q. Carl looks a little vexed, doesn't he?" Oscar sounded pleased with himself. "He's turned color."

Adelaide, she thought, *must be seething*.

Carl joined them and took Jacquette's arm, giving Oscar a curt little head bow. His touch was far from gentle. Jacquette could feel Oscar's eyes moving up from her wrist, fixing on the place where Carl's fingers were wrapped around her bare upper arm. She felt a little like a toy being pulled back and forth between children.

Not meeting Jacquette's eye, Oscar murmured, "Countess," and left.

The moment Oscar was gone, Carl released her. "Let me go find this footman who was spreading gossip. He is about to have a surprise audience with Charles Jean."

"Count Löwenhielm, don't." She never should have told him. There was already enough trouble between Oscar and his father, and she did not want to be the cause of more.

"Call me Carl," he said, "and come with me."

She followed, horrified, as he placed one hand on the red-haired footman's back and steered him across the floor to see Charles Jean.

"Tell the crown prince where you saw Prince Oscar and Countess Adelaide," Carl said to the terrified man.

Oh, no, Jacquette thought. *Nothing good can come of this.*

Suddenly, the booming voice of Crown Prince Charles Jean coursed through the suite of rooms. "Son, come speak with me, if you please."

Oscar dropped Adelaide's hand like a glowing coal. He rushed past Jacquette and presented himself to his father.

No matter what Oscar tells people, he fears Charles Jean, she thought.

Someone touched her waist. Aurora was back, or perhaps she'd never left.

"I thought you had gone," Jacquette said.

"Fortunate that I had not. What have you done, Jacquette?" Aurora's voice carried an unmistakable note of fear.

"What do you mean by that?"

"Don't you hear them?"

With Charles Jean silently watching, Oscar was shouting at Carl, his face twisted in anger. Ordinarily, he could barely be heard.

Aurora's friend Marianne, the eldest of the maids of honor, joined them, obviously full of news and anxious to share it. Her ample chest jiggled as she panted out her words.

"Adelaide will never see the inside of Stockholm Palace again if Charles Jean can help it. He is going to send the poor girl back home to be married."

"Married to whom?" Jacquette asked Marianne.

"It hardly matters."

Being Charles Jean's mistress, Marianne always acted as if she knew the innermost workings of his mind. It could be annoying at times. But her information must be true; Adelaide had joined the men and was, indeed, crying.

Aurora, who had not said a word since Marianne joined them, spoke under her breath. "Adelaide is not my principal concern."

Marianne looked pained. "What is it then?"

"The prince and Count Löwenhielm. They are about to come to blows."

It was true. Carl's stare could only be described as defiant, and Oscar's eyes were returning the gaze, flashing with French temper.

Aurora mopped her brow. "Quette, I fear you have unleashed something you won't be able to control."

CHAPTER SEVEN

Douglas House, Stockholm
February 1815

Jacquette shuffled through the afternoon mail and removed a note that had been addressed to her in Oscar's hand. She peeled away his red seal with her fingernail, putting the waxy disk in her pocket to be added to her little box of remembrances. It held everything that related to him—invitations, drawings, a libretto from the opera. Since his party on Saturday, he had sent three messages in three days, all asking her the same question—whether the printer she promised would really appear at Aurora's salon on Sunday. Exasperated, she scrawled the same reply she had written at the bottom of the others.

I don't know yet, O. Wait a few days. Q.

Patience was not one of his best qualities.

Finding a printer was turning out to be more difficult than she'd imagined. Brita was cagey on the subject of her acquaintances, a group that seemed to include everyone in the city, but Jacquette had no one else to ask. She needed to do it today or admit to Oscar she had failed. And nothing seemed more important than showing him she was different from the others. That she could operate in society. That she had value and could get things done. That she did not deserve to be left behind.

The drawing room door opened, and Brita emerged with Aurora's new gown for the opening ceremony of the Estates of the Realm. She slung it over one shoulder, complaining that Sophie had ordered her to deliver it to the dressmaker.

Jacquette saw an opening. "I'll take you in the carriage. I'm going that way. But I have something to ask you first."

Brita looked suspicious. "What is it?"

"After the Amaranth Ball, you mentioned some friends who work at a print shop, didn't you?"

Brita cocked her head as she twirled a strand of her long blonde hair. "No. All I said is that I walk past the print shops. I never said I knew anyone there."

"I think you know someone on every street in the capital."

Brita laid the gown on a bench and put her hands on her hips. "Jacquette, what is it you want?"

Jacquette took a deep breath. "I need to find out what Charles Jean is censoring. The Withdrawal Power, remember?"

"How am I supposed to help you do that? Why don't you ask Wetterstedt? You could just look in his folder."

"I'm sure Wetterstedt hates what Charles Jean is making him do. And I would never betray him."

"Does this have something to do with the prince?" Brita asked, pursing her lips into a thin line.

How had Jacquette ended up with a maid who had opinions about everything, even the heir to the throne? "Oscar wants to meet a printer. Someone whose shop prints pamphlets and such. Or newspapers."

"He's a prince, Jacquette. He can talk with any newspaperman he wants at his whim. He can send a message, and they will come scurrying up the steps of the palace to see him. So, why is he asking you?"

Oscar's intentions were none of Brita's business, but Jacquette could not help but defend him. "I expect he wants to find his own man. Someone not linked to his father." After glaring at the maid for a few minutes of cold silence, Jacquette walked toward her room.

Brita followed her and closed the door behind them. "He always wants something from you. Don't you see?"

"No, I don't." But she did.

"I haven't forgotten; he has been doing this to you since you were thirteen years old."

"He's my friend."

Brita pursed her lips and narrowed her eyes. "Listen to yourself. You always say royals don't have friends. What makes you think I know such a person, anyway?" she said in a gruff voice.

"I guessed."

"You're telling me the truth, right? This won't get anyone in any trouble?"

Jacquette took Brita's hand and locked their pinky fingers. "Break it if I'm lying." She opened her memory box and placed Oscar's note inside.

"Everyone knows you are a terrible liar. All right, then, I might know a printer. But I don't want to hear any more about how much you hate Prince Oscar. Ever. And stop saving every scrap of paper he touches."

Ignoring the insult, Jacquette pressed on. "Who is your man? Tell me."

"An Englishman named Peter."

"Peter? And he prints newspapers?"

Brita's voice grew soft, as if she did not want anyone to hear. "I think it's called Marquard's. He is a printer's apprentice there."

"Do you trust him?"

Brita nodded.

"Do you know him from working at the inn?"

"No. Before."

"All he needs to do is to come to my mother's salon on Sunday and meet Oscar. It will only be for five minutes."

"I cannot promise anything. Can you at least tell me why you are doing this?"

Jacquette toyed with the wax seals in her box. "To show Oscar who I am."

When Sunday afternoon came, Jacquette felt as nervous as a colt. More than once, she cornered Brita. Did Peter own a waistcoat? Speak a little French? Have money to hire a carriage?

And Peter was late. Jacquette could not stop wandering from room to room, sitting down at this card table and that sofa, distracted and unable to strike up a conversation. The third time she went to check the entry hall, Brita followed and laid her warm, rough palm on Jacquette's shoulder. "Act normally," she warned, "because the room is buzzing with talk. They all think you are waiting for Oscar."

"Don't be ridiculous," Jacquette lied. She could not resist a final look at the door, and that was when she saw him. A stranger trotting up the stairs to the apartment, taking them two at a time. Brita had told her that Peter was middle-aged, but this man's body did not betray his years. Trim, with a remarkable shock of long silver hair caught in an ebony clip, he could have been twenty-five or forty-five.

"That's Peter," Brita said, folding her arms, plainly amused by Jacquette's reaction.

"I suppose I should not have worried whether he would fit in." Jacquette noticed some of the other guests admiring Peter's exquisitely pressed white shirt, chestnut-colored silk waistcoat with fine gold stripes, and stiff black taffeta cravat.

Jacquette wondered how well Brita knew him. "Are you and he together? I mean, is he your—"

"Don't be daft. I've told you a hundred times, I'll not fall for a man, not ever. But as they go, Peter's a good one."

"Bring him to the front salon. Aurora won't look for us there, at least not right away."

As she walked away, it occurred to Jacquette that Peter had not met her eye even though she had been standing with Brita, even though he must have guessed who she was. *How discreet he seems*, she thought. *Good.*

When Jacquette entered the small salon, Peter and Brita were sitting on the narrow green sofa. He was perched on the edge, as relaxed as any person accustomed to moving in society. With his elbow resting on the sofa arm, he was chatting with Brita about some dark Christmas bread she'd baked for the *julbord* in December. They seemed to know each other well enough.

He stood for introductions and, in Parisian-accented French, told Jacquette his name, Peter Wells. And that he was from England. Liverpool.

She explained the need for secrecy and said that Oscar would have only a few minutes. His green eyes examined her.

"I am new to this city," he said. "Who would I tell?"

Jacquette would have expected a man of his station to be more apprehensive about meeting a prince, even a former commoner like Oscar. She stated her proposition anyway. For her plan to work, she would need to see Peter regularly. "My mother," she said, "wishes me to learn English."

"From the look in your eyes," he said, "I suspect there is more to it." She told him what she wanted from him, and he did not flinch, although the little crinkles around his eyes deepened. She wondered whether he was about to laugh at her, but instead, he said, "Let me ask you some questions."

"You may."

"You are right. The Gustavians bring pamphlets of that nature to my shop, and we print them, but why would I risk copying them? What of the Mandarin? And doesn't the prince know all this already?"

She shook her head. "His father tells him nothing. They disagree."

"I see. But that doesn't persuade me I should help him."

Jacquette dropped her voice. "You would have a prince in your debt. Just talk to him."

The salon door flew open. During the four or so years since Oscar had come to Sweden, he had lost the habit of knocking. With his hip, he pushed the door closed and took Jacquette's hand. She felt the friction of their palms, together and lightly touching. As he kissed the back of her knuckles, he lifted his eyes, which were clear and lively with interest. He always seemed happy at Douglas House. Closing a door, pouring a drink, returning a book to the shelf. Meeting people without the presence of cavaliers to buffer his connection to the outside world. She knew these were all things Oscar missed about his former life.

"Countess," he said, with a funny smile. He rarely addressed her formally.

When she bent a knee, he seemed about to laugh.

"Did you ride Odin here?" Jacquette asked him.

He nodded. "With the Life Guards."

"It's cold."

"The wind off the lake is strong today. He took one step onto the bridge and tried to go back to the stables." He laughed.

Jacquette had almost forgotten about Peter, who was now standing at her left shoulder, his head bent in a perfect bow.

Oscar raked at his windblown hair with his fingers, and said to Peter, "My apologies. I hope you have not waited long. Mr. Wells, I understand?"

"Your Royal Highness."

"Thank you for meeting me."

"What can I do, Miss?" Brita asked Jacquette.

"Just lean against the door. You will hear the floor creak if anyone is coming. Come," Jacquette said to Oscar and Peter. "It is sunny near the window, and you can speak freely." She strolled with them to the window seat, one on each side of her. They were a striking couple of men, Oscar and Peter.

"You are English, I understand?" Oscar said to Peter.

"I am."

"How did you come to work in Stockholm?"

Peter responded as if the question had been asked of him many times before. "I needed money, and the wages are good. There are many skilled printers in Liverpool, and fewer here."

"Where do you work?"

"Marquard's on Stora Nygatan."

Oscar rubbed his lips with his forefinger and thumb, as he often did when he was nervous. "I will be frank," he said to Peter. "I value a free press in Stockholm—it is in our constitution—but my father does not place the same importance on it."

Peter studied him. "People are saying the Withdrawal Power was not enacted properly. It is censorship."

"Debate about these things is important," Oscar said.

"But I am without power to do anything about it," said Peter. "You, on the other hand . . . people say you offer them hope of progress, a promise of more freedom."

Oscar pursed his lips. "I appreciate that, Mr. Wells, but at the moment, I seem to be unable to accomplish anything from inside the palace."

Peter looked down onto the square. "In my country, a popular heir is often viewed by his father as a threat."

Oscar did not reply. Jacquette suspected he was enjoying Peter's praise, perhaps a bit too much.

Peter said, "With respect, sir, why me? Why not speak to one of the owners of the presses? You know them all, I presume."

"Half are on my father's payroll, and he is having the other half followed by the Mandarin. I'm trying to find someone I can trust—someone my father does not have in his pocket."

Peter folded his arms across his chest and leaned against the wall. "I will do what I can."

"I need to find out what is being censored. My father will not tell me, and every copy is seized and burned."

"If I may ask, sir, what are you looking to find?"

"Whether these Gustavian conspiracies are real or just an excuse to stifle debate." He grinned. "I also must admit that I am a little curious about what they are saying about me. There is a rumor that I am dying, I understand."

"I did see a sketch of you lying on a table surrounded by doctors."

Oscar laughed just as Brita jumped away from the door to the hall. It opened with a bang, and Aurora burst in.

"Where have you been, Quette?" Seeing Oscar, Jacquette's mother dropped a curtsy, and her tone grew airy and sweet. "Oh, Your Royal Highness."

Peter bowed, and Oscar introduced him. "My lady," Peter said.

Jacquette exhaled in relief as Aurora's eyes took in every inch of Peter. She knew Aurora would have loved to touch the fabric of his fine waistcoat, to ask him whether they knew the same tailors in Paris.

Peter chatted to Aurora about England and charmed her thoroughly. She soon was compiling a list of guests for him to meet.

"Would you mind terribly, sir, if I took Mr. Wells away from you for a few moments?" Aurora asked Oscar, motioning for Brita to pour Peter a glass of champagne from the bottle on the brandy table.

"Of course not," Oscar said.

Jacquette feared she would burst into laughter if her eyes met Oscar's. Although Aurora was the De Geer woman most likely to keep her corset on and had not looked at another man since she married Wetterstedt, her old weakness emerged whenever she met a handsome foreigner.

After the others left, Oscar leaned back against the door, laughing. "Wells really knew how to handle your mother, didn't he?"

Jacquette giggled. "I think you give me too little credit. It worked, didn't it?"

Oscar brushed his hair back and unbuttoned his jacket. The tails of his white silk shirt fell softly against his tan riding pants.

"It did, and I give you all the credit. This uniform is damn uncomfortable, you know." He pulled at his collar.

"Well, aren't you going to thank me for introducing you?"

Oscar hesitated for a second, then seized her hands. Surprised, she looked down at their entwined fingers, then up into his eyes. They were dark and glassy, and she saw something that had not been there before. He threaded one arm around her waist and tilted her chin toward his face with the other.

She could hardly breathe as she waited.

"There is only one of you," he said in a gravelly tumble of words, then parted his lips and pulled her body against his. His kiss was light and deft, dancing along her lower lip until he covered her mouth with his. He smelled delicious and tasted even better. Her body relaxed into his, and a delightful energy surged deep inside.

"Q?" he asked.

She nodded.

He drew in a breath, and the marvel that was his tongue stroked hers, inviting her in. He guided her toward the wall, and she felt the small of her back flatten against the wood paneling. A tiny moan escaped from the back of her throat as he kissed her neck and the lobes of her ears. In the recesses of her mind, she wondered who else he had kissed, and when, and where.

Her eyes were still closed when she heard the door to the salon scrape the wood floor. Oscar pulled away, and she straightened her neckline, but not before she saw Peter standing in the doorway. He walked over to a table, picked up his forgotten glass of champagne, and left the room.

CHAPTER EIGHT

Douglas House, Stockholm
Late March 1815

Jacquette rushed into the dining room ten minutes after the dinner bell had sounded. She was late, but not as late as Emilie, who had not yet arrived to take her place at the round table. Aurora stood next to the fireplace, looking crossly at Christine, who was on her knees and holding a hot water bottle against Aurora's black-stockinged legs, despite what Jacquette felt was the extreme heat of the apartment. Rising to greet Jacquette, Christine blinked her eyes hard and rubbed her hip, making Jacquette feel guilty she was not the one attending to her mother, who was recovering from a spring fever.

Jacquette was seized by a fervent wish for Emilie to come down the stairs and fill the stuffy room with some gossipy news or idle speculation.

Wetterstedt started to rise from his chair, and Jacquette shook her head, hoping to dissuade him from standing on her account. He stood anyway, but that was Wetterstedt's way. This evening, he looked tired and distracted, so she walked behind his chair and hugged him. There was a leather folio at his place, open to a letter marked with blots of ink and interlineations. He rarely brought work to the table.

He sighed and closed the volume. "Ah, Jacquette. I must apologize for my rudeness."

"Has there been any sighting of my sister?" Aurora asked Jacquette.

"She's coming, Mother. I saw her rummaging through her shoes."

Aurora straightened a taper in the brass candle sconce on the wall behind her chair. "She probably won't be wearing any shoes, if she chooses to present herself at all."

"Mother, she is packing."

Tomorrow, Emilie would make the long journey to Himmelstalund with little Axel and Julie to escape the rumors of her upcoming divorce from Clairfelt. Few women received permission to end their marriages, yet both De Geer sisters had managed it, and the news had reached every salon and drawing room in Stockholm. It was a scandal Emilie would do well to escape, but Jacquette dreaded being without her again.

Wetterstedt pulled out Aurora's chair and held her tiny purse while she arranged her skirts. When he was home, he always extended his wife this courtesy, although he employed a dozen footmen to do it for him. Jacquette took her place at the round table, leaving an empty space between herself and her mother. Christine filled it.

"Well, Jacquette, how did you pass this gloomy day?" He coughed, and a maid rushed to offer him a cup of tea. He shook his head.

"I had my first lesson with the new English tutor," Jacquette said. "Peter Wells. I like him very much."

Wetterstedt pointed to Aurora's glass, and a server filled it with wine. "I knew you would find the right person," he said to Aurora.

She took a tiny sip.

"One of the bottles the former empress gave me from Malmaison. May God rest her soul."

"Papa," said Jacquette. "Don't forget your toast."

"To true love," he said, as he did every time he opened one of Joséphine's bottles.

"And in memory of all who have died of a broken heart," Jacquette added.

"One cannot die of a broken heart. Science has proven it," Aurora said.

Christine nodded in agreement.

Emilie drifted into the room holding a glass of brandy. To protest Clairfelt's latest betrayal, she had freed her hair from its pins and thrown her hair tongs in a trunk. Her bronze curls spilled over her shoulders and around her breasts, un-brushed and untamed.

Slurring her words a little, she asked, "And what does science know of passion?"

Jacquette hoped her mother was right. If anyone's heart was broken, it was Emilie's.

Emilie slid into the seat on the other side of Jacquette and squeezed her hand. "Don't fret about me. I have two children. I'm not at liberty to die."

❦

With a wink, Jacquette's favorite footman placed a small plate of smoked herring in front of her. She despised the stuff.

"Only four," he said.

She grimaced and saw Wetterstedt looking at her plate. He was probably about to ask the kitchen to send more of the slimy fermented fishes for her. She began cutting them into tiny pieces with a knife, wishing they were strawberries.

"And you, Papa? How was your day at the palace?" she asked him brightly.

"I spent it drafting dispatches to the Congress of Vienna and thanking Providence that your friend Carl Löwenhielm's uncle is representing us there, and not me."

"I would not call him a friend, Papa. He only brought me home from a ball," Jacquette protested.

"I hear he is making a trip to Vienna soon," Aurora said. "To assist his uncle at the Congress. Is that not so, Gustave?"

Aurora was the only one who called Jacquette's stepfather anything but Wetterstedt. She used the French form of his name, and made it sound like a cat purring.

"Quite right," Wetterstedt said. "The Allies are drawing the new map, and the tsar proposes to give Gustav a principality in Germany to rule. Charles Jean is furious. Carl Löwenhielm is going to carry his letter of protest to Vienna, and what a letter it is."

Aurora took another tiny sip of wine, drinking in Wetterstedt's adoring gaze as if they were alone in the room. "You cannot blame Tsar Alexander for protecting his wife's family."

Former Crown Prince Gustav was the Russian tsarina's nephew.

Wetterstedt said, "Charles Jean is threatening retribution if he grants Gustav a territory."

Jacquette's chest tightened. Who would threaten the tsar of Russia? Oscar might be right about his father after all.

"We cannot be thinking about objecting to him giving Gustav a small patch of farmland in the middle of Germany with a musty old castle or two. Please tell me we are not," said Emilie. "What can Charles Jean do about it?"

Wetterstedt said, "Embarrass the tsar. He says he has evidence that Gustav's father is illegitimate and will publish it."

Aurora said, "How would one prove that? People have been trying forever, but it is a fool's errand."

Wetterstedt put down his fork, rose, and shut the door to the hallway.

Aurora spoke again when he returned to his seat. "Not that I am suggesting our crown prince is a fool, of course. An impure bloodline would destroy any claim Gustav has to the throne."

"That old story?" Emilie yawned and returned to staring at her glass, which was empty. She turned toward the side table and motioned to the footman who was pouring the wine.

Wetterstedt looked at the folio, which was again open to the letter. "I hope to persuade Charles Jean not to send this, or at least to soften the language."

"Does he really have evidence that Gustav is from an illegitimate line?" asked Jacquette.

Aurora said, "Quette, how uncommon for you to show any interest in politics."

Emilie interrupted in a conspiratorial tone. "I heard something about Carl Löwenhielm."

"What is being said, Sister?" Aurora demanded.

"Oh, just this and that," Emilie said, draining her glass. "Carl has an eye for our beautiful Jacquette. But all the young men do, I suppose."

Jacquette swallowed.

"Carl Löwenhielm? Interested in Jacquette?" Aurora asked and looked at Wetterstedt. "I never liked that family much."

Wetterstedt held up both hands. "I know nothing of such matters. I am but a civil servant."

Aurora's features sharpened in the way they did whenever Wetterstedt made light of his importance.

Emilie responded to no one in particular, "I know Carl's father is odd, but it is a fine old family. Long Manor is quite large, even if it is practically in Norway. I have never been there, of course. It is something one hears."

Jacquette pushed a slice of herring onto the back of her fork and placed it in her mouth. She swallowed without chewing.

Emilie turned to Jacquette. "Oh, I see that little frown, Quette," she said. "I would not dismiss Carl Löwenhielm so lightly. Talk to him sometime."

Emilie seemed to have forgotten her belief in true love, probably because of Clairfelt's wanderings.

"But I understand Carl is making a long trip to Vienna, Aunt," Jacquette said with a smirk. "Papa just said so."

Not wishing to pursue the topic of Carl Löwenhielm any further, Jacquette was almost relieved when the double doors to the dining room flew open and two apologetic-looking Life Guards announced Crown Prince Charles Jean. Jacquette had never seen him in such a state. His tight black curls protruded from the sides of his general's hat, and he spoke so quickly that she could hardly understand a word.

"He's showing his temper, isn't he? He's lapsed into Gascon," Emilie whispered to Jacquette, obviously enjoying the show.

"Shhh," Jacquette said as she tried to make out the dialect, which sounded more Spanish than French.

"Marianne says he speaks Gascon to her sometimes. Late at night. In her apartment at the palace." Emilie loved a scandal, and no topic was more scandalous than Charles Jean's relationship with his mistress.

Aurora's withering stare silenced Emilie. Marianne was her dear friend.

Wetterstedt relinquished his chair to Charles Jean, whose breath was coming in ragged heaves.

"You have been riding hard, sir," said Wetterstedt in a soft, calming tone. "May I have some wine poured for you?"

Charles Jean nodded, and the footman filled his goblet. "Excellent red Bordeaux. It is too little appreciated by the French. I can see I am paying my chancellor well enough to afford it. Is that not so, Baroness?"

Aurora blushed. "You are too generous, sir."

"It is you who are generous for allowing me to disrupt your meal, but I just received word that Bonaparte left Elba and landed on the French mainland. He marches to Paris as we speak. I warned the tsar this would happen if we left the tyrant in Wellington's hands."

"He escaped?" asked Jacquette.

"In a manner of speaking. He got on a ship and left, and the English did nothing to prevent it," Charles Jean said.

With the lightness gone from his eyes, Wetterstedt said, "I feared we would be forced to go to war against Bonaparte. Again."

Emilie said, "The English permitted him to think he was the emperor of Elba."

No one disagreed. Emilie's shawl had slipped from her shoulders, revealing the deep cleft between her rounded breasts. Charles Jean's eyes darted in her direction.

The prospect of war terrified Jacquette. Would her brothers join the fight? Would Oscar? The peace had lasted only a year.

To Wetterstedt, Charles Jean said, "It is not so dire as you fear, Chancellor. War is far from a certainty. It strikes me that the French people are, as free men, entitled to choose the ruler of their own country, even if they choose Bonaparte. Are they not?"

Wetterstedt went pale and rested his elbows on the table. Jacquette could guess what he was thinking. Sweden had gone to war to dethrone

Bonaparte and send him into exile. Had Charles Jean just said he would support restoring him to power?

The crown prince's black eyes bored into Wetterstedt's. Jacquette could see that her stepfather was considering how best to disagree. "Of course, sir, but the Allies—"

It was one of the rare times when Wetterstedt chose the wrong words.

Oscar spoke often of Charles Jean's passionate side—his booming voice, the gesticulation, the throbbing vein in his temple. Jacquette had not seen it until now.

He stood, and Wetterstedt fell silent. "Allies? Whose allies? Russia and England did not ask my opinion before they put Louis XVIII on the throne to replace Bonaparte. The French people did not ask for another Louis, did they? He is a friend to Gustav, or that is what my spies in France are telling me. I would rather see Bonaparte return."

Uncharacteristically, Wetterstedt seemed to have run out of words.

Charles Jean asked, "You have seen the letter I am writing to Alexander? I will not allow him to give that pretender an inch of territory. He's not of royal blood, and I can prove it."

"I will review the draft tonight."

"It will put an end to the matter for all time. The tsar will see the proof I have gathered, and there will be nothing he can do, no matter how much his wife pleads with him."

"Proof, sir?" Wetterstedt asked.

"Yes. The Mandarin found a trove of evidence to show that Gustav's father is illegitimate. Once it comes to light, Gustav will be relegated to an obscure corner of history. Am I not correct? If I am not, may God strike the crown from my head."

"I am always reluctant to provoke the Russian bear," Wetterstedt said.

Jacquette could see the logic in what Wetterstedt was doing. He was stalling because he did not want Charles Jean's letter to be dispatched to St. Petersburg.

For the first time in years, she thought about the papers she'd found in the queen's letter box, the ones she'd hidden at Confidencen four years ago. They proved Gustav's bloodline was legitimate. If they were authentic, then the evidence Charles Jean wanted to use to blackmail the tsar was false. Was there a chance she could stop Charles Jean from sending his letter by revealing her evidence now?

If so, the peace could depend on it. At the same time, Gustav's legitimacy would make Oscar's crown less secure. Anything that helped Gustav hurt Oscar. It was as simple as that. Jacquette needed to speak to Oscar, and now.

CHAPTER NINE

King's Garden, Stockholm

The next morning, Emilie insisted Jacquette come for a drive. When they got to the carriage yard, Dawson, Emilie's coachman, objected to taking the four-horse landau on the city streets, protesting that its team was rubbed down and rested for their departure to Himmelstalund. Emilie patted the rear horse's rump and got into the carriage without responding. Jacquette lifted her skirts and climbed in behind her. As Aurora always said, "With my sister Emilie comes all that she is."

They entered the King's Garden through the north gates. Emilie knocked on the half-lowered side window, three quick taps.

"Stop there," she said, pointing to the corner of the old orangery.

"On foot, you would have been here a quarter of an hour ago," Dawson replied. None of the servants would have dared to suggest such a thing to Aurora, but people talked to Emilie without fear of condemnation or reproach. And it was true. The roof of Douglas House was visible over the park wall.

"I know, Dawson. I just . . . needed some time to think," Emilie said. Her hands were trembling, and she slipped them beneath her cloak.

They parked under an ancient chestnut tree, one of six that remained from the row planted in the last century. There had been a few sunny days, and the trees already had begun to flower and release the fine spring mist of greenish-yellow dust that always made Jacquette sneeze. She wrinkled her nose, filled with misgiving. There was nothing nearby except the orangery. *Surely*, she thought, *Emilie cannot mean to take me there.*

Emilie asked, "Do you remember coming here when you were small? It was a different place altogether. The thick lawns, the paths. We would picnic over there. The orangery was a dance hall then, and the gardens were lush and beautiful. Charles Jean seems intent on turning it into a military camp. *Quel dommage.*"

"I remember."

The King's Garden, now a bare, windswept rectangle carved from the city, had never been a proper English park like Haga or Finspång or Djurgården. Today, its dusty silence was broken only by the muffled crunch of soldiers' footfalls. The army was marching on the central field, where Charles Jean had recently had the grass replaced with gravel.

The soldiers were moving toward them, and their tall, slim commander caught Jacquette's eye. He rode alongside another officer, and the two were deep in conversation. She could not help but hope it was Oscar.

"Jacquette, come back to Himmelstalund with me. Please," Emilie said.

Jacquette's wish for an uncomplicated promenade evaporated.

Emilie did not wait for a response. "What will you do in Stockholm? You say you do not want to marry yet. You don't want to join the queen's household like your mother, either, I hope."

"Does it matter what I want to do?"

"It pains me to think of you at court."

"I can think of nothing worse."

Emilie looked out the back window of the carriage. "Then get away from here."

"I can't," Jacquette whispered, unable to look at Emilie. She felt her aunt's warm glove around her fingers.

"It is Prince Oscar, isn't it? I feared that."

"Of course not." She hoped Emilie had not noted the speed of her response.

"I adore the prince, but believe me, being around the court again will change him. It was different when you were thrown together during the war with everyone away. With the royals, these things do not often turn out as we intend."

"He kissed me. At my mother's Sunday salon," Jacquette said.

Outside the carriage window, dozens of soldiers in white breeches and gold-breasted blue jackets were marching up the center of the park, raising a cloud of dust. It was Oscar's company, the Second Regiment of the Svea Life Guard. He was astride Odin, his favorite horse, a long-legged chestnut Friesian with an arched neck and short ears. Frederik Due rode beside him.

Jacquette chewed the inside of her lip to stop herself from grinning.

Emilie released Jacquette's hand. "Don't seek him out. Don't look at him. Stop thinking of him this moment. Look what a mess I made of things by falling in love with Clairfelt. I will lose everything before that is all over."

It was true. Emilie's choice to divorce Clairfelt, in Jacquette's mind, was more courageous than Aurora's decision to divorce her father. When Aurora divorced Count Philip, she'd had Wetterstedt to lean on. Emilie would be alone, and with two children to raise.

"Believe me, you should get away from Stockholm and stay away until you forget him."

Jacquette could still feel Oscar's lips touching hers, and forgetting him was the furthest thing from her mind. "You have nothing to worry about. He still thinks of me as his childhood friend from summers at Drottningholm."

"Don't lie to yourself."

Jacquette raised a brow. No one was better at lying to herself than Emilie.

"It is good advice nonetheless, although I have not always abided by it, I admit."

"I'm sorry," Jacquette said. "I did not mean any impertinence."

"It's nothing, my sweet, sweet girl. I know how it is to be in love, to think you are so nimble and clever you can enter a forest filled with wolves and emerge unharmed. But you must realize that you are not your mother. None of us is."

"I don't want to be her."

Emilie waved her hand. "When I was your age, I imagined I was as strong as Aurora, that I could follow my heart at night and walk with my head high the next morning. That I could always win, always get what I wanted. But I found out that I was only Emilie. I so very much want to spare you that pain."

"Would you have me ignore Oscar? I have known him since he came to Sweden."

"Indeed not," Emilie said quietly. "I would have you run from him."

"Well, I cannot come with you to Himmelstalund. I need to stay in the city," said Jacquette. "What are we doing here?"

"I'm meeting Clairfelt before I leave. And don't tell your mother."

Jacquette followed Emilie's eyes and saw a lone man approaching. He was some distance away, near the east wall of the park. It was Clairfelt.

"Aunt, why?" Jacquette asked.

"We have children together, so we are married for life. Remember that if you ever take a husband."

"Don't see him. Let's go," Jacquette said, startled by Clairfelt's seething expression. She looked to the other end of the park, where Frederik Due had steered his horse away from Oscar's and was galloping toward them.

"I must speak to my husband, Jacquette."

A great pounding of hooves shook the carriage. Boots hit the ground and Frederik opened the door. As he helped Emilie down, he kissed her on both cheeks and said, "Baroness, Prince Oscar asked me to see if I might be of service." Jacquette followed Emilie and stood beside the carriage.

Clairfelt looked older than he had when she'd last seen him, but he was still handsome, with blond hair that brushed his shoulders. Pretty and penniless, Aurora called him. He was the illegitimate son of a Swedish general and a French actress, and Emilie could not resist him. Even now.

Addressing no one in particular, Clairfelt demanded to know what was happening. His eyes were narrowed, and his hands were clenched at his sides. He scowled at Emilie, and Frederik stepped to her side and placed a protective hand on her shoulder.

"Clairfelt, what are you doing here?" Frederik asked, not answering his question. "I beg you to stay where you are."

Clairfelt moved even closer. His steps were deliberate, slow, and threatening.

The carriage horses began to paw at the ground and snort. Dawson yelled some harsh words at Clairfelt and pleaded with Emilie to get back into the carriage. Then they were all quarreling—Dawson, Frederik, Clairfelt, and Emilie.

Frederik approached Clairfelt with his hand on his sword. Older than Frederik by at least a decade and a superior officer as well, Clairfelt went chest to chest with the Norwegian, barking at him to stand aside. He tore Emilie from her position behind Dawson. She cowered and tried to pull away, but Clairfelt half led and half dragged her by the arm to a bench under one of the chestnut trees.

Emilie screamed as he gripped her by the shoulders with both hands and pinned her to the tree. When he turned to look at Jacquette, his cruel leer terrified her.

Emilie's face had turned a mottled deep red. Was it anger? Embarrassment?

Jacquette opened her mouth to scream, but her breath was trapped inside her, and only a weak whimper escaped. Still trying to summon enough air to make herself heard, she tugged Frederik's arm as hard as she could.

"Help her," Jacquette croaked, pulling Frederik toward the tree.

When Frederik was almost upon him, Clairfelt released Emilie and she gasped, open-mouthed. She bent forward from the waist, choking and coughing, her face a grimace of pain.

Jacquette tried to run to her, but Frederik held her back.

"The prince ordered me to keep you away from him," he said.

"Look at what he is doing to her."

Clairfelt was pressing his body against Emilie's, kissing her, crushing her soft, round breasts. He was slim yet sinewy after years of enduring the rigors of military service and war, and Jacquette imagined the pain his granite-hard torso was inflicting.

"Maurice, no," Emilie panted. "I cannot breathe." She was squirming and trying to escape, with little success. With a loud cry, she raised her right knee, abruptly and with some force, and jabbed Clairfelt between his legs, but her heavy skirts and cloak must have softened the blow. Jacquette cringed, fearing Clairfelt's reaction.

He braced his forearm on the tree trunk above Emilie's head and snarled, "You bitch. You forced me to work among this swarm of flies you call a royal court, and now you say you'll divorce me? Do it. I dare you. You'll never see young Axel again."

So that was what he would use against Emilie. The only things that were really hers. Her children.

Emilie's legs buckled, and if it had not been for Clairfelt's body pinning her to the tree trunk, she would have fallen into the budding daffodils around its base. They had been cruelly trampled in the struggle.

"Strike me if you wish," Emilie choked. "But Axel is not strong. You know he needs me."

Axel was Emilie's firstborn, not yet three years old, and she doted on him.

Clairfelt's laugh was cruel. "Keep Julie then. It makes no difference to me. Raise her to be a whore like you are. But don't think you will get the boy or the house." He released Emilie, and she fell to her knees.

She looked up at him, her eyes clouded with confusion. "The house? But Wetterstedt bought Himmelstalund for me. It is mine."

Clairfelt laughed again. "Everything you own became mine the day we married. Do not think I will let you bend and twist the law like your sister did."

It was true; Aurora had somehow managed to avoid giving up even a sliver of her interest in Finspång.

Clairfelt groaned in mock sympathy. "I'm sure Baron Wetterstedt will allow you to live with him and Aurora. You can serve your sister. Another companion for her, perhaps?"

The color drained from Emilie's face, and her limp body crumpled. She crouched on the muddy ground, clutching her soiled white skirts and pulling them over her bare, bloody knees. Jacquette's head pounded. Seeing Emilie sob was almost worse than watching the physical struggle between her and Clairfelt. Emilie had been expecting this, Jacquette realized. It was not the first time.

Jacquette put her hands on her hips, suddenly filled with fury at Frederik and his detached, cool gaze. "You have to do something," she said.

"She's his wife," Frederik said to her, his face somber. "You cannot fault a man for taking charge of what is his."

"Frederik, she is ill and has been poorly for at least a month," Jacquette replied. "Please."

Frederik gazed toward the other end of the park, where the regiment had halted in front of the Arsenal Theater. He wiped his forehead, then swore under his breath. Odin was galloping toward them, and Oscar looked furious.

CHAPTER TEN

Oscar dismounted in front of the orangery, his hands folded over the hilt of his sword, surveying the wreckage of Clairfelt and Emilie's marriage. After a morning with his regiment, he looked like a soldier, flushed and sweaty and unnervingly handsome. His uniform jacket was open, revealing pearl-colored breeches that clung to the smooth hardness of his hips. Jacquette tried to meet his gaze, to will him to wrap his arms around her and take her far away from this ugliness.

She had spent every night since they'd kissed reliving the sensation of his lips pressing into hers. Beads of sweat formed on her forehead every time she thought of it. Oscar's kiss was not her first (that had been Adam Lewenhaupt last Midsummer Day), but it had revealed a world of unknown things, as if she had opened a book written in ancient Sanskrit and found she could read it. The kiss had been more than a superficial brush of skin on skin; Oscar's lips had burned with need. After Peter had left the room, she had been too enthralled to move, but when she recovered, she had wrapped her arms around Oscar. One hand had traveled down to cup his buttock, at first tentatively and then with a boldness that should have shamed her. Had she remembered that he would someday be king of Sweden, never would she have dared to touch him in that way. But she knew it had pleased him because his body stilled for a full few seconds. They had not spoken of it—not then, not since—and she wondered whether they ever would.

The kiss was not the first time she had touched Oscar, but it had been nothing like their youthful tumbles down the hill in front of the blue-striped copper tents at Haga Park. Nor had it been like the times when they'd clutched each other, sometimes in laughter, sometimes in shock, in the darkness of Aurora's box at the theater or the Royal Opera. And it had probably, or certainly, been a mistake.

He was looking at her now with a slight frown, and she sensed he could read her thoughts. Was he angry with her? Annoyed? Remorseful? Did he want her? Then she remembered that Frederik was watching them and turned away, her cheeks burning.

Oscar coughed. "Frederik, march the men to the barracks," he said.

"So early, sir?"

Oscar nodded. "Have ale served with their dinner. Convey my compliments and order them to report at eight tomorrow morning."

"Yes, sir," Frederik said as he remounted. He rode toward the Arsenal Theater, where the soldiers were probably spinning wild rumors about Oscar's detour to this end of the park.

Oscar pushed his hair from his eyes, and a passing frown knitted his brow. "Come. Let's go see about Emilie," he said after Frederik was out of earshot. They walked over to Clairfelt, who now was standing silently, a safe distance away from Emilie.

Oscar's words to Clairfelt were quiet but firm. "Is something the matter here, Colonel?"

Clairfelt bowed, his eyes never leaving Oscar's. His discomfort pleased Jacquette.

"Nothing amiss, Your Royal Highness," Clairfelt answered.

"Baroness?" Oscar asked Emilie.

"You are kind to inquire, sir," said Emilie. "I invited my husband to come here and talk with me. On neutral ground, as they say." Her cheeks grew red. "You are aware, I am sure, of our request to end our . . . to divorce."

It sounded so final.

Oscar hitched Odin to a post at the base of the chestnut tree and knocked some mud off his high black leather boots. Jacquette suspected he was thinking about the rumors that Charles Jean was about to divorce his mother.

He said to Emilie, "I am sorry to hear of it. I shall leave you to speak with him. That is your wish?"

Emilie nodded.

Oscar held up a hand to the wind. "It's blowing off the Baltic, much too cold for you to stand out here, Emilie. I know you haven't been well. Speak with Clairfelt in your carriage, and I will walk with Countess Jacquette. I am confident he will behave himself. And, Clairfelt, kindly check on Odin from time to time." Oscar patted the horse's rump, and Odin swung his head from side to side. Jacquette knew Odin, and he was looking for a carrot. Oscar reached into his saddlebag and fed the horse, who ate eagerly. "Clairfelt, take good care of the baroness. She is still your wife, you know, and she is dear to us all." He narrowed his eyes, and Clairfelt returned his stare.

Jacquette hugged Emilie and wiped the tears from her cheeks.

"Are you certain you wish to stay?" Jacquette said.

Emilie's brown eyes filled with tears. "I must," she said. "Leave me. Clairfelt will not hurt me. I promise you. He's not stupid."

Jacquette thought Clairfelt was quite insane. But Emilie was as serious as a nun.

"All right, I'll go. Send Dawson if you need me," Jacquette said.

"I won't need you."

Clairfelt climbed into the carriage without offering Emilie a hand, so Oscar helped her to mount the step, then closed the door behind them.

"Come, let us leave them to their problems," Oscar said as he turned to walk up the path to the other end of the park. "I daresay I have some of my own."

Jacquette tried to keep up with him, but he outpaced her with his long strides, and they had almost reached St. Jacob's churchyard before he spoke again.

"I'm sorry about all that. Poor Emilie doesn't deserve it," he said in a distant tone.

"What's wrong, Oscar?"

They often walked together, and he always offered his arm and wrapped his free hand over hers. Today, he did not.

"I'm fine, Q. It isn't you." He spun to face her, and his features drew into sharper lines. "I think my father wishes Magnus were his heir. I am not enough, or not good enough."

For someone with so many advantages, Oscar never stopped thinking about Charles Jean, the one person who had more. He was acting like a child, a spoiled only child.

"Magnus isn't your father's heir. He has only one son, and it is you."

"Right now, the two of them are at the palace deciding whether to go to war against Bonaparte, and they sent me here to march soldiers around the park."

He turned into the churchyard to avoid a group of young men who were rolling boules on the path. Oscar seemed in no mood to greet the Stockholmers today.

"Not the cemetery," she said.

He leaned against the iron gates of one of the large tombs in the churchyard, which faced the King's Garden. "No one has been buried here since I came to Sweden. Come on."

"Oh, all right." She picked up her skirts and hurried past a mildewed old tombstone to stand next to him.

"You have heard about Bonaparte, I presume," he said. "Probably more than I have."

She nodded. "Your father came to our house in the middle of dinner. He was saying the most perplexing things. Wetterstedt seemed quite vexed by it all."

The leather ball rolled off the path, and a boy came running to retrieve it. Oscar turned away and pulled up his jacket collar to hide his face, then motioned to her to come nearer. He seemed anxious to hear what she knew.

"Father didn't tell me he went to your house. What did he say to Wetterstedt?"

She tried to remember. "His face was red, and he was speaking so quickly. He told us the French are celebrating Bonaparte's escape and want him to rule France again. He thinks they have the right to choose him. Wetterstedt seemed quite shocked, as we just went to war to remove him."

"He has never forgiven the Allies for giving Louis XVIII the French throne instead of him. You know what this is all about, don't you?"

"No," she said.

"Gustav."

"What do you mean?"

"Louis XVIII is funding half the Gustavian spies in Stockholm, and my father will do anything to remove him, including supporting Bonaparte."

She almost didn't tell Oscar the rest but decided he had a right to know. "Your father has written a letter to the tsar. But I don't think he has sent it yet, and I don't think Wetterstedt likes it."

"What letter?" Oscar tore off his gloves and tucked them into the waist of his breeches.

Jacquette put her hand on his sleeve. "He's threatening to embarrass the tsar if he insists on supporting Gustav. He says he has proof that Gustav's father was illegitimate and will make it public."

Oscar wiped his brow. "I think he does have something. Damn spies. Secret police. I told him spying is a dirty business and we should stay out of it."

"But, Oscar, your father's spies are wrong, and I can prove it. I have some papers. Hidden."

"What papers?" he demanded. "Come on, Q, tell me. This is important."

Two ragged boys in felt caps, apparently having wandered away from their game, pressed their grubby faces against the gate to the tomb. One of them shouted at Oscar, "Are you the royal prince?"

Oscar took some coins from his belt and walked to the fence. "I am Oscar." He bent down, nodding and smiling as he gave each boy his money. "But don't tell your friends I am here. I am doing some important business with my . . . chief court mistress."

Eyes wide, they nodded. "May God save our prince," said the taller one.

"Bless his health," replied the other, and they ran off.

After they rejoined the other boys, the younger one cupped his hands to his chest like breasts and shook his backside, and the entire group broke into laughter. Oscar clamped his lips together, suppressing a smile. He wiped tears of laughter off Jacquette's cheeks and stroked her hair.

"Why didn't you tell me?" he asked.

"Why would you want proof that Gustav's claim to the throne is valid?"

"The Gustavians are searching for those documents, so wouldn't it be better if we got them first? It might stop my father from making false accusations. Where are they?"

"Drottningholm. At Confidencen," she mumbled. "I put them there the first time we met."

His lips parted. "Really? They were in the queen's box, and you didn't tell me?"

"I'm not sure the papers really belonged to the queen. The box was sitting in the library at The Birdcage. Anyone could have put them inside."

"You could have trusted me."

Jacquette decided she owed him an explanation. "I didn't know you then."

He leaned against the tall granite monument and folded his arms across his chest. "And you didn't think I would be a prince for very long."

"No, that's not—"

His voice was gentle, not filled with anger as she'd expected. "It's all right. Nothing is certain even now, is it? If my father threatens the tsar, or backs Bonaparte, or shuts down the newspapers, I expect we will be exiled ourselves. Meet me at Confidencen. You know me now."

"April's just begun, Oscar. Drottningholm is closed and shuttered and freezing."

"I shall have the caretaker unlock everything. Just get yourself there," he said.

She nodded, although she had no idea how to begin planning a secret trip to Drottningholm. "We should go back now. What if Clairfelt has done something to Emilie?"

"He would not dare," Oscar said. He straightened his collar and brushed off the back of Jacquette's cloak. She thought his hand lingered longer than necessary at the small of her back, but he did not kiss her. It seemed he had forgotten their first one, but she hoped it would not be their last.

Emilie went to bed with a headache as soon as they returned home and stayed there until it was nearly time for her to begin the fourteen-hour journey to Norrköping. Jacquette opened the bedroom door a crack and saw her sitting on the edge of her bed, her eyes red and swollen.

"What happened?" Jacquette asked. "Uncle Clairfelt didn't . . ." She could not continue.

Emilie was wrapping a long rose silk scarf around her shoulders, wincing every time she touched the red marks left by Clairfelt's fingers. "Wounds of the body heal, but the kind he has dealt me will not. Men will take things from you, Quette, things they do not even want or know how to care for. Just because they can."

"What has he done?"

"He is taking Axel to the south, to live with him in Skåne." She began to sob. "The poor boy is his heir, so I can do nothing to stop it. I should never have asked Charles Jean to make Clairfelt a baron. He would not have needed an heir if he were still a commoner."

"And Julie?"

Emilie looked away.

Jacquette knew the answer. It had been one of her first lessons from her parents' divorce. She was twelve years old at the time and had been living with Emilie. She had not seen Aurora in more than a year. When they had been reunited, Jacquette, frantic with joy, had crushed herself against Aurora. She'd felt her mother's fingers running through her hair, but when she'd looked up, she'd seen her tears.

"What is it, Mother?" she had asked.

Aurora had released Jacquette and stared at her sons with a chalk-white face. In a voice drained of emotion, she'd explained that, after the divorce, Nils and August would live with their father in a cold, faraway place called Härnösand.

"What of me?" Jacquette had asked.

"He did not make any arrangements for you," Aurora had said.

That was the moment when it had become clear. Boys mattered, and men made the decisions. Now, it had been almost five years since she had seen her brothers, and her father would not even allow them to write. Aurora never mentioned the boys, but she was strong and, apparently, content to give up her sons to keep Finspång. Jacquette did not think Emilie would fare so well.

Peter followed Brita into the library at Douglas House a quarter hour after Jacquette's lesson was due to have begun. Making no excuse for his tardiness, he simply pulled a thick book of English grammar from his bag. His ensemble, a white satin hair ribbon, blue velvet morning coat, and starched white shirt with ruffled sleeves, would have been the height of French fashion ten years earlier. Plainly, he had not been working in the print shop today. Even his fingernails, which Jacquette imagined as black with ink, were unstained.

"Ready to start?" Peter asked.

"Our young countess's mind is elsewhere," Brita said matter-of-factly.

It was a fair point. Since she'd left the cemetery yesterday, Jacquette's thoughts had been of Oscar. Why, with every opportunity to crush her against the stone wall behind the old mausoleum and kiss her senseless, he hadn't.

"Is my native tongue less fascinating than . . . let me guess . . . Prince Oscar?" Peter chided her.

Since Peter had seen their kiss at Aurora's salon, she had been expecting him to raise the subject.

"He's only a friend," she said, trying to sound unperturbed.

"And she has never spent five minutes thinking about another man since she was fourteen years old," said Brita.

Jacquette made a face and said, "It's not true. Let's just start."

When she tried to open her assignment book, Peter's long, elegant hand was planted squarely on its cover.

"What is bothering you, Jacquette?"

She decided to trust him. He had seen her and Oscar together and, to her knowledge, had not told a soul. He walked with Brita late at night when she went to help the pastry chef at the French Inn, to keep her safe. Even Oscar had come to rely on Peter, who gave Jacquette copies of censored pamphlets and articles for him to read.

"I have gotten myself in a mess, and it is all my fault, but I couldn't possibly burden you with the details of it," she said.

"Slow down and tell me. It will make you feel better."

"I need to meet a friend in an unusual place."

"And why is that so very difficult?" Peter asked.

"You cannot repeat this to anyone," Jacquette said.

With a knowing smile, he inclined his head and thumped his heart with a closed fist, and it was all Jacquette could do to refrain from stamping her boot. She hated to be mocked, and Peter seemed immune to her usual devices.

"On Tuesday, I must go to Drottningholm without anyone learning of it. To meet Prince Oscar."

Peter laughed out loud and raised his eyebrows at Brita. "It comes back to him, does it?"

"God save you if people find out, Jacquette," said Brita.

"I won't tell anyone you helped me, even if I am caught. All I am asking is how to get from here to there without anyone discovering my purpose. And I can't ask anyone else."

Brita said, "Obviously not. Your other friends can't tie a bonnet without at least a couple of servants to help."

"Can you aid me or not?"

Peter looked sympathetic but said, "I don't relish the idea of Wetterstedt finding out."

"Someone as worldly as you must have had his share of secret meetings."

"Hardly."

"Well, you must have been in love at least once in your life."

Peter looked away.

"Well?" Jacquette asked. When he looked back at her, his face was pale, and he seemed ten years older.

It seemed like a full minute passed before he spoke. "The harbor is still frozen, so you can't go by boat. Even the roads may be too muddy once you leave the capital. You should take the Royal Road, but not with the prince. Go by carriage and bring companions. You will have to tell your mother, you know."

"I was afraid you would say that."

"There's really no other way. Has the prince told you how he will get there?"

The palace was in a frenzy, planning for a ceremony to mark Oscar's oath of loyalty to the king. It would be easy for him to sneak away. "He sent me a note. Everyone will think he is riding out to Drottningholm to plan military exercises."

"May I see?"

"Here." She handed it to Peter.

He pointed to the last line.

Meet me at Confidencen. O.

"Why Confidencen, Jacquette?" asked Peter.

"There's something I hid there a long time ago," she said. "Some papers."

"How do you know they are still there?"

"I don't. But I need to get to Drottningholm on Tuesday to find out."

Peter did not ask what was in the hidden papers. If Jacquette were in his position, she would have been dying to know.

CHAPTER ELEVEN

No one in the capital was Aurora's equal as a hostess, and she was determined to keep it that way. She had been closeted with Christine and Sophie since breakfast, planning the seating arrangements for the luncheon to follow Oscar's ceremony in the Hall of State. The long table in the library, cleared of books and paper, now displayed a silk banner embroidered with the words On the Occasion of the Prince's Oath of Allegiance, Royal Palace Stockholm, April 20, 1815. Circles and rectangles were pinned to the silk to represent banquet tables, and stacks of tiny name cards were arranged in a neat row along the table's edge. When Jacquette slipped into the room, Christine gave her a tiny wave and a smile, but Aurora did not even glance in her direction.

Jacquette watched Aurora studying the table. From time to time, she exclaimed "*Mais non!*" or "*Que Dieu nous en préserve!*" and directed either Sophie or Christine to write a table number on a name card. Aurora relished nothing more than arranging people.

"Good morning, Mother."

"Quette, you are here—come see the three counts I am considering seating next to you. There's a Wachtmeister and a Hamilton, and that one—Daughter, are you listening to me?"

Good, Jacquette thought. *I have her attention*. "Pick the one who is most interesting to talk to, I suppose."

Aurora removed her reading glasses, which now dangled from a long chain around her neck. "If you were a maid of honor, I could seat you better. Won't you come visit Queen Charlotte some afternoon when I am in service? A position with her would offer you such advantages. I do not know why you resist it so."

"No thank you, Mother. Aunt Emilie has told me all about the *advantages*."

"Emilie made the wrong choices when she was young."

"I suppose I am fortunate she did. It allowed her to raise me while you arranged parties at court." Jacquette laughed and kissed her mother on the cheek.

Aurora threw up her hands. "My years away from you were not easy for me, either."

Jacquette hugged Aurora's delicate shoulders. "I am only teasing. Look at this letter." Jacquette removed a sheet of paper from her dress pocket. "It's from the foster mother in that dear little house in Drottningholm Village."

Aurora showed no interest in examining the letter, which was for the best. She might have recognized Brita's handwriting.

"I thought the widow was going to move those little angels to the city," said Aurora. "It's such a pity that Charles Jean never warmed up to Drottningholm. Soon there will be no one left in the village. When I was a girl—"

"I'd like to bring the children some books."

Aurora put down a stack of name cards and turned around to face Jacquette. "Books, you say."

"Yes, Mother. Books. A gift to the school to honor Prince Oscar taking the royal oath. You asked me to choose some charitable works, didn't you?"

Christine and Sophie drifted closer, and Christine wrote a table number on a name card. Jacquette didn't mind her curiosity. This plan involved her, too.

"Don't put Magnus next to Carl Löwenhielm," Aurora barked at Christine. "They will end the night in a duel, God forbid." Christine apologized, duly chastised for disturbing the social balance.

Jacquette wished Emilie were here. She would have found this amusing.

"Mother," she said in a quiet whisper. "Can I go?"

"Go *where*?"

"Drottningholm Village, just for the day."

"In April? None of society is there yet, and you cannot miss the prince's oath."

"I told you, it's next Tuesday. Two days before the ceremony."

Aurora narrowed her eyes and tilted her chin to one side, as she often did when she thought Jacquette was hiding something.

"I'll take Brita with me. And Christine as my chaperone."

"And Sophie," Aurora said. "She will tell me what you are up to. What *are* you not telling me?"

It was so difficult to hide things from Aurora.

Making sure that Sophie and Christine were not watching, Jacquette leaned over the table and touched the card with Oscar's name on it. Aurora would understand the unspoken message. Oscar would be at Drottningholm.

Aurora took a sip of her tea and set it down. "Of course you can go to see those darling little girls. And you will have a new dress." Reexamining the seating arrangement, Aurora slid Jacquette's name card closer to Oscar's. "But, Quette, let's not mention this to your papa."

"As you wish."

Wetterstedt adored Aurora but did not always approve of her political machinations. And Aurora did not even know about the documents at Confidencen.

⁂

At the end of the King's Road, the toll collector raised the barrier to the third and last bridge, an unsteady wooden structure that crossed a narrow neck of Lake Mälaren that separated marshy Kärsön Island from Drottningholm, which was on Lovön Island. Aurora had insisted they take her four-horse carriage with Queen Charlotte's insignia on the doors, which ensured that every gate along their route would be lifted and every window flung open. People were anxious to see the first spring arrival of highborn Stockholm society ladies.

Jacquette's companions were enjoying the attention, Sophie in particular. Dressed in Sunday finery, she kept taking coins from Jacquette's reticule and handing them through the window to hungry farmers' sons. They probably thought she was a countess. Christine found this hilarious, but Brita seethed with contempt. Jacquette just tried to keep her nerves calm.

Breaking the tension, Christine exclaimed, "There it is!"

Jacquette had visited the royal island dozens of times but never tired of it. It was a place to take your breath away.

The Duke's Stables had just come into view. The building had three stories with two wings and was painted, like the other buildings in Drottningholm Village, in a buttery gold limewash. It had a steep orange tiled roof, stalls for dozens of horses, and double doors that were wide enough to accommodate the largest gilded royal coach. When they neared the entrance, an officer in royal uniform tried to pull the door open, but a group of plump children filled the portal, extending their hands and crying out greetings.

With a squeal, Christine pressed her face against the carriage window and waved until she was winded.

"Here," Jacquette said, removing some sweets from her bag. She handed them to Christine. "Give them these."

"Is Versailles more beautiful than this?" Christine asked, pointing at the palace.

Jacquette shook her head. "I've heard Bonaparte had to restore all the rooms. We Swedes have the good sense not to sell off the furniture when we overthrow a king."

For Jacquette, Drottningholm brought good and bad memories. On the good side, there were happy times. Parties. Theater. Meeting Oscar.

But Drottningholm was a place of butterfly games. It was here, as a young child, that she had first seen her parents dallying with their lovers and realized their marriage was a facade.

The coachman's voice interrupted Jacquette's thoughts. "Countess, I trust you know the village?"

"Of course." Aurora had planned everything. The driver would park the carriage and wait for them upstairs, where there were rooms for coachmen and stable workers.

Brita pushed a basket of books toward Sophie's feet. "Stop staring at Christine," Brita said to Sophie. "You only have to act as her maid for a day. You'll be back with Baroness Wetterstedt soon enough."

"Remember, we are here to spread cheer," Jacquette said, directing her words at Sophie.

When Brita reached to get Jacquette a shawl, Jacquette shook her head. "Not for me. Thanks." She did not wish to cover her outfit, a high-waisted heather-colored gown with short puffed sleeves and a soft woven cape in the same tone.

Sophie scowled. "I won't be needing one," she said with a shrug. No one had offered.

"I wouldn't cover that cape either, Jacquette. It's too beautiful," Christine said.

"I hope the orphans appreciate it," Jacquette said to the others. She led them down the main road of the village and stopped in front of the Cavaliers' Residence, a long building that housed male courtiers when Drottningholm was teeming with royals in summer. She gave a tiny nod to a tall young man who was standing at the side of the residence, inconspicuous unless one knew where to look.

Swaying and off balance, Jacquette stepped on the sloped curb of the road. Making sure there was a post nearby for her to grasp, she allowed her knees to buckle.

"Ouch," she said, cradling her left foot in both hands.

"What is it, Jacquette?" Christine rushed to her side.

"It's these old streets. Something hard just bruised the bottom of my foot. Look, it was one of those." She pointed at some black iron knobs that protruded from the road. Wincing as if in pain, she leaned against a column near the entrance to the Cavaliers' Residence and took off her slipper.

Just as Aurora had arranged, the red-haired young man walked around the corner and appeared next to her.

"You should have worn boots. I told you," said Sophie.

"Have a little sympathy. She is hurt, don't you see?" said Christine.

"Adam," Jacquette said, trying to sound surprised. She looked at her companions. "You have been introduced to Baron Adam Lewenhaupt, I trust?"

Christine looked relieved to see Adam, whose tousled red hair was a poor complement to his dour gray lawyer's suit.

"What are you doing here, Jacquette?" Adam asked her. He was a good enough actor and seemed genuinely surprised.

"*Ack*, I do not know. I should have stayed in Stockholm."

"Are you bleeding?" he asked.

"I think it is just a bruise. But I don't believe I can walk," Jacquette said.

Christine and Sophie stood in silence, wearing matching frowns. Adam spoke to Christine in an authoritative voice that seemed, to Jacquette, older than his years.

"Let me take the countess to the apothecary's house, and Dr. Hedrén will look at it. It may need a poultice."

Dr. Hedrén, Aurora had assured Jacquette, would be nowhere in the vicinity of Drottningholm, being in Stockholm at a funeral.

"I suppose you should," said Christine. "Baroness Aurora will not forgive us if Jacquette is hurt."

Trying to sound brave, Jacquette said, "Take the books to the children's home and give the house mother my deepest regrets. I shall meet you back at the carriage after I finish with the doctor. And kiss the little angels for me."

"Oh, we can come collect you at the doctor's office. Where is it?" Christine asked, looking up and down the street.

Adam blushed until the color of his cheeks matched his freckles. For a moment, Jacquette thought he was about to betray their scheme, but he stepped forward and laced his arm under Jacquette's shoulders to hoist her upright.

"It is just up the street on the next block. But there is no need for you to go there. We will join you at the widow's house," he said. "Now let go of the wall, Jacquette, and let's try to walk."

Christine nodded.

Until the girls turned the corner and were out of sight, Jacquette hopped on one foot and grimaced in pain, leaning on Adam's arm. She hoped he would not press for details about why she was here. She didn't want to lie, but she would.

"Where to, my lady?"

This was the tricky part. "Adam, I need to go to Kina." Kina was the section of Drottningholm Palace Park where the China Palace, Confidencen, and the aviaries were located. There was no reason for anyone to go there, particularly in April.

His eyes narrowed for a second, and he scratched the back of his neck. "Kina it is, then."

Jacquette almost wished she had fallen in love with a simple, honest person like Adam.

CHAPTER TWELVE

With Drottningholm Palace looming behind Jacquette and Adam on the lakeshore, they walked across the park, past the large fountain, and around the maze. Lest Adam pose more questions, Jacquette changed the subject.

"You," she said, twirling on her heel to face him, "still owe me money."

He threw his shoulders back. "From our chess game? I do not. There was to be a rematch."

"I do not recall agreeing to that."

"Here, then," he said, reaching into a leather pouch slung over his shoulder. "Two riksdalers-banco, is it? A Lewenhaupt always pays his debts. But, Jacquette, I wanted to talk about what happened last summer—"

"I beat you fair and square, that's what happened."

He clasped his hands behind his back, always the gentleman. "I think you should give me a chance. And I don't mean at chess."

It was only one kiss, she thought. "Come, now. You were never this serious before you became a lawyer."

"I'm not quite a lawyer yet. Can we talk the next time we are at Haga?"

She made light of it. "Of course. The queen is planning a huge spectacle there for my birthday. Enormous. Boats, fireworks, a French comedy troupe. The fourth of July, you know."

It broke the tension, and he laughed. The elaborate party was for Oscar, not her, and she and Adam joked about it every year.

"Bring your money because I'm going to win this time. The chessboards are still at Noah's Ark."

She and Adam had played many matches at the floating swimming pavilion off the shore at Haga. "It's a deal."

They passed the rest of their walk in a comfortable silence. Adam probably was grateful for the reprieve from reviewing estate inventories of dead nobles.

Midway up the hill, before they entered the avenue of chestnut trees that led to the China Palace, she pulled open a narrow gate in a low stone wall. Her heart was pounding, and her hands were shaking from nerves. There was no sign of Oscar.

"I don't know what you're up to, but be careful," Adam said. He walked down the narrow, sunless path between the kitchen buildings and the rear of Confidencen.

She touched his elbow. "Thanks, Adam. I'll meet you in half an hour around the corner in the kitchen garden. There's a bench."

"I hope you find what you are looking for, Jacquette."

She had told him she was here to find something. He had not asked her what.

When he was gone, she pulled on the old plank door to Confidencen's basement, worried it might groan on its hinges.

It didn't.

❧

The basement was semi-dark, and dust hung in the air. In a corner near the stairs, Oscar's leather boots gleamed in the flame of a lantern that sat on the dirt floor near his feet. He was sitting on the bottom step resting his elbows on his long, thin legs, dressed head to toe in midnight blue with cloth buttons. For once, he wore none of his medals or insignia.

He brushed the dust from his trousers and hastened to her. They stood in silence with their bodies almost touching. She wondered whether he could see in her eyes what she saw in his—the mixed motives for coming to this place, the uneasiness, the exhilaration of having a secret, the desire that obliterated all other thought.

He took her hand and traced circles on the paper-thin skin in the center of her palm. When she held her breath, she could feel each stroke down to her toes.

She said, "I'd like for you to do that all afternoon."

"As would I." He took a deep breath before he continued. "How did you persuade Christine and Sophie to wait in the village? Brita knows what we are doing, I presume."

She nodded. "I told them I'd hurt my foot and that Adam was taking me to Dr. Hedrén. There wasn't much Sophie could do about it. I'm sure she would have liked to follow."

Oscar's lazy grin froze. This had been a tense subject ever since she'd told him Adam had kissed her last summer.

"Adam Lewenhaupt is out there?"

She nodded and chattered on, ignoring his cold stare. "My mother got him involved in this. I told him I'd come here to find something, and he has no idea that I am meeting you. He went to the kitchen garden to read a book."

Oscar folded his arms across his chest. "You didn't let him think he was taking you into the woods to—"

"Of course not." She huffed out a sigh and rolled her eyes for effect. "He's just a friend."

Oscar was jealous, and Jacquette was more than a little pleased.

He was so close. She yearned to pull him toward her but instead felt her way in the musty darkness toward the large wooden wheel that dominated the room. The papers were inside a storage box next to the hand crank. She had placed them there, confident no one had used the wheel in years.

From behind, Oscar's hands reached around her shoulders and underneath her cape, tracing the square neckline of her gown. With gentle strokes across her pleated silk bodice, he teased her breasts until she felt a dizzying fullness. Her nipples were raw and hard, and she wanted nothing more than for him to pinch them until they hurt. It was a new feeling for her, one she did not completely understand, and it was nothing like the grinding and squeezing Brita had told her about.

He hadn't forgotten their kiss.

"I hope Adam didn't do that," he said in a tantalizing voice.

His lips grazed the side of her neck, and her knees went weak. She needed to get hold of herself, for Oscar appeared to have forgotten why they were here.

"The papers," she said in a strangled little voice.

Oscar's hands moved down to her hips and guided her around to face him. She breathed in his scent of dust and citrus and pressed her body against his. *This is Oscar, and I am safe with him*, she reminded herself, although he seemed so much older now, so ready to take what he needed from her.

When he lowered his head to kiss the skin above her neckline, she opened her eyes and saw the top of the storage box where she had hidden the papers. The pebbles she had placed on its lid four years ago, so carefully in a circle, were gone. What, she asked herself, or *who*, could have disturbed them?

She placed both hands on his chest. "Oscar, let's get the documents out first."

He drew away from her, his eyes glazed and unfocused, and she could hear him breathing fast and hard.

"Q, for God's sake. I'm the one the Gustavians want. If I'm willing to take the risk . . . All right, give me a minute." He tucked his curls behind his ears and reached under his jacket straighten his dark blue silk shirt. His neckcloth had loosened, and he threw it over one shoulder like a scarf.

"I thought you wanted to do this," she said.

He grinned as he pulled his uniform jacket down. "I do want it. You have no idea."

She put her hands on her hips. "I mean the papers. I brought a pouch to put them in. What will you do? Will you tell your father they say Gustav is legitimate?"

"I don't know," he said. He moved away from her and examined the crank attached to the wheel. "Haven't decided."

"If you tell him the truth, he might abandon this crazy idea about supporting Bonaparte. Stop censoring the newspapers. Tear up his letter to the tsar. And he would give you the credit. Not Magnus."

"Or he just might put me in a cell at Vaxholm Fortress, divorce my mother, and find a wife who could birth a replacement heir."

"He wouldn't send you to Vaxholm. Don't be ridiculous." She wasn't sure about the rest. Charles Jean might well do those things.

Oscar shrugged and stuffed his hands in the pockets of his long jacket. "Let's just get them out of here so the Gustavians don't find them first. In there?" He pointed to the storage cabinet.

She nodded. "I put the packet inside the day I met you. You probably don't even remember—"

He stopped her. "I do," he said in a husky voice, almost a whisper. "I didn't have a friend in this country, and my father sent me up here with my men, who didn't want me around, either. You do not know how low I was feeling, but then I looked up and you were there. To me, you were the prettiest girl in Sweden. Still are."

She forgot all about the missing stones.

She turned around and drew him toward her, opening her mouth to meet his, teasing his lips, his tongue, his throat, for what seemed like forever. When she heard his low moan, she released him.

"God, Q," he said, trying to catch his breath.

"See? I can lead," she said. "Not just kiss back."

He said nothing and stood there looking at her with a blank, stunned expression as she knelt and lifted the lid of the box.

It was empty.

⁂

She stared at the clean rectangle of polished wood where the stack of papers should have been. All these years, the possibility that someone might steal them must have been in the back of her mind. Why had she ignored the risk? There were a thousand safer hiding places. If only she had moved them.

Something about the inside of the storage box nagged at her. A clean rectangle free of dust. A place where sediment had not had the time to settle. It meant that someone had taken the papers from the box recently.

"Oscar, when did you ask the keeper to unlock the door?" she asked.

"Frederik talked to him the day before yesterday, I think. He said no one has asked him to unlock it since he chained it a couple of years ago. Can I see inside?"

She rose and stepped away. "Look yourself—they're gone. I checked a couple of years ago, before they locked the basement door. The papers were here then."

"Well, we will all be bending the knee to Bonaparte soon, I suppose." His laughter sounded shaky.

"Who could have taken them? Who would think to look here?" she asked.

His fiery French look challenged her to answer her own question. "The Gustavians, perhaps?"

Tears sprang to her eyes.

"I expect they would be more than a little pleased to get their hands on the papers. You know, if they weren't trying to kill me, I don't know whether I would care. I wasn't born into this kind of life, and I'm far from sure I want it."

She didn't know whether to believe him. "You don't wish to be king?"

He shrugged. "I'm not sure I believe in kings."

If that were true, if he didn't want to be king after all, if he could find a way back to being himself, just a French soldier's son named Oscar Bernadotte, maybe, just maybe, they could be together.

They both heard it at the same time. Someone was outside the door.

The basement door did little to muffle the voices outside. Had the newcomers heard them? She rested her ear against a crack between the planks and stood frozen, like a hunted animal. There were two voices, maybe three, male, and none of them was Adam's.

"The door chain is off. Look. It's lying over there. I know I looped it over the doorknob." The voice sounded familiar.

"Leave it. Come, we must go."

Oscar pointed to the stairs and whispered, "I cannot be found here—you know I cannot. Tell Frederik I will wait for him in the upper basement. He is over by the aviary."

Then he turned and was gone.

Jacquette was alone, without anyone to help her, far away from the village, and she did not know who was on the other side of the door. Oscar had left her to take the blame for their misdeeds before. But that was different; it had happened before they were . . . well, whatever they were.

What if the men outside were dangerous Gustavians and had stolen the documents?

Deciding it was best to find out, she opened the door, shielding her eyes with her forearm to block the glaring rays that were just beginning to penetrate the trees.

It was past midday.

She sensed the men near her, standing by the stone wall near the gate. Not looking at them, she turned in the opposite direction, toward the kitchen garden.

"Adam," she cried cheerfully. "Come see. The wheel that lowers the table is in this basement." She turned toward the two men, making sure to gasp loud enough to be heard.

To her surprise, she recognized one of them, Otto Natt och Dag, a wild-haired young noble with low blond eyebrows that angled toward his nose.

"Oh, Otto," she said, rubbing her chest with one hand. "You scared me to my bones. What are you doing here?"

Jacquette vaguely recalled dancing with Otto once at the Karlberg Military Academy Ball. Even then, his darting, nervous eyes had unnerved her. He was from an old family, but she'd heard he had become a rebel, forever the source of intrigues.

"Jacquette." Otto smiled like a man winning at bridge. He told her he was now an army clerk assigned to the surveying office.

"What on earth are you doing here? Don't tell me they have you surveying the basement of Confidencen." She started down the path to the kitchen garden and hoped Otto would follow. He did.

The other man, a young officer about Otto's age, said nothing. Rather than follow them, he hurried through the gate and toward the palace.

"Well, if it isn't young Lewenhaupt," Otto said to Adam, who had just come around the corner.

Adam took Jacquette's elbow. "I see you have found Countess Gyldenstolpe. I thought I had lost her."

Jacquette moved closer to Adam. He hesitated for a moment, then seemed to understand what she wanted him to do. He pulled her closer.

Otto looked from Adam to Jacquette, and a lascivious smile spread across his face. "Pardon the interruption. I will not disturb your morning further."

Jacquette could not resist. "You didn't say why you were here."

"You didn't look like you were in the mood for talking. And you are right. I didn't say."

Adam opened the gate. "Jacquette, let's go back to the village."

Frederik would have to find Oscar on his own.

CHAPTER THIRTEEN

Douglas House, Stockholm
May 1815

While the Estates were in session, politics was impossible to escape in Stockholm, particularly on Sundays at Aurora's salon. Oscar and Charles Jean were late this week, and Jacquette found herself trapped on a long spindle-legged Gustavian-style sofa in the blue sitting room. She was wedged between a count, who was this session's Leader of the Nobles, and a prominent farmer, who was the Speaker of the Peasants. They had been arguing for a quarter of an hour about the proposed ban on coffee, and Jacquette was trying to steer their conversation in a more congenial direction.

"Is it true, Count," she asked the Speaker of the Nobles, fluttering her eyelashes, "that Claes Rudbeck recently fought a wolf off his dog?"

If there was one thing the Nobles and the Peasants could agree on, it was wolves.

"Indeed, he did," replied the count.

"Was Claes badly injured?" Jacquette asked. "I hope not."

"I saw him today. Not to worry, he is well," said the count.

"Praise God," said Jacquette. She was about to inquire after the unfortunate dog's health when Brita tapped her on the shoulder.

"Your mother's called Christine into her sitting room."

"Right," said Jacquette. "I'll go see."

The count and the farmer were now deep in conversation about the senselessness of wolf pits and seemed hardly to notice when she left the room.

Outside in the vestibule, Wetterstedt was wringing his hands. "My dearest girl, I saw you with the Speakers. Tell me, how are things going in there?"

"You need not worry, Papa," she replied. When she kissed him on the cheek, she saw beads of perspiration on his forehead. Bonaparte's return to Paris had destroyed the calm of victory, and Wetterstedt kept saying he wished this session of the Estates was over.

"My dear, if you were responsible for presenting Charles Jean's proposals, you would worry, too."

Hoping to reassure him, she said, "The Speakers are talking about wolf pits, Papa."

Wetterstedt's face relaxed, and Jacquette watched as he strode into the room amid murmurs of "the chancellor" and "Wetterstedt." Nodding to the Speakers, he announced, "Monsieur DuPuy is singing in the library. Do join me, gentlemen."

Wetterstedt gave Jacquette a little pat on the cheek as he led the count and the farmer out of the room. They were still chatting about wolves.

With Brita, Jacquette waited outside the open door to her mother's sitting room, watching and listening. Aurora sat in her favorite armchair, a carved French antique upholstered in needlepoint. Christine, wearing an expression of pure terror, was perched opposite her on the edge of an uncomfortable-looking bench.

In a voice shrill as a peacock, Aurora was imploring God, never a good sign. "*Mon Dieu.* I asked my Christine, a pious, godly young woman, to do one single task, to watch Jacquette, and look what has happened. Have I done something to offend the Heavens?"

Christine burst into tears.

After sending a sympathetic look in Christine's direction, Jacquette leaned closer to Brita. "What has happened? Christine was fine—she was downstairs until a few minutes ago."

Brita sighed. "It's about our trip to Drottningholm. Sophie told your mother something. Maybe she found out about those documents you hid and told her what you and Oscar were really doing there."

Jacquette shook her head. Brita would blame Sophie if it rained and the roof leaked.

"Sophie couldn't possibly know that. You probably should get out of here."

"Happy to oblige," Brita said and disappeared down the hall.

Jacquette walked into the room and draped her arms around Aurora's neck.

Aurora wheeled around in her seat, furious. "There you are. Perhaps, my dear, you can explain why the queen's maids of honor are spreading vile talk about you."

Jacquette's confidence melted away. Queen Charlotte's maids of honor—Aurora's friend Marianne and the Chatterati—were all downstairs. Marianne, she knew, would never speak ill of her, so Aurora must be talking about the Chatterati.

"Erica? Go on then. Tell me what she is saying, if you must."

"She is telling everyone you were alone with Adam Lewenhaupt at Drottningholm. What did I tell you about that young man?" Aurora said with an accusatory lift of her chin.

Jacquette hesitated to respond. Aurora knew Adam had been taking Jacquette to Confidencen to meet Oscar. She knew they would be alone. Indeed, the plan had been her idea.

"I don't know what you are talking about." She hung her head so that Christine could not see her eyes.

"Tell me, then, why I just heard Erica say that you and Adam were caught *in flagrante* in the kitchen garden at Kina. You are ruining yourself, I tell you."

Jacquette laughed. "*In flagrante*? That's ridiculously untrue. And why are you yelling at Christine about it?"

Poor Christine. The Chatterati had learned that Jacquette and Adam had been alone at Kina, and Aurora had been caught at her own game. She needed a scapegoat.

Aurora protested, "Because she allowed you to leave the village and go walking with a young man. Alone." She put her head in her hands.

"Nothing happened, I swear to you. It's not Christine's fault."

Aurora stared at them, wringing her hands. "You'll be the death of me, Jacquette. Christine, you may go."

"Would you like me to entertain downstairs?" Christine wiped the tears from her cheeks.

"No. Stay upstairs, away from the maids of honor," said Aurora.

"Yes, ma'am." As she left the room, Christine gave Jacquette a questioning look.

Jacquette mouthed the word "sorry" and then turned to Aurora. "That was unfair to Christine."

"I feed her and take her to the palace, don't I? And someday, I will find her a good match. Isn't that enough?"

Jacquette sighed.

Aurora asked, "Why didn't you tell me someone saw you and Adam?"

"You were at the palace for the last three nights. How could I tell you anything?" It was true enough. Queen Charlotte was getting older and wanted her court mistresses close by. Aurora was spending as much time at the palace as she had when Jacquette was a child.

"Who saw you?"

"Some cadets from Karlberg. Otto Natt och Dag and another one that I didn't recognize."

"What did they see?"

Jacquette thought a minute, replaying the encounter. "Nothing. I don't know. Maybe Adam holding my arm a little too tightly."

"Did they see the prince?"

"No. I'm pretty sure. No."

"I'm not so certain about that," said Oscar from the doorway. He entered the room and kissed Aurora's hand. "Baroness." Oscar treated Aurora like a substitute mother.

"Your Royal Highness. We are honored, sir," Aurora said.

"None of that. The pleasure is mine."

With her hands folded in her lap and a voice dripping with concern, Aurora said, "I was just telling Jacquette how difficult it would be if the Natt och Dag boy were to spread gossip about you."

"How could Otto know you were there?" Jacquette asked Oscar. "You were still inside."

"Inside? Inside where?" Aurora demanded.

"Confidencen," Oscar said. "And yes, Otto might know I was there."

"The basement of Confidencen," Jacquette added.

Frowning, Aurora said, "Did he see you?"

Oscar clasped his hands behind his back "Not me," he said. "My horse."

"Odin?" Jacquette asked.

"Yes. He was tied up near the guard tents. Otto knows he's mine. I mean, Otto's a Life Guard, for God's sake. He knows I would never permit anyone else to ride Odin out to Drottningholm."

Aurora wiped her forehead with a linen handkerchief.

Oscar was not finished. "Jacquette, what did Otto see? Did Adam touch you?" His jaw tightened when he said the last words.

"I was talking to Otto, and Adam came around the corner from behind the kitchen building and took my arm. Like this." Jacquette walked behind Oscar's right shoulder and grasped his elbow with both hands. He looked at her, his eyes widening.

They both looked at Aurora at the same time.

Her eyes were fixed on Jacquette's hands, which were still wrapped around Oscar's arm. Jacquette let go and took a step back.

Oscar kept pushing a stray curl behind his ear, and Jacquette could tell he was struggling with a decision. "Q," he said.

Aurora set her teacup down on its saucer with a clink.

"Listen to me," Oscar said.

"Yes?"

"Wouldn't it be better if the whole court didn't know I was there? If everyone thought you were with Adam?" he asked.

"What?" Jacquette asked. "You want me to *admit* I was with Adam?"

Oscar's voice was soft and filled with regret. "There's no other way. I can't let my father find out, not right now. If Otto tells people he saw

Odin, they will eventually suspect I was there to meet you. Unless they think you were with Adam."

Aurora hastened to agree. "We must protect the crown at all costs."

"Oscar, why does it matter if people think I happened upon you there? What aren't you telling me?" Jacquette was unsure whose betrayal stung more—her mother's or Oscar's. He had not seemed to care if people saw him with Adelaide, so why the sudden change?

He pretended to look at a portrait on the wall, his back to her. "What I can't figure out is why Otto was there in the first place."

Tears filled her eyes, and it took all her strength to hide her disappointment. But Oscar was royal, and she was not. There was no choice, no other option.

"I'll do it," she said.

Aurora said, "Now let me have a word with the prince, and you go downstairs and make everyone think you went to Drottningholm to meet Adam Lewenhaupt."

Without even a glance at Oscar, Jacquette descended the stairs to destroy her own reputation.

In the library, Marianne Koskull crushed the fine blue linen of Jacquette's skirt between her fingers. With an exaggerated sigh, she said, "It's lovely, Jacquette. Your gown, I mean. The waist wouldn't reach around my thigh. How many yards of this did your mother make Wetterstedt order from Paris? Enough so there is none left for anyone else to buy, if I know her."

"Don't be silly. I have enough for only one gown," Jacquette said. Hearing the raised voices of soldiers outside the room, she looked over Marianne's shoulder toward the stairs.

"That won't be Charles Jean. Not yet. But I saw the prince come in and sneak up the stairs," said Marianne with a knowing shrug of the shoulders.

Jacquette did not wish to hear Marianne speculate about her prospects with Oscar, so she listened to DuPuy, who was singing.

Marianne waved toward Erica and Hedda, together on a tiny settee, their faces rapt with admiration as they applauded DuPuy. "Those two have told so many people about you and Adam."

"Everyone here in this room knows?" Jacquette asked.

"No, *everyone everywhere*."

"*Ack*," Jacquette said. It was true; all eyes seemed to be on her. She touched Marianne's hand and said, "Watch. I'm going to come back in a minute and make it a thousand times worse."

⁂

She pushed her way down the crowded hall, returning the smiles of a dozen young officers, nodding to the elder nobles, accepting compliments from their wives. The sound of DuPuy's voice pursued her, now muted by the din of conversation. Where was Peter? Then, among the dozens of blue, gold, and white military uniforms, she saw him at a window that looked onto the square. Leaning casually against the wall, he wore a taupe-and-ivory-checked waistcoat and jacket with an upturned collar. Sophie was sitting in the window seat near him.

Jacquette rushed down the hall, trying not to call out too loudly. "Peter."

Could Peter possibly be interested in Sophie? Jacquette did not think so; he was a better judge of character than that.

"Jacquette, I was just looking for you," said Peter.

"Come. I need you," she said, tugging his arm. She ignored Sophie except for giving her a brief glance with narrowed eyes and a little frown.

She led Peter to the library and chose a place just behind Erica's settee.

"Who are they?" he asked, cupping his hand over his mouth so he could not be heard.

"Chatterati."

He raised his eyebrows and suppressed a laugh. "Them?"

She nodded.

Peter drew in a breath and took a glass of champagne from a tray passed by one of the kitchen maids.

Jacquette checked the door, wondering what Oscar and Aurora were discussing upstairs.

Peter said, "I can see why you chose the name. I didn't recognize them without their cipher pins."

She laughed as Peter sipped his champagne with the nonchalance of a duke.

He asked, "Your mother wants you to become a maid of honor? Like them?"

She bit her lip. "You can see why I resist. Would you want them gossiping about you?"

"Horrible. Never," he replied.

She took a step closer to Erica and said to Peter in a too-loud whisper, "I should have refused Adam, but he was so insistent, and he made all these promises to me. I went all the way to Drottningholm to meet him. *Alone*. And I feel terrible. My mother trusted me, and I lied to her. And Otto saw us, so everyone will know."

Erica leaned over to announce this to Hedda, whose tongue began to wag.

Peter raised his glass to Jacquette, then drained it.

Jacquette and Peter were standing in an alcove with Wetterstedt when the singularly strident, uniquely French voice of the crown prince cut through the buzz of polite conversation. She heard her stepfather take a deep breath. The cluster of young courtiers surrounding the door to the salon all bowed, instantly clearing a path for the heir to the throne, who strode directly toward them.

Charles Jean was the only royal Jacquette had ever known who could not wait to be announced properly. She smiled at the unfortunate young page charged with that duty.

"His Royal Highness the Crown Prince," croaked the boy, his voice breaking into a squeak. He blushed crimson, probably afraid that he would be sent back to Värmland, or whichever remote location he hailed from.

A wave of bows and curtsies responded. Charles Jean was with his usual entourage—Magnus one step behind him and a cavalier carrying his discarded cloak.

"*Eh bien!*" said Charles Jean. "*Buvez, messieurs, buvez!*"

It was Charles Jean's usual greeting, but today, the long-legged crown prince looked more like a cornered fox than a conquering hero. Under his black curls, which were darker and tighter than Oscar's, his eyes darted around the room, moving from noble to artist to opera singer, and Jacquette flinched a little when they rested on her.

He said to Wetterstedt, "Ah, the little countess, here she is. *La petite Gyldenstolpe.* And is this the Englishman you sent me the note about, the tutor?"

Wetterstedt, ever the model of cool-headed competence, whispered something to Charles Jean and exchanged an anxious glance with Magnus. Everyone in the room was staring.

Wetterstedt gave the back of Jacquette's hand a reassuring pat and said to Peter, "I trust your French is perfect? Of course it is. Just come and tell the crown prince what you told me." They followed Charles Jean into a corner where they could be alone.

Peter's face betrayed no line of concern. He produced a pamphlet from his waistcoat pocket and gave it to Charles Jean. The cover said, *Plan for a New Organization of the Swedish Army, by Otto Natt och Dag. Published by Marquard and Sons, Stockholm.*

"Certainly, Chancellor," Peter replied. "As you know, Your Royal Highness, I work for Marquard's publishing house. One day, a junior officer, Otto Natt och Dag, a Svea Life Guard, if I am not mistaken, brought a handwritten copy of that pamphlet to our business office. On Stora Nygatan. Number 31."

Magnus nodded, impatient. "We know where you work. Go on. Get to the point."

"The officer asked for a private run of a few copies. We printed them."

Charles Jean handed the pamphlet to Magnus, who dangled it between two fingers with obvious distaste.

"It's treason," Magnus said.

Charles Jean, rubbing his chin with his fist and pacing, announced, "The young man thinks his superiors are incompetent. His complaint is with the generals, not with me."

"They will be furious with him when they see this," Magnus said.

Peter clasped his hands behind his back and stood before Charles Jean. "I had no idea this was to be distributed. I was told . . ." He shook his head. "To be honest, I looked at the title and hardly read the rest of it. He said it was to be given to some friends from his days at the military academy. Sire, tell me what I can do."

Magnus snorted.

Charles Jean shook his head. "Monsieur—"

"Wells," Wetterstedt supplied.

Charles Jean folded his arms and looked down his long, straight nose at Peter. "You say this was being distributed in the market by a wool vendor?"

Peter responded, "Yes, and that surprised me, sire. Natt och Dag told me it was not for public distribution."

"Well then," said Charles Jean. "We will see what we can discover. Wetterstedt, you and Magnus will handle this. Now I must find my son."

Charles Jean looked Jacquette square in the face as he said this, turned on his heel, and walked away.

After Charles Jean left, Magnus turned to Peter.

"The crown prince wishes for you to perform a service to the kingdom. It would involve no disloyalty to your own country. I understand you are a British subject."

Peter replied, "I am, though I have often lived abroad. But what can I do for the crown prince? I am only a printer."

"Let me explain," said Magnus. "The crown prince believes that the public deserves to know the truth, something other than this flood of false and scandalous publications."

"I hope he feels we have cooperated with the Withdrawal Act."

"You should have reported this to the Mandarin before it was printed."

Peter nodded. "What can I do?" he asked again.

"We have been using the Withdrawal Power and will continue to do so, but the crown prince wants to speak to the people with his own voice."

"How?" asked Peter.

"By publishing our own views. Anonymously, of course. They must be printed and distributed by someone like you who is not easily associated with him. And the arrangement will be rewarding."

Peter nodded.

Jacquette looked at the empty stairs through the open door, willing Oscar to descend, but he did not appear. He had looked so proud when he'd made the arrangement with Peter to get information about the pamphlets. Peter was Oscar's contact, and like everything else Oscar loved, Charles Jean was taking him for himself. Maybe that was the reason Oscar had betrayed her so easily. He was used to being betrayed himself.

But now everyone thought she was sneaking around with Adam, and it was Oscar's fault.

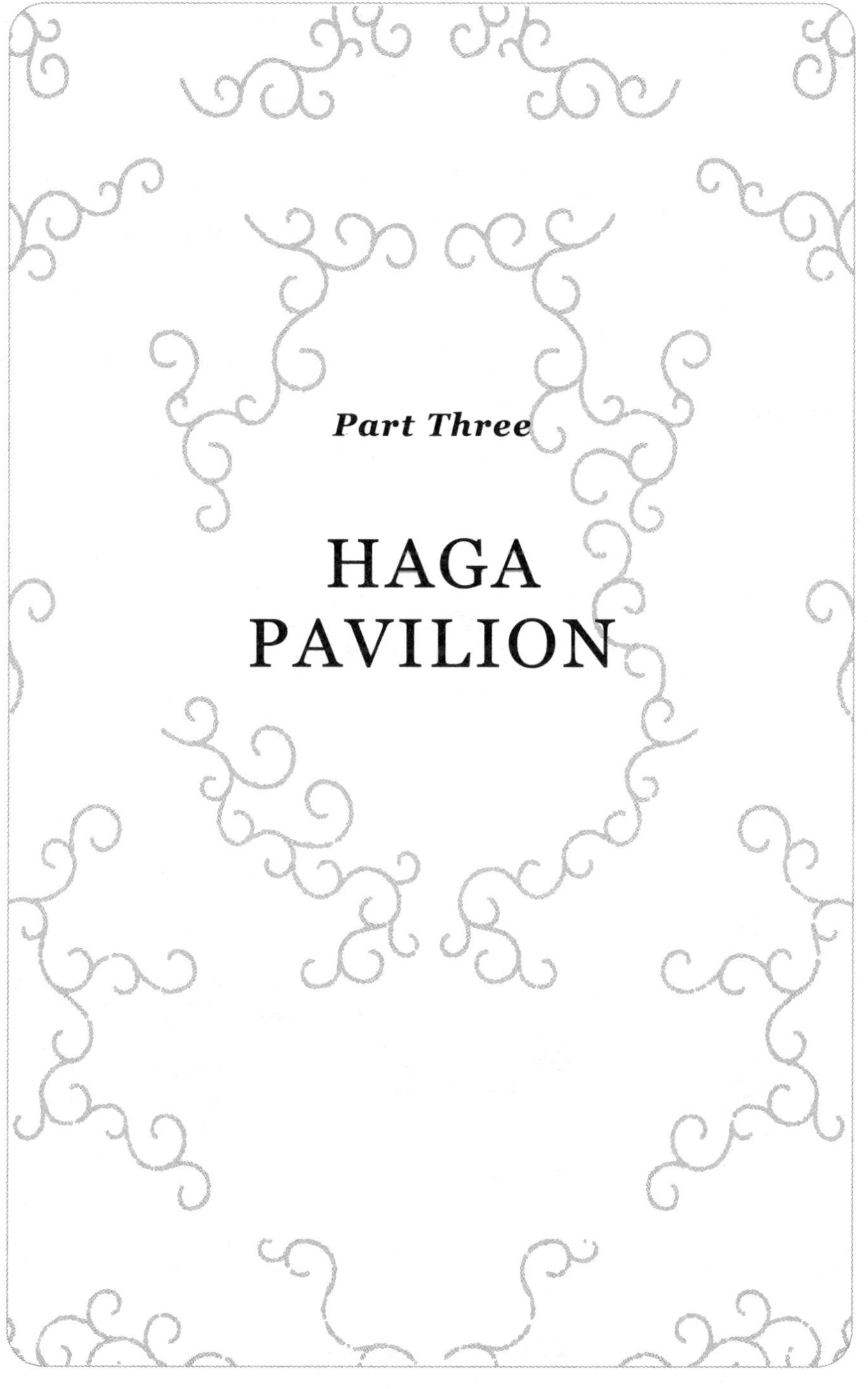

Part Three

HAGA PAVILION

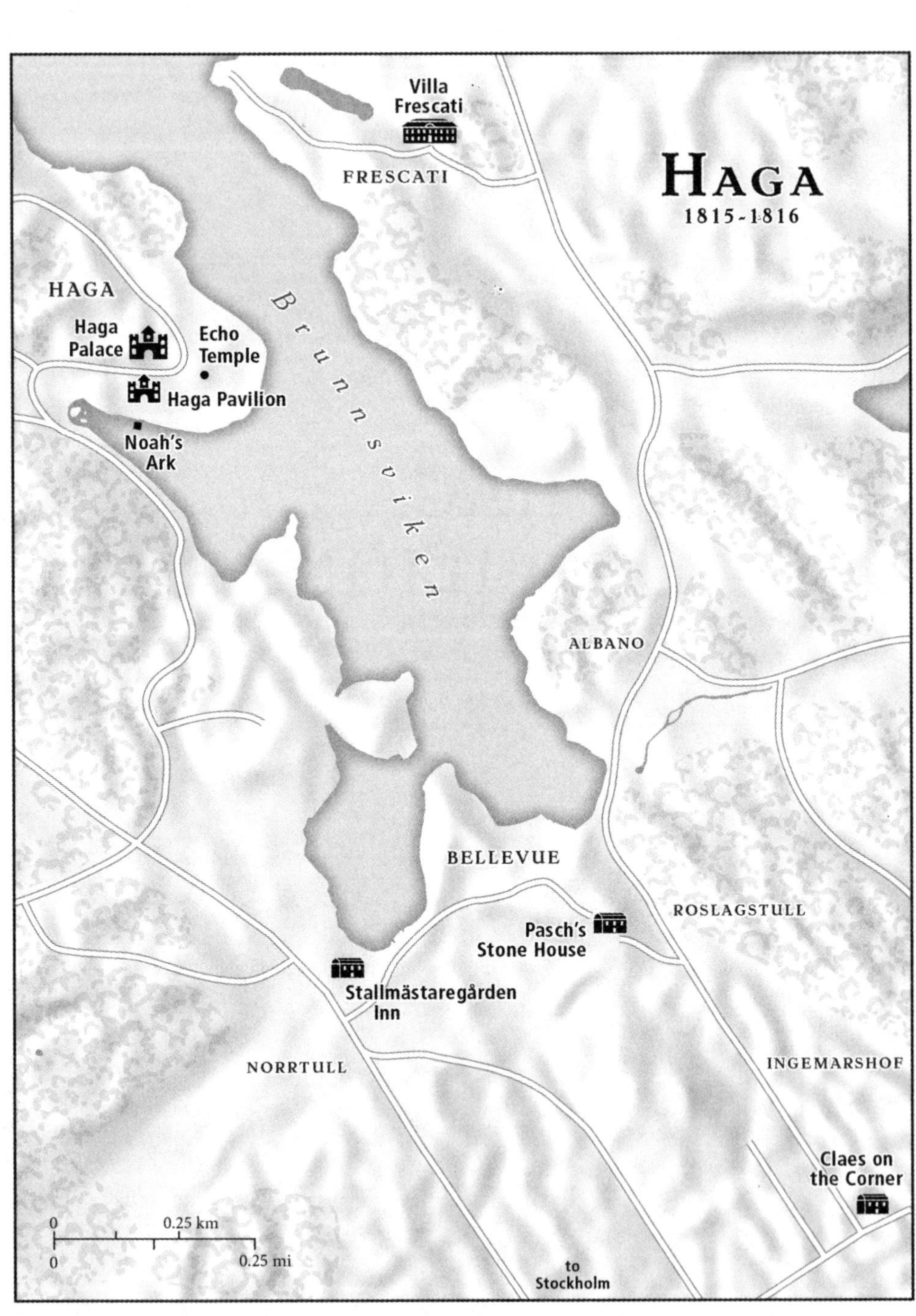

Haga
1815-1816
Villa
Frescati
FRESCATI
HAGA
Haga
Palace
Echo
Temple
Haga Pavilion
Noah's
Ark
Brunnsviken
ALBANO
BELLEVUE
ROSLAGSTULL
Pasch's
Stone House
Stallmästaregården
Inn
NORRTULL
INGEMARSHOF
Claes on
the Corner
0
0.25 km
0
0.25 mi
to
Stockholm

CHAPTER FOURTEEN

Haga Pavilion
July 4, 1815

Jacquette had a premonition that going to Haga for the fourth of July, her eighteenth birthday, would break something in her life. But the Estates of the Realm were still meeting, and there would be no trip to Finspång until the interminable session ended. She tried to swallow her disappointment and, with Aurora, Christine, Brita, and Sophie, made the short journey out of Stockholm on her birthday afternoon.

The moment the carriage door closed, Aurora began boasting about securing Jacquette and Christine a room in the queen's residence, Haga Pavilion. King Karl, Crown Prince Charles Jean, and most of the cavaliers would lodge at the adjacent and much larger Haga Palace, and Oscar and his entourage would be at Bellevue, a property on the hill on the opposite shore of Brunnsviken. The rest of the court would be scattered throughout Haga Park, cramped and miserable at a variety of farm cottages, inns, and manor houses that surrounded the brackish, choppy lake.

At least Oscar and I will not be under the same roof, Jacquette thought as she walked into Haga Pavilion's grand salon, the Hall of Mirrors. She would try to be cheerful, although everyone was here to celebrate Oscar's birthday, and no one was celebrating hers. She still could not believe Oscar had asked her to encourage the rumor about her and Adam, or that she had agreed. He had put himself first, at her expense. It was part of being a man and a prince, she supposed.

Aurora led Christine to the end of the room, like a recalcitrant pet, to show her Haga Pavilion's celebrated wall of glass with its spectacular view over the lake. Jacquette followed. Marianne, who was sitting on a blue-and-white-striped sofa against the opposite wall of the long rectangular ballroom, rolled her eyes.

"Jacquette, look." Christine had spotted the royal gondolas, the *Boar* and the *Dolphin*. The bow of each brightly painted boat was adorned with a figure carved from gilded wood, one a dolphin and the other a boar. They bobbed on the waves like nodding heads. "Are they really cursed?"

Jacquette loved a good superstition. She held up three fingers. "Gustav III brought the gondolas here, and he was shot." She folded her ring finger, leaving only two. "His son was overthrown and exiled." She waved her index finger. "And our present king, forced to adopt Charles Jean and turn the government over to him. It sounds like a curse to me."

Christine laughed. "Don't get us into trouble. I so want your birthday to be a special one."

"At least I have one friend who remembers," Jacquette replied with more than a bit of sarcasm.

"Don't be ridiculous," Aurora said. "It is an honor to share your birthday with Prince Oscar."

What an honor, Jacquette thought, *to spend every birthday at an interminable party for someone else.* Someone who seemed to be avoiding her. Oscar had not come to Aurora's salon in weeks, and Jacquette had seen him only once since the trip to Drottningholm.

When Aurora took Christine to the dining room to see the queen's porcelain collection, Jacquette remained at the window. She smelled Marianne's perfume before the familiar short, plump arms wrapped her in a hug.

"It's your day! Eighteen!"

Jacquette winced and turned to greet the fuchsia-gowned Marianne. "I doubt we will see my name in fireworks tonight."

Marianne looked out the window to the lakeshore, where large, gilded letters that spelled PRINCE OSCAR had been erected. She said,

"Forget about him. It's perfect weather, and I know of at least three counts who are waiting to congratulate you on your birthday."

Jacquette shook her head. "Not today. Why do you say I should forget about the prince?"

Marianne, who had an impressive tolerance for the lovesick, rubbed her thumbs over Jacquette's temples. "It's all right, little bird. I've heard she has a face like a muffin and bad teeth."

"Who?"

Marianne stepped back, a furtive expression in her blue eyes. "Oh, no one."

"You're lying. Look at me."

Marianne searched the crowd, probably trying to find an excuse to run off. When Jacquette tightened her grip on her arm, she turned around, biting her lower lip.

"I thought you knew."

"Tell me," Jacquette said.

"You cannot imagine the burden of keeping Charles Jean's confidences." Marianne clutched her gown's too-low neckline.

Jacquette pulled her into the corner. "I'm serious."

Marianne pursed her lips. "You cannot let on that I am the source of this. Charles Jean would be furious."

"I won't."

Her voice fell to a whisper. "It's Oscar. Charles Jean has sent General Camps to Prussia with a marriage contract."

The buzz of chattering women seemed to recede, and the sound of Jacquette's heartbeat filled her ears. She had a sudden urge to wring the information out of Marianne like a laundress twisting wet linens. Now she understood why Oscar was avoiding her. And why it was so important to hide their meeting at Drottningholm. The liar. He'd told her he would never let his father choose his wife.

She tried to keep her voice even. "An engagement? To whom?"

"There is a princess from Berlin named Alexandrine—"

Jacquette pulled Marianne down onto one of the cushioned sofas that lined the side walls. "I know who the king of Prussia's daughters are, Marianne. Tell me why."

"She's one of those stiff Germans. Big red cheeks."

"Why now? Why did he send Camps?" General Camps was Charles Jean's cousin, his courier of choice for things he wanted to hide from Magnus and Wetterstedt. *Maybe*, she hoped, *I was too quick to condemn Oscar. It is possible he does not even know.*

"Charles Jean must find him a bride now, Jacquette. Wellington's victory south of Brussels was the end of Bonaparte."

"What does that have to do with Oscar?"

"The throne of France is empty, my dear."

"And why would that mean that Oscar should get married?"

Marianne said, "Marriage into one of the old royal families would increase Charles Jean's chances of taking the French throne, although Tsar Alexander and England are threatening to restore that glutton, the Bourbon heir."

Oscar had told Jacquette that his father dreamed of becoming king of France, but she did not realize there was still a chance of it happening. "King of France? And Sweden, too?"

Marianne nodded. "And the pretender Gustav will lose his luster once Oscar marries into royal blood. Gustav certainly doesn't have anything else to commend him."

Jacquette was not interested in hearing about Charles Jean's political schemes. She had to ask her question, although she did not really want to know the answer. "Does Oscar know?"

Swallowing hard, Marianne nodded.

Jacquette's heart sank. *Damn him*, she thought. *The coward.*

Marianne was wringing her hands, and the black frankincense gum she'd used to darken her eyelashes was running down the ridge next to her nose. "It was bound to happen. You must accept it, Jacquette."

Acceptance might have been possible a few months ago, but not now. Almost to herself, she said, "I cannot believe I ever allowed him to touch me."

With a maternal smile, Marianne said, "What is a little kiss, or even a stroke of the bosom? Don't let it worry your—" The plump blonde frowned. "Wait. You aren't in love, are you?" She placed her hand over her heart.

Jacquette turned away. "I would not be so stupid. I am a De Geer."

Until dinner, it was easy to avoid Oscar, who was amusing himself at Bellevue with his men. But dusk came, and Wetterstedt showed Jacquette and Aurora to a mahogany table under the dome of the Echo Temple, the old gazebo on the hill above the lake. At the center table, Charles Jean was staring over the water toward Bellevue, and the seat reserved for Oscar, the guest of honor, was empty.

Finally, ten minutes after his birthday dinner began, Oscar arrived on horseback, drunk and accompanied by Frederik. As he walked into the Echo Temple, he braced his hand against one of the sets of double stone columns and surveyed the room. He looked magnificent dressed in a pearl-white court suit with silver trim, and he seemed unconscious of the many people watching. Jacquette knew he intended every move. Sliding into an empty chair three seats away from Charles Jean, he allowed his hair to shroud his eyes. When he looked her way, she avoided his gaze.

After the last toast, Aurora said, "The young people are going to Noah's Ark to watch the fireworks. Why don't you bring Christine?"

When Christine's face brightened, Jacquette knew she had no choice.

They left the gazebo without passing the center table, where Oscar was slouched in a chair next to a very agitated Charles Jean, who was making wild gestures with his hands. The defiant tilt of Oscar's chin, which Jacquette knew so well, gave her hope that he was telling his father he would refuse to marry the Prussian princess.

Squealing with excitement, Christine disappeared into the stream of young people who were teetering across the primitive pontoon bridge to Noah's Ark. Jacquette followed, but she was far behind, and she arrived alone at the crowded, noisy club room. It had been painted white and swept of the dust and squalor she recalled from her childhood. Brandy, wine, and sweets filled the sideboards, and the linens were embroidered with Oscar's coat of arms.

To avoid a group of young women at a table in the corner, she took a glass of wine outside to the diving terrace. News of her supposed tryst with Adam had spread, and she had endured all manner of insults over the past weeks. Marianne had advised patience, saying, "Tomorrow they will forget about you and resume talking about me."

It didn't work. The stares hurt.

She held on to the railing and looked into the water as the Ark rocked gently on Brunnsviken's waves. It was a clear, warm night, and the sun had set about an hour earlier, leaving a faint blue-gray glow in its wake. On Jacquette's birthday, the sky was never really black.

She thought she was alone until she heard a male voice. "He had to insist on fireworks. What a waste of money. It's not dark enough in early July."

It was Carl Löwenhielm, standing even more rigidly upright than she remembered. She placed a silent wager with herself that he would not remember her birthday. Still, talking to him seemed preferable to being alone, and he might even know something about this Prussian princess. She greeted him with an interested smile. Men like Carl thrived on attention.

"Who insisted on fireworks? Crown Prince Charles Jean?" she asked.

"No."

"Prince Oscar?"

"None other."

Oscar knew Jacquette loved fireworks. Had he ordered them for her? She asked, "Have you been at Bellevue?"

He scowled. "The prince is gambling with his new favorites, Frederik and Johan. They have the stone house at Bellevue arranged like some sort of gambling hall and played cards there all day."

Jacquette could not deny that Oscar had new friends. Frederik had recruited another cavalier, Johan Lindersköld, to participate in their wilder escapades, and the threesome had been frequenting society parties all over Stockholm.

She changed the subject. "Wetterstedt told me that you were called home to Värmland."

"Chancellor Wetterstedt spoke of me?"

She nodded. "You concluded things there successfully, I trust?"

He pursed his thin lips, which made his long nose seem longer. "My father is incompetent. I did manage to force him to allow my sister's husband to run the estate and the mills, but he still refuses to give me anything, even a place to live, although I am his heir."

"You have rooms at the palace, do you not?"

Carl snorted in derision. "It's hardly a place to call home. Last night I tolerated Frederik's and Johan's singing until dawn while I drew up plans for the prince's trip to Norway. Frederik and Johan are too busy chatting up married women to do their jobs."

Jacquette didn't know about any married women and hoped Oscar was not chatting them up too. He would be leaving soon on a long royal visit to Norway, and Wetterstedt had told her that Oscar was brooding about it, convinced his father was going to use him to win over the rebellious Norwegians. Wetterstedt would be traveling with the large royal entourage, and society in Stockholm would dry up like a parched field during a drought.

She asked Carl, "How long will you be away?"

"Until November or December. We are leaving next month, but I expect you know that."

"Yes, everyone at Finspång is preparing to receive the crown prince," she said, cursing the geographic coincidence that placed her family home directly on the road to Norway. Charles Jean and Oscar would be spending a night or two at Finspång, and Oscar still had not apologized for making her take the blame for the Drottningholm fiasco. And by next month, he could be engaged to marry the Prussian.

"Look. Something is happening over there," Carl said, pointing to a seating platform on the shore where the royal family was assembled to watch the fireworks. They were standing and watching Charles Jean, who was following the queen up the path to Haga Pavilion. Magnus and Wetterstedt were at Charles Jean's heels, and Aurora was holding the queen's elbow as she hobbled with her cane.

Jacquette leaned over the rail, where she could see dozens of young courtiers leaving the Ark and crowding onto the pontoon bridge. "Where is everyone going? The fireworks are just beginning."

Christine appeared on the swimming deck and eyed Carl with interest. "There you are, Jacquette. Come, everyone is going back to the Echo Temple."

"Why? Don't you think the fireworks will be better here?" asked Jacquette.

"Someone overheard Charles Jean say that the Allies are going to crown him king of France. Everyone wants to find out what is going on. Will we all be French?"

Carl stamped the heel of his boot on the deck.

Jacquette shrugged and said to Christine, "*Ack*. Let us stay here and watch the show while we are still Swedish."

It was not the first Jacquette had heard about Charles Jean's dream. Oscar had once told her his father would move to Paris if he became king of France and leave Oscar in Stockholm to rule Sweden after the king's death.

"Your life would be your own," Jacquette had replied. But Oscar had shoved his hands into his pockets and changed the subject. He'd looked terrified. And not long after, he had begun carousing with Frederik and Johan.

⁂

Carl straightened his uniform hat and bid Jacquette and Christine goodnight. Jacquette watched as he pushed to the front of the line of people leaving the Ark for the shore.

"What a curious sort of man," she said.

"Who? The crown prince or Carl?" Christine laughed at her own joke.

"Carl, of course. What do you think of him?"

"I daresay, he makes me nervous."

Jacquette leaned over the railing, allowing the ribbons of her hat to trail in the wind. "I doubt he ever has any fun. Well, we can watch the fireworks from here."

"Someone's on the platform with us," Christine said.

Frederik and Johan were standing in the shadows close to the building, away from the torches.

"Happy birthday, my lady," Frederik said. "You are too beautiful for your own good."

He was such a charmer, the type whose flattery was best ignored. Jacquette said, "Let me make introductions. Christine, you know Frederik, of course, but may I present Johan Linderskköld? He is also one of the prince's cavaliers. Johan, this is Baroness Christine Palmstierna."

Johan, an archbishop's son, was cursed with a prominent jaw, which made him look fearsome. He was actually a lot of fun, if a little bit wild.

"Happy birthday," Johan said to Jacquette.

Another one who remembered. She thanked Johan and even gave him a kiss on the cheek.

"Frederik, why are we hiding in the shadows?" she asked.

"The prince is aboard the *Boar*, and he asked me to bring you there."

How had Oscar managed to escape his family, his men, his birthday celebration? And why? "Give me a minute," she said.

Christine was playing with her necklace, her usual signal that she wished to speak to Jacquette in private.

"We will wait inside," Frederik said, and the two men retreated to the empty salon.

"You aren't going, are you?" Christine asked.

"I don't know."

Christine shook her head. "You said he is to be married. You can't."

Something about the droop in the corners of Christine's eyes and the uncertain slope of her shoulders spelled defeat, and every fiber in Jacquette's body rebelled against it. She untied her white straw bonnet and tossed it over the railing. It floated, with its multicolored ribbons trailing behind, on the surface of the lake toward the *Boar*'s stern, where oil lanterns were flickering. She waved to the gondola and thought she saw the gleam of silver buttons in the amber light. He was there.

"What are you doing?" Christine asked. "Emilie probably spent a month decorating that hat."

"The hat isn't important. Listen to me, Christine. There won't be any marriage contract, and there definitely won't be a Prussian wife."

"You mean you're going?"

"You are, too," replied Jacquette as the last of the fireworks exploded over the lake. An orchestra began playing near the Echo Temple, and she saw the guests dancing in the night. She remembered something Marianne had said about never giving up your dreams. The problem was that Oscar was at the center of two people's very different dreams—hers and Crown Prince Charles Jean's.

CHAPTER FIFTEEN

Frederik led them to the beach near the royal gondola, which was moored close to shore. He waded a short distance and hopped onto the deck, where he lifted the plank from its hooks and fed it over the side to Johan.

"After you," Johan said, offering Jacquette a hand.

With a shawl wrapped around her head and shoulders, Jacquette mounted the plank, displaying a good deal more confidence than she felt, not wishing to show the men her fear of water. She did not understand Oscar's plan. Had he wished their meeting to remain a secret, would he have chosen this showy gondola, the *Boar*, from among the dozen or so boats at his disposal? Someone was certain to see the vessel's gilded, snarling figurehead with its tall plume and bared teeth. In a nod to privacy, the deck canopies were raised, but the boat itself was impossible to hide, even in the dark. And, unlike some of the smaller royal vessels, it required three men to row. She looked down into the galley and acknowledged the "crew," noticing that Oscar had replaced the usual sailors with pages he knew and trusted. Why the change? He had seemed so intent on secrecy when he'd made her lie about why she was at Drottningholm.

For balance, she held on to the bulkhead, listening for Christine's steps behind her.

"I'll take Christine and Johan in another boat," Frederik said as he stowed the plank and hopped over the side.

Christine looked frantic, and Jacquette hoped she was not about to run off and tell Aurora her daughter was sailing on Brunnsviken, alone with the prince in the night. If anyone was more afraid of the water than Jacquette, it was Aurora, who would call out the navy if she suspected what was going on.

Jacquette poked her head into the space between two facing benches that ran the length of the gondola. Designed in the last century, the benches had deep cushions covered in velvet and tall, solid wooden backs designed to obscure the royal persons on board. From the water or the shore, one saw only the seat backs, each decorated with six shields depicting the labors of Hercules.

Oscar was there, watching her.

She looked straight at him, unblinking. Before she could speak, a wave rocked the boat, and she clutched the bench to regain her balance, narrowing the distance between them.

He held up both hands, which she interpreted as a conciliatory gesture. "You can sit at the other end if you wish. I know you are angry," he said.

She eyed a position as far from him as possible, but his long legs blocked the space between the benches, and she'd need to step over them to get there. As she passed, he caught her leg between his knees.

"Crouch down, or everyone will see you," he said with a sly smile.

"You are drunk. Let me go." She glanced up the hill to the Echo Temple, where his birthday celebration appeared to be over. People were beginning to come closer, to stroll along the shore. He was right; she needed to sit down.

"Proceed," Oscar ordered the oarsmen.

The narrow gondola was not the sort of boat that allowed one to stand on deck and chat. When the hull began bucking against the swells, Jacquette pitched toward him and landed hard against his shoulder. She sat up and straightened her skirts.

"Why would I be angry with you?" she asked in as sarcastic a tone as she could manage in a rocking boat. "You did pull me away from an interesting conversation with a very nice count. I'm a bit peeved about that."

"Carl?" he asked, unsmiling. "Really."

He was mocking her, which was infuriating. And irresistible.

"Carl—and others," she stammered. "And what are you doing out here on the water? Aren't you the guest of honor?"

"My father, as usual, has everyone's attention. I made my appearance for the speeches, and that is enough. Come on. Talk to me, Q."

"Where are we going?"

"Bellevue."

"Alone?"

He looked back at the other boat. "They are right behind us. I have something for you for your birthday."

She hoped he would not be so callous as to surprise her with news of his upcoming engagement. *He has kept it from me*, she fumed to herself. *I have been so stupid. I told myself I would not be stupid, and I would stay away. I thought he was different, but I was lying to myself.*

She pulled off her shawl and tossed it on the bench between them. "Is the surprise that you are getting engaged? Honestly, Oscar, a Prussian? Don't you think I had a right to know that before I let you—"

"Do this?" He looked her straight in the eye and pulled a single hairpin out of her coiled hairstyle. Her dark curls tumbled to her shoulders. "I saw you toss your bonnet in the lake."

All she could think at that moment was that Brita had put twenty-two pins in her hair this evening, and Oscar knew exactly which one to pull. Irate, she slapped him.

One of the pages stood up in the galley, but Oscar waved the young man away.

"Oh," he said, still smiling. "You really are mad. I like you this way, but I guess I should tell you. I'm not marrying anybody or getting engaged to a Prussian. Not now, at least."

"How was I supposed to know?"

"You could have asked me."

"I could have if you had come to Douglas House. It's been weeks and even longer since we—"

"I know. Every part of me knows," he said.

"You talked to your father about the marriage contract?"

"There's nothing he can do. I am stopping it—don't worry. I want you."

Then he pulled her onto his lap and kissed her. She closed her eyes, listening to the lapping water, the creak of the oars, the distant murmur of the crowds. He wanted to be with her. He'd said it.

"Come," he said. "Lie down and look at the stars."

When she nodded, he eased her onto the soft velvet cushions and lay on his side next to her, looking into her eyes.

"But you can't see the stars," she said.

"They're all right here for me."

Above her, the royal standard flapped in the summer wind.

About half an hour later, they docked in a secluded bay near Bellevue. Frederik helped Christine climb out of the other boat, and she pointed to Jacquette's disheveled hair with a frown.

"God help us if your mother finds out. Drottningholm will seem like nothing."

Jacquette and Oscar walked up the hill to the smaller of two buildings, the one everyone called Pasch's stone house. It was a hundred years old. He led her inside and shut the door behind them.

There was a piano next to the window with an ink-stained sheet of music lying on the bench. So, he was composing again.

"Play it if you like," he said.

She took it to the sofa. The piece was a sonata, titled in French.

Rêves de Toi. Dreams of You.

"Did you write this?" she asked.

He nodded. "For you."

"Play it for me."

Oscar unbuttoned his silvery-white coat and removed his diamond-crusted Seraphim Star. His white linen shirt hung in folds over slim white pantaloons as he slung one long leg over the piano bench.

"Take the music," she said.

"I don't need it."

The piece began at a slow tempo, a progression of bell chimes in an empty church. As Oscar's long fingers played the keys, the melody soared. It was beautiful.

He never asked to be a prince, she thought. *This is what he loves.*

"It's perfect," she said, her voice cracking with emotion. "My mother and Wetterstedt gave me shoes. The same ones as always."

They laughed together.

"Don't worry about them. We're here now," he said.

"But my mother—"

"She will be with the queen until morning. Poor Aurora. My father has the queen in a state."

"Oh."

"Stay with me awhile, Q. Or more than a while. Let's celebrate."

"May we always spend our birthday together."

He kneeled next to her on the sofa and gathered her hair in one fist to kiss the back of her neck. It was a tender place, never touched by a man's lips, and she did not expect the quiver of warmth that coursed through her center. Her spine stiffened, and she drew in a breath.

He pulled back his head, placing a warm hand where his lips had been.

"Is this what you want?"

She nodded.

"Relax for me." He kissed the tips of her fingers, the inside of her elbow, the base of her throat.

She sighed in pleasure and wrapped her arm around his waist, touching the bare skin under his loose shirt.

His eyes darted to hers.

"Just tell me if you want to leave. But do it now," he said. His voice was low and gruff.

She shook her head slowly and rested back on the sofa. He lay on top of her, but he didn't seem heavy. With his knees pinning her legs together, he pulled down her gown, cupped her breasts in his hands, and lowered his mouth to her nipple.

It was the most delicious feeling: the narrow sofa, the press of his legs, the urge to open hers.

She kept her eyes open, fearing she would not be able to remember this night, to re-create it from beginning to end. Oscar raised his head to look at her, and the man she saw was nothing like the shy boy she'd met four years earlier at Drottningholm. He tossed his cravat to the floor, lifted her from the sofa, and carried her to the bed like a precious thing. She felt him above her, but he was not close enough. Her body arched in need while her legs pulled him to her, finding an anchor just above his hips. His back was bare—she must have torn the shirt from his breeches—and her thin gauze gown was corded around her waist.

"My God, you're beautiful," he said. "Your skin."

Slick with sweat, their bodies moved against each other, first in unison, then in opposition, until she felt his mouth on her, his teeth teasing and pulling the tender skin of her nipples. She rolled him on his side, reaching for the buttons of his breeches, and told him she wanted him. It felt natural, inevitable, a reason for joy, not shame. When he entered her, something pinched and he grew still, but she begged him to go on. She heard herself moan, and then her moan became strangled and stopped. There was nothing more, just a dead, peaceful quiet.

She knew she was lost.

CHAPTER SIXTEEN

Stockholm Palace
August 10, 1815

In August, the Estates finally dissolved. For Jacquette, this meant enduring one last ceremony, the closing salute to the king, before leaving Stockholm to spend three months at Finspång. Though she had no love for court rituals, she would watch the procession and perhaps even dance with Oscar at the palace ball. His trip to Norway was nearing. Knowing it would separate them until Christmas, she could not stop thinking about what had happened at Bellevue.

At the ceremony, Jacquette sat on the Queen's Balcony, a high perch overlooking the Hall of State with rails draped in midnight-blue fabric with thin gold stripes. The narrow balcony was cramped and uncomfortable, and, at the end opposite Jacquette, the diplomats' wives were packed three deep, balancing on spindle-legged stools. The queen was in an armchair at the front with her ladies-in-waiting seated next to her in descending order of seniority. Jacquette's Aunt Lotten had pushed her chair as close to the queen's—and as far away from Aurora's—as possible.

Aurora sighed and said to Jacquette, "Remember, rank is rank."

No one respected or enforced the concept of rank more rigidly than Aunt Lotten.

Jacquette took a sharp breath when her aunt leaned over to speak to her. "You will have your wish, Jacquette. I understand your father is sending Nils and August to Aurora."

"I have yearned for that day, Aunt," she replied.

"Well, I only pray that my brother's good influence has taken root. People in the capital will pull the boys in the other direction, you know." Lotten stared at Aurora.

"I suppose your brother's desire to have me pay for our sons' education won out over his disapproval of my character," interrupted Aurora in a flat tone. "Do you ever see Philip's friend, the maid? Or her son? What is the young boy's name? Remind me . . ."

Aurora's eyes were cold, as they were whenever she spoke of Jacquette's illegitimate half brother, her father's *oäkta barn*.

Aunt Lotten folded her hands over her stout midsection. "The boy's birth got you a divorce so you could marry Wetterstedt. You should be glad of it." She tossed her head and resumed speaking to the queen.

Jacquette tried not to stare at Oscar, who was wearing a ceremonial dark blue velvet coat, which reached to mid-thigh, and high Hessian boots. He even had an ermine cape and crown. Usually, he preferred his plain blue military jacket with its gleaming rows of medals, but today, he looked like he was enjoying the feel of the heavy fur on his shoulders. Jacquette found it vaguely unsettling to see him looking so much like a prince.

The more he is a prince, she thought, *the less he is mine.*

As he passed the representatives of the four Estates—Nobles, Priests, Merchants, and Peasants—Oscar looked more than once in Jacquette's direction. Charles Jean, who was already on the dais next to the king, frowned and squinted. She suspected he was trying to figure out what, or who, had caught his son's attention. Flashing his father an irreverent smile, Oscar mounted the stairs two at a time and walked past him to the silver throne, where he kissed elderly King Karl's hand.

A red-faced Wetterstedt, hurrying behind the much-taller Oscar, looked older than his thirty-eight years. Supporters shook his hand, congratulating him on his reading of the crown prince's closing speech. Jacquette was pleased for Wetterstedt but wondered why Charles Jean had not selected Oscar as his reader, as he had at the opening ceremony last winter.

Aurora flashed a proud feline smile at Jacquette. "Stop dreaming," she said.

"Our Wetterstedt," said the petite, frail queen in a voice every woman in the box could hear. "I fear he is the only competent man on the council." She raised her opera glasses and leaned forward to watch.

Jacquette wondered how her mother could ignore the jealous twitches at the mouths of more than one of her fellow court mistresses, many of whose husbands served on the council with Wetterstedt.

"Wetterstedt has been well rewarded," said one of them. "Some say too well rewarded."

"With the opportunity for more," said another. "Who knows what he will be granted during Aurora's entertainments next week at Finspång? Wetterstedt will have Charles Jean's ear there, and all the way to Norway. Who will say a word to stop it?"

Jacquette jumped when Aurora swiped at her with her fan.

"Pay them no mind, and just consider yourself fortunate to be here," Aurora said. "You cannot imagine what I had to endure from these women when you were invited and their daughters were not. The jealousy. *Mon Dieu.*"

"Mother, don't provoke them. They have finally stopped talking about me and Adam."

Aurora leaned close to Jacquette and whispered, "The queen intends to appoint new maids of honor at the start of the year."

Jacquette suspected that it was Aurora who had planted that idea in the queen's mind. Now, she would try to force Jacquette to accept a place at court.

"I have told you. I don't want to—"

Aurora cut her off. "Take care not to make any missteps at the ball tonight. The queen will choose only girls with sterling reputations."

She looked at Jacquette for a long time after she said that.

Below, in the Hall of State, Charles Jean signaled to Magnus and spoke into his ear. Oscar looked in the other direction, his mouth set in a line. Jacquette imagined she could see the muscles of his neck straining.

"Poor Prince Oscar," said one of the women. "His father should be preparing him to rule, not grooming Magnus Brahe to run the country."

Erica, who was sitting with the Chatterati in the next row, tapped the woman on the shoulder and said triumphantly, "Speaking of Prince Oscar, I have it on good information that he is in love."

"Of course he is in love," said Aunt Lotten in a bossy tone. "He's getting engaged soon, I hear. To a princess from Prussia." She had little patience for her court mistresses and none for her maids of honor.

Erica spoke so everyone could hear. "I don't mean the Prussian. He's never even met her. No, Prince Oscar has fallen for a *Swedish* girl. A countess, and I don't mean Adelaide. Someone new."

All the ladies leaned closer to listen, apart from Marianne, who turned her head in the other direction.

As the ceremony dragged on, Jacquette could not banish the fear that the Chatterati knew what she and Oscar had done.

Jacquette and Oscar had been cautious after they'd left the stone house at Bellevue. Laughing in the gondola with Christine, Frederik, and Johan, they'd poured bottles of brandy into the lake and littered the deck with the empty containers. By the time they wobbled off the boat and onto the dock at Haga Pavilion, anyone watching would have thought they had been rowing around the lake for hours, eating and drinking and watching the fireworks. Each of them carried a half-drunk glass, and Christine even stumbled and supported herself on Jacquette's arm.

Jacquette's heart had nearly stopped when an irritated Charles Jean appeared with Magnus to meet them and asked Oscar where he had been during the fireworks.

"With my friends, as you can well see," Oscar had replied in a curt voice, staring at his father with eyes that sparked fury.

Charles Jean had retreated half a step, but soon collected himself and kissed Oscar on the forehead. "*Eh bien.* I am pleased to see you having fun with the young people."

Oscar had wiped his forehead. He hated it when his father kissed him in public.

Charles Jean had motioned to Jacquette and asked, "Was my son a good host on your birthday, Countess?"

"Thank you for remembering me, sir."

"You see, I keep my facts in here, as I learned to do on the battlefield." He'd tapped the side of his head. "But I seem to remember you were wearing a bonnet. Well, was Oscar a good host?"

"He made it memorable, sir." It was the best Jacquette could do in the circumstances.

She thought she'd seen Frederik blanch, and Oscar nearly burst out laughing. A blast of wind had blown off the lake, and Christine, who had spent part of the return trip trying to repair Jacquette's hair, looked with concern at her lopsided chignon. It had been about to fall around her shoulders.

"Ah, my son will make us proud. There will be good news when Camps returns from Prussia. We may be planning a wedding, the biggest one Stockholm has ever seen." As he'd spoken, Charles Jean had watched Oscar, and Jacquette had held her breath, praying that nothing was out of order. A button undone, a medal pinned upside down, anything.

"*Allons-y*," Charles Jean had said, tapping Magnus on the shoulder. He'd kissed Jacquette's hand and said, "I must rejoin your mother and Wetterstedt. They are with the queen."

When Charles Jean was halfway up the path, Oscar had moved to her side and wrapped his little finger around hers. "Don't worry," he had said. "He did not notice a thing."

She had said to Oscar, "Let's hope that no one did."

Now, after hearing what Erica had said on the Queen's Balcony, Jacquette was not so sure.

In the Hall of State, the trumpets were sounding the closing salute, and Charles Jean was watching Oscar with the same intense gaze he'd greeted them with when they'd returned from Bellevue.

"Stand up," Aurora said.

Jacquette heard a few of the women whispering behind her, still talking about Oscar's infatuation with the mysterious countess. She bit her lower lip, straining to hear them.

One said, "We deserve it for choosing these French commoners. Gustav would never have behaved so badly."

Another said, "And what of this countess? She must know she is just another medal on Oscar's chest."

Jacquette recognized the next voice as Erica's. "How could any noble family allow such attentions to be paid to their unmarried daughter?"

"The law does not allow the prince to marry her," said Diane.

"We must find out who she is," said Hedda. The others murmured assent.

Jacquette gripped the balcony rail, feeling ill. Could they be right about the law? Oscar's mother had promised him he was free to marry whomever he chose. Couldn't he choose her?

The minute the procession left the Hall of State, Jacquette pulled Marianne down the stairs and practically dragged her to the street. There was a great crowd assembled, and the heralds, in their medieval costumes, were just setting off on their ride through Old Town to announce that the Estates had disbanded.

Marianne brushed Jacquette's hand off her arm. "What is wrong with you, Quette? I have seen this a dozen times. It always turns into a riot, and I need to change my gown before the ball."

"Did you hear what Erica said on the balcony?" Jacquette demanded.

"I hardly listen to her."

"She told everyone Oscar is in love with a Swedish countess."

Marianne's face broke into a broad grin, making her cheeks seem even plumper. "Is it anyone I know?" She squeezed Jacquette's hand.

"Stop it. That's not all."

"What else?"

"Is it true that the law requires Oscar to marry a princess?"

Marianne nodded. "Act of Succession, 1810. The Estates passed it when they elected Charles Jean crown prince. The Noble Estate insisted that the new royal family gain some royal blood, and Oscar's marriage is the only way to get it."

"Couldn't Charles Jean give Oscar permission to marry someone else?"

"Oscar would forfeit his right to the throne. Then, you know who is left."

"Who?"

"The exile. Gustav. Who does have royal blood, in case you don't recall. Listen to me, Jacquette. Oscar is going to have to agree to this engagement."

Jacquette needed to think. And Oscar needed to explain why he hadn't told her this before Bellevue.

The heralds galloped by, chased by half of the young boys in Stockholm. Marianne laughed and pointed out a group of young women standing near the palace entrance. "Aren't they a ridiculous sight? Soon I am going to have to put up with them. They all will be maids of honor next year."

Rather than watching the heralds, the girls were prancing and preening around Oscar, who was standing with Odin near Wetterstedt's carriage, smiling and thanking the departing representatives. When he noticed the girls, he waved a hand and greeted them with a sideways glance and a half smile. Jacquette swallowed hard when she saw one of them blush and try to hide her coy giggle. She was positively simpering.

"He's going to be popular among the ladies," Marianne said.

Giving Marianne's hand a squeeze, Jacquette returned to the palace and found Frederik in the vestibule at the bottom of the half flight of stairs that led to the Hall of State.

Frederik held out a message. "Hide this somewhere. Don't read it yet," he said. He began to walk away, as if they had just exchanged a brief hello. Then he turned and, in a louder voice, said, "You look radiant today, Countess, I must say."

Oscar had affixed the seal to the note himself, and hastily. The lions on his monogram were tilted to the right, and an abundance of red wax was pooled around the edges. It was unlike him. Turning toward the wall so no one would see her, Jacquette read the message, which was penned in his slanted French script.

You will be pleased, I hope, to learn that I have been rejected by a certain princess.

That was all it said—no signature, no explanation. She slipped it into her bag.

"Frederik, I need to see him before the ball. It is urgent."

Without hesitation, Frederik replied, "Come to my apartment at a quarter before seven." His steady gaze betrayed nothing, not surprise, not alarm, not judgment.

"Thank you," she said, curious whether Frederik had arranged such meetings for Oscar in the past. She would owe Frederik a debt, she thought, and wondered whether it would be the first of many.

Charles Jean emerged from the Hall of State with Magnus and stood a few feet away from her. At fifty-two, he was still in his prime and handsome, but not in the refined way Oscar was. He had removed his robes of state, revealing a trim blue uniform with few adornments, just a wide gold silk sash circling a neat waist, epaulets crowning straight shoulders, and a hint of white silk flashing over a tall blue collar. The Seraphim Star hung at his breast, and his sash was tucked into his belt. She could not imagine him allowing his shirt to hang loose over his breeches. Jacquette prayed she was not the reason for his menacing scowl.

Magnus wiped his forehead and spoke a few words to Charles Jean, who snapped at him. Appearing relieved to see Jacquette, Magnus asked her, "Where in God's name is Wetterstedt?"

Jacquette pointed outside and gave Magnus a sympathetic shrug.

Charles Jean was shouting in French. "Louche? The princess's father refused the marriage contract and called my son's way of living louche? He does not even know him. I will not abide it. It was my victory at Leipzig that allowed him to recapture Berlin. Without me, he would be a king without a capital." He was pacing from one side of the vestibule to the other, clutching the hilt of his sword.

She heard Magnus say, "Someone in Stockholm started rumors about Prince Oscar. They spread among the nobles in Berlin, who said that the prince has gotten himself involved with a Swedish countess, and the Prussian king refused to entertain your proposal when General Camps presented it."

"Nonsense," Charles Jean bellowed. "Which countess? Frederik, get over here now. Do you know anything about this? My son's engagement was as much as arranged."

"No idea, sir," Frederik said, his face inscrutable.

"It is your job to know everything about Prince Oscar," Magnus said to Frederik. "Everything."

With the men arguing among themselves, Jacquette escaped outside to join Aurora. Never one to hesitate, Aurora snatched Oscar's message from Jacquette's bag and opened it. The seal was crumbling and would not be fit to save in her memory box. After reading the note, Aurora refolded it and placed it in Jacquette's bag, saying nothing. She pulled Jacquette into Wetterstedt's carriage.

Jacquette said, "Is it true that Oscar must marry a princess, under the law? Why didn't you tell me this?"

"What does it matter?" Aurora asked.

"How could you encourage it?"

"What?"

"Oscar. And me."

Aurora snorted. "I certainly encouraged nothing that has the slightest thing to do with marriage."

On the short ride home, Jacquette sat in the corner and looked out onto the water as they crossed the bridge.

"What *did* you want to happen between us, Mother?" Jacquette asked.

Aurora folded her arms. "There is nothing wrong with a little mystery—a bit of romance—with a person in a high position. He likes you, Jacquette. If you manage him wisely, he always will. He will be king someday, and he will favor you, your family, your friends. Think of your brothers."

"My brothers? You should have thought of them when you sent them away."

"Don't be ridiculous."

If Aurora had traded away her sons to keep Finspång, she would not hesitate to use Jacquette's closeness with Oscar to advance herself and Wetterstedt. But, Jacquette asked herself, did Aurora know how far it had gone? Would she continue to dangle her before Oscar like a shiny bauble if she knew? What would Charles Jean do? He would never blame Oscar; he would laugh and slap his back, dismissing it as a rite of passage. *No*, she thought. *If anyone finds out, the consequences will be mine.*

CHAPTER SEVENTEEN

At Douglas House, Sophie opened the door with a curious self-satisfied little smirk. "Brita is home," she said. "You won't have to dress yourself for the ball after all."

Jacquette interpreted this as "Heaven forbid you do anything without a maid." She reminded herself to speak to Aurora about Sophie. Aurora and Wetterstedt were at the shops and had not yet returned from the ceremony.

"Peter Wells is with her in the blue sitting room. He was not expected, was he?" Sophie asked.

Peter and Brita sometimes met at a coffeehouse in the Old Town near his print shop on Stora Nygatan, but she did not often receive visitors at home and always told Jacquette when one was expected. Jacquette gained a moment to think by fumbling with her hat ribbon.

She gave the ribbon a final tug and handed the hat to Sophie. "*Ack*, I cannot keep anything in my head. I must have forgotten Mr. Wells was coming today. I think he is helping Brita to organize her recipes. Don't tell my mother he came unannounced, Sophie, understand?"

"As you wish. But something's going on with those two, and I'm going to find out what it is."

Sophie never hesitated to cause trouble, especially when jealous. Jacquette checked the hall clock.

"Don't be silly. Peter and Brita? He's half a foot shorter than her, and I daresay he's prettier. Tell my mother I will be ready for the ball at six—we are sharing a carriage. Don't you have to press her clothes now?"

Sophie could be right. Brita insisted she would never trust any man, but Jacquette had seen her pinch her cheeks in front of the mirror on Sundays when Peter was expected. And Brita was good at keeping secrets.

In the blue sitting room, stacks of recipes were laid across the sofa, and Brita and Peter were peering into an open leather trunk in the center of the floor. His waistcoat was thrown across a chair, and his silver hair had come loose from its tie. Jacquette could see why an ambitious lady's maid like Brita might fall in love with him. He was above her station, but maybe not too much. Things in Stockholm, as Brita said, were changing.

Brita looked up from her work with an unrepentant wave of the hand. "There you are. Was it very boring?"

"Even more boring than when Wetterstedt was admitted to the Swedish Academy."

"You don't sound pleased," Brita said.

"I'm not. Do you know what Mother told me in the middle of the procession? She has persuaded the queen to appoint some new maids of honor this Christmas. She wants my name on the list."

Brita responded as Jacquette expected she would, with a friendly taunt. "Oh, poor you. And what about me? I'll be forced to move into the palace, too."

"You know that I—"

"I know you don't want it. I'm only joking. But your mother certainly is determined."

Jacquette rolled her eyes. "Hello, Peter," she said.

"I hope I am not here at an inconvenient time."

"You are always welcome. I am just irritated with my mother."

Peter said, "Ah, the royal court."

Brita asked, "Did you speak to the prince?"

Jacquette shook her head. "Maybe later, at the ball. And there is a supper." She did not say she was meeting Oscar in Frederik's apartments.

"Does Crown Prince Charles Jean still prefer French food?" Peter loved court gossip, and his eyes lit up every time Jacquette passed on the smallest item.

Jacquette smiled. "He never eats a morsel in the dining room. He forbids the cooks to prepare anything but Swedish food and then refuses to eat it. He has his own French chef in his apartments."

"Are there separate kitchens?"

"I think so." An odd question.

Brita yawned and said to Peter, "Aurora will be home in a minute. Would you mind taking the trunk upstairs? I can bring the rest of the cards later."

When he was gone, she said to Jacquette, "I imagined you would come back with better gossip, sitting on the Queen's Balcony."

Jacquette nodded. "I did hear something. There will be no engagement between Oscar and the Prussian princess."

Brita stopped tying her recipes into bundles and set the ball of twine on a table next to the sofa. "Did the prince refuse? I would have bet a year's salary that he would not stand up to his father."

"On my birthday, he practically promised me he wouldn't marry her."

"Did he tell Charles Jean that? Why is the engagement off?" Brita asked.

"What does it matter?" Jacquette asked. "There were rumors in Berlin."

"About what?"

Brita's interrogations could grow tiresome. "I must dress now," Jacquette said.

"I'm only trying to help you. God knows you don't think clearly when it comes to the prince. What were the rumors about?" Brita asked again.

Exasperated, Jacquette sank into a chair. "That Oscar is louche, or a libertine, or something like that. The king refused to take Oscar as his son-in-law."

"Louche? What does that mean?" Brita looked confused.

"Kind of disreputable and hedonistic in a way that can be very attractive. Like roguishly handsome, or something like that. That's the best I can do. I'll admit it's a good description of Oscar."

"Was the reason really so vague?"

Jacquette dropped her voice to a whisper and leaned forward in her chair. "No, it wasn't. He heard that Oscar is in love with a Swedish countess."

"Did you hear a name?" Brita was looking genuinely worried.

Jacquette shook her head. "They don't know anything about me. Don't even say that."

Something was bothering Brita, and Jacquette needed to know what it was. "What are you thinking?"

"I don't know. Nothing."

"It's something. Tell me."

Brita looked at the floor. "It's just that all these rumors are a little too convenient for Oscar."

"What do you mean by that?" asked Jacquette.

"You cannot deny that he is the person who most wanted to see the engagement fail." Brita sounded gentle, almost apologetic.

"You think Oscar spread the rumors? About him and me?" asked Jacquette, incredulous.

"Maybe. Think about when he asked you to spread gossip about yourself and Adam," said Brita.

"But this is different. Would he spread rumors about himself?"

"Maybe he doesn't think this would harm him. That it only reflects on you," said Brita. "That's how men see things." Her voice had a hard edge.

"He wouldn't do anything to hurt me so."

Brita showed no sign of giving up. "Well, from what you told me about what happened at Bellevue, it didn't seem he was trying very hard to keep your little tryst a secret. He let half the court see him with you in a fancy royal gondola, knowing rumors would start, sure as the sun rises. Easier than confronting the crown prince and refusing to marry, don't you think?"

Peter returned before Jacquette could answer. She wondered whether he had overheard them, but his face told her nothing.

"I must leave for an appointment," he said.

"Are you going back over the bridge? You are welcome in our carriage," Jacquette said to him. "I am riding with Aurora to the palace for the ball."

He hesitated, and she heard him take a sharp breath. "Thank you, but I'm not going to Old Town. I am meeting a friend for dinner on this side of the bridge."

Jacquette pressed the issue, suspecting he did not wish to answer. "Where is the dinner?"

"A friend's house. It's not a place you would know. Nothing as special as a court ball at the palace with Prince Oscar." He grinned, once again charming and confident. "And I would not be so quick to condemn the prince. Give the young man a chance. I've seen the way he looks at you."

"I have never trusted him," Brita said.

Jacquette could not dismiss Brita's opinion. Oscar had never said he had confronted his father about the engagement, not exactly. His argument with Charles Jean before they sailed to Bellevue could have been about anything. She felt like a fool for believing he was fighting for her.

"I almost forgot," Brita said a couple of hours later, in Jacquette's dressing room, as she handed Jacquette her long white gloves. "There's a letter from your aunt." She brushed some powder from Jacquette's shoulders and patted her cheek. "And I really hope you have a good time tonight."

Jacquette sensed that Brita regretted her harsh words about Oscar. "I cannot wait to leave for Finspång." She took the letter from Brita. It was written in Emilie's appalling hand.

My dear,

My little Julie and I are doing well at Himmelstalund. We read and sew and walk along the river at dusk. I only wish that young Axel could be here, too. I must admit I cried when I missed his third birthday. To think of him away from me in Skåne with Clairfelt's family!

Did you receive the fringe I sent for your birthday? Blue is such a good color for you. It brings out your large eyes, and you should always wear it.

Speaking about your birthday, as much as it pains me, and you are well aware of how much, I cannot avoid hearing news from the city and giving you my advice, which you must ignore if I sound like an old matron. On the matter of the gondola, and knowing your fear of the water, which is justified, I was rendered speechless by a note I received yesterday from an old friend. You have taken quite a risk, one might even call it reckless, and I pray you do not board that vessel again, even if it seems of the moment, as they say, a fashionable and attractive thing to do. Jacquette, listen to what I say. That boat is not safe for you, a young countess who does not know how to swim.

Forgive me my worries and burn this. I am for life,

Your devoted aunt and friend,

Emilie

Jacquette handed the letter to Brita with a nod toward the tile stove. She and Emilie had always understood each other, and the letter's message was obvious. Its words of caution had nothing to do with a boat.

Inside Stockholm Palace's gravel-paved central courtyard, an elderly general, a veteran of the Finnish War, passed the time, likely waiting for the ball to begin. When he was safely out of sight, Jacquette crossed the courtyard and entered a door in the far-right corner, where she mounted a narrow stairway. The Life Guard on duty, Anders, nodded and turned his back as she passed. On the stair landing, something skittered along the wall and ran into a crack in the plaster. This was no time for Jacquette to be squeamish; she needed to find out whether Oscar had used her, whether he was really the source of these rumors. She closed her eyes, gritted her teeth, and ran past it.

Frederik's rooms were directly beneath Oscar's, and a private staircase connected the two apartments. The other cavaliers lived on Frederik's corridor, but none of their small bedchambers had access to Oscar's apartment. Jacquette tiptoed the short distance along the cavaliers' hall, particularly anxious to avoid Carl, who was furious that Oscar had assigned Frederik the chief chamberlain's rooms.

The door to the apartment was ajar, and someone had drawn the drapes. Oscar was standing near the window next to Frederik's desk. She thought it best to stay away from him if she hoped to learn anything.

"Come closer—the sound travels in here," he said. "Unless you would rather talk in Frederik's bedchamber."

"No."

"No?" he asked, and she could see mischief, even excitement, on his face, which was lit only by the glow of an oil lamp. He looked at her the way he always did, clear-eyed and without reservation, as if he knew her soul. "I was hoping that was why you asked to meet. I'm disappointed."

She tried to stay angry but found herself eyeing him and fighting the now-familiar tug of desire. The usual shock of curls hung over one eye, emphasizing his thin, straight nose, which shaded a bit toward one side. Not yet dressed for the ball, he was wearing his riding clothes, shirtsleeves only, without his tailcoat. She wondered where he had been. She had an urge to run her hand down the buttons along the sides of his breeches and tuck her fingers in the flaps of his high boots.

Now as furious with herself as she was with Oscar, she confronted him. "Tell me the truth. Did you refuse to marry this Prussian, or not?"

Still grinning, he sat on Frederik's desk, his long legs nearly touching the floor. "Is that why you wanted to see me?"

"Did you even speak to your father?" She walked closer.

He laughed and patted the place next to him on the desk. "I don't know why you care so much. I thought you would be pleased that I am to remain a bachelor, at least for now."

"That's not what I mean," she said.

"You think I'm afraid of him, don't you? Q, try to understand. I'm just playing a game I can win. And I won. We won." He took her hands, and she did not pull away.

"I thought you were going to tell him—"

"But I got what I wanted. There will be no marriage, and by the time he figures out how to make me do it, the plump and lovely Alexandrine will be married to a Hapsburg. He will forget about marrying me off and go back to spending his time worrying about Gustav. I know him."

"You didn't refuse to marry her, did you? I knew you wouldn't."

"I fixed it. Why is it so important to you that I fight him?"

He got off the desk and faced her, placing his hand on the side of her waist. Her whole body tensed. Before she did something she would regret, she stepped back.

"It matters because of what everyone in the palace is saying about me," she said.

"They don't know anything."

"Well, they think your engagement fell through because you are—I don't know what to call it—*involved* with a Swedish countess."

He closed the gap between them and lifted her hand. She felt his lips brush her palm, the wetness, the heat of his breath. He whispered into her ear, "I admit I have been thinking a lot about one particular Swedish countess."

She wanted to slap the smile off his face. Instead, she stepped on his foot with her square wooden heel.

"Ouch," he protested.

"Did you tell anyone, Oscar?"

"Tell them what?"

"About us."

"Not I." He raised his hands in mock surrender, smiling. "Though I would like to."

"Well, someone sent a letter to Berlin about it, someone who has enough influence to cause the Prussian king to cancel your engagement. Was it Frederik? Did you tell him to do it?"

"I am not going to lie to you—"

"You did lie. At Bellevue." She folded her arms across her chest and leaned into the wall.

"No, I didn't. I told you that there would be no engagement."

"Is that why you took me there? So that people would talk about us and make you too infamous for any respectable princess to marry?"

She felt her back against the opposite wall. Short of fleeing the room, she had nowhere else to go.

"I don't understand you, Q. Have you thought, really thought, about what it would mean for us?" He braced his hands on the wall, one beside each of her shoulders.

Having him so near was unsettling, although it had never been so before Bellevue. He had been her best friend, and she was not sure what he was now. "It? You mean your engagement?" she asked.

"If we let my father get his way, I will soon have a wife, a person I don't even know. She will live with me, and they will expect me to—"

"I know what the palace would require of you. Your father would demand a grandson in the new year."

"If we want to stop them, we have to play the game better than they do," he said, wrapping his arms around her neck and pressing his body against hers. "We must fight for the things we care about. I care about this." He kissed her forehead. "And this." She felt his breath behind her ear. "And this." He ran his fingers along the base of her throat. "I don't want anything to change now. Do you?"

She did not hesitate. "No."

"Then let them think what they want. Dance with me tonight and think of what I am going to do to you at Finspång."

He bent his head and kissed her, a long, gentle kiss that made her dizzy. She had a momentary urge to ask him why he hadn't told her all of this before she had lain with him at Bellevue, but instead, she parted her lips. It was too late to worry about that now.

Jacquette paused halfway down the stairs and checked the landing, hoping the little rodent had departed. She heard a faint scraping coming from the ground floor, like metal on metal, so she descended a step or two, fearful of what, or, more appropriately, whom, she would find. It sounded like a latch. Someone had opened the door from the palace courtyard and was trying to enter quietly.

She peered around the wall where the stairway changed direction, hoping that the person who'd opened the door would pass through the stairwell and disappear into the ground floor hallway, where Oscar's kitchen staff lived, or go down to his kitchens in the basement. *Please,* she prayed, *let this be a maid, a cook, anyone who does not intend to come up these stairs*. She had no excuse for being in this wing of the palace, whose only occupants were Oscar's cooks and Oscar's men. And Oscar.

The soft footfalls in the entrance ceased, and Jacquette held her breath, certain that the newcomer was aware of her presence and waiting for her to emerge. Lacking any better idea, she decided to act like she belonged here. She was a countess, after all, the chancellor's stepdaughter. She adjusted her hat and descended the stairs to face the intruder.

It was Peter.

"My lady," he said. "I did not expect to see you."

Waves of relief and rage battled inside her. She thanked God it was only Peter but could not help but be irritated. Who was he to suggest she had no right to be here?

She held her head high and said, "I thought you were staying in Norrmalm for a dinner party."

"I ran into Magnus Brahe." He shrugged and gave her a bemused half smile, as if he were inviting her to share his frustration with the whims of the people who controlled their lives. "He told me the crown prince wanted to see me. My dinner plans were altogether ruined."

It was plausible. Charles Jean often summoned Peter to give him stories to print or to review the opposition's pamphlets and posters. Wetterstedt objected to the crown prince's motley band of unofficial "spies" like Peter. But if Peter had come to the palace to see Charles Jean, why was he in the east wing, not in the crown prince's audience room?

Before she could ask, Peter's eyes widened. "You were meeting the prince."

"Don't tell anyone," she said, becoming nervous.

"Of course not."

Anders, the Life Guard she had seen earlier, came in from the courtyard with a red-faced Aurora behind him. The stairwell was getting crowded, and it did not help that Aurora was shouting.

"Where were you, Quette? For the love of God, I do not know what will become of you." She looked at Peter and put her hands on her hips. "What are you doing here, Mr. Wells?"

"Countess, if I may say so, your gown is exquisite. From Paris, I would guess?"

Aurora loved it when people addressed her as a countess, although she had been one only while married to Jacquette's father. Her tone grew softer.

"Why, yes. You are so kind," she said, glaring at Jacquette, whom she obviously had not forgiven.

Peter said to Aurora, "I have a friend who works in the kitchens here, you see, and Jacquette was kind enough to show me the way."

At first, Jacquette was confused about why Peter was lying, but then she realized he had provided an excuse for each of them to be here. Wondering how he'd come up with it so instantly, she made a note to thank him for saving her from Aurora's wrath.

"We must go," Aurora said. "Until next time, Mr. Wells."

"I am indebted to you for leading me in the right direction, Jacquette. Have a lovely evening at the ball," said Peter. He bowed.

Peter did not follow them, nor had he explained why he was wandering around this side of the palace. And Oscar had been no more forthcoming. He had not fully denied that he'd asked Frederik to start the rumors that spread to Berlin. As she walked across the courtyard, Jacquette was no longer frightened of the furry creature who was building his nest on the stair landing. At least he seemed like an honest rat.

CHAPTER EIGHTEEN

Douglas House, Stockholm
August 13, 1815

Brita had been acting peculiarly, and now Jacquette could not find her anywhere in the apartment. They were leaving for Finspång later in the day to prepare for the royal visit, and Jacquette's travel trunks were lined up on her bedroom floor, ready to be packed. She went down to the carriage yard, where the horses were stirring and snorting in the stables, anticipating their morning hay. She was about to give up and feed them some carrots when something red attracted her attention, and she caught a glimpse of Brita's plaid dress through the gate. Lifting her skirts, Jacquette dashed into the square and grabbed Brita by the arm.

Brita's face was flushed, and there was an uncommon set to her jaw. She pulled her arm away. "Go back home. I'll get everything finished in time."

"Where are you going? You didn't even tell me you were leaving."

"I have something to do. It will take only an hour or two. I promise—I will fold every one of your gowns—just let me go."

"You're going to meet Peter, aren't you? Why didn't you tell me?" This time, Brita would have to admit that she and Peter were more than friends.

Brita shifted her basket from one hand to the other.

"And what do you have in there?" Jacquette asked. "Are the two of you having a picnic?" Grinning, she reached for the wicker handle.

When Brita spun away, the basket ended up on the cobblestones with one side of the lid open and its contents spilling out. Jacquette picked up a tiny girl's dress, not what she'd expected to find.

"Put that back!" Brita said.

"Why? Where are you going, and what is this? Where did you get a child's clothing?"

Brita picked up the basket, stuffing the gaily colored garment inside. "If you really must know, follow me. Maybe seeing the real state of things will do you some good."

"What do you mean?" Jacquette said, struggling to keep up with the long-limbed Brita as she crossed the King's Garden and turned north on Drottninggatan.

Brita stopped short, and Jacquette almost ran into her. "This is not a picnic, Jacquette. And we are not going to the park."

In silence, they walked along the noisy streets of Klara Parish, past old mansions and overgrown gardens. The air was teeming with summer flies. Had the Estates not been in session until yesterday, no person of means would be in Stockholm in August. Feeling dizzy from the heat, Jacquette stopped near Klara Church.

"Tell me, then, or I will not walk one step further. Where are you going?"

"Come through here with me. You'll see."

Brita turned off the street and climbed a short flight of stone stairs between two buildings. She smoothed her hair, patted her cheeks, and knocked at the side door of a yellow two-story house with a red roof and mullioned windows trimmed in brown. It, along with the connecting buildings, had been painted recently, and there were brushes and pails stacked near the iron fence that separated the churchyard from the street.

"Wait, Brita. This is the cantor's house." Jacquette pointed to a small wooden plaque that hung next to the door.

"Be quiet."

"Are we not going to call at the front door?" Jacquette lifted her dove-gray silk gown. "It is dusty here."

"We are in a cemetery, Jacquette."

There was no cause for Brita to insult her intelligence. She had been in Klara churchyard before and knew the house was the cantor's residence. She pursed her lips and raised her skirt higher as she walked toward the shade of a linden tree.

It had been some time since Brita knocked, and she seemed nervous. When the door opened a crack, she motioned to Jacquette and said, "Stand behind me."

There was an urgency in her voice that caused Jacquette to obey.

A thin old woman opened the door and said, "I figured it would be you, early as usual. She's not here yet. Anna has gone to fetch her, but we can't have the vicar seeing you loitering in the churchyard."

Brita put her hands in her pockets, appearing downcast.

Jacquette fumbled in her pocket for a calling card and stepped forward, anxious to assure the poor confused creature that she had come from Douglas House in Blasieholmen, had every right to walk in the parish garden, and certainly had no need to hide. Indeed, some of the De Geer relatives were significant patrons of Klara Church, and Wetterstedt knew the new vicar. Before she could say a word, the old woman realized that Brita was not alone. Her mouth fell open, and she grabbed the door latch with both hands like someone about to tumble from a boat into the sea.

Brita interrupted the woman's stammering. "Do not worry, Madame—"

"Oh my, oh my. I have offended. And I am sorry." She kept apologizing to Jacquette and was acting as if the queen of Sweden had just arrived at her doorstep.

The poor woman dropped into a deep curtsy, and her nose nearly touched the hem of her skirt. Dressed in a clean roughhewn smock of brown linen, she could have been a maid, or even the cantor's housekeeper.

Whoever she was, Jacquette could bear her distress no longer. She stepped between Brita and the woman.

"You are to tell me right now," she addressed Brita. "What is going on here?" Taking the old woman's hand, she helped her to stand erect. "Let us sit down and get you a drink."

"Madame Lindgren, this is my young mistress, Countess Jacquette Gyldenstolpe," said Brita.

The woman bowed her head. "My lady," she said.

"I am honored, madame," said Jacquette. The woman had collected herself and was beaming like a proud mother cat.

"Bring her inside, then, and I'll pour her tea," said Madame Lindgren to Brita. "I can't very well leave a countess pounding at the door, can I? Oh, my daughter will be so disappointed in me when she returns with the girl. Mark my words, I meant no offense." She continued muttering to herself as they walked through the door and entered the house.

Inside, rather than the cantor's living quarters Jacquette had expected to see, they passed through a large room with thirty or so desks and tiny cupboards along the walls. Above the cupboards hung placards with the letters of the Swedish alphabet, each letter written in uppercase and lowercase, and quotations from the Bible. Next to the door was a sign that said KLARA PARISH SCHOOL FOR POOR GIRLS.

A school, Jacquette thought. *Did Brita bring the basket of clothes as a donation?*

"Where are the children?" Jacquette asked.

"It's Wednesday, the half day," said Brita.

Curious as to why her twenty-two-year-old lady's maid knew so much about a poor girls' school, Jacquette did not protest when Brita led her into a sitting room. They sat on a sofa under an open window. Madame Lindgren returned with the tea, then announced that she needed to attend to her elderly mother, who was bedridden in the next room.

As soon as they were alone, Brita bit her lip and said, "I'll just get to it. We're here to see my daughter. She's three."

Jacquette took this in. "You never told me." She had to admit she had not told Brita everything, either. Particularly about Oscar, at least not the extent of what had happened at Bellevue.

"She's the reason I could not continue as your maid after the summer at Drottningholm."

Jacquette counted in her head. The girl would have been born in 1812.

"Is she Peter's?" Jacquette asked.

"What? No." Brita shook her head, looking appalled at the suggestion.

"Whose then? What is her name?"

"Elin."

"Does your daughter—Elin—go to school here?"

Brita shifted on the sofa. "She's too young, but she will start when she's six."

"Where does she live?"

"With a foster family, but they don't want me around. The schoolmistress, Anna, is Madame Lindgren's daughter. Anna knows the foster parents, and she brings Elin here sometimes so I can see her. She's a kind woman."

Jacquette had never heard Brita speak this way. There was a soft edge to her words, and her eyes looked moist.

"You must have been increasing—"

"That's right," Brita said. "The summer you met the prince. You were all gangly arms and legs in those days." She smiled.

Jacquette nodded. "I always thought you refused the position because you hated me."

"You drive me crazy, but of course I don't hate you. I knew I was with child and reckoned that Aurora would not want a lady's maid in that condition. So, I ran away. I lied."

"You did not appear pregnant to me."

"I was only just so. It happened before Midsummer Day, in early June."

"Was it Peter?" Jacquette asked again, still not convinced that this had nothing to do with him.

Shaking her head, Brita looked at the floor. "I told you it wasn't. Let's not speak of the father. He does not deserve that title. And I swear to you, it wasn't Peter. But Peter was the one who saved us."

"I don't understand." Jacquette heard dishes clatter in the bedroom and supposed that Madame Lindgren was still feeding her mother.

Brita sighed. "After I refused your mother's offer, I made my way to Stockholm. My boat landed at Djurgården, and I met some of the women who worked in the alleys outside the French Inn."

"Prostitutes?" asked Jacquette.

"You can call them that if you like. They were my friends. Still are to this day. They gave me a home until Elin was born, and in return, I did their laundry, made their beds."

"Then why did you give Elin away? Could you not have stayed there?"

"Have you ever known a child who grew up in a brothel? No, of course you have not; nothing like this ever happens to people like you. I had to work, Jacquette. Or I would have starved."

"Oh."

"And no one was going to hire me with a nursing baby strapped to my back."

"So, what did you do?"

"I suppose I would have had to sell myself eventually, though I could not bear the sight of a man then. I think Elin was about a month old when one of the women introduced me to Peter. She brought him over to the brothel from the dining room. I'll never understand what made him want to help me, but, God bless him, he brought me here to meet Anna, and she found a place for Elin to live."

"Why couldn't Elin live with you?"

"I told you, I had to make money. Peter got me the job as a pastry apprentice at the French Inn, and it worked out for a few years. So, now you know why I trust Peter. And you know what happened to spoil my good luck."

"You got thrown in the palace jail?"

Brita picked up a child's ball off the ground and tossed it from one hand to the other. "I will never understand how that happened. Misfortune, I guess."

"You never told me how it happened."

"No? I had been taking a rest from the kitchen, standing behind the French Inn talking to the workers from the brothel, and some guards came into the alley. They called me a prostitute and took me to the jail with the others."

"Then why did you have on that dress?" Jacquette asked.

Brita laughed. “My smock had torn, and one of the girls lent the dress to me. I was going to give it back. I was just in the wrong place with the wrong people, I suppose.”

Jacquette heard a young child’s excited voice outside the window, followed by the thud of boots stamping off the Stockholm dust. Brita ran to the door, and a girl fell into her arms. *This must be Elin*, Jacquette thought. She was the most perfect little doll Jacquette had ever seen, with straight, chin-length black hair and blue eyes. For some reason, she was dressed in boys’ clothing, but she had the manners of a queen.

Brita whispered to Jacquette, “If Anna did not bring her here and tell the foster parents she was teaching her letters, I would never see her. She does not know I am her mother.”

“But her clothes,” said Jacquette.

“I know, I know. It’s what she prefers. That is why I brought her these.” She held up one of the little dresses.

Elin laughed and said, “Can’t you bring me some trousers, kind miss? Mr. Wells told me he would teach me to ride a pony.”

“You’ll need to choose your gloves,” said Brita, a few hours after she and Jacquette returned to Douglas House. “Look at this list. Your mother has even arranged for the crown prince to tour the cannon foundry.” She read from the itinerary for Charles Jean and Oscar’s royal visit to Finspång. “And then there will be a dinner, and a ball. A hunt and a performance the day after that. Do you even own enough gloves for this?” Brita flung open a cupboard and began rummaging.

“Peter visits your daughter?” Jacquette said. “Elin told you that Peter promised to teach her to ride a pony.”

“When she is at the school. Just sometimes.”

A wasp buzzed in through the open window, and Jacquette hid her face against Brita’s shoulder. “Please. Get him out.”

“You are such a baby about bugs.” A pair of old bellows was leaning in the hall, and Brita went to retrieve it. She blasted the wasp with air, and he zigzagged back out the window toward Blasieholm Square.

Jacquette released Brita. "So, if you are not in love with Peter, why did he find Elin a foster family and promise her a pony ride? There must be a reason."

"Believe me, there is no romance between Peter and me." Brita's grin grew into laughter, and she covered her face with a silk skirt patterned with tiny lavender flowers.

"You'll wrinkle the gowns," Jacquette said.

"I suppose that will be my problem to fix, won't it?"

"That skirt is the one that Oscar likes best."

Brita propped her hands on her hips. "What am I going to do with you? I brought you to meet Elin to teach you something."

"Oh, but you did."

"Not the right things. I wanted you to see what can happen if an unmarried woman gets herself a baby. Even a countess. What happens is that other people make decisions for you. What's yours is not yours at all."

Jacquette cocked her head and narrowed her eyes. Brita did not have any cause to be lecturing her, and she was beginning to develop an odd sort of quivering ache in her stomach.

"A baby? Don't be so ridiculous. Why would you think that?"

"Bad things never happen to people like you, I know. But you and the prince—it worries me. You do know how you get a baby, don't you?"

Jacquette tossed her head. "Help me with my shoes. I think I must take a nap before we finish packing."

It seemed like hours had passed when Jacquette heard Brita's voice. "Let's get you up. Your mother is waiting for your trunks to be loaded."

A sour taste crept down the back of Jacquette's throat. Above her bed, the colors of the paneled ceiling seemed to bleed together, and she tried to blink them away. Her head felt so heavy.

"Now?" The afternoon light was waning. "Tell her I need to rest. I'm feeling queer."

"I did, but she insists."

"Oh, very well. I can see this is not going to be a pleasant journey."

She placed her feet at the side of her bed, searching for her slippers.

The floor felt cold and smooth. She longed to lie on it, to press her forehead to the cool planks. When she stood, a wave of dizziness sent her crawling back onto her pillows.

"You are unwell," said Brita. "Can I get you some water?"

"Just let me lie here a few minutes." The pressure of the cool, firm pillows against the back of her head seemed to steady the spinning of the room.

Brita sat on the edge of the mattress and held her hand. "My young miss, I worry about you. You drink too much, and dancing all night in those hot ballrooms is bad for your health."

Jacquette rolled over on her side and looked up at Brita. "After we got home, I looked in Wetterstedt's desk drawer for the note the Life Guard brought to the council chamber when you were in the palace jail. He showed it to me that day, but I couldn't remember who signed it. So, I checked."

"What made you look at that? I never saw it," Brita said.

"You told me how much Peter helped you with Elin, and it got me wondering. Brita, the note to Wetterstedt was from Peter. I didn't know him then, so it meant nothing to me at the time, and I forgot about it."

"From Peter? How did he know I was in the jail? I certainly didn't tell him."

"You should ask him," said Jacquette, resolving to figure it out when she felt better.

Brita helped Jacquette to her feet, pulled a traveling gown over her head, and moved behind her. "I'll never get these buttons hooked if you are not still."

"Nor if I faint from lack of air." Jacquette felt sullen, still mulling over her questions about Peter.

"You haven't bled this month. Shall I bring some cloths for the carriage ride? It's been some time." Brita began counting on her fingers.

Jacquette thought about the weeks. "Oh, my courses never arrive when I expect them. The last time was before my birthday, was it not?"

Brita dropped her hands, and the gown slipped off Jacquette's shoulders. "It's August," Brita said, frowning.

"Only the middle of August." Jacquette chewed on the edge of her little fingernail. "It has not been that long. Six weeks? Seven?"

"Have you done anything to cause you worry?" Brita took Jacquette's face in her hands and looked into her eyes. "With the prince? God forbid, Jacquette. Tell me you haven't."

"Um, I don't think so."

Had she? Emilie had once told her that the man must not be allowed to finish in the woman's body, lest she fall pregnant. Had Oscar finished, whatever that meant? At Bellevue, she had listened to his ragged breath as she lay under him with her knees pressed against his sides. When he'd gotten up, he'd reached for a folded cloth on the table beside the bed. But even if he had finished, she told herself, they had done it only once.

Brita patted the back of her hand. "Jacquette, what happened?"

"We did do something. Oscar and I."

Brita's eyes grew wide, and she placed her hand on Jacquette's belly.

"It is flat," said Jacquette.

"It is early. Now, pardon me, but I need to touch your bosom. Is that all right?"

Jacquette nodded.

"Tell me, does this hurt?"

Brita reached inside the top of Jacquette's shift and squeezed one of her nipples with her thumb and forefinger. Her nipples had been feeling chafed and swollen for days, and Jacquette had suspected that the tenderness signaled the coming of her menses. Even her clothing seemed to irritate them. But when Brita pinched her, a searing pain shot to the center of Jacquette's body, and she swatted Brita's hand away.

"Ouch. Why did you do it so hard?"

"I didn't. I hardly touched you." Brita began to wring her hands and looked away.

As the terrifying possibility presented itself, Jacquette made vow after vow, silently hoping Brita was wrong.

"God have mercy," Brita whispered.

Jacquette put her head in her hands.

Brita must be wrong. There was no possibility that she was going to have Oscar's child. Absolutely none.

But in her heart, she knew two things. It was true, and it was just the beginning of the lie.

CHAPTER NINETEEN

Finspång Castle
August 16, 1815

Despite everything that had been sold off and all that had been lost during the lean years before Aurora married Wetterstedt, Finspång was still a magical place. It would always be home, a haven where nothing terrible could happen. Jacquette loved every fragrant row of flowers, every tree, and every one of the hook-nosed Walloon cannon makers who crowded around Wetterstedt's carriage to welcome them when they arrived from Stockholm. She did not even mind that the lilacs were wilted, long past their prime, or that Henry, her Uncle Gerard's gangly new wife, had turned her old room into a nursery.

The footmen deposited Jacquette's trunks near the end of the women's wing in a small bedchamber with a view of the creek. The eldest footman, a man who had worked at Finspång since Jacquette had lived there with Emilie, looked apologetic. "Do not worry about me," she told him. "The size of the room means nothing." With a confidential wink, she told him to be patient, that Wetterstedt would restore the castle and the park to the sparkling treasure it had once been.

"Funny thing," the old footman chided her. "I never met a De Geer woman who was patient, and I do not think you will be the first."

She started to laugh but, remembering her present dilemma, picked up the corner of the silk bedcover and began twisting it like a rag. He gave her a funny little frown and shook his head.

"If your grandmother could see you at the ball tonight," he said. "Dancing with the cavaliers on the terrace."

"She prefers princes to cavaliers, this one does," Brita said with a husky laugh.

"Well, she does favor her grandmother, then," he said, unruffled. "I'll leave you to settle in, my lady."

Jacquette had not lied. Despite, or perhaps because of, its small size, she felt safe in this room. It was a gem of dainty Dutch perfection, nearly unchanged from its prior life as her grandmother's private library. The ceilings were of modest height with smooth white cornice moldings decorated in carved laurel wreaths, and the walls were painted a soothing tone of celery. She stooped to check a low shelf, relieved that her old French novels were still there.

She would wait here for Emilie and beg for her advice, for she had experience handling problems like this. No one had ever told Jacquette the full story of Emilie's disgrace, but bits of it had reached her. It had happened when Emilie was a young maid of honor, and it had involved a man, one deemed inappropriate for a girl in her position. "Inappropriate" to Jacquette could mean anything—old, poor, married, royal. When one of Emilie's friends had become pregnant, they were both sent away from court. They'd suffered a lot of abuse, and to add to the sting of it, the king had replaced Emilie with the older and already married Aurora. Emilie had never gotten over it.

Jacquette could trust Emilie.

Brita was treating Jacquette's predicament as an unfathomable catastrophe, and Christine had no idea what was going on. Both were unpacking, and Jacquette could see they were decidedly less enthusiastic about their accommodations than she was.

"Your wardrobe won't fit in this room, Jacquette. I don't know what your uncle's wife was thinking, putting all three of us here," said Brita, standing on her tiptoes to open one of Jacquette's trunks. To save space, the footmen had stacked the cases in a corner, one atop the other, and even the unusually tall Brita was straining to reach them. She fetched a chair, pulled up her skirts, and climbed on it. When she came down, she had a gown in her hand.

"Jacquette, can I do anything?" asked Christine. "You hardly spoke all the way from Stockholm."

Brita, who had been watching Jacquette's every move, coughed and muttered, "Fetch her some juniper. I hear it works."

"Why? My stomach feels fine." Jacquette prayed Christine did not know that a pregnant woman might take juniper berries. Or why.

"What are you talking about, Brita? Jacquette, what is going on?" Christine stopped unpacking Jacquette's toiletries from her travel case, a smooth mahogany box with brass fittings.

Jacquette needed to speak to Emilie before she told Oscar, so she was reluctant to make her situation known to Christine. The girl could not keep a secret and spilled every fact to Aurora. So, Jacquette crinkled her eyes and forced a smile, trying to act like her old self, something she was finding difficult now that she carried the burden of her secret. She sat on the bed next to Christine.

"Nothing is going on," Jacquette said. "Don't you like this room? I think it is just right for us. It used to be my grandmother's favorite hideaway."

"God rest her soul," said Christine.

Brita frowned. "I hope she haunts your Aunt Henry for putting us here. That woman is so odd."

Christine threw a tiny fringed pillow at Brita. "Henry is really quite a dear. You just don't know her."

"I'm not sure I want to," said Brita.

"Wetterstedt needs Henry and my Uncle Gerard. He hasn't the time to run a cannon foundry and the country, too," said Jacquette.

Christine stopped swinging her legs and planted her feet on the floor. "I feel kind of sorry for Henry, having to be married to Gerard. Sorry, Jacquette. I know he is your uncle."

"Oh, no, I agree," Jacquette said. "What a man. He spends most of his time staring at his easel down by the lake. He used to yell at me if I so much as touched his brushes. And he wants fifteen children."

Christine went pale. "Surviving one childbirth is hard, but fifteen?"

Jacquette had not contemplated childbirth. Her upper lip began to quiver, and she tried to push it out of her mind, for the prospect filled her with dread.

Brita spoke before Christine could go further. "I still say Henry is a funny duck." She was working to loosen the buttons of a flowered tea gown she had hung up to freshen. "This will have to do, Jacquette. It's the only thing I can reach to unpack until I find a footman to help me."

"I need riding clothes to wear when Oscar gets here, not that dress." Jacquette knew she sounded impatient. "I'm sorry. I did not mean to snap."

"Riding clothes?" Christine had been here for royal visits before. Aurora expected everyone to put on their gowns and gather to receive Charles Jean.

"I will find your habit; I think I packed it in that one." Brita's eyes were steely as she pointed toward the ceiling at the second trunk.

"You really don't seem like yourself today, Jacquette. Are you sure you aren't ill?" Christine asked.

"Just tell her," Brita said.

Jacquette covered her face with her hands.

"You may need her help, assuming she can manage it without getting us all in trouble." Brita's voice grew clipped when she spoke to Christine. "Not like you did after we went to Drottningholm. Can you at least try to keep a secret?"

"What kind of help do you think I need?" Jacquette asked Brita.

"For one thing, how are you planning to get away from here to tell Oscar?"

"*Mon Dieu.*" Jacquette was tired of them both and wished Emilie were here.

Christine put her hand on Jacquette's cheek. "Tell Oscar what?"

Jacquette lay on the bed and stared at the ceiling to avoid Christine's eyes. She needed to talk to Oscar in private, and Aurora might not object if she and Christine organized a ride with Oscar and Frederik before the reception. It was worth taking the risk.

"Do you remember when we went to Bellevue on my birthday?"

Christine nodded.

"Well, something happened there. Something I didn't tell you about." Jacquette rubbed her eyes and looked at Brita. "Go ahead. I can't say it."

Brita said, "What she's trying to say is that she's nearly two months gone."

When Christine did not react, Brita rocked an imaginary baby in her arms.

Christine's eyes widened, and she turned to Jacquette. "With the prince?"

Rolling over on her stomach, Jacquette groaned. "There wasn't anyone else with me in the house at Bellevue that night."

"Are you sure? About the baby?" Christine asked.

Jacquette buried her face in the pillow.

Brita said, "I am."

Christine clutched the tiny cross she wore around her neck. "I'll pray it is not true. But if it is, do you think the prince will acknowledge the child is his, or—"

"Not now, Christine." Brita's voice was harsh.

"I don't know what he will do. Right now, you are the only ones who know," Jacquette said. "Please, let us speak of something else."

The door opened, and Emilie glided in wearing her usual gauzy white dress. The girls fell silent, and Emilie said, "Oh, no. I insist you continue discussing whatever it was. It sounds so interesting."

Jacquette climbed off the bed and buried her face against the familiar solid shoulder. When Emilie asked to have a look at her beautiful niece, tears were running down Jacquette's cheeks.

Emilie held her at arm's length. "What is it? You had better tell me while your mother is still barking at poor Henry about putting you in this room. I wouldn't unpack yet, Brita. My sister is beside herself about this."

Jacquette pursed her lips and brought her head close to Emilie's. "I must ask you something. The king sent you and Mademoiselle Kaulbars away from court when you were my age, didn't he?"

Emilie hesitated before answering. "I was a wild young girl, and my friends were, too. I am ashamed to think of it now. But what has that to do with—"

Jacquette bit her tongue and tasted blood. "Let's sit on the sofa, Aunt."

Emilie said, "Brita, please close the door." She folded her hands on her lap, the joy on her face suddenly gone.

"Oscar and I—"

"You'd best not say his name."

Even Emilie was suggesting she face this alone.

"How can I not name him? I am carrying his child," Jacquette said in a voice so soft that, to her, it sounded like it came from another room.

Everyone was silent, so she said it again. "A baby. Oscar's." Speaking the words out loud gave them a life they hadn't had before. Her hands were shaking now.

Emilie was holding her head. "He is only—"

"He's old enough," Jacquette said.

"I suppose he is. I told you to stay away from him, didn't I? Oh, Quette." Emilie stroked Jacquette's hair, and her eyes moved toward the chair where Christine was sitting.

Jacquette said, "Christine knows. And Brita, too."

"When?"

"My birthday. It was the only time."

Emilie held out her hand. "Don't. I don't want to know all of it." Jacquette could tell her aunt was counting the months. "It is still early."

"Then you'll help me?"

Before Emilie could answer, the door opened, and Aurora walked into the room, still lecturing Henry. "Henriette, how could you be expected to understand that Jacquette is not a little girl anymore? You have not been to Stockholm in—how long has it been? If you had been out in society, you would never have put her here." She waved her hand, indicating the small size of the room.

Emilie intervened on Henry's behalf, speaking to Aurora as only a sister could, part patience and part exasperation. "Henriette is still a new bride, Aurora. Gerard will guide her, and soon she will know Finspång as well as you or I."

Aurora snapped, "It is not only Finspång she needs to learn about. It's everything else, what is happening in the great world. The court. How did my brother marry such a woman?"

Disregarding the chaos, Henry walked into the room, clear-eyed and with a placid face nearly devoid of expression. She said, "I'm sorry. Really, I am, Aurora. And Jacquette. There are so many in the crown prince's traveling party. There was no more space."

"It's all right, Henry," Jacquette said.

Henry acknowledged her with a tiny smile.

Brita was still trying to reach the trunk that contained Jacquette's riding ensemble. Just as the teetering stack appeared to be about to fall, Henry braced her hands on one of the leather straps and climbed up the first case, gaining a toehold on each and pulling herself up to the next. When she reached the top, she lowered the cases to Brita one at a time. When she finished, Henry jumped down to the floor with a thump. Tall and skinny with a bosom as flat as the lake, she was dressed, as was her preference, in a straw Sunday bonnet, brown kidskin trousers, and a frayed checked shirt.

Aurora was raking her hair with her hands, something she resorted to only when she was truly vexed. "Hasn't my brother taught you anything? Or is he at his easel painting, leaving you to manage our guests? This is a royal visit, Henriette, and a royal visit at Finspång is like no other. And if the daughter of the house"—she hugged Jacquette—"happens to enjoy the favor of the prince—"

Emilie cocked her head and spoke in a droll tone. "You cannot even imagine, Henry, what high favor our Jacquette enjoys with Prince Oscar."

Brita laughed, and Christine looked stricken. Jacquette swallowed hard. Now her stomach really was churning.

"As I was saying." Aurora tossed her head as she spoke. "You must accord Jacquette every courtesy, and certainly not lodge her in this cupboard."

"Honestly, Aurora, I am sorry," said Henry. With her hands stuffed in her pockets and her loose hair chopped off at the jaw, she could have passed for a tall young lad. She did not look sorry, or in the least bit perturbed, and that was one reason Jacquette admired her. Though she was married to Gerard, who was more than thirty years her senior, Henry was the same age as Jacquette, but she was unapologetically different.

"I like this room, Henry," Jacquette said.

Emilie pulled Jacquette up from the sofa by the hand. "We were just going to take Jacob for a walk."

The Leonberger's enormous head emerged from under the bedcovers, and the dog followed Emilie and the three girls out of the room.

"We must see Mamsell," said Emilie to Jacquette as soon as they reached the carriage drive.

From the castle, they walked a short distance past the modest two-story buildings on the drive. About halfway along the row, Emilie knocked on a freshly painted set of narrow double doors. Painted in pale green limewash, they were decorated with sprays of brilliant blue cornflowers.

"Why are we here?" Brita asked. "Will you at least tell me that?"

"The foster children live in this cottage with Mamsell," said Jacquette.

"Which foster children?"

"You will see. They are quite darling."

Brita shook her head. "But the baby, Jacquette. Emilie hardly raised an eyebrow when you told her."

Christine stepped between them. "It's just how they are about such things."

"Who?" Brita asked.

"Emilie, Aurora, Jacquette, probably even the grandmother. I didn't know her." Christine lowered her voice. "I have never seen a De Geer woman answer to anyone for her actions."

"Oh, stop," Jacquette said. She had heard this all her life, and it just was not true. "We are no different from other women."

"Don't tell me that. Most girls would be dragged to the pastor for wickedness," said Brita. "Now why are we here?"

A stout, square woman with silver hair and a black dress opened the cottage door and covered Emilie's face with kisses. When she recognized Jacquette, she held out her arms.

"Mamsell!"

"Countess Jacquette! My dear, it has been too long. And Christine. And who is this?"

In a guarded tone, Brita said she was Jacquette's lady's maid.

Jacquette ducked under the door header and stepped inside, offering her cheek. "Oh, Mamsell," she said. "How are the little angels?"

Mamsell shook her head. "They are fine, just out rambling in the park, I expect. They will be the end of me, but I do adore them. I'll go call the two girls. They're inside." She offered her visitors seats on a rose-colored Gustavian sofa carved with the De Geer crest.

Brita nudged Christine and said, "Whose children are they? And doesn't Jacquette have more to worry about than making afternoon visits?"

Christine, who was trying to avoid being knocked over by a jubilant Jacob, put her finger over her lips. "Leave her be."

"Just stop fretting about me," Jacquette said.

When Mamsell returned, she was followed by two young girls wearing identical green dresses and shiny black shoes. They charged into the room and fell to their knees, hugging Jacquette's skirts.

"Quette! I knew you would come," said the older one.

Mamsell planted her hands on her hips. "You must call her 'my lady,' Lisa. She is a young woman now, and so beautiful. Look at her. That long neck is just like her grandmother's."

"But we are old friends," Jacquette said, hugging both girls.

Emilie gestured toward the hallway and asked Mamsell, "Would you show me the empty room?"

Mamsell's eyes darted to Emilie's, and she led her toward the back of the house.

The little girl's plump face reddened, and her eyes filled. "I was so afraid you would not visit this summer."

"Don't cry. We had to stay in Stockholm until the Estates ended," Jacquette said, moved by the child's affection. "But a De Geer never misses a summer at Finspång." She knelt, wrapping an arm around Jacob's neck.

"I have never been to Stockholm," said Lisa.

The girl had been born there, but Jacquette saw no need to tell her that. "It's dirty, and there are no trees, and it smells bad except in the dead of winter. Stockholm is no place for a Leonberger. Jacob doesn't like it there—that's why he stays here at Finspång."

The girls grimaced in unison at the mention of Stockholm's bad smells. Jacquette could not help but smile.

"I may have to leave early this fall," said Jacquette.

The girls squealed with disappointment, but Lisa brightened up and asked, "Can Jacob sleep here in the cottage? He did last year after you left."

Jacquette nodded.

"Every night?"

"Yes. Unless I'm able to visit. Then he will sleep with me." Jacob nuzzled Jacquette's skirt in agreement.

"Are you going away to live in the palace like a princess?" asked Lisa.

"Who knows what my future will bring?" The answer depended on Oscar.

⁂

Outside the cottage door, Brita, whose mouth had been clenched in a frown since they'd come here, snagged the hem of her skirt on the fence. She pulled to dislodge it, and the sound was like a bandage being torn off a wound.

"Who are those children in the lodge?" she asked Jacquette.

"Some of the *oäkta barn*. The mothers were unmarried and cannot claim them, so they live here."

"Where are the mothers?"

Jacquette shrugged. "A few live in Finspång village, but others are in Stockholm and other places. It depends."

"How many children are there?"

"Sometimes seven or eight."

Emilie said, "There are only six now. And the single room is empty."

That answered Jacquette's curiosity about the mysterious visit to Mamsell's cottage. Emilie was going to propose that her baby live here at Finspång.

"We care for our little angels," Jacquette said in a clear voice, steadying herself on her aunt's elbow.

"Are you all right, Jacquette?" asked Christine.

Emilie asked Brita and Christine to return to the house, then brushed off a place on the stone wall for Jacquette to sit.

"You have not told the prince?" Emilie asked in a soft, tender voice.

"You will get your gown dirty," Jacquette said.

Emilie waved away the concern and sat down. "You must tell him. It is his right as a father."

The word hit Jacquette like a blow. She could not imagine it. A father. His rights.

"And make sure he does not run off and tell his friends. I doubt he will, but men do not always think at such times. If you must, bring him to me. I can reason with him."

"What do you mean?"

"Men tend to receive such news unkindly. They think only of themselves. Try to overlook it, though it will sting."

"What should I tell him?" Jacquette asked.

Emilie placed her hand on Jacquette's thigh and leaned close to her. "I assume Oscar will agree that Charles Jean must never learn of it. The child's existence is a threat."

"What sort of threat?"

"Oh, Jacquette, I wish you had thought more about this. It is so much more than a boy falling in love with a girl." Emilie pulled a blade of grass that was growing between the stones of the wall. "The Gustavians already say that Oscar drinks and gambles and accuse him of going from one girl's bed to the next. Your little prince or princess would play right into their hands."

"You make Oscar sound like a terrible rake. It isn't true."

"Haven't you been in Stockholm long enough to learn that the truth does not matter? Charles Jean's opponents would rejoice to know Oscar is already fathering royal bastards. It is fortunate that he is going to Norway with his father, and that they will be gone for so long."

Jacquette had almost forgotten that Oscar would be gone for four months. Nothing, it seemed, could make one feel more alone, more abandoned, than this curse that had come upon her.

"When he returns, will I look different? Will I be sick?" She touched her midsection.

"You will not be able to see the prince at all. It is out of the question."

"Why not? What will happen to me?"

Emilie stood facing Jacquette, and her voice, ordinarily so quiet and playful and breathless, grew clear and strong, like a priest exhorting directionless souls. "I can help you, but here is what you must do. And your mother will not be easy to persuade, believe me. Come to Himmelstalund and live with me. We have no visitors there. It is just me and Julie, and she is too young to understand scandal. Everyone believes I am still hysterical over my divorce, so let them think what they will; it is to our advantage. In Stockholm, Aurora can make it known that she fears for my sanity and has sent you to comfort me. That will ensure that no one will call on us—no one will know you are with child. Henry visits occasionally, but she won't speak a word of it to anyone. She is a friend."

"And when my time comes?" It frightened Jacquette to think of it.

"The birth itself, that may have to be in Stockholm, but we can bring the baby to live here with Mamsell as soon as it gains strength."

"But I am here only in the summer."

"Don't return to the city. You can live at Himmelstalund with me and visit Finspång whenever you choose, if you are discreet. It's a different sort of life, but you will be free of the prince. You won't have to play the Butterfly Game at court or become a maid of honor. And you can marry someone here. There are counts I know who live on their estates and have no use for Stockholm."

Across the circular carriage drive, Jacquette saw Aurora and Wetterstedt open the castle doors and descend the stairs. She felt the ground rumble and turned to look at the bridge to the village. The first of the black royal traveling coaches was crossing it, and Oscar was in one of them.

"I will think on it, Aunt."

"Now run. They will be waiting," Emilie said.

Jacquette was breathless when she took her place next to Aurora and Wetterstedt at the bottom of the castle steps. Oscar was traveling in his own carriage, and she watched the dust rise as his men jumped to the earth, first Carl, then Frederik. When Oscar emerged, he shook his head, refusing their offers to take his cape, store his sword, give him his hat, which was still lying on the carriage seat. His eyes were sparkling with adventure, and he was looking straight at Jacquette.

Aurora touched her shoulder and whispered, "How well you have done, my girl. Go and greet him."

CHAPTER TWENTY

Many times before, in darkness, in fog, in the heat of the day, Jacquette had waited here with her family to greet honored visitors between Finspång's twin curved staircases. But today was different. Today she would tell Oscar about the baby, and everything would change.

Although he had traveled for two days, as he walked across the dusty drive, he never took his eyes off her. He stopped to greet Aurora, who seemed not to notice his hungry look or the impatient way he tapped his thigh with his fingers. When he slipped his hand under the wide, flat band of his gold corded belt, Jacquette's entire body reacted, drawn to him in ways she had not known possible. She shivered in the August heat and pulled her light shawl around herself, thankful that Charles Jean had not yet emerged from his coach. The crown prince had earned his fame by reading his opponents' intentions on the battlefield, and she was beginning to fear that her connection with his son would be impossible to conceal.

There were so many people crowding the circular drive. All the residents of Finspång village had assembled to receive the royal party. Opposite Jacquette, a cannon maker was leading a group calling Oscar's name, and Oscar returned their admiration with an easy wave. Many among the crowd were young women. They had begun to cluster around him in Stockholm as well, and his obvious satisfaction with their attentions always made Jacquette uneasy.

Confidence was something she would need today. That, and courage. She tried to avoid catching his eye, certain he would sense something amiss. He had explored her body, so it stood to reason that he would also know her mind. But at the sight of him laughing with her mother—he was so carefree, so excited to be here, so optimistic—she realized he suspected nothing about what was to come.

The mere thought of the coming conversation with him left a knot in her chest. The moment she told him about the baby, she would know whether he was with her in this undertaking, this affair of the heart, this life. His answer would be in his eyes, his long, narrow hands, the set of his delicate shoulders. She was uncertain whether she could bear to learn it. In the past, when confronted with the consequences of his actions, Oscar had wavered in his convictions so many times.

Time was short. The royal party would leave Finspång the morning after next, and a hunt was planned for tomorrow. From then until the end of the year, when Oscar returned from Norway, she could not hope for more than a distant secondhand greeting passed on in a letter from Wetterstedt. No matter the outcome, she must tell him now, at Finspång, where they were as close to being alone as they ever would be. The estate offered protection, an unwritten code of silence that forbade guests to take away what they learned on their visits, what they heard, what they suspected. Here, she could walk with Oscar, touch him, cry with him about their futures, if only she could find the courage to begin.

When Oscar finished talking to Aurora, he offered Jacquette the usual polite greetings in his public voice, one loud enough that the surrounding family could hear. Still, she did not meet his eye, so he pushed his hair behind his ears and cocked his head to the side, pursing his lips and frowning.

When she started to look away, he grinned.

"Oh, don't tease me," she said, exasperated.

"I hope we can find some time together soon," he whispered.

She nodded. "This afternoon. Before the reception."

He drew closer. "Are you cross with me? I could apologize for whatever I did, I suppose."

"But you won't, will you?" she asked, not expecting an answer. He had always taken to heart what she'd told him the first time they had met, that long-ago day at Drottningholm—royals never apologize, and they do not have friends. Long ago, she had concluded she had been too forthright as a young girl.

With a smile, he nodded to her and moved on to talk with Christine. It would have been risky to linger at her side. People were envious, and they were watching. Wetterstedt had invited twenty overnight guests to the castle, counts and diplomats, scholars and government men with their wives. They were lined up on one side of the circle opposite the villagers, waiting to have their moment to bask in the glow of power.

The crowd stirred as Charles Jean alighted from his carriage. The tall crown prince hopped to the earth, thanked the driver, waved to the crowd, smiled at his hosts. Before approaching the castle, he strode over to Oscar's carriage, where the cavaliers were loitering. The majority were stretching their legs or leaning against the vehicle in various states of lethargy, drunkenness, and dishevelment. Even Carl was yawning. Charles Jean's cold gaze was a direct reproach to them, and his own pristine appearance a subtle one. His midnight-blue general's uniform was spotless, his gold sash was straight, and his fringed epaulets crowned his impeccable posture. As always, every tight curl of his black hair was in place, and his boots gleamed with polish.

He greeted Aurora like an adoring brother, smiling at her and admiring her hat. After praising the lush park and the beauty of Finspång village, he reviewed the assembled family as if they were a regiment summoned for inspection. Jacquette had to admit he was remarkable.

"Wetterstedt," he said. "Tell me, why is our good cousin Emilie not here to receive us?"

Charles Jean called everyone his cousin, a mannerism that Jacquette found decidedly un-Swedish.

The family fell silent, and she and Christine exchanged worried glances. Emilie had rushed past them up the stairs and probably was shuttered in her old bedroom with her daughter. The reason, she had told Jacquette, was her ex-husband, Clairfelt, who was now standing across the courtyard, whispering with Carl as they brushed off their coats. He was traveling with Charles Jean as his adjutant, and Emilie did not want him here.

After a few words with Aurora, the head housekeeper hurried into the castle to fetch her.

When Emilie finally descended the stairs, Clairfelt's insolent, gin-fueled laugh grew louder. Though Jacquette had thought her opinion of him could sink no lower, he was proving her wrong. Emilie's fiery glare could have melted ice.

In a booming voice, Charles Jean ordered Clairfelt to go and help groom the horses. The task should have fallen to a stable hand, not to the crown prince's adjutant. It was demeaning. Clairfelt began to protest, but Charles Jean ignored him and turned to Emilie to kiss her hand, calling her his dearest of friends, saying that the beauty of Finspång would pale for him without her presence. Clairfelt blanched when Charles Jean remarked that any man who did not prize Emilie De Geer's company was a fool.

Jacquette had been furious when she learned that Charles Jean was bringing Clairfelt to Finspång, but now she understood. He never did anything without a reason.

After speaking to Emilie, the crown prince embraced Wetterstedt, kissed Aurora's hand, and tapped Oscar on the elbow.

"Go, Son, enjoy yourself," he said. "Wetterstedt and I have work to do." He motioned to Magnus, who was carrying his paper-case, and Magnus hurried behind him. Wetterstedt kissed Aurora on the forehead, and the three men climbed the stairs to the castle.

Dismissed by his father, Oscar looked at Frederik, who pulled a brandy flask out of his coat. He opened it and turned it over, demonstrating it was empty. Next to Jacquette, Christine giggled, and Oscar rolled his eyes.

Frederik's lighthearted mood did nothing to relieve Jacquette's anxiety. Before this, her secrets had been innocent ones—a stolen kiss, a secret meeting, a trivial lie. Now, as Emilie had pointed out, she was carrying the offspring of a future king, not any ordinary *oäkta barn*. If knowledge of it spread, every Swede would own the story, and she and the child would become the property of the nation, of its lore, of its scandals.

After a tour of the cannon works, Jacquette and Christine joined Oscar and his men in the castle's entry hall. She felt his eyes burning through her gown and knew Christine had noticed, too.

"I have to speak to him now."

"I'll say you do," said Christine.

Jacquette said to Oscar, "I have a new horse I'd love you to ride. He's a little devil, but so, so remorseful after he has been wild."

His mouth curled into a smile, and he took a deep breath. "I've not met one I couldn't handle."

Carl interrupted, "The prince is tired from the journey."

"Not at all. Never a better time for some air." Oscar laughed without even looking at Carl. His black lashes glistened. "Let's ride out. Frederik, do you want to come?"

"Of course, but—"

"It is only five o'clock," Christine said, "and the days are still long."

She was trying her best to help, the dear, shy girl.

"Let me change my boots," Carl said.

Oscar motioned to Frederik to hand him his shoulder bag. He removed a leather folio and handed it to Carl.

"Another time. I need you to attend to this."

"What, sir?" Carl asked. He opened the folio and frowned at Frederik.

"Wetterstedt finished my father's speech. I need you to copy it in Swedish for me. It is not long; you may be able to finish it before the reception." Oscar took Jacquette's arm, not waiting for Carl's answer.

From behind, Jacquette heard Carl say, "But, sir, there is plenty of time for me to do that in Norway. We have two weeks."

"Nonetheless." Oscar handed the bag back to Frederik.

As they were leaving to dress, Carl stood in the stairwell gazing up at the castle architect's dedication, which was carved on a stone tablet that hung on the wall. He was holding the speech Oscar had handed him as if it were on fire. Jacquette feared there would be trouble between the two men someday and hoped Oscar took seriously the stories of the rebellious Swedish nobles from Värmland, who had toppled more than one king. When Carl was not yet twenty, he had ridden with the Western Army in the coup that had sent Crown Prince Gustav into exile. Ruthlessness ran in his blood.

From the stables, they rode through the park and into the forest, and when they reached the first fork in the trail, Christine and Frederik disappeared. Jacquette and Oscar continued to the northeast, Oscar astride the latest addition to Finspång's stables, a spirited gray stallion. His black leather riding boots hugged his long legs to the knees, and Jacquette imagined the strength of his thighs as they squeezed the horse's sides.

They dismounted in a clearing. Turning his face toward the sun, Oscar unbuckled his saddlebag, folded his plain black riding coat into a precise bundle, and tucked it into his pack. His white silk shirt, as usual, was loose. It billowed in the wind, and Jacquette could see his skin and a trail of tiny dark curls above his tan breeches. The summer's military exercises had toughened him, made him into a man. She wanted to touch him but pushed away her desire. Touching him was what had brought her to this point.

She shivered.

"Are you cold?" he asked.

"No, it's not that." She untied the ribbon of her riding hat and gave it to him. It was wheat-colored, made of corded bands of straw, and had a tall crown like a top hat and a tiny furled brim. She debated whether to allow herself one kiss before she told him.

"There's a wind off the lake." He walked over to his horse, patted the stallion's rump, and offered him a carrot. The stallion reared his head in appreciation as Oscar tied the hat to his reins. "I can tell this one is going to be a fine boy. Give him a year," he said.

"Hmm, yes. A year is a long time," Jacquette said.

"What do you mean?"

She waved her hand. "Nothing. Carl seemed out of sorts, didn't he?"

"He thinks his job is to tell me what is best for me. And he's not getting on with the others, especially Frederik."

"I can tell."

"Frederik is the only one who noticed what my father did. When he took Magnus with him and sent me off to amuse myself."

"He wasn't the only one."

"You saw?"

She nodded. It was difficult not to notice Charles Jean's preference for Magnus.

"He ignores me now, but when we get to Norway, he will expect me to ride with him at the head of the parade and dance with all the noblemen's daughters."

"I hope they are all fat and wear plaid wool," she said.

"It doesn't matter what they look like. They won't be you." Button by button, Oscar loosened the tight military-style cuffs of her short green riding jacket and removed it. He spread a blanket under an ancient oak tree and sat, leaning against the trunk. "Come here," he said. He bent his knees, leaving a space just wide enough for her hips to nestle neatly between his thighs.

She tried to forget why she'd brought him here, the news she needed to share. One last time could not be too much to ask of the gods, she told herself. *One last time before I tell him, and it becomes real.*

"You seem so far away," he said and spread his feet a little wider, pulling her closer to him. His breath was coming hard and fast.

"Bring me back," she said and leaned into him.

Feeling his chest against her shoulder blades, she wished away their white silk shirts and imagined their bare skin touching. She wiggled her toes in her boots, wanting to free them, to rake them through the grass. With lazy strokes, Oscar teased her breasts until they were hard and full, then withdrew his hands.

When she could wait no longer, she squirmed against him and guided his hands back to her, and he loosened her shirt without touching any of the places that burned with need for him. He dangled one of her white silk ties before her eyes, asking her what she wanted in husky French. Her stores of willpower depleted, she arched her back and eased her hips farther into the space between his legs. She wanted to feel him.

"I like this," he said as he unlaced her corset bodice, a narrow band of white linen that opened in the front. "It's different."

He ran his fingers down her neck and past her collarbone, cupping her breasts and massaging her nipples with his thumbs. He lowered his head, and the invitation he whispered in her ear would have made a courtesan blush. After he stretched out on the blanket, she climbed on top of him, moving against his body to feel his desire. Slipping his hands under the loosened waistband of her riding skirt, he cupped her buttocks and asked her what he was going to do without her for the rest of the year.

She froze, picturing his return to Stockholm this winter. She wearing the green wool cloak she always wore at Christmas. He running his hands around her, feeling the swell of her pregnancy. She rolled off him and took a deep, sorrowful breath.

"Oscar, I have to tell you something."

He blinked. "Now?"

She nodded.

"Just . . . give me a minute." He raised himself on one elbow, and they faced each other on the blanket. With a confused look, he stroked her hair. She heard his sharp intake of breath and saw the need in his eyes.

"Stop it, Oscar."

He pouted, a mock show of hurt.

"I'm pregnant."

"Pregnant." He said the word and stared at her with his lips parted. "Pregnant."

Slowly, his eyes refocused. "You are certain of it?" he asked.

She nodded.

"There's no mistake?"

"I don't think so, no."

"But, how? I mean, it was only the one time, on your birthday."

"Just so," she said.

He did not look angry, only stunned. After a moment, he sat up and took her hand. "When will the . . . When will it happen? The date, I mean."

"It? Our baby is what I think you meant to say, and you can count as well as I can."

He looked bewildered, and his eyes darted from the horses to her abdomen to the path that led back to the castle. "I can," he said. "I wasn't thinking."

As he stumbled over his words, she answered his question. "The beginning of April, I think," she said.

"Wait," he said, leaning closer, the vein on his forehead throbbing. "You haven't told anyone, have you?"

She did not answer. It hurt too much. Of all the things he could have said, this. But at least he had not asked whether the baby was his. He knew better.

"Wetterstedt does not know, does he?"

"No. I don't know how I will ever tell him. *Ack*." She covered her eyes with her hands.

"Dr. Pontin?"

"No, I have not been to a doctor yet." Tears were running down her cheeks, but he did not comfort her. Instead, he lay back and stared at the sky through the trees. After what seemed like an hour, she felt his fingers link with hers.

He said, "That did not come out as I meant it to. All I mean is that we must keep this from my father, if that is even possible."

"Am I to be hidden, too?" she asked. With Oscar, everything, even this, was about his father. It stung.

He placed his hand on the flat area between her hip bones. "I need to think."

"There isn't much to think about, is there?" she asked. "I suppose they will send me away somewhere. I can't very well stroll in the King's Garden when I am as large as a cow."

"You'll never be that. You're perfect." He ran his hand along the side of her hip.

He sounded sincere.

"Emilie knows. I told her today."

"What does she think you should do?"

Oscar trusted Emilie.

"She says the baby can live here at Finspång in the orphans' cottage. I would move out of Stockholm and live with her at Himmelstalund.

She thinks getting me away from the capital would save me. I don't know. Maybe it would."

He swallowed. "What does your mother say?"

"She doesn't know yet, but we can talk to her. She adores you."

"I'm not sure she will adore me after this."

"She will find an advantage in it, somehow. And she won't blame you."

"Look at it this way. I'm a prince. There is not much they can do to us, is there?" he asked.

"Not to you," she said.

He did not speak for a while, just lay on his side, twirling her hair around his finger. Then he rolled on his back and said, "Maybe I should take a cold swim before we go back." He sat up and unbuttoned the fall of his trousers, beginning to undress.

"Oh, I suppose I could have just kept it to myself." She tried to sound annoyed but could not take her eyes off what he was doing. It had been dark at Bellevue, and she had not seen all of him. Now she did and wanted him with a fierceness she could not ignore. Even now.

"That's not what I meant. Don't be cross." Kneeling, he put his arms around her neck, and she rose to face him.

"I'm not cross, Oscar. I've got a problem. We've got a problem." As she lifted her breast to drop it back into her corset, his eyes followed. She smiled and cupped her hand around her other breast.

He kissed her, and she could not resist running her fingers along the bare skin below his navel. The news she'd delivered had not quelled his need for her, it seemed. He held her chin, and his eyes filled with mischief.

"Once a woman is pregnant, she cannot become any more so, can she? Let's not waste time talking about things we cannot change, Q."

"Let's not talk at all."

She kissed the tender skin under his ear until he moaned and asked her not to stop. Then she was underneath him, her legs wrapped around his back, urging him to give her what she needed like she needed air, or water, or the warmth of the sun. This time, what she felt was more than a tingle; it was a long, slow cascade—waves of sheer bliss.

When it was over, she opened her eyes. He was looking at her with a determined set expression.

"I don't care what they say. You can't live with Emilie. For God's sake, it's fourteen hours from the palace. I love Emilie, but you can't do that. I need you in Stockholm. Take me to Aurora. I'll speak to her."

Oscar had said nothing about the baby, but the knowledge that he needed her meant everything. He'd said it: He was a prince. He would sort it out.

When the sun began to sink below the trees, Oscar set her riding hat on her head in the French style, tilted a few degrees to the right. He had grown pale and looked a bit nervous, but the way he tied the ribbon was so careful and deliberate that she was sure he recognized their new bond. One that could be severed only by death.

CHAPTER TWENTY-ONE

They handed their horses off to the grooms and walked toward the rear of the castle under the shade of the ancient elm trees. Oscar plucked a dried lilac blossom and gave it to her. She tucked it in her hat.

"During your long absence," she said, "this will remind me of you."

"Please, no," he said, laughing. "It's dead."

She could not help but giggle and indeed felt a bit hysterical after the events of the day. She was catching her breath, bent at the waist and resting her hands on her knees, when she heard someone call her from the castle's back terrace, where the reception was to begin in an hour.

It cannot be him, she thought.

He called again. "Quette. We are here!"

Oscar took a step away from her. "I expect this will be your brothers," he said, smiling.

Nils, the family's eldest son, who was eighteen months her junior, had grown into a robust young man with shaggy blond hair. He was running toward them, down the wide stone stairs that led from the terrace to the castle park. August, still only fifteen, was at the top of the stairs, facing away from her with his head thrown back. He was looking at the grand rear facade of Finspång Castle, with its central round turret that housed the main salon. August had been only ten years old when their father took the boys.

Still running toward her, Nils said, "You look so grown up I almost did not—"

Suddenly he stopped, and his arms flew in every direction. He straightened the double rows of buttons on his blue jacket, pulled down his white waistcoat, and checked his black cravat. Jacquette had to admit that he looked altogether dazed. He bowed to Oscar.

"Your Royal Highness."

Oscar laughed. He was a few inches taller than Nils, more fine-boned, darker. "Count Gyldenstolpe. I have heard so much about you."

Nils said only, "Sir."

The young men were the same age, but Oscar seemed so much more like a man. From the terrace, she could hear the staff preparing for Aurora's party: the chime of crystal glasses, the melody of stringed instruments. She broke the silence.

"I didn't know whether Father would really allow you to come."

Nils glanced at Oscar as if he were hesitant to speak.

"It's all right," Jacquette said. "I have known the prince since just after you moved to the north."

Nils said, "Father could not wait to be rid of us. He went away to the army for, I don't know, about two years. We had to live with the governor in Sänna, if you can believe that. And then, when he finally came back this winter and realized what it would cost for me to study at Uppsala next year, he started talking about sending us back to Mother."

"He wants Wetterstedt to pay your fees, and Mother will not agree unless you live with us. Well, at least Father fed you," Jacquette said.

Oscar looked sympathetic. He had his own problems with Charles Jean. He said to Nils, "I visited your father when he was at his command on the Norwegian border. He performed a brave service."

"Thank you, sir," said Nils.

"You may call me Oscar."

Jacquette added, "But not in company."

Nils nodded. "I was on my way to the stables to visit Fury. Aunt Emilie says he is still as feisty as ever."

"Well, bravo that you are finally here. That is all that matters now." Jacquette linked her arm with her brother's and said, "Let's go see August."

Oscar interrupted her. "Wait a minute, Q. My father is coming."

Nils dropped Jacquette's arm and frowned. Oscar had used his private nickname for her. No one else called Jacquette Q.

"I told you. We are friends," she said to Nils.

From around the side of the castle, with a Life Guard on each side, Charles Jean was approaching them at a brisk pace. Carl was trailing behind, trying to hand him some papers, but Charles Jean looked less than interested in whatever Carl was offering.

"My son. I have been looking for you," he called to Oscar. He peered at Nils.

"Your Royal Highness," said Nils, appearing overwhelmed. *That,* Jacquette thought, *is the fault of our father, who should never have taken him to live in the north for so many years. He probably saw more horses than people there*. She could fix that now that he had returned.

"Young Count Nils," said Charles Jean. "Could that be you? You have grown since I last visited your father. Was it only three years ago? You will be old enough to become a cavalier soon."

"Thank you, sir," Nils said. "I would really rather be a cavalry officer."

Charles Jean gave him a severe look, and Jacquette cringed. One did not decline the crown prince's offer to serve at his court. If Aurora had been here, she would have shaken Nils by the shoulders.

Then Charles Jean burst into a solicitous chuckle and slapped Nils on the back. "I'll tell you, son, I cannot blame you. You would face more danger from my courtiers than you would in the cavalry and enjoy yourself less. Have you applied to our riding academy in Skåne?"

"Not yet, sir." Nils's eyes gleamed.

"We will arrange it when it is time. I'll wager you could manage both court service and a military post. Like Carl here."

Carl said, "Your Royal Highness, I have finished translating the speech, if you would like to review it."

Charles Jean took Jacquette's arm, and her knees began to shake. "How can I have time to discuss such matters when I could be speaking with our beautiful young hostess?"

Jacquette murmured her thanks. "You flatter me, sir." She tried to be discreet as she brushed grass off her riding skirt. Her hair, she feared, was a mess, too.

"Oscar," Charles Jean said, "Nils will show you to your rooms, and I will escort the countess."

Oscar looked alarmed, but before he could object, Charles Jean had led Jacquette over the little arched bridge and down the path to the orangery. He guided her to a bench, where she sat down. He stood, towering over her.

"I imagine that your mother and Wetterstedt are fighting off the young counts who are asking for your hand. How old are you now, Countess?"

"Eighteen."

"*Eh bien*, eighteen is a fine age for a young woman to marry, but sometimes a young man needs more time."

"That is very true," she said, but in fact, she did not understand his meaning. He had been trying to persuade Oscar to marry Princess Alexandrine, not urging him to wait.

"You have been spending a good deal of time with my son."

"We have known each other since we were children." Her hands were beginning to shake, and she thought she knew what the crown prince was going to say.

He gazed at her and let his words do their work.

"Ah," he said, "the situation is a difficult one. Were he a young soldier, I would not hear of a marriage at his age, but he is a prince, and the circumstances demand it. He tells me he has no interest in princesses. You see my problem?"

She nodded.

"Of course you do. You are your mother's daughter. You understand." He swept his arm toward the castle, a grand gesture.

"What can I do, sir?" she asked.

"There are agitators, outsiders who seek to stir up sentiment against us. They slander Oscar's bloodline and exalt the exiled king's son. It is all over Stockholm—I am sure you have heard them say that Gustav should inherit the throne after me." He gave her an amused conspiratorial look. "Some would even replace me now."

"That cannot be," she said, opening her eyes wider.

He threw back his head and laughed.

"I like you, Countess Jacquette. I can see why my son does, too. And I would look the other way when he strays a bit if he were not the heir to the throne. But he is."

"Yes."

"And he must behave himself and attend to his studies so that these Gustavians have nothing to start their rumors about."

"Of course."

"I want nothing to mar his reputation. There have been rumors already. And I think you can help me to secure the best sort of marriage contract for him."

"Oh, I am not sure what I could do," she said. Having Oscar's baby was probably not what Charles Jean had in mind.

"He must leave behind his childhood friendships."

Was Charles Jean telling her to stay away from Oscar? Jacquette sputtered, "But the prince will return to Stockholm before Christmas, will he not?"

"Yes, and I hope my cousin Camps will have a marriage treaty for him by then. He needs to behave like a vicar at the New Year's balls this year. There can be nothing for the gossips to talk about."

"Yes, sir."

"You will have the young counts sighing for a dance with you, and you will not even miss Oscar. I will speak to Wetterstedt; perhaps the time is right for him to arrange a match for you. Though I'm sure there will be many aspirants." He looked at his watch, the one Bonaparte had given him. "Now, I must dress for your mother's party."

"I think I will stay here for a minute and take the air," she said.

"Very well."

He turned on his heel and left her shaking. The man who led the nation had just ordered her to stay away from the father of her child.

She walked around the castle to the front entrance but got no farther than the vestibule. The doors to the round salon were open, and Emilie was waiting to pull her inside before she could escape up the stairs or turn into the corridor leading to the women's wing. Her aunt's face was grave, and Oscar was standing next to her.

"Baroness Aurora is inside, Your Royal Highness, and she has ordered some refreshments. How was your ride?" Emilie asked Oscar.

Oscar muttered, "I feel like a different person."

Emilie looked alarmed.

"Was my mother watching us ride in from the park?" Jacquette asked Emilie.

"She has been standing at the window for an hour."

"Who told her?"

"Christine."

"Everything?"

"Yes."

Jacquette groaned and saw Oscar bite his lower lip. Aurora, dressed in a silver ball gown, rushed across the room to curtsy to him, dipping almost to the ground. When she rose, her face was placid and serene, without a hint of opprobrium.

Oscar spoke first. "I can explain, Baroness Wetterstedt. It was my birthday, and we—"

Aurora placed a motherly hand on Oscar's shoulder. "There is no need for you to say a word, sir."

Jacquette looked at Aurora, astounded.

Ignoring Jacquette, Aurora said to Oscar, "I want you to enjoy everything we have planned for you. Go, dress, have a glass of champagne. It is chilled and waiting in your room. Jacquette and I will attend to everything."

When she spoke Jacquette's name, her eyes narrowed.

Oscar said, "This idea that Jacquette will move to the country, I . . ."

"Don't bother about that for a moment. My sister has many ideas, not all of them good."

Emilie looked out the window, drumming her fingers on the sill. It occurred to Jacquette that no one had asked her where she would prefer to live.

Aurora continued, "When Jacquette's health permits, she will return to Douglas House. You can trust in our absolute discretion, sir.

Now go be with your men and enjoy yourself. We will see you at the reception."

As he walked from the room, Jacquette noticed a lightness in Oscar's step, and when he said goodbye to her, he looked everywhere but at her eyes.

Aurora spoke in a low voice, keeping her eyes on the salon doors. "You should have told me."

"I didn't know how." Jacquette could hardly blame Christine for betraying her secret; the fact that Aurora already knew relieved her of having to speak the words and admit her stupidity.

"You confided in Emilie. Don't you think I deserved to be told first?" Aurora's voice was distant, like she sounded when planning her traveling wardrobe or plotting the downfall of another lady at court.

"Aurora, please. She needs your love. She is only eighteen," said Emilie as she slid into a salmon-colored silk armchair and set her glass on a polished dark wood table.

Aurora, who never drank spirits in the daytime, picked up the glass and sniffed its contents before she spoke. "This is so typical of you, Emilie. Did love solve your problems, or did my husband come to your rescue? Tell me, how are we going to break this news to Gustave, and what is he to do about it?" Aurora's first thoughts were always of Wetterstedt.

Emilie's eyes filled with tears.

"Where is Christine?" Jacquette asked, changing the subject to give Emilie time to collect herself. With Oscar gone, Emilie was the only one available to defend her.

Aurora sat up straighter in her chair. "Don't blame the girl, Jacquette. You know she cannot keep a secret, and I sensed something was not right with you. All I had to do was to remind Christine about who paid her father's debts."

"I don't blame her. It is all my fault," said Jacquette.

"You should have married last year when I wanted to find you a husband. You and the prince would have been free to do as you pleased. No one would have cared then."

"Perhaps my husband would have," said Jacquette.

"There is a lot a prince can do to make a husband look the other way. Titles, commissions, positions in the government, the army. Really, I am surprised you got yourself in this mess and are still so naive about how the world works."

Emilie looked pained. "Is this necessary, Aurora? The poor girl. She needs—"

"Of course it is necessary. Did you think I would waste this opportunity by sending her to hide out in the country with you?" demanded Aurora.

The word "opportunity" settled heavily on Jacquette's chest. She must have frowned, for Aurora came to kneel beside her chair.

"I do believe the prince is smitten with you," Aurora said.

Emilie sighed. "You make young love sound so tawdry, Sister."

"Hardly," replied Aurora. "Jacquette, your child could put an end to all of Charles Jean's plans for Oscar. He's too young for this, unmarried, and you are not just any coffeehouse girl. We may find our situation advantageous. That is all I am saying."

Jacquette's eyes filled with tears. "Don't you care about me or the baby at all? What will I do?"

Aurora looked offended. "I love you like the moon and the stars, my dear girl. But we cannot have you quit Stockholm and move to Himmelstalund at the same time as Mamsell takes in a new infant at Finspång. People will connect the two." She looked at Emilie. "The baby will come in March or April, you say?"

Emilie nodded.

"Until your confinement in the spring, Jacquette, you can stay at Himmelstalund with Emilie. We will say you are poorly and cannot have visitors. You can return to Stockholm when your time is near."

"And the baby? Can Mamsell raise the child? I can visit when I am here in the fine season." Jacquette was finding it easier to breathe, and her hands had stopped shaking. Her mother's idea made good sense.

When Jacquette hugged Aurora, Aurora stiffened and pulled away.

"There is one thing you must realize. If anyone figures out what you and the prince have done, we will all be ruined," Aurora said.

Jacquette rubbed her brow. "I'll never tell anyone."

Emilie smiled at Jacquette, but her eyes were sad. "This is what I feared would happen when you went to Stockholm."

Aurora said to Jacquette, "If anyone suspects this, if stories spread, then you will never find a husband, Wetterstedt's hopes of becoming foreign minister will be gone, and heaven knows what would happen to my position at court. And what of your brothers and their futures?"

"I see. I understand," said Jacquette.

Emilie gave Jacquette a queer look as Aurora continued, "I'm not sure you do."

"What do you mean?" Jacquette looked at her mother and her aunt, neither of whom would meet her eye.

"I mean we must find a home, someone to love the child and raise him or her as their own," said Aurora.

"Not here at Finspång?" Jacquette asked Emilie, confused.

Emilie said, "I know this is a shock, Quette. But your mother knows someone, a kind woman who will take the baby into her home. Do you remember Countess Meijerfelt?"

Jacquette knew the elderly widow, who was one of Aurora's friends from the old days. She frequented the King's Garden on Sundays, assisted by her companions and a walking stick.

"My baby would live with her in Stockholm? Why not here?" Jacquette's eyes were burning, filling with scalding tears.

Aurora turned red. "Jacquette, you must understand. It will be impossible for you to see this baby. Ever. You cannot visit, send a gift, carry a portrait. You cannot admit you are its mother or speak of the child, not even with friends or family, not even in private. You are not the first person to be in this situation, you know. There are rules. We will talk again. Now go to your room and dress. And put cucumbers on your eyes. They are swollen."

Jacquette didn't understand. The words passed by her like dried leaves in the wind.

Emilie led her to the largest of the sunny bedrooms overlooking the castle park, telling her that her room had been moved. Christine's and Brita's possessions were nowhere in sight, and a dazzling sapphire necklace was laid on the bed.

"Where did this come from?"

"Oh, it's from your grandmother's vault," Emilie said. "I suspect you will receive more. You just became the family's most valuable asset."

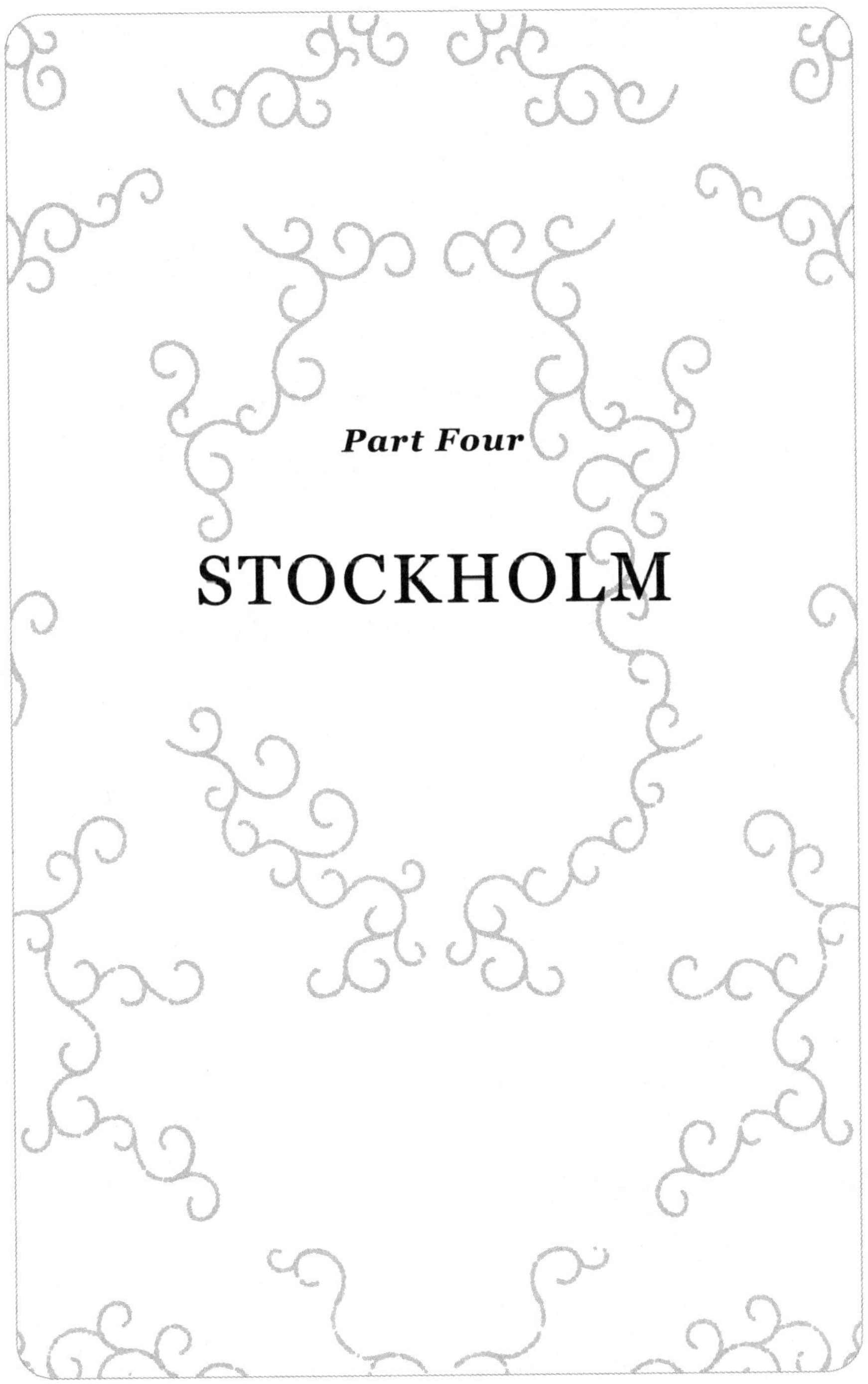

Part Four

STOCKHOLM

CHAPTER TWENTY-TWO

Douglas House, Stockholm
Seven Months Later
March 22, 1816

My return to Stockholm has left me more alone than ever. Last night, Papa Wetterstedt, who had been nervous and distracted during the entire journey from Aunt Emilie's house, asked the driver to stop just as our carriage was entering the courtyard through the arched passage under Douglas House. The tight, narrow space is quite dark, a good place for a secret conversation.

I asked him why no one was outside to welcome us, not even Aurora or Christine. He took my hands and, in a sober voice, told me I would not be going to my rooms. Your mother, he said, has prepared one of the carriage houses in the courtyard for you. Just until your confinement has passed.

There is no other way.

In delicate situations, Papa is normally as deft as a tailor working a needle and thread, but not last night. He gave me a firm hug, pulled his gloves on, and got out of the carriage, mumbling his regrets. Before closing the door, he begged me to be patient, saying it would break my mother's heart to be apart from me. We would be separated by only a few yards, but she would have to stay away.

He told me I am a treasure, but one that must be hidden.

Whether Oscar is aware of my return, or whether he cares, I do not know. In my isolation, I am not even certain he is in Stockholm. It is morning now, when he always spends an hour writing music. With a stack of paper engraved with rows of blank staves, he sits near the window on his piano bench, toying with the graphite stick he uses to fashion the tiny connected notes. When I last spoke to him at Finspång before he went to Norway, he was composing a march. Since then, I have heard nothing. Someone is keeping us apart.

With my eyes closed, I curl my hands into tight fists, trying to feel his presence. I am forbidden to go outdoors but dream of escaping around the corner to gaze across Lake Mälaren at the tall windows of his bedchamber in the east wing of the palace. I know exactly the spot on the shore where I would stand and which of the palace's long rows of windows is his. Though I try, I cannot calm the part of me that fears I will never see him again.

Brita says these disordered thoughts are a sign that my time is near. Aurora has allowed her to sleep on a sofa next to my bed, and she complains that it is too short, that her feet dangle off the end. She tries to amuse me by lying on her back and kicking her legs in the air, hoping to lift my spirits, but the prospect of what I must face is becoming real to me now, no longer an abstraction. It fills me with terror, and I try not to think of it, but still, I sit and wait for the first grip of pain to seize me.

Papa Wetterstedt, as always, was true to his word. Despite horrid piles of melting snow and the miserable state of the roads, he collected me three days ago from Emilie's house, Himmelstalund, as he said he would. For this, I am grateful. We endured an uncomfortable and dangerous journey, fourteen unbroken hours of driving, because lodging overnight at an inn was too risky. Someone could have recognized me, even as large and misshapen as I am. Still, driving through the dark, frigid night was terrifying. More than once, Papa's driver had to urge the horses forward to avoid a pack of wolves.

Leaving Emilie was unspeakably sad, and someday I hope to repay her for her kindness. When this is over, I must apologize to her, for I did not bear the trials of my condition cheerfully, but she never scolded me. I pray she finds peace. Papa arranged for the king to sign her divorce proclamation last month, but she is inconsolable. Despite professing her disdain for Clairfelt, she speaks of him endlessly and cries through the night. I asked her to come visit Stockholm soon, but she shook her head.

My absence during the winter social season, I fear, cannot have gone unnoticed. In our circles, no eighteen-year-old countess would choose to forgo the balls, the opera, the intimate dinners at the palace, the opportunity to meet one's mate. I wonder whether people are talking about me, whether rumors are spreading in Stockholm Palace.

Outside my window, hooves clop on the pavement. Buckets of water are set down with a metallic slap, men whistle to summon the drivers. I miss the quiet of my large suite of rooms across the courtyard on the fifth floor. The carriage house where I am staying, which once accommodated the kitchen maids, has been decorated in blue, my favorite color, and a few of my things are here. Someone left a stack of shapeless gowns with a note telling Brita to wear them, presumably to cast suspicion on her should there be talk of a pregnant woman living in these quarters.

I burn to speak to my mother, to ask her the questions that plague me at night. Aunt Emilie ventured no answers, and I was reluctant to embarrass Papa by asking him. So, I am alone with my slow, plodding thoughts, immersed in the sadness of what is and has been, unable to contemplate what could be. And although it is almost two weeks early for the birth, I feel swollen and push my food from one side of the plate to the other, hoping that I will fall ill and die. I have not seen Oscar for almost seven months. Now, all I can do is avoid thinking about which day God has chosen for me and whether our baby and I will survive.

Today is Wednesday, washing day at Douglas House, and I wake to the sounds of the laundry maids laughing. My curtains are drawn, as always, but Brita has been outdoors and tells me the weather is fine. "It is the false spring of Stockholm," I say. She spins to face me, most likely frustrated with my perpetual crossness of late. Just as I am about to apologize, something tightens deep inside me. My spine draws forward and I seek protection, one hand under my belly and the other reaching for Brita. I tell myself it cannot be my womb; it is still a week early.

"Don't go near the window," she says and leads me to a chair. "Did you feel something?"

I nod and take a deep breath. "It passed," I tell her. "It was so strange."

"Sit there, and do not move while I go to the house."

Unlike me, Brita moves freely around the main house and courtyard. Papa told the household staff that he brought her back from Himmelstalund to help with the spring cleaning, and she would be staying in the carriage house until my return. According to Brita, this explanation was embraced with enthusiasm by the other servants, especially Sophie, who had no desire to see her nemesis enjoying the comforts of my large and airy bedchamber in my supposed absence.

The door from the courtyard slams, and I hear my mother's voice on the stairs. I go to her, and she rocks me like a baby. Filled with emotion after being apart for so long, I sob against her thin shoulders, and my knees go weak. The little clenching pain seizes me for a second time.

"Has it returned?" she asks.

"I think so," I answer. "Mama, help. I don't want to die, and I'm afraid."

She takes off her gloves, turns to Brita, and says, "Go find the midwife, and if she tells you she is busy, remind her that Chancellor Wetterstedt paid her enough to buy brandy for a month."

Brita, usually so bold, fusses with the buttons on her cloak and declares that she is nervous. Aurora fastens them herself, and I see Brita's hands shaking as she puts on her boots.

"Go quickly, Brita, and if the midwife is not in her apartment, look for her book of accounts. I don't care if you must climb into the window. Visit every woman who has paid her since Christmas and figure out who she is attending. Bring her to me. Wetterstedt will send someone else to help the other women."

Brita says, "But it is early for a first child—"

Aurora cuts her off. "The child must live. So must my daughter."

I sense she wants us alive to use us, not love us, and I lie back, waiting for the next spasm of pain.

⁂

My daughter is here, a bit small, perhaps a week early, and I am alive. In fact, Barnmorska Ekebom, the most discreet and trusted midwife in the capital, said I performed admirably for a first-time mother with hip bones set tight. My success makes me proud, although I find it troubling that after the baby came, Aurora kept asking the midwife whether I was damaged. When the old woman replied with a question—"What woman, my good baroness, has not been damaged by a man?"—my mother's patience gave way. In a haughty voice, she demanded to know whether the midwife had allowed me to tear. Alarmed, I reached under the covers to touch the place between my legs but felt only layers of damp cloths and numbness.

Barnmorska Ekebom said no, the skin did not tear, and I heard my mother mutter, "We shall count our blessings that she is not ruined for him."

I do not know whether she was speaking of my possible future husband or of Oscar.

Aurora coos to the baby as she carries her to the wet nurse, who is waiting in a chair. As she passes my bed, she pats me on the cheek with a triumphant nod and a smile that seems genuine. My daughter is her first grandchild, and the De Geer family, unlike many others, prizes its female babies, perhaps more than its males. I share in her pleasure and wonder why she does not give me the little one when I reach out my arms, although I know the baby must go to her new home with Countess Meijerfelt soon. I tell myself I am fortunate that she will be raised in a noblewoman's household, that things could be so much worse.

The midwife departs, promising to return in the morning. Without asking my opinion, Aurora announces that my daughter's name will be Oscara. It will protect her, she says. And us.

I decide to call her Cara.

⁂

After three days, it is determined that I am strong enough to move into the big house. Even this is handled in secret. A hired carriage waits for me behind the back wall of the courtyard, near the old bridge to Fredrikshov. Brita, who has already loaded my possessions, sneaks me out of the gate and holds my hand as I get in. Emilie's maid, who appeared in Stockholm without warning, sits next to me in the carriage. She explains the charade, which my mother has gone to great lengths to plan. We will drive around the King's Garden, and when we return, I am to say I have been at Emilie's house recovering from an illness. The need to deceive people saddens me.

Once it is over, I go to my room and sleep until dawn, when I wake to voices outside my door. Wetterstedt must have returned from the palace.

He sounds anxious. "My dear," he says to my mother, "I cannot tell you why. All I know is that Countess Meijerfelt paid me a visit in the queen's salon last evening and told me our plan must wait for a couple of weeks."

"How is the crown prince's mood?" Aurora asks. She sounds wary.

"In a tirade since late afternoon."

"I told you he would hear about the baby from his spies."

"His agitation may have nothing to do with us."

"What else could it be?"

Wetterstedt says, "Otto Natt och Dag has joined Gustav's household in Germany and declared his allegiance. He is calling for Charles Jean to be assassinated. Oscar, too. We got word of this yesterday, and you can imagine how Charles Jean took the news."

"How can we keep the baby here any longer? What if someone sees her? There is talk about Jacquette and Oscar, you know. And the crown prince is not deaf." Aurora's voice is shrill.

"It is only two weeks," Papa says.

To me, two weeks is like a gift of immortality. Fourteen precious days, maybe more. I vow that I will see Cara again before they have passed, although that, Aurora tells me, is strictly forbidden.

CHAPTER TWENTY-THREE

Douglas House, Stockholm
April 1816

Days go by, and no one takes Cara to Countess Meijerfelt's house. One moment, I hope she will be claimed; the next, I fear it. Something has gone wrong, the dread inside me screams.

As I am now deemed fit to be seen in public, I walk in the courtyard and look up at Cara's window and even venture across the King's Garden to Drottninggatan, where I keep watch on the old countess's town house. After an hour in the cold sun, Brita pulls on my sleeve and urges me to return home, lest we arouse suspicion by missing the midday meal.

When Aurora praises my harp playing, I inquire about why Countess Meijerfelt asked Papa to keep Cara for these additional weeks. She refuses to tell me anything, and I receive a sharp rebuke for eavesdropping. It seems I am not to know such things, although they concern my daughter, whom I carried inside me and delivered onto this earth. I do not dare to ask to see her before Aurora sends her away. I know what the answer will be.

In my solitary hours, of which there are many, I sketch baby girls with thin, straight noses, slim cheeks, and wide-set brown eyes. They all look like Oscar.

At Easter, Aurora sends Nils and August, both now studying in Uppsala, to visit our father in the north. She hates to grant Father any small accommodation but says the boys must be shielded from the grim truth of my situation. Knowledge, she explains, gives other people power over you. She does not want my recklessness to weigh on my brothers, she says, adding that they have already suffered enough. I choke back the angry words that come to my lips. I want to tell her she is the true cause of their pain, that giving them up to preserve her share of Finspång was far worse than anything I have done. Mine was an act of love, hers one of greed.

But am I not making a similar choice in giving up my own child? The word "choice" rings hollow, for I've never had the luxury of choosing.

At dinner on Easter Sunday, tears stream down my face, and Christine holds my hand under the table. Aching to know where Oscar is and with whom he is celebrating, I go to my room before coffee is served. There, I gather up my sketches, all the brown-eyed babies, and cross the floor to the tile stove, which is still lit every night to fight the early spring chill. It is so easy to open the little trapdoor and burn them.

A person with a secret as terrible as mine is not entitled to record it.

As I watch the drawings crackle and their edges furl in a feral glow, I stifle a hope that has been growing inside me, a faint and flickering dream that Aurora and Papa Wetterstedt will allow Cara to stay here at Douglas House. Brita warns that I must not indulge in fantasies. I would like to do as she says and refuse to hope, but I cannot.

Each day, while my mother is out visiting, I walk to the rear of the upstairs hall and look through the window. The curtains of Cara's hiding place are drawn, and I never see anyone coming and going. Brita says that there is no need for comings and goings as the baby has a full staff, including a nanny, a wet nurse, and a maid. "As if she were a princess or some sort of royalty," Brita says with a smirk.

I cry, as I do most days, and Brita seems truly sorry.

Aurora, who cannot understand my melancholy, tells me I must lace up my boots and walk along the lake, go out in society, even attend a play at the Arsenal. She summons the brilliant and kindly Dr. Pontin to visit me, and he tells me that my body will heal; it is young, it is strong. He looks sad when I place my hand over my heart, but he does not address the thorny topic of my heartbreak. I wonder whether he has guessed the father's name, then chastise myself for thinking a man like him would allow himself to speculate. Pontin, as the king's doctor, will protect Oscar at all costs.

Just before he departs, he grips my hands. "I have known you since you were a baby, Jacquette, so I beg your leave to speak freely."

"But of course," I say.

"Do not let them do to you what they did to Emilie. People in the great world will invite you into their circle. You are beautiful—you have that spark they are chasing. Refuse them and I predict you won't regret it."

I nod and tell him what I have been yearning to say. "Dr. Pontin, they have not allowed me to hold her."

He does not answer, but as he leaves the room, he pulls a handkerchief out of his jacket pocket and wipes the corners of his eyes. He turns and looks back at me.

"The prince is in residence at Stockholm Palace now," he says.

Overcome with relief, I nod my thanks, my eyes burning with tears.

"He and the crown prince will attend General Adlercreutz's memorial service on the eighteenth, but they are planning another trip to Norway soon after that. They will not return until the Norwegian Parliament closes."

I must see Oscar before he leaves, whatever the cost.

⁂

The plan has been delayed again, it seems. On the twentieth morning after Cara's birth, I sit at my dressing table fretting about whether Countess Meijerfelt took her away last night. I wait for Brita to gather my hairbrushes and combs, and when she takes her place behind me, I meet her eyes in the mirror and ask the question I pose every day. Her answer is the same. My baby is still in the carriage house. She is not yet gone.

"We must do it today," I say.

She nods, and I wonder whether it is fear that causes her to drop the brushes as she pins up my hair.

When the house is finally empty, Brita comes into my room wearing her walking cape. She looks at my hands, which are shaking, and I draw them into my sleeves.

"Hurry, it is time," I say.

"You should see the pamphlets Peter gave me. The things the Gustavians are bringing him to print! You'll get to hold your baby today; I'll vouch for it," Brita says.

It was my idea to ask Peter to help me. My plan is a simple one, but I know a thousand things could go wrong. "Do you think the maids will leave Cara alone with you?" I ask Brita.

"They won't be able to resist. Here, look at this one." She removes a pamphlet from inside her cloak and unfolds it. It is a printed sketch, a cruel, lewd lampoon showing Charles Jean and Marianne eating in bed while Magnus sits in a chair writing correspondence. The caption reads: *Make Gustav V Sweden's next king.*

"Mother of God," I say.

"I know. And this is only one of them." Brita hurries to return the pamphlet to its hiding place.

The servants minding Cara have been confined in the carriage house for weeks. When Brita tells them a boy just left a stack of leaflets under a rock in Blasieholm Square, they will jump at her offer to watch the baby, anxious to learn the latest gossip. They will go to the square, never seeing me run across the courtyard and into the carriage house to meet my daughter.

Brita tells me to hurry, and I mount the carriage house stairs two at a time. The room where I spent my confinement has been cleansed of the detritus of birth. One wall now features portraits of Charles Jean and his wife, Désirée, and a golden baby cradle sits in a corner. Fine, fluffy white blankets of the softest French merino spill over its sides. Brita was correct: Aurora has overlooked no detail in arranging Cara's care, except that she needs a mother. I hold the door frame and take a deep breath before I look at her. I want to remember it all, for I do not know what is to come.

Brita rocks the cradle and speaks to me in her softest voice. "Go ahead. Pick her up."

Cara, who is swaddled up to her chin, peers at me with wizened eyes. Her face is round and sweet, more dainty by far than my crude sketches.

"Her eyes are blue like mine," I say, surprised. I had expected to see large brown ones like Oscar's.

"You cannot tell what color they will be," Brita says. "Elin's eyes changed."

"She's beautiful this way."

Someone or something is whistling from outside.

"We do not have so much time." Brita has reverted to speaking in her country accent, and I can tell how apprehensive she is.

I step closer to the cradle, which rocks gently on its stand when I touch it. Brita holds it steady, and I slide my fingers under my tiny girl.

"One hand under the neck. She is not yet strong," Brita says.

I draw away, afraid I do not know how to hold her. "What if I drop her?" I ask.

"Here," she says, and scoops Cara into her arms.

"*Min fina lilla flicka*," I whisper.

My beautiful baby girl.

Brita and I stand face-to-face, and together, we hold Cara close. I drink in the scent of talc and lavender. Her eyes are clear and alert; to them, I am the world, and I am certain she knows I am her mother.

My body knows, too. It responds to her within seconds, struck like a lightning conductor atop a burning house. I pull Cara to my breast, and she follows her instinct, nuzzling for my nipple through my thin cotton bodice. The feeling is glorious.

Brita holds out her arms. "Oh, I have really shit in the blue cupboard now. Give her back to me."

"What do you mean?"

"Your milk still might come in if you let her do that. Your mother would kill me."

"Won't it just dry up?" I ask. Every cell in my body wants her back.

"Your bosom will never be the same. Now, give her a kiss." Brita takes her from me and unwraps the swaddling.

My daughter is wearing a lace-trimmed white shift with a small nameplate pinned to it. *Oscara,* it says. I kiss her face, her hands, her toes. Brita pushes me toward the door.

I pass the bureau, where I see two letters. The longer one is written in fancy script:

> *Highborn Countess Meijerfelt, with hope in God and your well-known kindness, venerable lady, Oscara lifts her hands to the ruler of the world and the one who resembles him in all things and calls for protection. Her mother is from a good family plunged into misery by this accident.*
>
> *Mercy, mercy on them both.*

The shorter note reads, *She eats best with a spoon.*

"A spoon?" I ask.

Brita points to a small cabinet, which has an assortment of pewter items on top. "A pap boat, like one of those. It is like a little ladle, and you pour the milk from it into the baby's mouth. You wouldn't use it if she were nursing well."

"Will she be all right?"

"She will. She will be a fine, strong girl." Brita strokes my cheek.

My fear grows that today will be the last time I ever see her.

"Do you know who wrote them?" I ask, pointing to the notes.

Brita's eyes widen, and a furrow appears between her brows. "I'll wager it was the wet nurse who wrote the one about the spoon. But the letter is Sophie's writing. I would know it anywhere."

I look again at the longer note, and suddenly, it appears familiar. The writing matches two others I have seen before—the note that threatened the life of Dorothea's father, the foreign minister, and the one my father's mistress showed me when she introduced me to their son.

Does my mother know more than she has told me? The delay in Cara's departure for Countess Meijerfelt's house, the nameplate she is wearing, the notes on the dresser—none of it makes any sense. Why would a letter begging for Countess Meijerfelt's help be necessary if the arrangements for Cara's care had been settled in advance?

The fact that Sophie is involved makes me even more suspicious.

CHAPTER TWENTY-FOUR

Stockholm
April 18, 1816

My reentry into society takes place on a balcony high above Drottninggatan, in an apartment my mother has rented to host a party for the ladies of the *beau monde*. The occasion is the one Dr. Pontin told me about, a memorial procession for General Adlercreutz, a one-time traitor who betrayed the exiled royal family but later found favor with Charles Jean. From my seat near the balustrade, I hear trumpets blaring in the distance, and Charles Jean turns the corner on his white horse. Ignoring Aurora's chattering guests, who have been pestering me with intrusive questions, I lean over the railing to catch a glimpse of Oscar. He stopped some distance behind his father and dismounted Odin, and he is now speaking with a man in a military uniform.

I want to talk to him, to hear his laugh. Most of all, I want to tell him about Cara.

As he walks back to Odin through the sea of dignitaries, he seems different, comfortable playing the role of a prince. The change in him shakes me to my core.

Brita appears on the balcony holding a silver tray filled with glasses. She hands one to me and says, "Have some of this." Her lip quivers as she steadies the tray, and I know something is wrong. She calls to another maid, who relieves her of the refreshments, and she kneels next to my chair.

"Tell me," I say and gulp the brandy, wincing at the woody, medicinal smell of the stuff.

She strokes my shoulder with her rough, wind-chafed hands. "After you and your mother left this morning, I checked the carriage house. No one was there. They must have come and taken the baby during the night."

I am not prepared for the crushing weight on my chest, though I have known for months this would happen and have even persuaded myself that the countess's home is the best place for Cara.

Brita's eyes are grave. "At least you got to hold her once."

My arms come together as if they're cradling my baby's warm body. I still remember how the tiny, solid bundle felt against my chest. Tears spring to my eyes because I know that this, like all memories, will fade over time from a palpable form to a still image, then to nothing.

Brita taps my arm, asks whether I feel ill.

I must know more, so I ask, "Is she well? Have you spoken to Countess Meijerfelt's maids? Was the countess's household ready to receive her?" I try to control my voice, which is rising with panic.

"I tried."

Countess Meijerfelt has at least a dozen servants, and Brita is a regular visitor in their kitchens, her friendships cemented by her frequent gifts of pastry. I cannot imagine them refusing to receive her.

"What do you mean, you tried? You did not speak to anyone?"

With a helpless slump, Brita looks down the street at Countess Meijerfelt's dark house. It is shuttered, and the oil lamp next to the door still burns.

"Jacquette," Brita says, "Cara isn't at Countess Meijerfelt's."

I stare, waiting for her to correct this outrageous lie. She does not.

"She must be there. You said you did not even speak to the maids, so how can you say such a thing? You cannot know."

"Peter told me."

My words die in my throat when I hear Peter's name. He always seems to have access to every whisper in Stockholm, and I have never had reason to doubt his information.

"What did he tell you?"

"That she was found on Countess Meijerfelt's doorstep this morning when the staff opened the house. In her basket, with the name badge, the letter Sophie wrote, and her blanket."

"It was so cold this morning. There was frost on my window." I cannot contain my anguish at hearing that my baby was left to freeze on a doorstep, and my garbled sob draws the unwanted attention of my mother, who is boasting to some baronesses about her party's success. Our eyes meet across the balcony amid the roar of cannons, which are being fired in honor of the dead traitor.

She weaves through the women on the crowded balcony until she stands behind my chair. "After the party, please unpack all of Jacquette's ball gowns, Brita," she says.

"Am I going somewhere?" I say, confused.

Aurora barks at me. "Ambassador Moreno has invited you to a dinner party next week, and I responded that you will be delighted to attend." She points at my glass. "And now you are drinking brandy? You will ruin your health." She shakes her head and returns to the other end of the balcony.

Brita takes my arm. "Peter told me the governor of Stockholm went there this morning. Without his clerks."

"Why would he visit Countess Meijerfelt?" I ask.

"Well, I am no authority, but Peter says the governor is the only one authorized to sign an abandoned baby over to Allmänna Barnhuset."

I brace my hand on the balcony railing and whimper, "No, no."

My mother tells her friends I need rest, and I hear murmurs about my recent illness. Erica holds her hands in a large semicircle in front of her abdomen and shakes her head, and the Chatterati laugh. I ignore this, for I have more important worries. I try not to jump to conclusions, as I so often do, but I cannot quiet my suspicions about my mother's involvement. Does she know where Cara is? Is Aurora behind the whole plan? Would she condemn her own granddaughter, her most valuable asset, to that awful place?

For Allmänna Barnhuset, the public orphanage, is an infamous haven for every plague and malady imaginable. If Cara is there, it is a death sentence.

CHAPTER TWENTY-FIVE

Residence of the Spanish Ambassador, Stockholm
April 25, 1816

At Ambassador Moreno's party, men in livery are serving dinner in the large dining room where I am seated between two brothers, both members of the tsar's legation in Stockholm. One is coughing and swatting away the thick smoke of the tallow candles, and the other is staring at my bosom. Both speak incomprehensible Russian-accented French.

The doors open, and from the entry hall, I hear boots scuffling and the clatter of long swords. The conversation around me ceases and every guest rises, thick chair legs raking against the ancient wood floor. I place my goblet on the table and stand like the rest. Someone from the palace has arrived, and I am praying it is Oscar. He is the only one who can help me get Cara out of that place, for my mother and Wetterstedt say they are powerless and know nothing.

The anticipation in the room subsides as quickly as it grew. Without a shout of greeting or even the usual toasts, everyone sits down. Turning toward the door, I see it is only Frederik and another cavalier, Johan, who have arrived. Oscar is not with them.

As the two cavaliers walk behind me to their seats, I am deep in conversation with the Russian brother who seems less interested in my breasts and more interested in my mind. He's heard talk about the foundling abandoned in Countess Meijerfelt's doorway and wants the latest gossip. To hide my reaction from the Russian, I turn my head just as the hilt of Frederik's sword passes my ear. My eyes meet Frederik's as Johan says, "I fancied the girl, I'll admit as much, but I'm not stupid enough to think I can compete with Prince Oscar. But tell me, does he intend to take all the actresses for himself—"

Frederik cuts Johan off mid-sentence. "Idiot," he growls. "Now you have done it."

With a stern look at his indiscreet friend, he bows to me. "Countess, what a pleasure. I had not expected to see you. You are restored to good health, I trust?"

Frederik will make a good diplomat someday, I think. *He recovers so quickly.*

I try to hide my shock, telling myself I do not know Oscar anymore—what he thinks, what he has been doing, who he is with. Eight months of silence now separate us. I assure Frederik that I am well and strong, resolving to ask him my questions later.

The footmen serve a trio of delicacies prepared by Moreno's Spanish chef. As I eat, I ponder Johan's meaning, although it seems perfectly clear. I glare at Frederik, who looks alarmed when I leave my table to speak to the dance master. I insist on a waltz with Count Frederik Due, preferably the first.

When we take the floor to dance, Frederik seems uncomfortable as he wraps his arm around my waist. I pull him even closer and whisper into his ear. The room is watching us, and I hear people questioning my long absence, saying I do not look ill. I am not deaf to their implication.

"Where is the prince? Is he coming?" I ask Frederik.

He shakes his head. "The palace is in an uproar over the Gustavians, and the crown prince called a meeting. He hardly ever asks Oscar to attend these things, but he did tonight. Quette, I am sorry about what Johan said. He's a drunken fool."

I know when Frederik is being evasive, and I refuse to accept his excuses. "Tell me exactly what he meant. I insist."

"It was nothing of importance."

I use the only ammunition I have.

"It would be a shame if your father learned that you have been playing cards at Sällskapet until dawn and losing, would it not?" I ask.

Frederik frowns. "How can you know about that?"

"My mother's brother, Jacques, talks too much when he drinks," I say, squeezing Frederik's hand as we twirl around to the music. "But I thought you were my friend, Frederik, and my friends' secrets are always safe with me."

"As are yours," he says. "And I *am* your friend."

"I heard most of what Johan said."

"You will hate me if I tell you the rest."

"I won't."

He raises his brow and begins. "While you were indisposed—"

"Ill," I say. "I was ill."

"As you wish. After you left Stockholm, Charles Jean began insisting that Oscar dine with him every night. I accompany the prince some evenings, and Johan takes the rest."

"What about Carl?" I ask.

"He left in January and won't be back until next year. Oscar gave him leave to join his regiment."

"What happens at these dinners?"

"Every night, Charles Jean implores Oscar to choose a wife. The prince has not taken his father's entreaties well, if I may say so."

Swaying on my feet, I swallow hard and demand, "The actress. Tell me about her."

"Never mind her, she's an *actress*, for God's sake. Jacquette, are you well? I know you have been through a lot."

So, it is true, and so predictable. The arenas of theater, music, and art are places Oscar prefers to halls of state. They are escapes from the burdens of his position, doors his father would never enter. He has someone else at the Arsenal Theater, I am convinced of it.

He was to be the one to share my secrets, but he has abandoned me.

Before the waltz is over, I break away from Frederik's grasp and run back to Douglas House through Blasieholm Square.

Papa Wetterstedt's tall black hat is hanging from its hook outside our apartment. I edge the door open, using my weight to push it against its hinges so that it will not creak. From behind the closed doors of the blue sitting room, I hear their voices. Papa's, as always, is soft and measured, but my mother's is piercing.

I hear my name, burst into the salon, and slam the door behind me. I want them to notice me and to listen.

Wetterstedt is sitting on a wooden stool next to my mother's big chair, fingering a glass of brandy. *Odd*, I think. *He so rarely drinks anything stronger than red Bordeaux.* Holding the heavy glass tumbler between his hands, he leans forward with his elbows resting on his knees.

"My dear," he says to me, staring into the amber liquor as if he'd expected my arrival.

The instant he speaks, Aurora turns and attacks me. "What are you doing here? You should still be at Ambassador Moreno's."

I want nothing more than to beat my fists against her chest and scream, but I restrain my anger enough to ask, "How could you send me there, among all those people from court? Everyone was talking about the foundling who was sent to the orphanage. Even the men. What have you done?"

She places her hand on her heart. "Can you really think so little of me? I may not want the world to find out about your baby, but that does not mean that I wish her dead. If your grandmother knew she'd gone to the orphanage, she would strike me down from the grave."

"You must have known," I say, turning to Wetterstedt and hoping for an honest explanation.

He sets his round-bottomed glass on a side table where it wobbles a bit until it finds its balance. When he runs his hands down the sides of his face, I see distress there, as plain as it was on the day when he told us that Charles Jean had declared war against Bonaparte. Always the peacemaker, he offers me his hands, and I pull mine away.

"My dear girl, your mother and I are your most true allies—I can assure you of that."

As allies are the principal advantage I lack, I cannot help but lash out at him. "You let the baby be taken to the *barnhuset*! What did Charles Jean promise you? That you will become foreign minister? Or be raised to a count?" As I speak, my voice falls to a weak murmur. Already, I am ashamed of what I have said. He has already denied knowing that Cara would be taken to the orphanage, and Wetterstedt never lies.

I think of Aunt Emilie, who always tells me Wetterstedt is the least of my oppressors and should be spared the weight of my punishment.

"Gustave, talk some sense into the girl," says Aurora.

Without a hint of rancor despite my harsh words, he says, "If you will only hear me out, I'll tell you everything I know." He loosens the knot of his cravat. "First, let me assure you again that your mother and I did not know that she—your baby—would be sent to Allmänna Barnhuset."

"Cara," I say. "I call her Cara."

My mother, who has been reclining in her chair, sits upright to address me. "To you, from this day forward, that baby has no name. You shall not speak of her. What would be her worth if people learned she is your daughter?"

"If she could only live at Finspång with Mamsell and the *oäkta barn*," I say. "No one would know."

Aurora shakes her head. "Someone would make the connection. You saw the baby."

I take a sharp breath, cursing her for knowing my every move. "You found out that I went to her? How?"

"Never mind that."

As pursuing this would be useless, I try again. "No one would connect her to Oscar."

"With that tawny skin? That dark hair? She looks like a Bernadotte. A secret like her has no power once it is revealed."

"You will not even try to help?" I ask her, near tears.

Her voice softens, and I realize she is not completely without a heart. She asks, "Do you believe it so easy? This may be beyond your comprehension, but there are consequences to what you have done, and not just for you. What about your papa and your brothers? Even your father?"

Her rare mention of my natural father, and particularly the show of concern for the man, leaves me speechless. It occurs to me, for the first time, that she is afraid.

"Aurora," Wetterstedt interjects, "just let me explain to Quette what I know. In my experience, that is the best place to begin."

She shrugs. He turns to me.

"At Adlercreutz's procession, I asked Magnus about the foundling and why she had been taken from Countess Meijerfelt. He didn't give me a reason, and I was in no position to demand one. He snapped at me, said Allmänna Barnhuset was good enough. I was stunned. At that point, I couldn't be sure how much he and Charles Jean knew about the baby or about you and the prince. But I assure you, I knew nothing of the plan to take her to the orphanage, and I could not have prevented it," he says. "I know a little more now."

I sink into a nearby chair, staring at him. "Did the crown prince send her to the orphanage, then? Was it him?"

"I don't know," Wetterstedt says. "Last Friday morning, the day after the poor child entered the *barnhus*, I went to Charles Jean's rooms, as is my custom. I was determined to find out what was going on. He was closeted with Oscar and Magnus. Ordinarily, I would have been shown in. I wasn't, so I grew a bit wary."

"Did you speak to Oscar?" I ask.

Wetterstedt shrugs. "I saw him, but we didn't speak. After I'd waited for ten or fifteen minutes, the door to Charles Jean's bedchamber opened, and Oscar came out. He was not himself. Usually, he will stop and joke with me about his father for a few moments, but not that day. He seemed in low spirits, quite pale and dressed all in black, without any of his regalia or even a sash. He told Frederik to open the brandy table to everyone, even the guards. I must admit I suspect the prince had already been drinking. On the way out, he said something about the orphanage. In language he rarely utters."

"So, Oscar knew about the orphanage?"

Wetterstedt nods. "I don't know when he found out. She had already been there overnight when I heard him say that."

Oscar could have sent a note or called on me. He found out at least six days ago, and he should have done something.

"Did Charles Jean receive you after they left?" I ask.

Wetterstedt sighs. "Yes, and when I inquired about the foundling, he spoke of her like she was any one of a thousand other problems in the city. Not like a man speaking of his granddaughter. He was livid about some Gustavian pamphlets. Apparently, there are sketches of an abandoned baby labeled *Stockholm's Moral Decay under the Frenchman's Rule*. Charles Jean told me Magnus would be handling the issue of the foundling from now on, and he no longer needed my help. He knew Cara was in the orphanage, but I do not know whether he sent her there, or when he found out about it. I'm sorry, Jacquette. I didn't want to upset you. You have endured so much."

"Papa," I say, "I cannot live knowing she is in that place."

My mother's hand reaches over the arm of her chair until it rests on Wetterstedt's thigh. "Gustave, speak to the crown prince, please. I will not have Magnus Brahe deciding what happens to that baby. After all, *oäkta* or not, she is a De Geer and of royal blood. Families have made their fortunes on the wings of such children. Look at Carl Löwenhielm's uncle, what favor he brought to that family."

Papa says, "You must let me do it my own way, Aurora. It may take time."

I mumble, "I am sorry I have caused you such trouble."

Papa asks, "Jacquette, might I suggest you find out what the prince knows?"

I say, "Oscar is the last person I wish to see."

Together, my mother and Wetterstedt say, "What?" Wetterstedt adds, "Have you talked to him?"

I toss my head. "He has been busy, I hear, with one of the actresses at the Arsenal Theater. That is the reason I left Moreno's party. I could not endure the talk."

If Oscar loved me, he would have done something—anything—to get our baby out of that place, but he let it happen. It is unforgivable.

I say, "I do not wish to have anything to do with Prince Oscar. Not ever. And I am going to tell him that the next time I see him."

My mother's eyes open wide, and she looks at me as if I am mad. She raises her arm, seemingly about to slap me in the face, and then drops it limp against her side.

"You will do nothing of the sort, Jacquette. You got yourself into this, and in it, you will stay. Everything that has been given to us can be taken away."

Her words are true. The De Geer title, the land, the iron mines—all of it can be taken from us. When people break rules, as Aurora always says, fortunes disappear, monarchies fall, lives are lost.

"I mean it, Jacquette. Make him want you," Aurora says.

"I will do no such thing."

"That is what we De Geer women do best."

Wetterstedt, looking distraught, says, "Aurora, perhaps it is not so dire as that." He turns to me. "Jacquette, give me time. I will find a way."

But time is something I do not have, and as much as I wish to obey him, I cannot. Every day that Cara spends in the orphanage brings her one day closer to death.

A commotion erupts in the hall, footmen shouting for the butler, who undoubtedly has retired for the night. Then I hear Oscar.

"She will receive me." His voice is firm, that of a person accustomed to others doing as he asks.

Oscar enters the room, dressed as Wetterstedt described, in black from his hat to his boots. His medals are nowhere to be found, and there is not even a hint of his usual white cravat peeking from the neck of his high collar. His hair is tucked into a hat I have never seen him wear. This is a disguise, I decide, one he wears when he visits his actress at the theater.

My mother curtsies. Wetterstedt nods, and I simply stare. Oscar waves a hand as if he were impatient with the formalities and addresses Wetterstedt. His words come quickly, and he lapses into French.

"*Mes plus sincères excuses*, Chancellor, for the intrusion. Baroness, *je suis désolé*."

Wetterstedt says, "Think nothing of it, son. You must treat our home as your own." He takes my mother's hand in his and leads her out of the room, but when she looks back at me, I can see unspoken words on her lips. Then, after a gentle tug from Wetterstedt, she is gone, her advice lost forever.

Looking into Oscar's eyes is too dangerous, a risk I must not take. My hair is down, and I toss it behind one shoulder, sensing he is watching.

"Has the show at the Arsenal run late?" I ask him. There is a hard edge to my voice.

As I intend, my question throws him off guard, and he draws back and frowns. "What do you mean by that?"

"Never mind. It does not matter." I am certain he understands that I am speaking about the actress. He bites his lower lip, and his earlier hubris dissolves.

"Frederik came back from Moreno's and told me you misunderstood something Johan said." He stumbles over the words.

"And you rode all the way to Blasieholmen to straighten me out? Or did you have other business on this side of the bridge?"

I hear him exhale. "Forget about her. She never meant anything, and it is over, in any case."

Is he so isolated, so surrounded by sycophants, that he believes I will accept this?

"Perhaps I could overlook your philandering, but, Oscar, I have not had a word from you since I told you I was to have a child. *We* were to have a child, I mean."

"I couldn't come to you, Q."

"Don't call me that."

When I look at him, his jaw is set, and his eyes are flashing in anger. "All right, then, *Countess*. Just hear me out, and I will leave. I knew nothing about the orphanage until she was already there."

"That was last week. And you must have known something before they took her there."

"I admit I knew she would not be able to live at Countess Meijerfelt's house. That is all. But my father—"

"So, your father knows about us?"

He nods. "That is what I am trying to say."

"And he knows the baby is ours?" This is my deepest fear.

"Yes."

"How did he find out?"

"His spies, I believe. Or perhaps it was Magnus," he says.

"I see you know she is a girl."

He nods.

"And her name? Do you know it?"

He nods again. "Oscara."

A sob escapes from my throat, and I cling to the back of the sofa to gain control. "She is so tiny and vulnerable, living at the *barnhus* while you play the Butterfly Game. How could you?"

He shakes his head and stands behind me, placing his hand over mine. "You have it wrong. Listen to me for a minute. I couldn't come to you or do anything—"

I interrupt him, furious, and without thinking, I turn to face him. "It doesn't matter what you knew or when you knew it. You did not even try to tell me."

Moving closer, he wraps his arm around my waist, and my heartbeat pounds in my temples. His voice rings soft in my ear. "We never could have stopped them. Didn't you tell me that when I was twelve years old? They have the upper hand, and for us, so much is inevitable. Let us take what little happiness we can. Let us survive."

I know he wants me, and I am drawn to his urgency. His lips are so near, his clean, citrusy scent so intoxicating. It would be easy to say this is our destiny, to disavow everything that drives us apart. To lie back on the sofa and allow him to bring me to fulfillment. It has been so long. As his hand moves down my back, and he pulls me against his hips, my eyes close, and I abandon myself to my craving.

About to crush myself against the hard length of him, I stop. If he cared about me, he would have prevented his father and Magnus from taking Cara. He would have told me.

I push him away and watch his face reveal his desire, his shock, his disbelief.

"Go ahead—play your games, bed your actresses. I will find Cara myself."

"Q. Jacquette. Listen to me," he says. His breathing is shallow and rapid, and he winces as he pulls at his black trousers.

"The last thing I should do is listen to you."

"What will you do?"

"I'll marry if I have to," I say. "As you say, that has always been in the cards. It is as inevitable for me as it is for you."

He goes pale, and I know I have made the correct decision. "Get out," I say.

There is a knock on the door, and Magnus enters the room. His face is taut with worry, but he need not fear that I will be the ruin of Charles Jean's precious prince. Silently, I vow to have nothing to do with Oscar; I vow to call on widows, read books, perhaps study my English, find a suitable husband. And I will search for Cara and bring her to Finspång, with or without Oscar's help. For I am a Countess Gyldenstolpe, and a De Geer on my mother's side, and I will not allow any of them to control me. Not Charles Jean. Not Magnus Brahe. Not Wetterstedt or my mother. And especially not Oscar.

Part Five

HAGA PAVILION

CHAPTER TWENTY-SIX

Haga Pavilion
Midsummer Eve, June 21, 1816

When Jacquette and Aurora arrive at the miniature lakeside palace, Queen Charlotte is perched on the edge of her silvery-blue velvet-curtained bed wearing a stiff gray gown and a warm printed shawl. Always tiny, the queen seems reduced, older and less venomous than when Jacquette last saw her. The queen brushes aside a gray ringlet, exposing her large, keen eyes, which are fixed on Aurora.

"You've brought me the young countess."

"As you asked." Aurora pulls Jacquette into the center of the room, squeezing her hand until it hurts.

Jacquette pastes a demure smile on her lips and curtsies. Aurora has told her nothing about the queen's request to see her, just as she has told her nothing more about Cara. In fairness, Aurora probably has nothing to tell, for news is scant. With Wetterstedt, Charles Jean, and Oscar away attending the Norwegian Parliament, Jacquette has listened in vain for any word of her daughter, ready to seize any opportunity to change the baby's woeful fate. The talk in the city is that the foundling remains at Allmänna Barnhuset, so Cara is alive, at least. And although nothing could interest Jacquette less than celebrating Midsummer Eve with the queen at Haga, she and Aurora will soon depart the capital until fall, so this may be her last opportunity to hear the court gossip. For a chance to learn even a sliver of information, she is willing to endure the Chatterati, to smile at the stoutest old count.

She is powerless and can do no more.

The queen strokes Jacquette's hair as if she is one of the palace lap dogs.

"Tell me, how is your health, Jacquette?"

"Much better, ma'am."

"Good, good. I was disappointed it prevented you from accepting my nomination last season. You look strong now." The queen narrows her eyes. Is she skeptical or merely squinting? Jacquette cannot be certain.

"The girl was terribly ill, Charlotte. Wetterstedt and I feared for her life." Aurora's fingers toy with the buttons on her glove.

The queen claps her hands. "And now she is recovered. Would you permit me a few moments of your daughter's company? This correspondence never ends." She points to a rosewood lap desk on the bed. Unfolded to double width, it is cluttered with quills, ink, miniature wooden boxes, and paper.

Clutching her satin reticule to her chest, Aurora backs out of the room. Jacquette senses her mother's disquiet. She is out of her element now, not in control of the situation she created.

Queen Charlotte circles her fingers around Jacquette's upper arm. "You are even more lovely than I remember. A little heavier, perhaps? The weight looks good on you."

"Thank you, ma'am," says Jacquette, uncertain whether the queen's flattery is a signal she knows about Cara.

"Keep yourself healthy this year. I intend to announce the Christmas List early, and you will be one of my new maids of honor."

"So gracious." A deep curtsy allows Jacquette to hide her dismay. As a maid of honor, she will be forced to live among the Chatterati at the palace and face Oscar's indifference every day.

"My dear, can I trouble you to take a little package and letter downstairs for me? A messenger awaits it." The queen removes a blue signet ring from a compartment inside the lap desk and holds it up to inspect it. Apparently satisfied, she slips it into one of the small wooden boxes and locks it inside.

The ring's design, the letter *G* and a Roman numeral five, is unfamiliar to Jacquette, unlike any of the royal seals she has seen.

"Of course I will deliver it, ma'am."

The queen hands the box to Jacquette with a folded letter that has a large wax seal. "I understand you know how to be discreet."

Jacquette nods, suspicious of the queen and her cryptic comments, and hurries out of the room.

At the front entry, without so much as a nod, the messenger takes the letter and the wooden box and buckles them inside a worn saddlebag. He pats his horse and speaks under his breath, probably not imagining that a young woman like Jacquette would be minded to listen.

"To Baden, then."

Baden is in the new German Confederation, home of the exiled Gustav. Hearing this, Jacquette understands the meaning of the ring the queen placed in the box. Its seal, GV, is the one the former crown prince would adopt if he ever became king. His father was the fourth Gustav. Only a Gustavian sympathizer would possess such a ring. It occurs to Jacquette that Charles Jean's suspicions about the queen may not be as far-fetched as Oscar believes.

If Aurora has taught Jacquette anything, it is that knowledge is currency. She files this away.

❧

She wanders through the dining room to the Hall of Mirrors, hoping to find Marianne. Outside the vast windows facing the lake, three women in plaid kerchiefs are washing the lower panes, which are splattered with spring mud. She cannot see Oscar's house at Bellevue but knows it is there, across the water. Empty.

Today the Hall of Mirrors contains a smattering of the queen's household—maids of honor, court mistresses, cavaliers. The young men are playing cards, and tobacco smoke hangs in the air. From the moment Jacquette enters the room, the Chatterati, who are gathered around the gambling tables, snicker and whisper behind their fans.

"If you are looking for Prince Oscar, he is in Norway. Strengthening the union, one countess at a time, I'll wager," Erica says. The others laugh.

Jacquette looks for a friendly face.

In a corner away from the windows, a scrawny, pale young woman dressed in black sits alone on a settee, reading a thick leather volume. It is Dorothea, Foreign Minister von Engeström's daughter, whom Jacquette has not seen in over a year. She looks up from her book and removes her round wire spectacles from the bridge of her nose, smiling. *She has been abroad with her mother and may not have heard the rumors,* thinks Jacquette.

"You are here. I understood you went away for a while, or that is what everyone says."

Jacquette sighs. If even a mouse like Dorothea knows, the situation is beyond repair. "Now where would I go? We drove up from Stockholm this morning."

"Don't worry about them. It is just talk," says Dorothea, looking at the Chatterati.

Erica and Hedda are staring at Jacquette, perhaps looking to find an extra half inch on her hips. She turns to the side and looks over her shoulder at them, confident that her belly is as flat as it was last Midsummer Day. They grimace and roll their eyes.

"Dorothea, I was looking for Marianne. Have you seen her?"

Dorothea lowers her voice. "She's been sent to Drottningholm. The queen is furious with her."

"What has she done now?"

"I thought Prince Oscar would have told you."

"Can we not talk about him? Tell me about Marianne," says Jacquette, becoming impatient.

Dorothea leans close. "Charles Jean suspects the queen of helping the Gustavians. The Mandarin have even interviewed her like she is a criminal."

"What does that have to do with Marianne?"

"Everything. The queen blames Marianne for putting the suspicions in Charles Jean's head. She's banished Marianne from Haga. And that is not all." Dorothea's still-peachy cheeks glow. She's not used to knowing the court gossip.

"What else?" Jacquette demands.

"To provoke Charles Jean, the queen sent a messenger to Paris to urge Crown Princess Désirée to move back to Sweden." Dorothea's eyes widen. "You can imagine what Marianne did when she heard. She has had him to herself all these years."

"Does Oscar know?" Jacquette had not intended to speak his name.

Dorothea nods. "He is taking the queen's side. He wants to see his mother, I suppose. But Charles Jean is doing everything possible to stop it. The prince didn't tell you? You were such good friends."

"Oscar and I have not spoken in ages."

"I see you still call him Oscar."

Adam Lewenhaupt's arrival relieves Jacquette of having to explain. His infectious smile is the same, but his fiery red curls have faded to a distinguished auburn. He is in the queen's service now, a newly appointed cavalier. He bows to Dorothea, then kisses Jacquette's hand.

"They do not pay junior lawyers enough to gamble with the queen's men," he jokes.

"Adam," says Jacquette, "it has been an age since—"

"You owe me a chess game, Jacquette," he says. "How about you, Dorothea? You can play me after I beat her."

"No. I'll see you both later. Stay friends, Adam. I think she needs one now."

The impudence of the bookish younger woman riles Jacquette, but she knows Dorothea is an ally at heart.

Adam leads Jacquette through the crowded room, nodding here and there, saying the right things to the right people. Selecting a table, he offers her a chair, sits down, and sets a marble chessboard between them.

"I'm sorry I missed your birthday last year. I couldn't get here, and we never got to have our rematch. Or our talk."

Her eighteenth birthday at Haga, now almost a year ago. Or a century. The gondolas. Bellevue. Oscar. She does not tell Adam she'd forgotten all about their plan to replay their game of chess that day. Nor does she tell him who made her forget.

Jacquette selects two pawns, one white and one black, and hides one in each fist. "Choose."

His eyes soften, and he extends his hand across the table to touch her bare elbow. "You."

"What?"

"I choose you. There, I've said it."

Her cheeks burn. Before Cara, she'd received compliments so naturally, and now they only raise a host of doubts. A tear runs down her cheek.

One at a time, Adam removes the pawns from her fists. He pushes the chessboard to one side and leans close to her, his forearms resting on the table. "Are you going to tell me what's wrong? You never could hide anything from me, you know."

"It's nothing," she says, intending not to tell him, but the words spill out anyway. "The queen is putting me on the Christmas List again."

"Court life is not for you, no matter what your mother thinks." He looks toward the Chatterati. "I could get you away from them and protect you with my life."

Could he be serious? She'd had a feeling Adam might declare himself but never imagined it would happen today.

"You wouldn't want me if you knew what Erica and Hedda are saying."

"I've heard. I don't care. I know a couple of counts have turned down Wetterstedt's invitations for their sons to court you."

"What?"

He reaches for her hand. "You didn't know. I'm sorry."

"I'm sure Wetterstedt didn't want me hurt." But she is. Before Oscar, any count in Sweden, and many elsewhere, would have welcomed her as a daughter-in-law.

Adam is direct, like a man with nothing to lose. "I would be a fool not to ask whether you feel anything for me. A year ago, your mother never would have allowed the match, but now? Just say the word and I'll speak to Wetterstedt."

Adam has analyzed this like a lawyer, and it makes her smile. Because she likes him, what she must say seems even harder.

"You are a good friend. The best of friends. But—"

"I knew you would say no." His lip curls, and he looks away.

"I'm sorry," she croaks.

He pushes his chair back from the table, reddening. "Is it because I'm not rich enough? Because I'm not a count? Or the real problem, because I'm not Prince Oscar?"

Her answer catches in her throat. She cannot encourage Adam because he loves her, always has, and her feelings for Oscar would destroy him. She shakes her head.

Adam leans toward her, and she sees Erica looking in their direction.

"Adam—"

"One day, you'll forget about the prince, and we could be happy. It's your move."

She suspects he is not talking about chess.

At that moment, a Life Guard hands Jacquette a letter. "Your morning mail, my lady," he says.

She thanks him and slides the letter into her pouch.

"Carl Löwenhielm writes to you?" asks Adam with a scowl. "That's his seal."

"Sometimes."

Adam looks up at the Life Guard. "Where is the courier? I have the queen's daily bundle for Stockholm."

The man seems overheated and exhausted. Moving on to the next table, he barks, "Did you not get word? The horses needed water, so he had to stop at the inn. We brought all our mail to him there. Could be gone already, for all I know."

With a frustrated sigh, Adam pushes back his chair and says to Jacquette, "I knew I was wasting my time, but I had to try. Just forget everything I said. I must take this down to the inn now." He picks up his leather bag and slings the strap over his shoulder.

"Be careful," Jacquette says. "It's so hot today."

He does not say goodbye.

She remains at the table, alone and unable to shake the feeling that something bad is going to happen. Through the window, she sees Adam riding along the lake toward the inn at full gallop.

⸙

From Carl's letter, she learns he will soon leave his regiment to rejoin Oscar's household. With Oscar and Carl so frequently at odds, she suspects the idea to bring him back to Stockholm was Charles Jean's. He asks her about vacant posts in Wetterstedt's office and complains about his father, as he always does. One thing stands out: There is no mention of her recent absence from society, not even an inquiry after her health. Carl may be the only person on earth who did not notice she disappeared for six months. And, unlike Adam, he isn't in love with her. Those two things weigh in his favor.

In a short, scrawled reply, she tells Carl she looks forward to seeing him again in the capital.

⸙

While folding Carl's letter, she hears a commotion on the swimming platform at Noah's Ark. Everyone runs outside, leaving the Hall of Mirrors almost empty. The card table next to her is in disarray, and a chair lies on its side. She turns to the window. One of the queen's small boats is tied to the dock, and the cavaliers and Life Guards are lifting something—no, *someone*—onto the wooden boards.

She runs outside to the platform and pushes to the center of the crowd, where a prone body, a man, lies on the deck. He is naked to the waist, his face bloated and blue, and blood is trickling from one of his ears.

It is Adam.

"Save him," she cries, to no one in particular.

A Life Guard leads her inside to a chair. On one knee, he explains that he and a fellow soldier rode with Adam on his return to Haga Pavilion. From the moment they left the inn, Adam seemed agitated, pushing his horse hard and refusing to rest. He insisted on stopping near Villa Frescati and dove into the cold, dark waters of Brunnsviken. When he did not surface for nearly a minute, the Life Guard plunged in after him, fearing the currents had carried the young cavalier away. Adam's red hair surfaced once, but he sank again before the Life Guard could reach him. When he and the other guard pulled him out, Adam was already blue like that, the man tells her, pointing out the window at the gruesome body. His eyes are sad as he tells her that he is sorry, he knows she was Adam's friend.

The doctor announces that Adam is dead and asks everyone to return to their lodgings.

None of it makes any sense to Jacquette. Half an hour ago, she and Adam were playing chess. Now, they will never complete their game. No one will win.

CHAPTER TWENTY-SEVEN

Douglas House, Stockholm
Autumn 1816

After the summer at Finspång, the family's return to Stockholm, where rumors about the foundling's true identity are swirling, deepens Jacquette's gloomy conviction that Cara deserves a better mother. Unable to field one more question about Adam's drowning, she feels herself sinking, but in guilt, not water. In her dreams, she sees the dark, choppy waves of Brunnsviken that consumed her friend. Could she have prevented his death by persuading him not to love her? Should she have told him about Cara to discourage his attentions? No one can know, but she saw the wild look in his eyes as he galloped away from Haga Pavilion with the mail. She failed him, just as she had failed Cara. Her self-doubt grows and haunts her, making her question the goodness of her soul.

Aurora insists that Adam's death was only a tragic accident and counsels Jacquette to return to society. She refuses to admit she is trying to push Jacquette back to Oscar. When Jacquette meets her suggestions with a cold stare, Aurora writes to Finspång and asks the housekeeper to send Jacob to the capital, as if the Leonberger will lick away her daughter's cloak of shame. When the enormous dog arrives, Jacquette leads him to her room, latches the door, and stays there.

Cara, if she is still alive, is six months old.

Jacquette yearns after her daughter night and day, and she even sends a message to Peter begging him to take her to the orphanage. He warns against the idea, and he is right, for going there could only endanger Cara. Charles Jean, who recently returned to the capital with Oscar, would learn of it in an instant. She has little choice but to wait for another opportunity to arise.

One afternoon, too exhausted to read, she is curled around Jacob's warm body for a nap when she hears Marianne's voice. She struggles to her elbows, ready to protest.

"What is it now? I am so tired—"

"Come and give me a hug."

Jacquette kisses Marianne on both cheeks. "I thought Charles Jean sentenced you to stay at Drottningholm until winter."

"The queen ordered it; Charles Jean would never do such a thing, I assure you. But he sent for me. I suppose he could not wait," Marianne says with a smug smile.

"The crown prince is coming here? Aurora did not breathe a word."

"You need not start selecting your undergarments, my dear. Oscar will not be with him," Marianne drawls.

"You are incorrigible."

"At least I am dressed," Marianne says.

"I still have time before dinner." Jacquette rests the side of her head on the mattress.

"Charles Jean wishes to speak with you."

Jacquette shoots to her feet, fumbling to button her gown. "Why would he want to see me?" she asks, fearing it has something to do with Cara.

"I don't know, and I am not about to ask him. He is in a rare temper about the Gustavians and says he must leave as soon as possible to speak with the king at Haga. I am beside myself. Furious. I came all the way from Drottningholm to see him."

Jacquette can tell Marianne has been crying. "I'm sure the crown prince has a lot on his mind," Jacquette says, draping her arm around her older friend. "I'll come to the blue sitting room in ten minutes."

"He wants to see you here."

The idea that Charles Jean is about to visit her bedroom is so shocking, so unusual, that she does not know what to say. Avoiding Marianne's eyes, she looks at the disorder that surrounds her.

"In my room? Why? It is in a state."

"Well, so is he."

They coax Jacob off the bed and remove most of the stray clothing from Jacquette's small conversation area. There is nothing either of them can do to prevent Charles Jean from coming, going, or whatever else he sets his mind on doing.

Marianne clears her throat and casts her eyes toward the floor. "He doesn't wish me to remain."

"He wants to speak with me alone?"

"So it seems . . ." Marianne's voice trails off, and she fumbles to remove a handkerchief from her bag.

Jacquette wraps her arms around Marianne's neck.

"Oh, don't worry about me," says Marianne, brushing away Jacquette's embrace. "I cannot claim ignorance. I knew from the start what part I would play. Call it mistress, harlot, or whore—there's nothing but pain in it, pain and condemnation. And don't think power makes it worthwhile—domination by a man who will someday be king is no different or better than being misused by any other unavailable man. Stay away, that's my advice."

Marianne's words strike a chord in Jacquette, but they come too late. She says, "I told you, I'm finished with Oscar."

As she tosses shoes into a closet, Marianne looks unconvinced. "Don't cross Charles Jean when it comes to his son, Jacquette."

Someone knocks on the door. Magnus Brahe's self-satisfied voice announces, "His Royal Highness, Crown Prince Charles Jean."

"*Bonne chance*," whispers Marianne to Jacquette. She touches Charles Jean's arm as she passes, and he smiles at her as one would regard an impulsive child. Magnus looks away during their exchange and adjusts the collar of his jacket, which is buttoned up to the neck.

The crown prince crosses the floor in three long strides. He is in shirtsleeves, wearing a dark green velvet waistcoat embroidered in gold and tight white breeches. His hair is shorter, curled by the moist air of summer, and is growing whiter at the temples each time Jacquette sees him.

After dismissing Magnus, Charles Jean looks at Jacquette in silence. To her, the seconds seem like hours, and she feels suffocated by the scrutiny of his narrowed eyes. They are smaller than Oscar's, darker, set more closely together. Piercing, where Oscar's are soft and soulful.

"Sit a moment, mademoiselle. I know you have been mourning the loss of your young friend." He rests his hand on the back of her favorite ecru chair, which is covered in scarves.

"*Ack*," she says, tilting her head so that her better side faces him. She leans closer and smiles. "Adam would have served you long and well."

He calls for Magnus, who must have been listening at the door, for he appears as if by magic.

"Have you sent the gift to the dead boy's family? If so, send another. Double the usual amount."

"Yes, sir," Magnus says, appearing disappointed he was not summoned for a weightier task.

"Go now and leave us. Truly leave us this time." Charles Jean looks down his very large French nose at Magnus, who, Jacquette is confident, will now stay away from the keyhole.

The crown prince stations himself a respectful distance from Jacquette's chair and folds his arms before his chest. He expounds on the weather and horses. All very cordial, all in French, all in the same matter-of-fact tone he uses when he speaks to men. He is a soldier, not a lover like Oscar.

Jacob rolls over on his side and sighs.

"Is that one of the famous Finspång Leonbergers?"

Jacquette nods. "Emilie got him when I was ten years old. He always preferred me to her."

"Your charms are difficult to resist, I understand, or so my son tells me." He raises his eyebrows.

So, she thinks, *the crown prince is finished with pleasantries. And he knows everything*. She shivers, remembering Oscar's warning during their last conversation.

He lifts a silk scarf that is draped over the back of her chair. "From Lyon, no? I must have your mother order one for Marianne. Ah, my dear Marianne, who is so magnificently uncomplicated. Unlike my wife." The word "wife" falls like a dove shot from the sky. He rarely speaks of Désirée.

"I understand the crown princess may return to Sweden," Jacquette says.

"What am I to do?" he asks. "I hold my wife in the highest regard, but I do not think her presence at court would make us stronger against the Gustavians. I must act for my son and his future. Not for myself."

Everyone remembers how unpopular Désirée was during her time in Sweden, which lasted a mere six months. Jacquette's corset is beginning to pinch the tender skin under her breasts, now moist from anxiety.

"Of course you must, sir."

He laughs. "There are no uncomplicated women in your family, at least none with whom I am acquainted. But there are times when a complicated woman can be very useful. *Eh bien*?"

"I leave that to you, sir."

"I will be frank, then. I need to place a woman in the queen's household. One who is loyal to me or at least has good reason not to betray me. My delightful Marianne, I regret, is not suitable. The queen would see right through her. But you are good with secrets, *non*? And you have every reason to help me, do you not?" He lifts his chin, and the charming smile disappears.

She had expected him to threaten her, but she did not expect this. "Of course, sir. Whatever I can do."

"The queen has a place for you as a maid of honor, but your mother tells me you wish to decline. Can that be true? You must tell me why."

Charles Jean's hand drops to Jacquette's shoulder. She shivers at the weight, hoping he does not notice.

"I mean no disrespect," she says.

"Of course not. You do not see my dilemma. Marianne tells me you are aware that I question the queen's political leanings."

"Oh, just that. I know nothing more." *Marianne talks too much*, she thinks.

"You see, I opened an inquiry, but the queen wishes to stop me. It is as simple as that. She is flailing in every direction, as women are wont to do."

"How regrettable. For both of you."

"Quite." Charles Jean picks up the large roll of paper that Magnus had placed on a table before he left. "Look and see. Stockholm Palace, of course." He unrolls the parchment and points to a large apartment near the East Stairs. On the plan, Jacquette's name is written in pencil.

She frowns. "A senior court mistress always lives in that apartment, not someone like me."

He shrugs. "Your reward for helping me expose the queen's treason."

The apartment is a bribe, plain and simple. But it is not what she wants.

He continues. "The queen only nominated you to displease me."

"I am glad to have some value, even if it comes from my notoriety," she says in a wry tone, unable to suppress her puzzlement about how she got herself into this position.

She expects him to be angry, but he laughs, and his voice loses its edge. "You see, she thinks she can make me close my investigation. She would release you from court, and that would keep you away from my son. It's blackmail."

"Then perhaps it is better I decline the offer now."

He taps his lower lip with his index finger. "The queen has miscalculated. You will actually be useful to me as a maid of honor."

"How, sir?"

"You will report all the queen's activities to me. Where she goes, what letters she receives, the people she meets, the correspondence she writes. All of it."

Jacquette decides to gamble. "With respect, sir, wouldn't I be committing treason?"

He rubs his fingers along the ridges beside his nose and sighs. "Countess, what you lost could be yours again."

Cara.

He has offered Jacquette what she wants, placed all his cards on the table. She must not show her satisfaction. She adjusts the sleeve of her gown and gathers her courage.

"I would so treasure having it returned to me. I would keep it safe at Finspång."

His upper lip twitches. "If you meet all my conditions, that could be arranged."

"Tell me."

"Join the queen's household and bring me what I need to know. You will not need to remain long in your position; my inquiry will be over in a few months' time."

If she were to tell Charles Jean about the queen's ring, would that persuade him to return Cara? If Oscar were here, he would advise her to test his father.

"No other conditions?" she asks.

"Two things. When the inquiry concludes, you will marry and leave Stockholm. And, Countess, from this day forward, you will stay away from my son. And never breathe a word to him of our discussion."

"Sir, I have not seen the prince in months. May I think about your proposal for a few days?"

"*Bien sûr, mon amie*," he says and kisses her hand. "We will talk again the day after the Leipzig Ball."

Oscar once told Jacquette that Charles Jean had learned from Bonaparte to keep his enemies close. Is that what this was? She wonders where it will end.

Her instincts tell her not to trust his vague assurances, and to find another solution. Charles Jean stole Cara and ruined what she had with Oscar, and she has reached her limit. She tells herself, *I will not let him frighten me or bribe me with gifts. He is only a man, and I am not for sale.*

CHAPTER TWENTY-EIGHT

Douglas House, Stockholm
October 1816

Charles Jean's offer to return Cara troubles Jacquette. Is he lying? Until now, every one of his moves has pushed Cara farther and farther outside Jacquette's reach. He had her baby kidnapped from Countess Meijerfelt's doorstep and committed to Allmänna Barnhuset, yet now he dangles the prospect of a reunion before her like a necklace of pearls. Why the sudden change of heart?

Midway through her next English lesson, she tells Peter her problem. He falls silent, pacing in front of the library window with his hands clasped behind him. Finally, he asks a question.

"Consider the man. Crown Prince Charles Jean did not become a Marshal of France or crown prince of Sweden by taking unnecessary risks, did he?"

"I imagine not." Jacquette closes the doors to the foyer.

"This bargain with you—does it give him the things he desires? What does he fear? In English, please."

The conjugation of English verbs has never taken root in Jacquette's brain, and she fears she may never learn the cursed language. She wrinkles her nose, and he raises his brow.

She says, "He fear that one more blow to Oscar's reputation could end their dynasty."

"Not exactly. The verb should be *fears*, not *fear*. I fear, he fears."

"*Ack*."

Peter says, "I agree with your point. When he summons me, Charles Jean speaks of little but Oscar, and half the articles I print for him are intended to bolster Oscar's position. But allowing Cara to live at Finspång would increase the chance that someone might identify her, would it not? Making his worst fear come to pass. And, you say, he offered this freely?"

"What do I really know of the crown prince? You meet with him every second Monday."

"You know everything Oscar ever told you about him."

He is right. "Yes, then. The crown prince did not hesitate before saying he could arrange it."

Peter, who is turned out in an impeccable gray waistcoat and light blue silk cravat, leans against the stone fireplace surround and crosses his arms. "Maybe there is no risk to him. Because his promise is illusory."

Jacquette understands what he means, even in the English language. Her response is spoken through tears. "You think Cara is already dead." Her tiny creation, born of her weakness for Oscar, lost through her powerlessness against his father.

Peter's eyes crinkle, sad and silvery, and he places his hand on her arm. "It's time to go to the orphanage and find out. We'll need Brita."

On the appointed day, leaves are swirling around a forlorn, empty Blasieholm Square. It is a dark morning, fittingly gloomy for the mood that has not left Jacquette since Charles Jean made his demands. She has not yet responded to his proposal that she join his society of spies, and his deadline looms. Tomorrow, after the celebration of the third anniversary of Charles Jean's great victory over Bonaparte's army in the Battle of the Nations at Leipzig, he will expect her answer.

The silence in the square is broken by the eerie shriek of hundreds of geese. Like a cloud, they obscure the sun, and Jacquette gathers her skirts around her thighs for warmth. She and Peter are waiting for Brita, who has been skittish all morning.

"About the queen, Jacquette. Nothing I have seen at the print shop implicates her in any plot."

"Who, then, is leading the Gustavians?"

Peter says, "Otto Natt och Dag. Look at what got dropped off at the print shop yesterday. Gustav gave a ring to Otto to reward his loyalty, and the Gustavians are planning to distribute these while the court considers his sentence." He pulls a pastel drawing out of his coat pocket and gives it to Jacquette. She recognizes the subject matter.

"I saw the queen send a ring like this to Gustav. She must be involved."

Peter rubs his chin and looks closely at the drawing. He pauses before he speaks, as if he were weighing his words.

"That's not enough to prove treason, not against a queen. It's surmise."

"I suppose." Jacquette hopes Charles Jean will feel differently about it if she decides to tell him.

Brita comes out of the house with Jacquette's favorite slate-blue pelisse over her arm, the one with the taupe cording across the chest. Jacquette presents her arm, and Brita helps her don the coat while Peter secures the door against the wind.

"We must hope my parents do not return from the palace before midday."

Peter glances at the upstairs window. "I would not be so concerned. Wetterstedt has been with Charles Jean day and night, and Queen Charlotte always keeps your mother close."

Peter's words are true. Last week, Crown Prince Gustav issued an edict from his court in exile. It proclaimed his intent to seize the crown, and the capital is holding its breath. Since the wars with Bonaparte, Jacquette has not felt such tension in Stockholm, such a feeling that something is about to change. According to Wetterstedt, the antagonism between Charles Jean and Queen Charlotte has become undeniable, and everyone who can avoid being around them is staying away.

Peter offers Brita his arm, his eyes shining. "If I didn't know better, I would take you for an aristocrat, Miss Nielsen."

Although Brita puckers her lips in protest, her eyes soften, and Jacquette can sense her pride. The emerald-green wool gown, a find from Emilie's trunk, suits Brita to perfection, as Jacquette knew it would. She wears it like a duchess.

"Hmph. No one will believe I'm anything but a maid. I don't know why I let the two of you persuade me to do this," she tells Peter. "Let's go around the north side of the King's Garden. If we see anyone I know, I will never hear the end of it, I tell you."

Brita, usually so bold, balked at Peter's plans from the start, and Jacquette does not understand why.

"We need you," Peter says to Brita. "Jacquette is too well-known to go to the orphanage just to ask questions. They would send word to Charles Jean immediately. With us there, she has an excuse."

They walk north on Drottninggatan until the shops become sparse, then disappear, and the paved avenue gives way to a dirt track lined with elm trees and red-painted wooden houses. They pass small farms with bleating sheep and out-of-place summer palaces built by newly rich merchants. In the distance, Jacquette sees Klara Lake.

"There. Allmänna Barnhuset." The color drains from Brita's face. Her hands tremble visibly, despite the black leather gloves she is wearing. "I must be cold," she mutters under her breath.

The orphanage stands alone, some distance from the street, a two-story stone building painted a drab shade of beige with endless rows of identical windows and at least six white chimneys. The bleakness of the place is magnified by what lies beyond. On a hill, two derelict, rotting windmills—called Big Adam and Little Eva—loom over it like grand albatrosses. A strong wind blows, and one of the windmills emits a yawning creak, as if warding them away. Brita stares toward the hills with her mouth agape. Peter takes her hand.

"What is it?" Jacquette asks.

"I thought I could do this," she says.

"You must. For Cara," Jacquette says.

Brita takes a deep breath and adjusts her bonnet. "All right, then," she says. "I'll try."

Someone has seen them coming. As they cross the gravel courtyard, they are met by a slight man of about forty with oily blond hair and a monocle that keeps falling out of his eye. Holding a handkerchief over his mouth, he invites them inside, where they stand in a corner of the entry hall. He tells Jacquette he is the director. She suspects him of lying.

"May I introduce myself?" she asks. "I am Countess Gyldenstolpe."

He wrings his hands. "A person who holds your position, you . . . you should not be here. We have a sickness in the wards." He pulls a handkerchief out of his pocket and offers it to Jacquette, who shakes her head.

"I have brought my friends here from Norrköping to inquire about the foundling." She points to Peter. "This man is a well-to-do iron trader. Who could provide a better home for the baby?"

"You are Wetterstedt's daughter."

She nods, exasperated.

The man's monocle clatters to the floor, and he stoops to pick it up, refusing to meet Jacquette's eye. "I regret I cannot help you. For your own well-being, you must leave now. And, Countess, your family should be proud of you for offering help to your friends."

She cringes when he tries to flatter her, ashamed of her failure, and hangs her head as they depart. They accomplished nothing. Outside the orphanage door, she hears the bolt slide into place.

As they cross the yard, Brita hands her bonnet to Peter and waves at a man who is hacking at some roots with a hoe. Jacquette looks to Peter, seeking an explanation.

"Mr. Bengt," Brita calls, but her voice sounds odd.

She repeats the man's name.

He turns slowly, coughing as he leans his hoe against a ramshackle black shed. It is as if he knew they would come but hoped they would not.

"Viti," he says. "It is you?"

Brita nods.

Jacquette asks, "Why did he call her—"

Peter squeezes Jacquette's arm, and she understands he means her to listen.

"But that man is sick, Peter, and the director said there is illness in the wards. What if Cara catches the disease? What if she succumbed to it already?"

The dull pain of foreboding increases a thousandfold. If Cara is already dead, Jacquette will have nothing.

The caretaker turns away from Brita. "They told me not to talk to you if you came."

"Tell me why, and I'll leave," Brita says. Her voice is different, almost childlike, and she folds her hands in front of her as she speaks.

In a nearly inaudible voice, he says, "The highborn men who are behind this said you might come here with a countess and ask questions. About the foundling."

"Which men?" Brita asks.

"All I can tell you is that the baby girl is gone. They sent her to live with a farmer and his wife. Out in the country somewhere." He picks up the hoe.

"Where is the farm? Is the farmer prosperous? When did she leave?" Jacquette calls.

"Just a few days ago." The man shrugs and walks away.

So, Cara is still alive. The wave of relief is brief. "Peter, you were right. Charles Jean was never going to take the risk of leaving her here."

"Right. This place is too close and too accessible. You knew she was here. So, he moved her."

"We have to find that farm," Jacquette says to Peter.

"We need to leave. Now," he says.

She sees a quartet of Life Guards at the corner and saves her questions for later.

On the way home, Brita is pale and hollow-eyed, but Jacquette needs to know the truth. "Why did that man call you by that other name? How does he know you?"

Brita mumbles, "Bengt doesn't know anything."

"Answer my question."

Brita sighs. "Viti is my Finnish name. My mother was a Forest Finn from Värmland. Near Long Manor, the place where Count Carl Löwenhielm has his estate."

Being from an iron-mining family herself, Jacquette has heard stories about people from Finland who moved to the forests of Western Sweden, near Norway, hundreds of years ago. Because they slashed and burned trees to fertilize their fields, they were much despised by the nobility, who needed forests to make their iron. Jacquette never would have guessed Brita was one of them. She knows so much about the maid, and yet so little, she realizes.

"I thought you never knew your mother," Jacquette says.

"I didn't. She left me at the orphanage when I was not yet two."

Another revelation. "You lived at Allmänna Barnhuset? Why did you never tell me?"

"Because I made myself forget." Brita leans on Peter's arm as they walk back to Douglas House.

"We must find the foster family." Jacquette quickens her steps to catch up to Peter.

"Jacquette," he snaps. "There are thousands, tens of thousands of farms. If we get close, the palace will just move her."

Brita manages a wan smile. "Wherever she is, it is better than the orphanage."

Peter's tug on Jacquette's sleeve tells her to leave the conversation for another time, and they fall into a tense silence until they get to Douglas House.

When Jacquette enters her bedroom, a *hovdräkt* is spread across her bed. It is a court gown, the one worn by maids of honor: a square-necked, high-waisted black velvet with the signature of the Swedish court—short puffed white satin sleeves crisscrossed with black windowpane trim. A gilt-edged letter summons her to the queen's service immediately, though it is only October. Attached to it with a sky-blue ribbon is her new diamond-encrusted cipher pin, the twisted *C*s. Blinking away tears, she clutches it. She knew this day was coming, but its inevitability does not soften the blow. A position at court is everything she never wanted, yet her own actions assured it would happen.

Aurora and Wetterstedt, just home from the palace, appear in her doorway.

"Mother, you know I cannot do this. Not right now."

"Do what?"

"Join the royal household. Play the Butterfly Game."

Aurora pulls the black netting away from her face and removes her hat. In a cold tone, she says, "Then tell me, Quette, what game *were* you playing with the prince?"

Jacquette cannot hold back any longer, and she braces her hands on her dressing table, sobbing.

"It wasn't a game, not to me. But it's over now."

Aurora sighs, then turns to Wetterstedt. "I cannot face another problem tonight, Gustave," she says and marches to her bedroom.

CHAPTER TWENTY-NINE

Royal Opera House, Stockholm
October 18, 1816

The performance to mark the anniversary of Charles Jean's Leipzig victory, an appallingly boring spectacle about the union with Norway, is to begin in half an hour. Jacquette has seen it countless times. Seated at the rear of the queen's grand box, she watches the attendants moving around the orchestra level below. They skirt the edges of the hall, snuffing candles and attempting to quiet the boisterous rows of diplomats and military officers who have just come from a dinner Charles Jean and Oscar hosted at the Stock Exchange.

Hoping no one will notice, she allows herself a look into the box to her right, which is Oscar's. He is sitting in a silk-embroidered armchair with his legs crossed and one arm slung over the empty seat next to his. Young men from his household hover, clamoring for a moment of attention, a morsel of power. He must know she is here, but she tries not to wish he would turn his head. Only the half wall between the two boxes separates them in physical terms, but in every other possible way, she and Oscar are leagues apart.

She squeezes Marianne's hand, grateful there is at least one person here whom she trusts. Someone taps her shoulder, and she half expects it to be Aurora. It is Erica.

"What now?" Marianne asks Erica, leaning over Jacquette to speak. "The queen needs to find you something to do." She has no patience for Erica's scheming.

"I want to tell Jacquette something," Erica says. "Don't you always say we maids of honor need to defend each other?"

Marianne's eyes dart to Jacquette, who laces her fingers in front of her and says, "Say what you must."

Erica's face is a mask of false sincerity. "I will tell you what people are talking about because I think it best to be truthful about such things."

"What things?" snaps Jacquette.

"Erica, leave her alone," says Marianne.

Erica stoops to whisper in Jacquette's ear. "It concerns the foundling. I am hearing she was born at your house. Is the mother one of your maids? Your kitchen staff? Or even someone in your family? Or even you? Is it true that two counts forbid their sons to court you? What do they know that I do not?"

Jacquette knows she must strike back, but it gives her no pleasure. "At least their sons were interested in me, whether or not the fathers approve."

"I haven't heard of any counts calling on you," says Marianne to Erica.

Erica places her hand on Jacquette's. "And I hear rumblings that the foundling's father is highborn. Very highborn." She stares into Oscar's box, turns back to Jacquette, and smirks.

"Don't be a beast," Jacquette says to Erica.

"Oh, look," Erica says, pointing to the left side of the stage. There, a petite blonde actress wearing ringlets that reach her shoulders is standing near the curtain and gazing at Oscar. "That is the little tart who has the prince so besotted."

In the next box, Frederik kneels to speak to Oscar, his face full of excitement. Oscar, blushing, lifts his hand to the actress in a discreet greeting.

Jacquette pushes past Erica and looks for a drink, unable to watch.

Marianne faces Erica. "Out. Go back to your friends or I will speak to the crown prince about this." She rarely threatens to involve Charles Jean.

Erica smiles, showing no reaction to Marianne's ultimatum, and rejoins the Chatterati at the end of the box.

Jacquette has never felt so exposed and alone. And this is only her first day at court.

This morning, she moved out of Douglas House, her home for the last six years, and into her palace apartment. As she feared, the cavaliers escorted her to a suite of large rooms, the very ones Charles Jean described. With tall windows looking onto the palace courtyard and a sitting room with French crystal decanters on silver trays, it is far too large and far too close to the East Stairs, which Oscar uses to go to and from his apartments. All morning, visitors kept knocking, and Aurora hovered, rearranging Jacquette's few paintings like a proud sparrow admiring its nest. When Frederik came by this afternoon, Jacquette held her breath, expecting Oscar to appear in the doorway behind him. He did not.

Marianne sent a painting of a vase of purple tulips, Jacquette's favorites. The card said, *Beware, my child. I know Charles Jean. Your fine lodgings come with a price.*

Jacquette snaps to attention when Marianne pokes her in the ribs and points to the rear of the box. There, Carl is holding open the red curtains and studying her with an intense gaze.

⁂

Carl looks distinguished in his trim ceremonial uniform with its rows of medals across the chest, tight white breeches, and high polished boots. Three of the Chatterati turn and look as he enters, and one rolls her eyes when he stops beside Jacquette. He is handsome, if a bit menacing, and Jacquette does not doubt he has done the things he describes in his letters, like fighting Napoleon's Grande Armée and walking to Finland over the ice. She rises to greet him.

"The gown suits you," he says in a gruff voice.

She thinks of joking about her disdain for wearing the *hovdräkt*, but Carl does not impress her as a man amused by irreverence. "Thank you."

"If you were my sister, I would tell you to raise the neckline."

Aurora had the dressmaker lower it. "But I'm not your sister, am I?"

Finally, a smile from him. "Would you like to go to the front of the box? It will be quieter there," he says.

He holds out his arm, and the Chatterati gawk and whisper as he leads her to the rail. They are exposed, in full view of the entire house.

He says, "I must leave for my regiment's headquarters tomorrow. Until December. I wanted to see you before I go."

Frederik and Johan, who are in Oscar's box and leaning against the half wall, nod to her but ignore Carl. They whisper to one another.

Carl says, "I guess I'll be living in the palace the next time you see me. I've put up with Frederik before, and I suppose I will have to tolerate him again."

"Frederik is not so bad," Jacquette says, and Carl raises his brow. He folds his arms across his chest, and his medals jangle.

"Why did you begin your court service now? Were you not to start with the other girls in the new year?"

She bites her lower lip, unable to suppress a conspiratorial smile. "One of the maids of honor is getting married and is in a great hurry to do so." It was Hedda, one of the Chatterati.

"Pregnant?" he asks.

She nods. "I think so."

Carl's eye twitches, and he swipes a hand across his face. With cold eyes, he says, "Another quick wedding to legitimize a birth; one fewer *oäkta barn* in the church books." He is silent for a few seconds, then says, "Forgive me. I just find the court reprehensible. I'd love to leave the capital, I tell you. Nothing would make me happier."

So, she thinks, *he is not fond of gossip. That is fortunate.*

"I thought I heard your voice, Löwenhielm. I understood you were to sit with the generals."

Even with her eyes closed, Jacquette knows the stony voice is Oscar's.

⁂

Oscar is standing no more than three feet away and appears furious to see Jacquette with Carl. She hopes his narrowed eyes are hiding more than jealousy. If he feels even a tenth of the pain she suffered when Frederik told her about the actress, it would be deserved. She waits for the wave of regret, some pang of embarrassment, a twinge of guilt. It does not come. *Maybe*, she thinks, *I really am over him.*

How tragic that her first love, the father of her child, could look at her with such cold eyes. What is she supposed to do? He cannot marry her, and she cannot wait for him forever. She does not flinch from his scrutiny, and he turns his attention to Carl.

"Pardon my intrusion. I did not realize . . ." Oscar seems to lose his train of thought.

Carl greets Oscar formally, giving no hint of unease. His composure seems to catch Oscar unguarded.

With a cross between polish and long-limbed awkwardness, Oscar looks at his boots and mutters, "I understand you are to return to my service after the New Year."

"Is that not your desire?" Carl asks, pressing.

Oscar says, "It is my father's wish."

He does not want Carl back, Jacquette thinks.

"I trust the crown prince is well," Carl says, changing the subject, apparently unbothered.

"My father?" Oscar's voice is too loud, his laugh too ready. "Since Gustav declared his right to the throne, he has fretted in his bedchamber, sent spies to France to prevent my mother's return, and periodically threatened to abdicate and make me crown prince. That is how he is faring."

Oscar deserves this, she tells herself. *For everything he has done to me and to Cara.*

"Countess," Oscar says, acknowledging Jacquette's presence for the first time. "I'll let the two of you enjoy the rest of your evening. You seem to be fitting in well here." He waves a hand in the direction of the Chatterati.

Carl watches Oscar return to his box. "I would think he was jealous if I didn't know better."

Jacquette believes Carl knows nothing about the rumors, so his accusation takes her by surprise. She needs to be sure. "Don't be ridiculous. Oscar's probably been drinking all afternoon and won't even remember this tomorrow."

"I was not aware you knew his habits so well. I remember now. You were once one of his circle."

"We were just children then," Jacquette says. Carl's face tells her nothing.

CHAPTER THIRTY

When she returns to the palace after the ball, the sitting room of her new apartment is dark, but she senses Oscar's presence, just as she did in the basement at Confidencen that long-ago day. Since then, six changes of season, a lifetime. In the tile stove, she ignites a flame with one of the long twists of paper she keeps in a vase. She touches the makeshift torch to the wick of a candle before she faces him. In the unsteady glow, he watches from the sofa, still wearing his uniform from the opera.

He bows his head and rubs his face with both hands. "You said you would never serve at court. I asked you once to change your mind, and you refused. Why now?"

Her reasons are none of his affair, and Charles Jean ordered her not to tell him, anyway. Let him wonder. With a shrug, she sheds her gloves.

"The queen nominated me. What was I to do?"

"Both of us at the palace? How pleasant. Were you not thinking?" The soft French words, spoken bullet-fast, drip with anger.

She, too, is angry. "I've had a lot of time to think, Oscar."

His reply is fast and straight as a missile. "Shall we attend court balls but not dance together? Join the afternoon walks in the palace gardens but take different paths? What about dinners, when our eyes meet across the table? How can we live so close and be apart?"

"I never wanted this." She unpins the queen's cipher from her bodice and tosses it on the table in front of the sofa. "You know that." Her new apartment is sparsely furnished, so she sits with him on the sofa, leaving a generous space between them. She will show him he has no effect on her now.

He slides closer to pick up the brooch and transfers it from one hand to the other. She thinks of the Seraphim Star he once tossed at Drottningholm.

He says, "I won't watch you dance with him."

So, this is about Carl. Her lips part, and she clamps them shut. "You have no right." She lists his betrayals, all etched in her mind. "The actress you were waving at tonight, the Prussian princess, the country countess—I forget her name—Adelaide. Oh, making me tell everyone I was meeting Adam in secret." She rubs her chest, finding it difficult to breathe. "Cara."

He closes his eyes and leans back against the sofa, lifting his chin to the ceiling. He groans. "Q, Cara is why I am here."

The possibility that he knows something sets her heart racing. "You found out where she is?"

He covers his eyes with one hand, rubbing one eye with his thumb and the other with his fingers. "No, no. I don't know who has her now. Fuck, I've made a mess of this."

It is a confession, one she never expected to hear, and it sounds heartfelt. If he speaks the truth, she will do likewise. Not a child anymore, she must accept her part in this.

"We both have." She tries to stand, but he places one slim hand on her stomach and the other on her lower back, guiding her down. The pressure of his touch, unexpectedly welcome, leaves her speechless.

"I need you to know you can trust me about the things that really matter. Everything else is a Greek chorus—it's just the life here. You know that's true because you taught me about it. Just trust me. Suspend your hatred long enough for me to say what I came to say."

An apology would have been better, but she accepts what Oscar can give, as she always has. She crosses her ankles, hoping to steel herself against the sensation caused by his thigh pressing on hers.

"All right. Go on, then."

The mask of pretense disappears from his face. "I never should have burst into your house after you got home from Moreno's party. I had to leave Stockholm the next day."

"Sophie told everyone in the capital you were there, and we were alone."

"I wasn't myself that night." He bites his lip, the picture of remorse.

It is easier not to look at him. "You should have gone to your actress instead."

With his elbows on his knees, he cradles his head in his hands, and a vein at his temple pulses. "At the Arsenal? I told you that was over. You never listen."

"How can I believe you? About us? About Cara, the daughter you deny?" She knows this will hurt him, but Oscar's pain is a speck of dust compared to the weight on her soul.

"I never denied her. I was trying to tell you the truth when I came to your house that night. I wish I could have made you listen to me."

"Oh, that would have helped. I so enjoy being browbeaten."

He ignores her sarcasm. "Q, listen. I know I have failed you ever since you told me the baby was coming. I have been an ass."

"Tell me the truth, then. What happened to her?"

His voice grows tense. "I didn't know a thing about the orphanage, not until she was already there. All I knew was that they were not going to let her stay at Countess Meijerfelt's house."

"You told me that the night of Moreno's party."

"I still don't know who decided to send her to the orphanage." His dark eyes pierce hers, and she is sure he is not lying.

"Wasn't it your father?"

"I don't know. It may have been Magnus."

She tries to distance herself from the inviting lemon scent Oscar dabs at the base of his throat. This proves impossible, as she is already pressed against the tall arm of the sofa and lacks the will to stand. Her voice breaks as she answers.

"You did not come to me after she was born. You left me alone." She has never spoken of this to anyone.

He holds her hands. "I don't expect you to believe me, but I had to stay away. For your sake. It's the reason I have traveled for months. I was trying to tell you the night of Moreno's party, but you threw me out."

When Cara was born in March, Oscar had been in Stockholm.

Why hadn't he come? She opens her mouth to protest, but he places the tips of his fingers over her lips. She catches her breath and resists the urge to part them.

He removes his hand. "There are things you don't know, and you deserve to. Just before she was born, I overheard my father and Magnus talking. They knew everything—I could tell from their conversation. About you and me. That you were with child. I walked in unannounced, just to let them know they aren't in charge of my life. I think my father actually felt guilty, and he gave me his word that if I stayed away from you, he would let the baby live at Countess Meijerfelt's. In a few years, he promised me, he would let her move to Finspång. I thought you would want that, so I agreed. That's the reason I never came to you."

"What changed?"

He hesitates. "It was my error. Frederik told me you were safely delivered, and I could not stay away. A couple of weeks after Cara was born, I went to see her in the carriage house. My father found out and was furious. He said I'd broken our agreement and could not be trusted to know her whereabouts. So, I knew he would not let her stay with the countess, but I didn't know where they would take her. Honestly, I thought she would go to a family in the country. About a week later I found out she was in the orphanage. The day after Adlercreutz's memorial procession."

Jacquette weighs the meaning of these revelations. Did he really stay away to protect her and the baby?

"You visited Cara? Who helped you get in?"

"Sophie. I swore her to secrecy. You were in the main house seeing the doctor that day."

Sophie, that disloyal traitor.

"Q, I held her." Oscar's eyes shine, and he gives her a crooked smile.

Then she sees it in his eyes. Oscar knows what she felt the day she hugged Cara to her breast. He feels what it is to be a father. Jacquette reaches for his hand, and he strokes the inside of her wrist. It still drives her mad, she finds.

"I held her, too. Only once, the little angel," she says.

"She is as beautiful as you. Will be. I can tell."

His shoulder is so near, and she yearns to rest her head on it. "Can't you do anything to help me find her? I expect you know they've moved her to a foster home somewhere."

He nodded. "Have I ever been able to stop my father? But this is what I was trying to tell you after Moreno's party—just let me say it now. I did do something."

"What?"

"When Frederik told me she was in the orphanage, I lost my mind. He tried to control me, but I ran to my father's apartments. As usual, he was working in bed, and I lunged at him. Magnus had to hold me back from fighting him with everything I had."

"Did he tell you anything about Cara? Anything at all?"

He shakes his head. "I'm not even sure he knew she was in the orphanage. He looked shaken when I told him, and he glared at Magnus."

"You said you did something about it."

He rubs his thigh and looks away when he speaks. "I did. Before Magnus dragged me out of there, I threatened to renounce my title and leave him heirless."

So, Oscar has finally confronted Charles Jean. Jacquette never thought he would do it and certainly never imagined he would threaten to renounce. Does he appreciate the consequences? For himself? For her? For Sweden?

"Why would you give up your throne? Oscar, your power to oppose him comes from being a prince. Don't act rashly."

The words spill from his lips, ready at last to be heard. "It's not only about Cara. Being seen as Bernadotte's only son, blessed more with luck than talent, is eating away at me. Just as I am not him, he is not me. I want to be my own person, and I cannot abide the ways he is destroying our freedoms. From outside, I could fight him."

"It would be foolhardy to walk away. You would not have him to fight. Gustav would return, and things would only get worse. I used to think a coup against your father could never succeed, but Wetterstedt tells me what is happening in the streets."

Oscar sets his jaw, and his slim shoulders slump. "It doesn't matter.

I can't renounce. My father played his trump card as soon as the threat was out of my mouth."

"What do you mean?"

"He swore he would ruin you if I ever quit the royal family."

"Am I not already ruined?" She laughs but feels no joy.

"You don't understand. He would destroy your mother, Wetterstedt, your brothers. I didn't doubt him. I don't."

Jacquette nods. "And what of Cara? Do you have a way to find her?"

"I don't."

"You must get your father to do something."

"We hardly speak. I avoid him, except when he summons me to his apartments. Magnus and Frederik carry messages back and forth. Q, I despise him."

"Don't say that, Oscar. All we have in this sad, broken world is family."

And that, Jacquette sees, is the heart of the matter. Cara is family and deserves a mother who will do everything in her power to find her. If Wetterstedt and Oscar can do nothing, she will have to meet Charles Jean's conditions. But right now, Oscar is so close, and she is so weak.

"Q, I've been avoiding him since our fight, but today he did something I didn't expect. Out of guilt, I'd wager. To prevent me from renouncing my place in the succession. He promised me freedom. I don't have to marry for five years, he says. I was going to tell you at the opera tonight. That's why I came to your box." His mouth clenches. "You were with Carl."

"Who are you to accuse me? You were waving at that actress."

"It is what everyone expects of me."

"And what about Hedda, the maid of honor? Was it you?"

He gives her a blank look.

"Do you know why the queen called me to her service early?"

He shakes his head.

"Because Hedda was sent home. Pregnant." Oscar will understand the tilt of her head; it is a demand to know whether the baby is his.

He tears off his cravat and twists it in his hands. "God, no. There's no one else. Only you, Jacquette. Don't you feel it?" He leans toward her and runs his hands through her hair. His lips are close, almost touching hers. "Say you want me to kiss you."

She parts her lips and cradles his face in her hands. Between them, it is answer enough. His kiss is bold, not too firm, not too gentle, and his tongue sends shivers everywhere, darting and stroking the tips of her teeth.

His low groan is filled with need, and his gaze holds a spark she has not seen for a long while.

"Every night, every morning, I want you more than anything," he says.

He tosses his jacket behind the sofa, and she straddles him, closing her eyes to feel the miracle of his hard body against hers. He scrapes his thumbs against her nipples through the thin velvet bodice of her court gown.

He runs a finger along the bottom contour of one breast and says, "So small and perfect. I love how they point at the sky."

She is paralyzed by her need.

He pulls down her bodice and takes her nipple into his mouth. "I hate that these have been so neglected. For so long."

She smiles and rocks against him. Panting, she says, "Please, Oscar."

"What, this?" His teeth meet, and when he tugs, she loses control, throwing back her head and surrendering to pulsating waves of pleasure. She opens her eyes to see his broad smile.

"How I have missed you," he says.

"Let's not stop."

"I don't intend to."

From the corridor, heavy footfalls signal the patrol of the night guard. To cover herself, she reaches for the shawl on the sofa back.

"Will they come in?"

Oscar eases the sleeves of her court gown from her shoulders, grinning like the devil. She is naked to the waist. "Not even if Gustav invades Stockholm. I made sure. It seems I am able to have a few things go my way around here."

"Don't be a prince tonight. Wait until tomorrow." She lifts his shirt and runs her hands along the sides of his hips. "Let me touch you. Lie back."

She kneels and, moving up his body, kisses his taut stomach, running her hands along the ridges of his chest muscles as his breath rises and falls. Button by button, she opens the fall of his trousers. His body stiffens when she takes him in hand.

"Tell me how."

He places his hand over hers, and she has never felt such power. "Just so."

"This?"

"Harder," he says.

"I think I must have you now, Oscar."

"But what if—"

"I don't think it can happen again. I haven't had my courses since Cara was born, and the midwife says they may not return."

"Are you unwell?"

"I am quite well, and I want you on top."

He places her head on a cushion and kisses her most private places until she can tolerate no more. She lifts her hips, seeking contact, and he pauses at her entrance, teasing her with his finger.

"That's not what I asked for," she says.

"You're killing me," he says as he enters her, filling the hole he left in her heart. She coaxes him. Deeper. Harder.

She braces her hands against the sofa arm and wraps her legs around his neck. He growls in her ear, his breath ragged.

"I won't be able to wait if you do that," he says.

"Don't wait, then."

They are left clinging to each other like drowning sailors sharing a piece of driftwood. When his breath slows, he whispers, "I love you, Q. Stay at the palace. Be with me. My father promised me five years. Why does it matter what happens after that?"

She pulls away, covering her bare breasts with her hands. She is no longer the girl in the gondola, dazzled by the prince who showed her fireworks over Brunnsviken. She knows what Oscar is asking. A life of late-night meetings, notes passed under covered trays, lies. Facing scorn, isolation, shame. And the irony is that despite all this, she would do it for him. She would play the Butterfly Game.

But they are three now, her and Oscar and Cara.

Accepting Oscar's love, the prize she has chased since she was a fourteen-year-old girl, would mean sacrificing their baby. She remembers

Marianne's advice: *Do not cross Charles Jean when it comes to his son.* The only solution is to break a promise to Oscar, one she made long ago. She must lie to him. He must not learn that Charles Jean is using Cara to blackmail her into leaving him. She knows what Oscar would do if he ever found out—remove himself from the succession and go straight back to Paris.

And that, she has come to realize, would be a disaster for everyone.

She bats his nose with a playful touch of her index finger, putting on her most alluring smile. She looks around the apartment.

"Well, I'm at the palace already, aren't I? But let's be discreet. I'm unmarried."

"We can find you a husband who doesn't care. My father is going to give me the command of the Life Guards soon; I'll be able to make the man a general."

He brushes his hair aside, and she sees the hope in his crooked smile. Allowing him to believe they will be together is wrong, and she wonders whether he will ever forgive her for lying. "Oscar, whatever happens, just remember that I love you, too."

She crushes her head into the crease of his neck so he cannot see her tears. There is no other way she can save Cara. She must do as Charles Jean asks. Marry. Leave Stockholm. Stay away from Oscar.

After Oscar leaves, she sees a book, a rare French translation of *Sense and Sensibility*, on her bedside table. None of the Stockholm booksellers have been able to find her a copy. She holds it up to examine it, and the pages fall open to a bookmark.

Her smile freezes when she reads the unsigned inscription.

Written in Charles Jean's familiar rounded hand, it contains his usual charming salutations—he insists that he see her, learn about her experiences at court, ensure she is faring well. Magnus, he writes, will collect her at eleven o'clock the next evening.

The hours pass, but her indecision does not. Should she tell Charles Jean about the queen's ring? Will it be enough to convince him to release Cara?

CHAPTER THIRTY-ONE

Stockholm Palace
December 1816

Christmas Eve turns somber when the king falls ill. There are whispered rumors of another stroke, but Aunt Lotten forbids the maids of honor from speaking of it. On her way to the queen's salon for the holiday soiree, Jacquette passes a tense Oscar in the gallery between the men's and women's wings. She suspects he has been waiting for her. Fearful of angering his father, they have met several times in secret since the Leipzig Ball, grateful that the constant state of Gustavian unrest has brought the social life of the palace to a near halt. So far, she has not told Charles Jean about the queen's ring, fearing it would end his investigation. This, she acknowledges, is selfish, but she has no one in mind to marry and does not want the crown prince to choose. Instead, she placates him with innocuous details about the queen's daily life. A teapot painted with Gustav's picture hidden in a cabinet. A miniature portrait in a drawer. Things like that.

Oscar's eyes dart to the ends of the empty gallery, and he leads her through a door hidden in the wall paneling. In the dark half-height service corridor, he kisses her—brief, but his lips are hard with yearning—and tells her the old king has not uttered a word since he was stricken. Oscar seems lost in his thoughts. For so long, he has pushed away the reality that he will someday be crown prince. It is a reality he finds, most often, unwelcome.

They decide to arrive separately at the queen's celebration and to sit on opposite sides of her large salon. He allows her to go first, waiting in the gallery until it is safe.

At the party, people whisper that Charles Jean is in his bedchamber with the chief of the Mandarin discussing the Gustavian threat and demanding the capture of Otto Natt och Dag, who is under a death sentence for treason. The king's incapacity hangs over the room like a shroud, but the queen distributes *julklappar* as if nothing has changed. Jacquette senses her fear, for fear is something she now understands. No one knows what the queen's fate will be if her feeble husband dies, especially now that her feud with Charles Jean has escalated.

After the party, the queen sends Jacquette home to Douglas House for the rest of the season. It is a welcome respite from the constant unease at the palace. Six weeks of freedom.

❧

On a foggy January morning, Sophie bursts into the blue sitting room.

"You have visitors. The palace coach just pulled into the courtyard."

"Who is here?"

Sophie shrugs. "Some of the court ladies. Chatterati. Brita can serve them. It's her job."

Jacquette rehearses what she will say, listening for the sound of cloaks being hung, bonnets being placed on shelves. When the double doors to the salon open, she thanks the footman and swallows hard.

Erica appears jubilant. Johanna, walking behind her and carrying a leather folder, is pale, with sweat spotting her silk fichu along the neckline.

"Jacquette, *bonne année*! Your first new year at court. One wonders how long you will remain." Erica's embrace carries a strong medicinal smell. The Chatterati, according to Marianne, have been partaking of some sort of intoxicating gas procured by the Life Guards, and their conduct has been even more unpredictable than usual.

Jacquette nods at the door, and Brita leaves.

"Tea?" Jacquette lifts a cup from the sideboard.

"Just had some," says Erica.

Johanna, who obviously would have accepted the offer, frowns at Erica.

"A seat, then," says Jacquette. They sit in the semidarkness on silk cushions.

Erica's voice is shrill. "The king does not recognize Queen Charlotte, and he cannot speak."

Jacquette has heard this from Aurora but merely nods.

"He will die, some say," says Johanna.

Erica raises her hand. "So crass to speculate."

The purpose of this visit, Jacquette knows, cannot be mere gossip. Something has happened. She waits and offers a cake to an embarrassed Johanna, who is pouting like an angry child. She snatches the plate from Jacquette.

"You must be so frightened," Erica says to Jacquette.

A burning pain grips Jacquette's gut, and she presses her hand against her abdomen, wishing she had a hot water bottle. "Frightened of what?"

Erica nods to Johanna, who removes a paper from the folder and hands it to Jacquette. "About what will happen when this is handed out at the taverns."

It is a letter dated last week and sent to one of Oscar's cavaliers by Mörner, the former governor of Stockholm. Jacquette knows him well. He is the man who visited Countess Meijerfelt's house the morning Cara was sent to the orphanage.

"Where did you get this?" says Jacquette.

"What does it matter? And don't bother burning it; it's only a copy. It seems Mörner, even in Norway, heard you'd become a maid of honor."

Could there be more to Mörner's recent appointment as governor-general of Norway? Did Charles Jean send him away because he knew too much about Cara? Jacquette reads the letter, her eyes drawn to her name.

Jacquette is correct to grieve that she has been named a lady-in-waiting. God knows how that can succeed. It must have been difficult to hide her at home for so long. She cannot control herself, and if she becomes accessible now, there will be a lot of quarrels and jealousy at court. She is just like her mother.

Chatterati, by their nature, can sense terror, so Jacquette keeps her tone light and conspiratorial. "Everyone knows Mörner's wife wanted to stay in Stockholm. He's angry with Wetterstedt about the transfer. He probably wrote this to hurt him and my mother."

Erica takes the plate out of Johanna's hands and sets it on the table. To Jacquette, she says, "I suppose you De Geer women need to take such slurs lightly. You endure so many of them. Mörner is ready to tell me what he knows; I only need to write and ask the questions. And I'll write him unless you resign. And I'll send this letter to the opposition."

"You wouldn't dare."

Erica gives her a coy look. "Tell me. Does your baby look like the prince? I hope so, for her sake. How unfortunate for her if she looks like Oscar's mother."

Why would Erica risk Charles Jean's wrath by threatening Oscar? "Leave him out of this. It is between you and me," Jacquette says.

Erica crosses her ankles to one side and smooths her hair. "Oh, I don't see how that is possible. I cannot leave the prince out of it, not with you holding a position at court."

"Erica's sister would fit in so much better," says Johanna. "There would be a spot for her if you were gone."

Jacquette wonders, *Could Erica be doing this just because her sister wants to become a maid of honor?*

Erica gives Johanna a fierce look. "If you resigned, Mörner's letter would be irrelevant. Not worthy of pamphlets on the street corners, certainly. It might even disappear." She waves the paper.

"I won't resign." Jacquette cannot know all of Erica's reasons for threatening her, but she realizes what this means. She must act quickly and figure out how to tell Oscar his dream of five years together is just a fantasy. He will not understand what has changed, why she must get away.

Panic sends a surge of pain from Jacquette's shoulder down her arm, and she hears her voice wavering. "You don't know anything. Now get out."

As they don their capes, Johanna says, "Not everyone is as enamored with these Bernadotte royals as you are."

Erica's eyes flash, and she practically pushes Johanna down the stairs to their carriage.

Wetterstedt, who can fix anything, is stammering like a young priest in church. He hands the letter back to Jacquette and says, "At court, things like this grow, and they grow."

"The Chatterati will ruin me, like Aunt Emilie, won't they? They know."

Wetterstedt does not answer the question. He does not have to.

For him, the letter opens an old wound: his long affair with Aurora while she was a married court mistress. *She is just like her mother*. But Jacquette is no fool; Aurora is Aurora, and she survived the scandal. Jacquette predicts she will not. She knows the damage these people can do with their cliques and their gossip.

"We will get you out of Stockholm. It's the only way."

"Papa, there is something I have been hiding from you," she says.

He raises his brow, and she knows he is asking himself how there can be more. But he says, "Trust me."

She does trust Wetterstedt, more than anyone else. "In the fall, October, I think, Charles Jean told me I must accept the queen's nomination. He asked me to report to him about the queen."

Wetterstedt rises from the window seat and rubs his face with his hands. He scratches his ear and arranges the papers on his desk.

"He spoke to you privately? I see." He opens a drawer, selects a long, feathered quill, and snaps it in two. It is so unlike him that Jacquette would not have been more shocked if he had leapt through the window.

"I am sorry I am so much trouble, Papa. But he said he will allow Cara to move to Finspång if I do this for him. And meet his conditions. He insists I marry after he finishes investigating the queen. And that I must leave Stockholm."

"It is not you who causes my anger, my dear. Have you told the crown prince anything yet?"

She shakes her head. "Nothing of significance. Everyone knows the queen speaks of Gustav and keeps his picture on her bedside table in a box. So I meet Charles Jean whenever he sends for me and tell him about a new picture or a harmless family letter. He still says he needs me at the palace."

Wetterstedt places his hand on her shoulder. "He will change his view when he hears of this. My dear, you must understand what this letter means." He turns Mörner's letter over and inspects the other side.

"That I must marry now."

He nods. "Imagine the pamphlets the Gustavians will print. Charles Jean will want you as far from Oscar as possible. This letter was not written by a bunch of gossiping maids of honor. Charles Jean cannot ignore a dart thrown by the governor-general."

"Is it true that two counts have forbidden their sons to court me?"

He sits on the edge of his desk and folds his arms across his chest. "The fathers, not the sons. Those men do not deserve you as a daughter-in-law."

"Who else is there to consider? Once everyone knows this—"

"We must act quickly." Wetterstedt's French clock begins to chime, and he checks his watch. "I am sorry. We must prepare for a dinner guest. We will talk more about this later."

"Who is expected?" Jacquette asks. She prays it is not Charles Jean.

"Carl Löwenhielm."

Young courtiers rarely come alone to Douglas House for dinner. "I saw him at the New Year's Ball."

Wetterstedt tilts his head, his affectionate way of asking Jacquette what she is about.

She says, "It's nothing. He wrote me a few letters from his regiment last summer."

"Does your mother know that?"

She shakes her head. "She does not like him much, does she?"

Wetterstedt rubs the bridge of his nose and takes a ledger from the shelf. He turns to her and says, "She thinks Carl just wants to use me for my influence, whatever it is worth. And there was bad blood between the families years ago. Carl's grandmother's and your own."

"What do you think about him?"

"I have no reason to think ill of him," Wetterstedt says. "He asked to see me. I know not what about, but I invited him to dinner."

Jacquette takes a deep breath. "Carl wants to leave Stockholm and run Long Manor. His father will not yield it."

Wetterstedt pulls his tailcoat together and nods. "I have some work to do and expect you wish to dress." He kisses her hand. "If I were you, my dear, I would make my own judgment about Carl Löwenhielm, but don't tell your mother I said that. He could solve a lot of your problems with the crown prince. And I could solve a lot of Carl's problems. There are marriages founded on less."

"I had hoped for a marriage like yours, Papa. But I understand." *Marriage to the stiff count from Värmland*, she thinks. *I've no other choice.*

Wetterstedt says, "Jacquette, before I speak to him, I need to ask you something else."

"What?"

"How much does Carl know about you and the prince?"

She shakes her head. "I suppose I will find out one day, won't I?"

CHAPTER THIRTY-TWO

Douglas House, Stockholm
January 1817

In Jacquette's estimation, Carl Löwenhielm is, quite possibly, the only person in the royal household who has not yet heard the whispers about Mörner's letter. He and Erica are far from friendly, and he is not part of Oscar's circle of popular young cavaliers. When he arrives, he boasts to Wetterstedt about his year with his regiment and hardly casts a glance in Jacquette's direction. The two men shutter themselves in the library, where they remain until the butler rings for dinner at precisely three o'clock.

Conversation revolves around the Gustavians, the rumors of a plot, and the whispers that Charles Jean's days as crown prince are numbered. Jacquette, who has listened to such discussions all week, talks with Christine until dessert is served. Brita has prepared one of her recipes from the French Inn, orange peel halves filled with sugared orange segments and shaved almonds. Carl takes only a small bite of the confection, then pushes his porcelain plate toward the center of the table. From her post at the sideboard, Brita stares at him like an enemy in close combat.

Jacquette lifts her head when she hears Wetterstedt say her name, not expecting anyone to take notice of her. Her tiny silver dessert fork is still in her mouth, and she slides it out, pressing it between her lips to clean it. As she lays it across her plate, she sees Carl watching her.

Wetterstedt waits until she swallows, then nods to a footman. Her plate disappears.

"The count would like to know whether you are disposed to walk with him along the lakeshore tomorrow," Wetterstedt says.

"The weather should allow it. About noon?" Carl seems confident she will accept.

Jacquette looks at Wetterstedt, who nods his head. "That would please me," she says, but she feels like a cow being prodded to slaughter.

"It is freezing, and she must not fall ill before the king's name day," says Aurora to Wetterstedt.

Carl begins drumming the side of his thumb on the table. *Tap. Tap.* He meets Aurora's eyes with an icy stare.

"Do not fret, my darling," Wetterstedt says, as he places his hand over Aurora's. "It is just a walk."

Aurora's closed-lip smile looks strained, but Wetterstedt rarely asks anything of her, and his message is clear.

"It is all right, Mother," Jacquette says. "It is only a walk."

Jacquette and Carl are two people who know little of each other, brought together by exigency. Not an auspicious beginning. Wetterstedt's open sled delivers them to Strömgatan, where the royal palace dominates the skyline on the opposite shore of Lake Mälaren. As Carl barks instructions to the driver, Jacquette imagines Oscar is watching her from his window, perhaps through the telescope he keeps in his study. Carl chides her for her inattention and lifts her to the ground, setting her between the icy patches on the road. After months with his regiment, he has the arms of a rider, long and strong and hard. She feels weightless in his hands, like a dandelion gone to seed and caught in the wind.

Brita, her chaperone, sets off into the King's Garden.

Being long-legged and energetic, Jacquette is well matched for walking with Carl. People admire his captain's uniform as they pass, and for the first time in ages, she does not feel like the pariah society has made her out to be. When the wind whips her fur-lined cape over her shoulder, he stops and pulls it around her. January in Stockholm, the middle of winter. Something about his touch makes her shiver, and she hopes this midday promenade is worth the chill she is sure to catch by tomorrow.

"I've not seen you at the balls since New Year's Eve. Were you not at the Amaranth or the Innocence?" he asks.

"I get migraines, you know," she says.

It is not a lie. Not exactly, anyway. And it is the only excuse she could think of to avoid dancing with Oscar under Charles Jean's watchful eye.

"Ah, migraines," Carl says, taking her hand. "As did my mother. I lost her, you know, when I was only nine."

"I'm sorry. God takes the good ones. He makes them angels."

With a slight grimace, he turns his face into the wind and looks toward the palace. "If only the season were over. The prince insists we go to every ball on the calendar, and I have been out until dawn every night. I prefer to work, unlike the others."

She suspects Carl does not approve of Oscar's sense of fun, nor of Frederik's aversion to his duties. She is about to ask him for news of the balls but decides it is a bad idea. They fall silent, and the wind stills. In the distance, she hears a chorus of banging, like crude music driven by sticks beating on metal.

"What is that?" she asks.

They turn the corner in front of the Royal Opera House, where the Gustav Adolf statue is surrounded by a ragged crowd, perhaps fifty or seventy-five strong. Men with weather-worn faces, aged beyond their years, wear caps pulled low, scarves wrapped high. Jacquette cannot make out their muffled chants, but they seem to represent different factions of the opposition, both of which are demonstrating against Charles Jean. Young boys carry sticks and rocks, and she sees a sign that says CROWN PRINCE GUSTAV BELONGS IN SWEDEN. Another says PRINCE OSCAR—THE FUTURE—OUST CHARLES JEAN.

Carl shields her body from the mob with his own, and they move to a quiet doorway just off the square. No one seems to notice them. She can see the tiny red veins in the whites of his eyes.

"This filthy city. Charles Jean sees them for the cancer they are," he says.

It is no surprise that Carl and Oscar do not see eye to eye, she thinks. Oscar wants to listen to the demonstrators, to know their concerns. But she is not here to argue with Carl about the dissenters.

"Come with me. I know a place that is quieter. And warm." She points to a door on the side of the opera building across from St. Jacob's Church. "In there."

At first, he does not follow, so she tugs his hand.

Once inside, he looks around the stairwell. "What is this?"

"It leads to apartments for the opera staff."

"My uncle's apartment is upstairs. He is not often in Stockholm, but as long as he is the opera director, it will be his. You are familiar with the building, I gather." He says this with some measure of suspicion. She cannot tell him that she and Oscar used to meet here during breaks between acts.

"I got us away from the mob, didn't I?"

"You did."

Carl's abrupt manner allows for little levity. They sit on a small wooden bench in the entry, and she tries to move the conversation in a different direction.

"Do you still hope to leave court?" she asks.

"Never more than now. Frederik would celebrate my departure, I'm sure. I don't know what the prince would think. I suspect he realizes I am the one who does all the work." Carl's voice sounds strained.

"What would you do if you left?"

"Go where I am allowed to do things my way. Where there are no favorites or relatives asking for promotions. Where people aren't resolved to despise me before I arrive."

She brushes it off with a joke. "I don't think there is such a place for women, certainly not maids of honor. For you, where is this place?"

He looks impatient. "Long, as I said in my letters. But it is a poor estate, and my father still won't turn it over to me. His incompetence has run it dry. I could do something with the business if he only allowed it."

"Would you move there if you could?"

"If I had a family. A wife."

This is her opportunity, but it is a small one. "I am sure my papa could help you."

"Before dinner yesterday afternoon, I asked him to help me get the estate out of my father's control," Carl says. "He remembers my work in his office during the campaign against Bonaparte and said he will consider it."

"Wetterstedt always delivers on his promises."

"He has an ardent interest in your future. And is willing to do a great deal to secure it."

"I quite adore him."

"There is little he would not do for you."

Carl is seeking a guarantee, testing how far she will go.

"He has always been a great help to those close to me."

For Carl, this seems to be sufficient confirmation that she will meet her end of the bargain. He loosens his scarf, and she notices his eyes, which are a dull shade of hazel.

"I presume you will attend to the wedding arrangements?"

She nods. "I'd like to announce it on the king's name day. And then I want to leave Stockholm. And stay away."

He does not ask what she expects from their union. Perhaps he believes that for a woman, the marriage bond is reward enough.

"Nothing could suit me more. It is settled," he says.

With that, she is engaged to a self-important, not-very-rich count from Värmland who has barely touched her and seems more interested in discussing Wetterstedt than their future. She asks herself, *What does Carl really want? Why is he marrying me? Does he know about Cara?* None of her answers are good. Does he want to claim her, perhaps control her, put her in a cherished niche, display her to the people who own him? To take her away from Oscar and feel he has bested a prince? To gain what Wetterstedt has to offer him?

But marrying him will secure Cara a home, and staying with Oscar would only lead to Jacquette drowning in her own pleasure and weakness.

She scolds herself for thinking these thoughts, for she has no choice. Her well has been poisoned, and Carl is the last drop of pure water left. She must marry him or suffocate in the mess she has made.

In the salon at Douglas House the following night, she is met by a chorus of eyes—Wetterstedt's steadying gaze, Carl's hesitant glances, Aurora's glare.

"Welcome, my dear," Wetterstedt says and introduces the other man in the room, Carl's boyhood friend, Malmborg, who kisses her hand and tells her he is honored to be part of such a happy event. Carl, who looks nervous, offers his arm and directs Jacquette to the long blue sofa. She sits, less stunned by what is about to happen than she is by the way she feels.

She feels nothing.

While Carl and Wetterstedt talk at the small table, pushing a paper back and forth between them, Aurora moves closer. She looks over her shoulder at Wetterstedt, then turns to Jacquette.

Their eyes lock, and she whispers, "There is no need to give your answer tonight, not before we speak. There are other men, Quette."

Aurora lists her objections: Carl's family is stingy and provincial, he is intractable, he will take Jacquette away from Stockholm, worthier candidates are available. Emilie, were she here, would say that Carl is exactly what Jacquette needs: a man who is impossible for Aurora to control and who will get Jacquette away from the palace.

On the other side of the room, Wetterstedt says to Carl, "It is settled then, as far as I am concerned, but you will need your father's and grandmother's consent, and you must also seek Count Philip's approval. Jacquette will write a letter asking for his permission. You can carry it with you to Örebro, providing she is amenable to the arrangement, of course."

Carl is in front of her with Malmborg at his side. This is moving so fast.

With everyone watching, he bows to her and drops on one knee. She feels his large hands, the hands of a cavalry officer, calloused from holding the reins. They circle hers.

In a strong, clear voice, he says, "Countess, will you tell me what I most wish to know?"

She makes the tiniest nod of her head, and it is done.

CHAPTER THIRTY-THREE

Douglas House, Stockholm
March 1817

When Jacquette arrives at Douglas House for her English lesson on a rainy day in March, Peter is in the salon. He looks troubled. Instead of his usual modish clothing, he is dressed in the drab uniform he wears at the print shop.

"I hope you were not waiting too long," Jacquette says, shutting the door. "The queen made us walk with her around the palace garden for hours."

"The lively adventures of a Swedish maid of honor," says Peter in a dry tone. "You should have seen what went on at Versailles."

"Were you there? I didn't know."

Peter scratches his forehead. "No. I knew someone."

"Were you at the print shop this morning?" She points at his clothes, which are less than suitable for a day in the capital.

He looks surprised at her question. "No. So, how proceeds the engagement?"

She shrugs. "Wetterstedt is Wetterstedt. He could reach a treaty with the devil himself."

Peter's laugh does not reach his eyes. "So, the young count's father will turn the estate over to him?"

She nods. Värmland is a faraway place, one she does not know, and she has had little contact with Carl. Since the engagement, he has traveled frequently to finalize the arrangements and make improvements to Long Manor, and he speaks of little else during his visits to Stockholm.

Peter taps the toe of his boot against the leg of the coffee table. "And the prince? What does he say?"

Her hand shakes, and she spills the tea as she pours. "Carl wasted no time in announcing our move to Long. Oscar is furious with me. Not so much because of the engagement as because of the groom and the fact that Carl is taking me to Värmland. We no longer speak." She does not repeat the hurtful things Oscar said when they danced at the king's name day ball. Carl had whispered something in Oscar's ear early in the evening. She can still hear Oscar asking her, as they twirled in a waltz, "Värmland? Why, Q? Why are you leaving? You were supposed to stay here. What about our five years? Did you lie to me?"

Peter touches her hand. "And the crown prince? Has he agreed to return Cara, now that you are engaged?"

"Nothing about Cara," she says.

"I delivered some pamphlets this morning. They said that Russia is about to attack us and will place Gustav on the throne. Reading them, Charles Jean grew agitated, almost to the point of panic."

"Did he say anything about me?"

Peter frowns. "No, he didn't."

"Oscar?"

"No."

"The queen?"

He crosses one leg over the other and folds his hands over his knee. He seems vigilant, somehow on edge. "No."

Jacquette says, "Mörner's letter changed his view. He released me from reporting on the queen. Instead, he wants me out of Stockholm as soon as the roads dry up. I'll go to Finspång after Easter and return just before the wedding. So now you'll be the only one of us who is still his spy."

Her joke unsettles Peter, or seems to. He uncrosses his legs and sits forward in his seat with his mouth agape. After a fraction of a second passes, he composes himself, sitting back in his chair, smoothing his ponytail with both hands.

"Whatever do you mean by that? Me, a spy? Hardly." He laughs.

"You print pamphlets Charles Jean wishes to be circulated around the capital, do you not? Things to counter the Gustavians. And you tell him what the opposition is printing."

"Well, ah, yes, but that does not make me a spy."

"What if Queen Charlotte really is part of a plot?"

Peter shakes his head and sighs. "There's just no evidence that the queen is involved with the Gustavians, not in any meaningful way. I told you that. She may have a soft spot for her nephew, but that is all."

Christine comes into the room and sits on the piano bench. Coughing and wheezing, she says, "Sorry, pardon."

"Christine, are you still sick?" Jacquette asks. "It has been months."

"Just the cough."

Jacquette rubs her friend's back. "Why did you run up the stairs then, silly?"

"Wetterstedt says the Mandarin are on their way to Countess Rålamb's house. The crown prince thinks the countess is part of a plot to kill him. And Prince Oscar, too."

"Has anything happened to Oscar?" Jacquette asks.

"No. Wetterstedt said there have been meetings at Countess Rålamb's house." Christine opens her eyes wide and shrugs. "It seems this group is planning something. Wetterstedt is not one to exaggerate the gravity of a thing."

Jacquette looks at Peter, anxious to hear what he has to say. His fingers are wrapped around the window ledge, his knuckles white. He is leaning his forehead against the glass as if he's watching for something in the square below.

Without warning, he straightens and says, "Forgive me. I must go," before rushing past Jacquette and out of the room.

"Peter!" Jacquette calls, but he is gone. She hears quick, light steps on the back stairs and the bang of the door to the carriage yard.

"Why didn't he use the front door?" Christine asks.

Brita walks into the room and asks, "What happened? He pushed past me as if a demon were chasing him."

"I don't know. Something I said, I think. It rankled him," mumbles Christine.

"What did you say?" asks Brita.

"That Charles Jean thinks Countess Rålamb is plotting to kill him and replace him with Gustav."

"Oscar, too," says Jacquette.

"Countess Rålamb? Are you sure?" Brita poses her question to Jacquette.

"As soon as Peter heard her name, he ran out of the room," Jacquette says, not understanding why any of this would matter to Brita, who has no interest in the Gustavians and always busies herself elsewhere when the subject arises.

Brita drops the parcel she is carrying and sinks into a chair. "Then I think I need to tell you something. It's about Peter."

Brita removes her hat, a black straw bonnet Aurora gave her when she moved to the palace with Jacquette. She balances it on the arm of her chair. Pulling on the tip of each finger, she peels off her fashionable black kid gloves and places them on the table. Her eyes rest on them for a moment, and she runs her thumb over the embroidery on the back of each glove, a colorful nosegay with trailing ribbons. They were a gift from Peter for her last birthday; she had turned twenty-three.

"I loved every minute I wore these on my hands," she says with a wistful expression. "But he's gone."

"Did you and Peter quarrel?" Jacquette stands by Brita's chair, sensing something is very wrong.

Brita's usually confident demeanor has vanished, and she is biting the inside of her lip, something Jacquette has seen her do only twice before: once when they visited Brita's daughter, Elin, and again when the caretaker from the orphanage called Brita by her Finnish name. Brita likes to pretend she is invincible, but Jacquette knows she is hurting now and is about to cry.

"Christine, would you mind if I spoke to Brita alone?" Jacquette asks.

Christine agrees to leave. After allowing enough time for her to reach the other end of the hall, Jacquette asks, "Peter is not involved in this plot of Countess Rålamb's, is he?"

Brita looks away. "There's a chance of it." Then, after a moment, she says, "Yes, he is."

Jacquette wonders if Brita is jumping to conclusions, like a neglected wife who imagines mistresses hiding in every closet. "You think Peter is a Gustavian?" she asks, incredulous.

Brita nods.

"Then why did he tell us he is helping Charles Jean? Printing all those articles supporting him?" Jacquette considers what she has just said and murmurs, "Oh, I see what you are saying."

"Like the double agents in your novels," Brita says. "He only pretended to be on the crown prince's side. Must you tell Wetterstedt?"

Jacquette thinks it over as she walks the length of the room. "Yes, of course, but I need to know everything first. Where is Peter now?"

Brita shrugs. "I think he is probably already on a boat or riding toward the toll gates. Gone, like I said."

"Should we go after him?" Jacquette takes Brita's hand and tries to pull her up from her chair, but Brita resists.

"Do you really think we could catch him? He's part of the plot, I am telling you. He stopped when he was running down the stairs and offered to take me with him. And Elin, too. I refused."

Jacquette freezes. "Take you where?"

"America. A place called Vermont." Brita makes a keening sound and draws her knees close to her chest. It hurts Jacquette to see Brita's hands shake as she tangles and knots her bonnet's long black ribbons.

Jacquette says, "Just tell me whatever you know. I promise I will help."

"I'll try." Brita sits straighter in the chair, her chest rising and falling as she takes deep breaths. "Cook sent me on an errand to Countess Rålamb's house this morning, and the maid who answered the door looked terrified. I asked her what was wrong, and she said she was afraid to open the house."

"Why?"

"She told me she lives in fear of the crown prince's secret police."

Everyone fears the Mandarin, Jacquette thinks. She says, "Christine told me the police are there now. Questioning the countess, I think. So, they already know about the plot, and maybe about Peter."

Brita nods. "The maid told me to be quiet because the countess was having one of her meetings. She took me past the door to a salon, which was open a bit, and I could see inside. People were sitting on chairs in a circle, and right in the middle was Peter. He was standing and speaking to them."

"Would he have any honest business at the Rålamb house? Something that would explain him being there?" Jacquette asks.

"None that I know of," says Brita.

Jacquette's mind begins racing. "Who else was in the salon?"

Brita seems calmer now, her answers more precise. "People you would never expect to see together. I don't know their names, but there were nobles and soldiers, even a Life Guard, and police, and common working folk. About fifteen in all. I saw Erica there, too."

Erica, a Gustavian. Now Jacquette understands why she threatened to expose Oscar for fathering Cara. But do Erica and Peter really wish Oscar dead?

She faces Brita. "Peter is English. Why would he care whether Gustav is our next king, or Charles Jean, or the tsar, for that matter? Think with me; you know him better. Why would Peter, of all people, do this? It makes no sense."

Brita says, "I can answer that one. If he did it, he did it for money."

"He does have such fine clothes, too fine for a printer's assistant."

"And he pays for Elin's school." In a halting voice, Brita adds, "I never asked him where he gets the money."

Jacquette had never questioned it, either.

"What else seems out of place?" Jacquette asks. "Things he said, little coincidences?"

Brita is silent for a long while, and then she taps her finger on the table. "There is something," she says. "It struck me as odd, even at the time." Brita rubs the back of her hand and blinks her eyes slowly, as if she is deep in thought.

"What?"

"You told me Peter wrote Wetterstedt a note when I was in the palace jail saying I was in a cell and asking for him. But remember? I swore to you I never told anyone at the jail that I knew Wetterstedt. And I don't see how Peter could have known I was there. I asked him, and he wouldn't tell me."

Jacquette thought of the possibilities. "He knew you spent time with the ladies at the brothel. Could he have arranged the raid somehow? Your arrest got him close to my family, didn't it? If you had not been in the jail, you would never have come to work here again, and you would never have introduced Peter to me. And that is how Peter met Oscar, and then—"

"That's how he met Charles Jean. Jacquette, this is all my fault. I trusted him," says Brita.

"No, it is mine, and I must figure out how to fix it. And what about Erica? She was at the meeting."

"I don't know about her," says Brita. "But there's not a reason on earth why Peter would have this if he weren't doing something underhanded."

"What?"

Brita unties the twine and removes the brown paper wrapping from the package she brought into the room. "He gave it to me in the hallway just now when he asked me to go to America with him. He said it was safer for me to hold it."

The package appears to be very old, and scraps of the wrapping fall away as Brita unfolds it to reveal what is inside. She frowns and holds up the first page.

"I think this is what you and Oscar were looking for at Drottningholm a few years ago."

Jacquette shivers as she realizes Brita is holding the documents that were stolen from Confidencen. "I'll wager that Peter stole them to help the Gustavians prove that Crown Prince Gustav's bloodline is pure."

"What I cannot understand is why I did not suspect him. But he never asked me anything—not a single question, Jacquette."

"I imagine that is a most excellent quality in a spy." Jacquette looks at the window where Peter was standing only half an hour ago, and her knees begin to tremble. "You saw Peter leading a Gustavian meeting this morning and you still allowed me to meet him? Why didn't you tell me?"

"I'm telling you now."

"You left me here with him. Alone."

Brita is silent for what seems like an eternity.

"Peter would never harm you, Jacquette. You're right—I saw him at Countess Rålamb's. At first, I wasn't going to tell you. But I didn't know about the documents then, and he had not asked me to escape with him. That happened just now, in the hallway. And I didn't know they planned to kill anyone."

"How could you keep it from me?" Jacquette demands.

"Because of Elin," Brita says. "I asked myself, if Peter is gone or in prison, who will pay for Elin's board? I was planning to let him escape and tell you he'd disappeared with a woman. But I couldn't do it. I couldn't hide it from you. I couldn't go with him to America, either."

"What made you change your mind?"

Brita rises from her chair and puts her arms around Jacquette in a brief, firm hug. Surprised, Jacquette stares at the normally undemonstrative maid.

"I suppose it was because of you," Brita says. "You would have taken all the blame for introducing him to the prince. And how could I leave you now? With this mess about Cara, and the prince, and Carl, and you thinking about marrying, and all of it. Now that Peter is gone, you are the only friend I have."

Jacquette cannot suppress a smile. "Does this mean you are moving to Värmland with me?" Until now, Brita has insisted she would have no part in joining Carl Löwenhielm's household and would remain in Stockholm.

"Someone needs to watch out for you. Jacquette, have you talked to your aunt about the engagement?"

"Emilie? She likes Carl, and the fact that my mother despises him makes her even more enthusiastic. She told me Aurora is going to throw me at Oscar until my heart is dried out like tinder. I cannot deny that, can I? Come with me to Long." Brita's eyes dim, and Jacquette asks, "What is the matter?"

Brita frowns. "Elin. I won't have the money to pay the schoolteacher. I vowed I'd never put myself first, ever again. Carl won't have her living at Long Manor, I'm certain of that."

"Let me take care of it," Jacquette says. "Elin can live at Finspång with Mamsell, and when Cara gets there, they will be friends."

"You would do that for me?" Brita is beaming, her face filled with hope.

"At least someone will be happy while we are in Värmland. Every day, we will be terrified a white moose will trample us." Jacquette rubs her face as if washing away the vision.

"What should I do with these?" Brita asks, holding the documents Peter stole.

"Leave them with me," Jacquette says. "This time, I'll put them to better use."

Could the long-lost documents from Drottningholm be the key to solving her problems? Jacquette needed to think about it. Nothing could be more threatening to Charles Jean than the proof they contained about the legitimacy of Gustav's claim to the throne. But if she used them as leverage to make the crown prince release Cara, the consequences would extend far beyond one tiny girl. He would punish her family. And Oscar would find out that his father had threatened her, which might be the last straw for his fragile relationship with Charles Jean.

Wetterstedt looks up from his desk as Jacquette enters the room. "What is it, my dear?" He checks his watch. "I have to go back to the palace soon."

Jacquette says, "I will not be long, but I must speak to you, Papa."

"Of course." He takes a pile of books off the settee.

"It is about the plot, the Gustavian plot."

He looks surprised. "Did Carl tell you about our suspicions? Or the prince?"

"Christine."

"Ah," he says. "She was in the room when I told Aurora, and I should have known better. Discretion has never been her hallmark, has it?"

He smiles, seeming unconcerned. He rarely keeps secrets from Jacquette.

"Is there still danger?" Jacquette asks.

Wetterstedt's smile fades. "I am afraid that is a possibility. There are rumors that the Russians are going to mount an attack in the south and put Gustav on the throne. I don't think it is a serious threat, but Charles Jean does. It is nothing for you to worry about, though."

Jacquette nods and says, "Peter was here today."

"Yes? I did not get to see him. I would have shown him my newest volume of Hegel."

Jacquette feels a sudden wave of remorse, knowing that her mistake might harm her dear, kind stepfather. "He is part of the plot, Papa. And when Christine told me about the raid at Countess Rålamb's house, he ran."

Wetterstedt takes this in silently, then says, "Tell me."

She explains her suspicions, leaving out the part about the documents. Wetterstedt listens, inclining his head at certain points, taking notes.

When she finishes, she says, "I swear I didn't know he was a spy. And there's someone else. Erica, the maid of honor. She was at Countess Rålamb's meeting."

"You couldn't have known, Quette. Leave it with me."

The courtiers call Wetterstedt a mender, a fixer, a patcher of holes. No one is better.

"What will you do?" she asks.

"The right thing. I will report it," he says, without hesitation. "You do not need to do anything—I will attend to it. There are lists being made of the conspirators, including people who work at the palace. Two more added to the list won't matter. No one will blame you for bringing in Peter when people far closer to the crown were a part of it."

"Oscar will." Jacquette hugs herself, covering her breasts, and says, "Papa, I have made such terrible mistakes."

It feels good to finally admit it.

CHAPTER THIRTY-FOUR

Stockholm
March 13, 1817

The next day is the eighth anniversary of the coup that exiled Gustav, and Stockholm is tense. Each year, the demonstrations grow larger. At the morning assembly, a herald reads Charles Jean's order canceling the day's activities, and the queen dismisses her household, keeping only Aunt Lotten and a cavalier with her. The Chatterati slink into a salon with Anders, a Life Guard, and Jacquette decides to spend the day at Douglas House. It is the only sure way to avoid Oscar.

Arm in arm, she and Brita walk across the bridge amid the appalling disorder of the capital. At the taverns, so-called liberals wave pamphlets and cheer while Gustavians, on opposite street corners, throw rocks and set fires. Outside St. Jacob's Church, a Gustavian wearing a tattered infantry jacket from the Finnish War jostles Jacquette. The bare gray wool where his brass buttons used to be reminds her of losses, the sort that are irretrievable. It is a sad thought. She asks him whether he can see the future, and Brita grabs her arm, telling her she has lost her mind.

The man's rheumy eyes gleam as he predicts, "Green coats for Gustav on our southern shore." She has made the old man happy, she thinks. He has been seen. Maybe Oscar is right to want to place these people in the light. Nestled as he is in the sanctuary of Stockholm Palace, can he have any idea what is happening outside his walls today?

For hours, she pretends to read in the library at Douglas House, where Aurora and Wetterstedt join her to drink their nighttime port. A footman announces a late visitor, never good news. It is after ten o'clock when Carl strides in wearing his full battle uniform. His shoulders are thrown back, and he looks inexplicably proud. With only a brief nod to Jacquette, he whispers in Wetterstedt's ear.

Jacquette puts down her book and watches as Wetterstedt's face turns ashen. Something is wrong, and horribly so. When she rushes over to Wetterstedt's chair, Carl looks surprised. He eventually bows to kiss her hand, and she tries to look like a girl in love, to grow comfortable with his touch. Aurora must think it real or she will shatter their arrangement, watch it wither and die. She does not trust Carl and says so daily, but she has great respect for love. Two things are stopping Jacquette's mother from ending the engagement: Wetterstedt's advice and Jacquette's lie. She has told Aurora Carl is the match of her heart.

Jacquette asks Carl, "What has happened?"

He drops her hand. "There has been an attempt at assassination. A plot against the crown. I must go now."

She grasps the gold cords of his uniform jacket, but he looks down at her with narrowed eyes. Her vision blurs, and she feels the dull throb of a migraine between her brows. She removes her hands and is careful in choosing her words.

"Charles Jean—is he safe?"

"Yes. We stopped them in time."

"And the king?"

Carl leads her to a sofa, but she refuses to sit. "All of them are safe."

She tries to be content with this answer. "How did you stop it?"

"We had information from the raid at Countess Rålamb's home. A cook and a Life Guard from the palace tried to carry it out, but we arrested everyone."

"What was their plan?"

Carl's eyes move to hers. He probably thinks her disinterested in politics, wonders at her questions.

"The Life Guard, a man named Anders, provided pulverized crystal to a cook in the palace kitchen. To be put in the food."

Anders, she thinks. The man she saw with the Chatterati today. The Life Guard on duty that day she saw Peter at the palace.

She asks Carl, "Is pulverized crystal a poison?"

"Not exactly. The Gustavians suspect that Bonaparte drank small amounts of the common poisons to build immunity. Charles Jean probably takes this precaution, so they needed something new. Who knows whether it would have worked."

"You captured the assassins?"

"The two of them, the Life Guard and the cook, will hang as soon as the city is calm."

Jacquette should not ask him about Oscar. But she cannot do otherwise. "What of the prince?"

Plainly annoyed, Carl barks, "To my surprise, the prince acted courageously. Charles Jean, on the other hand, is distraught."

She is relieved. For she is the one who caused this by bringing Peter into Oscar's world. This is her fault, perhaps even more so than when she let Adam ride off on a fast horse after dashing his hopes.

"What of the city?" Jacquette asks.

"It is not a night to be on the streets. I am to bring Wetterstedt back with me, and the palace is to be locked against the riots."

"Will you be with the prince?"

"Yes. I am to be posted outside his door all night."

She must wait until morning.

Without eating breakfast, Jacquette searches Douglas House for Aurora, whom she finds lying on a chaise with the latest fashion sketches scattered around her. A red-faced Christine is balancing on her knees in the middle of the rug, fetching and sorting them at Aurora's direction. Christine looks relieved to see Jacquette and struggles to her feet.

Aurora exclaims, "Pulverized crystal! Who has ever heard of such nonsense? I cannot imagine why Charles Jean summoned the troops to the streets—he must have lost his head. 1809 was a true uprising, nothing like this farce."

"I need to go to the palace, Mother. To Oscar."

Christine raises her eyebrows and takes a deep, audible breath, then sits next to Jacquette on the window seat. "God help you, Quette."

Aurora offers no resistance and asks no questions. "I'll come with you or you'll never get past the guards. Wear your court gown and cipher. And apply some rouge." She orders Wetterstedt's carriage to be brought round, outfitted with the royal standard and the chancellor's seal.

Charles Jean has summoned every regiment within fifty miles, and the city is teeming with soldiers on foot, cavalry on horseback, and even naval boats patrolling the partially frozen lake. The Stockholmers have flooded onto the streets, blocking Arsenalsgatan, looking terrified and confused. Soldiers stop their carriage at every corner and twice on the bridge, but Aurora asserts she is traveling under the queen's authority and is needed in the royal apartments without delay. When they reach the western gate of the locked palace, the Life Guards do not hesitate to remove the chains from the heavy wood doors, and an escort walks them to Jacquette's apartment.

"Did I not say I would deliver you here?" Aurora asks, examining a broken fingernail.

"Thank you." Jacquette kisses her mother's forehead.

"I will speak to Wetterstedt and make sure you find only Frederik at the prince's door. And, Jacquette, I'm happy you've come to your senses."

"Don't jump to conclusions, Mother."

"Express my joy to the prince that he is safe," says Aurora matter-of-factly. "And your own."

Jacquette takes a leather folder from a shelf in her sitting room and tucks it under her arm. Aurora does not notice, seemingly caught up in thoughts of her daughter's renewed influence over the prince, of the rewards she and Wetterstedt will gain.

Oh, how disappointed she will be, Jacquette thinks as she walks to Oscar's rooms.

CHAPTER THIRTY-FIVE

Stockholm Palace
March 14, 1817

Perhaps, Jacquette thinks, *I could have done no better. As young as I was, as privileged, as alone. But I ducked in and out of palace life, broke my promise to shun it, pretended the rules did not apply to me. It was folly of the highest order, akin to a man playing at dice while denying he gambles. But I am older now. I can do better. I must, lest more people suffer. Aunt Emilie said the Butterfly Game is not for the halfhearted. If I had only mastered it, everything might have succeeded for Cara. And for Oscar. At the very least, I would have seen through Peter, not let him wiggle his way into Oscar's life and threaten to destroy him.*

Despite the chasm her engagement has opened between herself and Oscar, he needs to know. She looks at the leather folder in her shaking hand, wondering what would have happened if Peter had given its contents to the Gustavians. The scandal might have sent Charles Jean and Oscar back to France as exiles. And now that she has the documents, the burden is on her to choose how she will save Cara—by marrying Carl or by using the documents to force Charles Jean's hand.

In the guard room of Oscar's apartments, where she has not set foot for months, Frederik greets her. He touches her shoulder, looking almost surprised to find she is flesh and bone. Since she agreed to marry Carl, she has become a statue from the Royal Museum to him, a ghost from the past. A disloyal one, at that. Frederik will never understand her reasons for coming to Oscar today, and she does not explain them. She is a woman, and women do not hide from the ripples that spread from their actions.

Frederik turns to her before he opens the door to Oscar's bedchamber. "Quette, the prince has not been himself since the last time he saw you. You know, your engagement. He—"

The handsome courtier does not finish his sentence. He falls silent when she kisses him lightly on the cheek and says, "Thank you, friend, for keeping him safe."

Wetterstedt and Aurora announced her engagement to Carl six weeks ago, at the celebration for the king's name day. Jacquette tries not to remember the pain that shot through her chest when Oscar congratulated them, turned on his heel, and left the gallery.

When she looks at him now through the open door, all the words she planned to say escape her. He is not as he was, not as she expected. On the other side of the surprisingly spartan room sits the boy from Drottningholm.

He is writing at his enormous French desk with its black velvet blotter, set against a row of frosty windows that look across the lake to Blasieholmen. Stripped of his finery, he wears a loose white shirt and brown leather breeches with a black arm garter buckled at the elbow. He looks healthy but thinner than when she saw him last, and he wears a hint of neatly trimmed beard along his jawline. His hair is loose, dark curls that swing past his shoulders as he turns his head toward her.

His face is open, earnest, vulnerable.

After capping his inkwell, he stands, running two fingers back and forth across his lower lip. She cannot look away, though she knows she should. When he does not move toward her, she places the folder on a table and runs to him, burying her tears in his chest. He lifts her face, holding her cheeks, silently resting his forehead against hers. Their other parts do not touch, and she is conscious of the distance. Were she honest, she would admit she cannot abide the few inches that separate them.

He speaks first, after her sobs subside. "It has been a long time since we talked. Come, sit down with me, Q. I'm glad you are here."

He takes her hand and leads her to a sofa in front of a white tile stove. His piano sits in a corner, and his landscape paintings are stacked on the floor under a window. He has been working. They sit, their hips touching. She tries not to think about how it felt to wrap her legs around him. When he reaches for her hand, she does not withdraw it. The faint scent of lemon tickles her nose, and her eyes fix on the olive skin above his loosened collar. It used to be her favorite spot to kiss.

He watches her but does not move to fasten his collar or tie his cravat, which is hanging loose and crossed in front.

She takes her eyes away from his throat, coughs, and says, "Thank God you are safe."

Another hot tear runs down her cheek, and he wipes it away, then leans back against the sofa and laces his hands behind his head.

"Don't cry. You know it breaks me. It's hard enough to see you at the palace. Why did you come? Why now?"

"I have things to tell you, Oscar."

"Go on."

"It is my fault that the Gustavians did this to you."

"Don't be ridiculous."

"I put you in danger. I am so, so sorry."

He frowns. "How?"

"It's Peter. He was spying for Gustav. I swear to you, I didn't know."

Oscar's mouth tightens. "Magnus told me he was part of it. Wetterstedt added him to the list."

Jacquette looks away. "And now he has fled. I introduced you to a spy. It is far worse than anything you have done to me."

"It's nothing compared to what I've done to you, Q."

It is easier not to look at him.

She says, "Have you seen the streets? The soldiers?"

He bites his lower lip and shakes his head. "My father didn't need to summon the garrison. It's his obsessive fear. This is only agitating the people."

He does not seem to realize how close they had come. "The Gustavians are real. They tried to kill you."

"The Gustavians are fanatics who yearn for a Sweden that does not exist anymore. My father's vision is just as outmoded. It is time for a third point of view. For change."

Oscar has always had his opinions about things—censorship, the rights of the unrepresented, the justice system. But she has never heard him speak like this.

"Are you going to oppose him? But how?"

"I am going to act this time. Do something."

She draws in her breath as he rises, withdrawing the warm comfort of his body. From his desk, he retrieves a long sheet of paper and hands it to her. It is covered with his slanted handwriting, which runs across the page and up the side margins, and is addressed to the editor of the *Stockholm Courier*.

"A prince cannot write to the newspapers. It will cause a scandal."

"Anonymously, I can."

"Your father controls them."

"Not all of them. Not anymore."

"Be careful, Oscar." She thinks of what happened to Cara when Oscar defied Charles Jean by visiting the carriage house.

"It's something I'm working on. Not for now. I'm thinking about university. Uppsala."

His decision surprises her, coming from the same Oscar who used to avoid his studies and have his tutors do his assignments.

"My brothers say you have quite a society of young admirers at the school. The students think you're a liberal."

"Maybe I am," he says. "As much as a prince can be. I still don't know whether someone like me can learn to be a prince."

Jacquette frowns. "What do you mean?"

"Before all of this, in Paris, I was just a regular person. Not a count, or a prince, or anything. Just Oscar."

He paces with his hands clasped at the small of his back, looking for all the world like the son of Marshal Bernadotte.

"Bloodline doesn't matter," she says. "Whether you are a prince comes from your brain and your heart. But why go to university now?"

He straightens his leg and pulls up his long Hessian boot. "You. Carl."

She expected Oscar to ask her why she'd agreed to marry Carl or even shout at her for her foolishness—but he says Carl's name without rancor.

"You knew I would have to marry. We talked about it."

"Not to him. I thought you were going to marry some ancient field marshal and stay at court with me. Carl could not wait to tell me you asked him to take you away from Stockholm. Värmland? Is it true?"

"I need to leave. You must have heard about Mörner's letter."

"I'm not afraid of Mörner. And I'm not afraid of a bunch of maids of honor, Q. But I swear to you, if my father is making you move away, he will pay. I told you I threatened to renounce the damn title. And I will. I'll tell everyone Cara is mine, and he will have to give her up. You and I can go to Paris."

"What would he do to my family?"

"Think about it, Q. If I renounce, he has no heir. No power."

Oscar's threat to renounce is real, and Jacquette knows what it means. It means she cannot use the documents, for Charles Jean would tell Oscar that she used them to obtain Cara's release, and she would have to admit the truth to Oscar. All of it. That Charles Jean lied about giving him five years of freedom, that Charles Jean dangled Cara's safety before Jacquette like a precious jewel. That Charles Jean will never allow them to be together. And she cannot tell him why she is marrying Carl. If she tells Oscar these things, the ripples of her misjudgments will spread. He will renounce the throne, and everyone will suffer.

She is left with only one way to save Cara and avoid destroying Oscar and her family. So, she tells the biggest lie of all.

"I didn't expect this to happen, Oscar."

"What?"

She avoids his gaze. "I fell in love with Carl."

As he stares into her eyes, his frown relaxes, and the anger leaves his face. "I refuse to believe that. Jacquette, no. Don't do this." His voice breaks, and the desolation in his words rips her apart. He pulls her to her feet, and they stand face-to-face, their bodies touching. His hands run through her hair, and he says her name over and over, his eyes searching hers.

As well as she can, she puts on a mask. If she hopes to survive, to save Cara, to preserve Oscar's crown, she must cut their ties, no matter how much it hurts.

When he sees her expression, he groans, a sound that comes from the back of his throat, speaking his need and frustration. He throws down his hands and steps away.

"I must go," Jacquette says. If he touches her again, she is uncertain she will have the strength to leave.

He strokes her hair, and it does not feel wrong. "May I kiss you farewell?"

This hits her like a blow. "You may."

"I am sorry for all of it. For my part, and my father's, and everything." He cups her face in his long, slender hands. Their lips meet, and she is surprised by his gentleness, the soft, velvety feel of his mouth on hers. It lasts for only seconds, and he steps away with a bittersweet smile and tears in his eyes.

"What?" she asks.

"You're not in love. Not with him. I can feel it. You always were a terrible liar."

He offers Jacquette his arm, and Frederik meets them at the door. "Take care of her," he says to Frederik, rubbing the bridge of his nose. He rests his hand on Jacquette's waist, and before he turns and walks back into his room, he says, "And, Q, do what you must, but don't think this is the end."

⁂

Jacquette walks through the east wing of the palace on the way to her apartment. In Oscar's vast, empty dining room, she finds what she is looking for: a fat tile stove still lit to banish the late winter chill. She opens the tiny metal door and looks inside. *Good*, she thinks. *The embers are glowing, the fire is hot.*

She removes the papers and looks at them, thinking of the lone man she saw as her carriage pulled up to the palace. He was holding a sign with a picture of Oscar. It said PRINCE OSCAR. THE FUTURE.

Gustav is part of Sweden's past.

She came here intending to give the evidence to Oscar and to make him choose whether to give it to Charles Jean and save Cara or give it to the press and expose his father's slanderous campaign against Gustav. If Oscar disclosed the documents, the Gustavians could replace Charles Jean as crown prince, and Oscar would be freed from the butterfly games played in his royal prison. But today, Oscar showed Jacquette what he could become. He could make things different, change things so people, even women, did not have to live this way. She decided then that she would do anything to protect him and Cara, even if it meant marrying Carl.

"Burn it all down, my prince," she says. "Set us free." She tosses the papers onto the hot coals and watches them curl into ash.

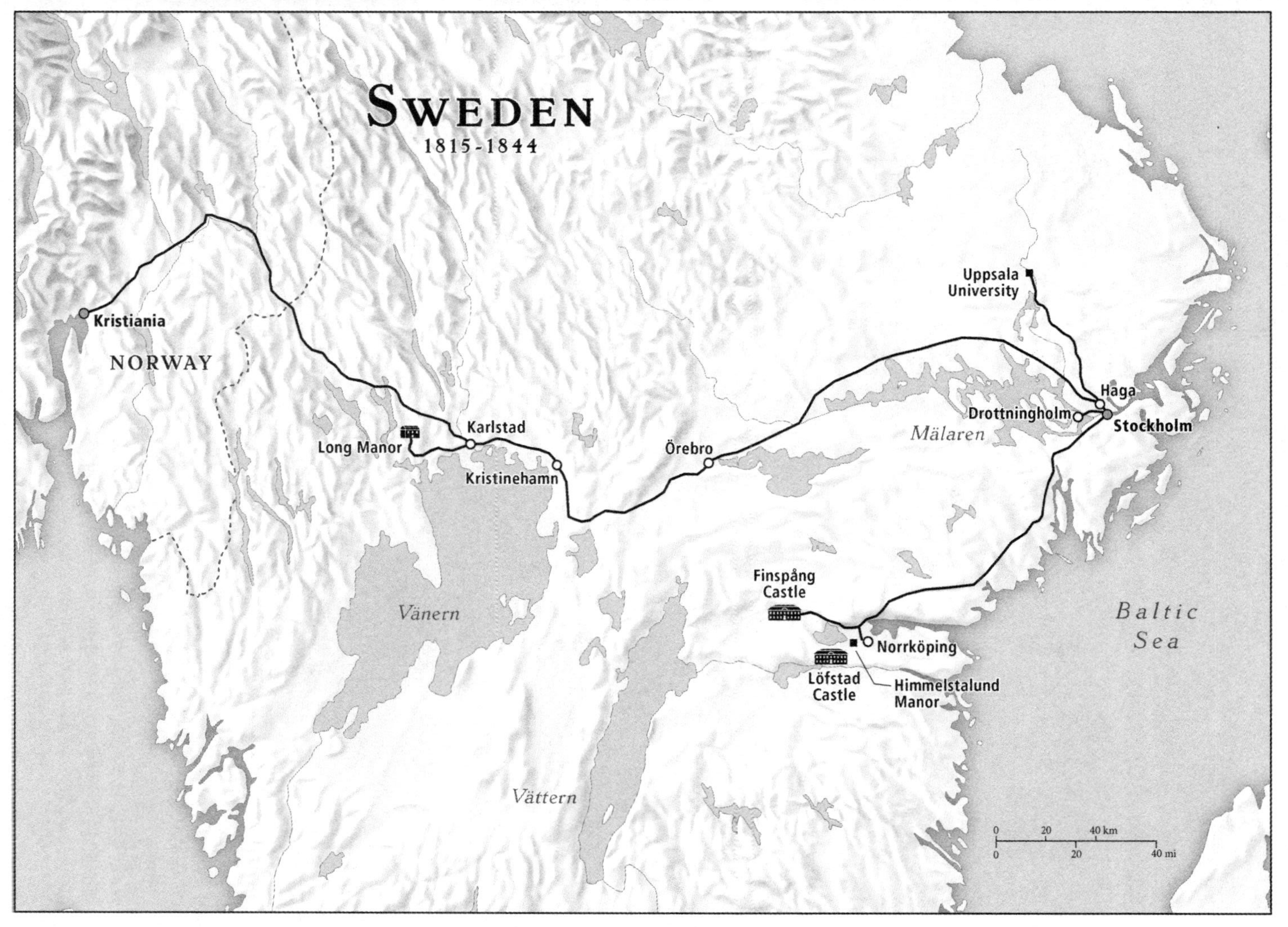
SWEDEN
1815-1844
Kristiania
NORWAY
Long Manor
Karlstad
Kristinehamn
Örebro
Uppsala University
Haga
Drottningholm
Stockholm
Mälaren
Vänern
Vättern
Finspång Castle
Norrköping
Löfstad Castle
Himmelstalund Manor
Baltic Sea
0 20 40 km
0 20 40 mi

AUTHOR'S NOTE

I found Jacquette at three thirty in the morning while I was at my computer drafting a legal document. It was 2014, and I lived in a high-rise mid-century apartment in Phoenix, where the city lights twinkled through walls of glass. My husband was away on business, and my children were sleeping in their rooms down the hallway. This was my peaceful time, the hours when I did my best work, but that early morning, I was stressed and tired.

As they have so often throughout my life, my thoughts turned to books, and I remembered one very special black leather-bound historical novel that had belonged to my mother. It was *Désirée*, by Annemarie Selinko, originally published in German in 1951. As a young teenager in New Jersey in the 1970s, I had loved reading about the silk merchant's daughter from Marseilles whose first love was Napoleon Bonaparte. Through a series of improbable events, she overcame the heartbreak of losing him to Joséphine and ended up being crowned queen of Sweden. Désirée's descendants still occupy that throne today, and her fourth great-granddaughter, Her Royal Highness Crown Princess Victoria, will become the nation's first female monarch since 1720.

Oscar was Désirée's son. That early morning in Phoenix, I asked myself: *What happened to him?*

The answer was Jacquette, and after a bit of internet research, I embarked on the project that resulted in this novel. During my journey, I made several trips to Sweden, where I visited the exquisite locations in the book, including Finspång Castle, Stockholm Palace, Drottningholm Palace, Confidencen, the China Palace, and Haga Pavilion. I walked in the King's Garden and strolled past Douglas House and Bellevue, all of which still exist and are preserved in pristine splendor. I translated more than 150 letters written by Jacquette and others, many of which are preserved in the magnificent Swedish National Archives. And I amassed a collection of antique Swedish memoirs and diaries that left Stockholm's antique booksellers wondering what an American who spoke little Swedish intended to do with it.

I hope you enjoyed reading Jacquette's story. If you want to learn more about her world, and where truth and fiction meet in the novel, please visit me at https://kellyscarborough.com/.

Thanks for reading. For my latest book news
and to access exclusive content and offers, sign up at
https://kellyscarborough.com/readers-club/.

HISTORICAL NOTE

I wrote *Butterfly Games* to give readers a window into what Countess Jacquette Gyldenstolpe's life might have been like and to explore, in fiction, her connection with the former Oscar Bernadotte (later His Majesty Oscar I, King of Sweden and Norway). For more than 200 years, allegations and suggestions of a romantic relationship between the two and the possible birth of a daughter have persisted in legend, popular culture, and other accounts of the early years of the Bernadotte dynasty.

In her iconic 2017 BBC Reith Lecture series, Dame Hilary Mantel described the challenges of creating fiction from history:

> *As soon as we die, we enter into fiction. Just ask two different family members to tell you about someone recently gone, and you will see what I mean. . . . [History is] "the record of what's left on the record. . . . It's the plan of the positions taken, when we stop the dance to note them down.**

In writing historical fiction, what Mantel "wasn't prepared for were the gaps, the erasures, the silences where there should have been evidence." The record of Jacquette's life, as one would expect, is replete with gaps and probable erasures, and Sweden's extensive and orderly archives contain no letters or messages between her and Oscar. Few

* For historical fiction lovers and skeptics of the genre alike, Mantel's five Reith Lectures are fascinating and illuminating, and can be read or viewed on the BBC website at https://www.bbc.co.uk/programmes/b00729d9/episodes/guide.

eyewitness accounts of their encounters exist. Vis-à-vis each other, their actions, inner thoughts, conversations, and intentions are a mystery.

No one can know the truth.

What is known is that Jacquette and Oscar met sometime after December 1810, when Oscar and his mother, the former Désirée Clary, sailed from Helsingør/Elsinore, Denmark, and arrived on Sweden's southern shore. Based on Jacquette's letters to her mother and Carl Löwenhielm's nearly 1,000-page handwritten memoir, we know Jacquette spent the summer of 1811 at Drottningholm Palace, and that Prince Oscar and Carl Löwenhielm were also in residence during those months. While it is possible that Oscar and Jacquette met elsewhere before June 1811, I chose to place their first meeting at this magical place, where Oscar's birthday was celebrated in the ballroom of the exquisite Drottningholm Court Theater. The novel's depiction of the events at Drottningholm (including the story of Confidencen and the evidence in the queen's letter box) is fictional, but the sparse record convinced me that a seed was planted that summer. Jacquette mentioned Oscar in a letter to her father written in October 1811, shortly after her summer at Drottningholm. Jacquette's letter no longer exists, but we have her father's response, which criticizes her lack of punctuation in her discussion of various parties and Prince Oscar. Was Jacquette already in love with Oscar at Drottningholm in 1811? I think so, but it was a forbidden love that, by its nature, needed to be hidden.

The historical record of Jacquette's life, her association with Oscar, and evidence about her alleged daughter, Oscara Hilder (born Meijergeer)—including the child's journey from Countess Meijerfelt's doorstep to Stockholm's public orphanage to Finspång Castle—may be found in Anna-Lena Berg's comprehensive biography, *Jacquette Gyldenstolpe: romantik och tragik i skuggan av tronen* (Santérus Förlag 2022, in Swedish). The book was invaluable in helping me to write *Butterfly Games*. When I learned of its upcoming publication, I was midway through writing the first draft of my novel. I had by that point translated hundreds of Jacquette's family letters and amassed a collection of Swedish historical texts, but I needed a key to help me unlock the story. Berg's fine work was that key, as I believe she was the first to unearth much of the evidence relating to the early years of Oscara Meijergeer's life.

The scenes and events in *Butterfly Games*, although fictional, align in most cases with the locations of the actual historical figures depicted at the time in question. Despite any resemblance to historical events or figures, however, what happens between those people in those places is fiction, a product of my imagination. That includes all the conversations, meetings, thoughts, and personal traits of every character in the novel.

In a few cases, I elected to change names, create a character from more than one historical person, place characters in locations where they probably or certainly were not found at the time, or take imagination to the level of the "possible but improbable." Without attempting to create an exhaustive list, the following instances deserve mention:

With respect to names, I refer to His Majesty Karl XIV Johan, King of Sweden and Norway, as Charles Jean, which is how he styled his signature.

I changed the name of Jacquette's birth father, Nils Gyldenstolpe, to Philip (which was his father's middle name), to avoid confusion with Jacquette's brother Nils, who is also a character in *Butterfly Games.*

To improve the experience of readers not familiar with Swedish history and language, I Anglicized many names and location references. Examples are Gustaf Wetterstedt (known in Sweden as Gustaf af Wetterstedt), and the King's Garden (Kungsträdgården, in Swedish).

I created nicknames and changed proper names for the same reason. Although Jacquette's family called her Quette, for example, there is no historical evidence that Oscar (or anyone else) ever called her Q. Jacquette's paternal aunt, Chief Court Mistress Christina Charlotta Stierneld (born Gyldenstolpe), was called Charlotte by Jacquette and other family members. Aunt Lotten is a fictional nickname, one I chose to avoid confusion with the queen, also named Charlotte. Adam Lewenhaupt's name was Carl Adam, but I elected to use his middle name to reduce the number of male characters named Charles and Carl. For the same reason, the book refers to His Majesty Charles XIII,

King of Sweden and Norway, as King Karl, using the modern Swedish spelling. My labels for the queen's maids of honor (the Chatterati) and secret police (the Mandarin) are fictional.

In addition to the story of Jacquette and Oscar, some of the novel's other major fictional plot points follow:

While it is true that Crown Prince Charles Jean began an investigation into possible Gustavian collusion by Queen Hedvig Elisabeth Charlotta (or, as she was called, Queen Charlotte) in 1816, there is no evidence that his suspicions were well-founded. The alleged cipher ring sent by Queen Charlotte to the exiled Crown Prince Gustav in the novel is fictional. Charles Jean's interactions with Jacquette and his efforts to enlist her as a spy are similarly fictional.

Although it is documented that Prince Oscar had numerous political disagreements with Crown Prince Charles Jean, the novel's depiction of Oscar's efforts to undermine his father's implementation of the Withdrawal Power are fictional, as are all of Oscar's views relating to the political opposition. In addition, no concrete evidence exists that Oscar was father to (or even aware of) Oscara Meijergeer. Because Oscara has no known descendants, any connection or lack thereof with the Bernadottes likely will remain in the realm of rumors and fiction.

Long after the events in question, Carl Löwenhielm wrote a memoir translated by his daughter and entitled *Minnen*. Presumably, Löwenhielm relied on his diaries, a fascinating set of tiny books with details of his life, in the writing of his manuscript. Unfortunately, the diaries relating to most of the period covered by *Butterfly Games* no longer exist and are not part of the Long Archive held at Carolina Redviva Library at Uppsala University. Like any memoir, Löwenhielm's *Minnen* recounts his subjective impressions of personalities and events, and in some cases I chose to disregard his version of the truth, or to supplement it. For example, Carl's memoir indicates that he spent the entire year of 1816 away from Stockholm with his regiment. The novel places Carl at the celebrations of the anniversary of the Battle of Leipzig in October 1816. It is possible, though unlikely, that he returned to Stockholm to attend these celebrations.

The tragic drowning of Count Carl Adam Lewenhaupt in 1816 is recounted in Queen Charlotte's famous diary. A newly appointed cavalier to the queen, twenty-four-year-old Lewenhaupt set off from Haga Pavilion for Stockholm on a royal errand on a hot day in late June 1816. He requested permission to go swimming in Brunnsviken near Villa Frescati and accidentally drowned. While Jacquette plainly knew and liked Lewenhaupt—she wrote in one letter that the two were in the middle of a game (probably cards or another parlor game) before he died—the novel's depiction of the entire relationship between the two, including any suggestions or rumors of a romance between them, is fictional. It seems likely that Jacquette was absent from Haga the day he drowned (the Wetterstedt family departed Stockholm for Finspång in late May). The unfinished game between the two may have occurred at an earlier date. In addition, the story of Adam accompanying Jacquette to Confidencen and later proposing marriage to her is wholly fictional. While he was a second son, the real Carl Adam was a count, not a baron, as depicted in the novel. I changed his title to give Aurora a reason to oppose him as a marriage partner for Jacquette.

A major event in the early years of the Bernadotte dynasty occurred in 1815, when Count Jacob Otto Natt och Dag wrote a pamphlet called *Plan for a New Organization of the Swedish Army*. Jacob (he was not called by his middle name, Otto) had the pamphlet printed at Marquard's in Stockholm, which distributed five copies against his instructions. The event ignited a well-documented conflict between the young noble and Crown Prince Charles Jean, who accused Natt och Dag of treason for aligning with the exiled Crown Prince Gustav. In November 1816, while in Germany, he was sentenced to death for conspiring against the Swedish order of succession. He escaped to Cincinnati, Ohio, and, despite Charles Jean's general amnesty issued in 1835, remained in the United States until he died at the age of seventy-one. It is possible that Jacquette was acquainted with Natt och Dag, although the novel's events involving him, particularly those at Confidencen near Drottningholm, are fictional. It is noteworthy that his descendant, Niklas Natt och Dag, is the author of the wonderful Bellman Noir series of Swedish historical mysteries, which are published in

English as *The Wolf and the Watchman*, *The City Between the Bridges*, and *1795*. The Natt och Dag family is the oldest surviving noble family in Sweden with wholly Swedish roots.

A key to the novel's characters, including a list of fictional characters, can be found on my author website, www.kellyscarborough.com.

ACKNOWLEDGMENTS

To thank every person who supported me on this journey would require another chapter in the book, but I deeply appreciate every kindness shown to me by friends and colleagues in Sweden, the United States, and England. I particularly value the friendship of two incredible Swedish women, Anna-Lena Berg, a multi-published author who has written biographies of both Jacquette and Wetterstedt that were essential to my research, and Elisabeth Daude, Stockholm guide extraordinaire, who, among other things, managed to arrange a tour of Finspång Castle, which is owned by Siemens Corporation and generally not open to the public. *Tack så mycket.*

I learned early that legal writing and novel writing are different skills and benefited from the talents of some truly great professionals: Louise Dean, who is the reason I started the book, and Lindsey Alexander, who is the reason I finished. Without the help of my dear friend and French tutor Anne-Françoise Bewley, I never would have discovered the true voices of Jacquette and Carl. Together, we translated hundreds of letters to and from Jacquette and her family and continue to work on the thousand handwritten pages of Carl Löwenhielm's memoir. My deepest gratitude and admiration go out to the publisher of She Writes Press, the downright inspirational Brooke Warner, and to my amazing project manager, Shannon Green. No book is created without a skilled editorial team, and I thank Alison Jack, Signe Jorgenson, and Julia Gibbs for getting the project to the finish line.

The book's beautiful cover art, designed by Holly Dunn, was created from embroidery samples worked on blue velvet by needlework artist and costume designer Maxence Benoit. I'm in awe—thank you. Erin Greb, a master cartographer, drew the historical maps that bring Jacquette's world alive. I'm so grateful to her, and you can visit my website to see Erin's work in full color.

I am fortunate to work with a group of public relations, digital, and marketing professionals who make me better every day. Thanks for bringing Jacquette's story to the world: Simon Appleby and his team at Bookswarm, Andrea DeWerd, Amanda Livingston, and the marketing team at the future of agency, Kellie Rendina, Andrea Kiliany Thatcher, and Rachel Fischer at Smith Publicity.

Writing requires a flexible and understanding partner, and no one could do more than my husband. Larry, you are the best. And to my wonderful children, stepchildren, and mother, thank you for listening to me, reading my work, and being there.

ABOUT THE AUTHOR

Photo credit: Kaitlyn Casso Creations

Kelly Scarborough worked for more than two decades as a law firm partner and white-collar prosecutor, but her real passion is reading and writing historical novels about the lives of fascinating women in challenging times. *Butterfly Games*, her debut novel, took her on journeys to Swedish castles and archives, where she walked in her characters' footsteps and translated hundreds of their letters. Along with the people she met, those experiences inspire her stories.

A lover of coastlines and sunsets, she lives on the Connecticut Shoreline and in South Carolina's Lowcountry, where she tries to keep track of her workaholic husband and appease her stubborn Shih Tzu.